A. J. Profeta

NeLkie's Quest

Legend of the American Elf

outskirtspress
DENVER, COLORADO

Nelkie's Quest
Legend of the American Elf
All Rights Reserved.
Copyright © 2014 A.J. Profeta
v2.0

Outskirts Press, Inc.
http://www.outskirtspress.com

ISBN: 978-1-4787-3086-6

Outskirts Press and the "OP" logo are trademarks belonging to Outskirts Press, Inc.

PRINTED IN THE UNITED STATES OF AMERICA

For Annie
Her love was unconditional
Her creativity inspirational

ACKNOWLEDGMENTS

Many thanks to Andrea Abbott (wife of the real R. J. Abbott) for telling me, "No, I cannot write this for you – you have to do it!"

To my dear friend and mentor, Kristie Petersen Schoonover, and the Pencils Writing Workshop for showing me real talent and for teaching me how it is developed.

To my beloved sister, JoAnn, for being an uncomplaining typist, proofreader, financial consultant, and landlady. I love you, sis.

As promised, heartfelt thanks to "Uncle Dutch" Jordan for curing a terminal case of writer's block by asking, "hey, did you ever consider a love triangle?" I miss ya tough guy!

And, of course, to my wife, Annie, for making me realize that Albert was from Flushing, not Houston! I miss you too, baby!

The true measure of one's existence is revealed in the mural he paints in the minds of those he has touched. If one paints that mural with the brush of compassion, he will surely leave behind a masterpiece.

Daido the Elder
1853

Prologue

In the days before medieval times, when men were barbaric and unenlightened by the wisdom of compassion, honesty, and justice, there were legends, stories, and rumors of a mystical race of creatures that were not human.

These beings, although diminutive in size (about one-third the height and weight of the average-sized man), were said to possess abilities far beyond the reach of mere humans. Legend has proclaimed them to be a benevolent race, and stories have been told that on occasion, they have bestowed their benevolence upon humans.

The legend of these creatures, dubbed woodland elves, grew out of stories told by travelers and minstrels, and were told and retold from generation to generation. A popular minstrel song told the story of Kalaya, the great warrior. Wounded in battle, he became separated from his defeated army. He wandered through the Scandinavian woods aimlessly for days without food or drink. Hopelessly lost and sick with fever, he lay down to die. Until his actual death many decades later, Kalaya swore that his life was saved by a band of "little people," who levitated his body (presumably because they were much too small to lift him), and treated him with salves and potions.

There were other tales that prevented all but a few brave souls from venturing into the vast woodland, believed to be a thousand miles deep--stories of evil trolls and ogres. Men who set off into the wood, never to be seen again, were said to have been eaten alive by these monsters. Such was the fear and superstition of medieval man, that the woodland elves lived undetected for hundreds of years.

The elves rejoiced in life's simple pleasures. Although the gifts and knowledge they possessed could easily garner them great wealth and power, the accumulation of wealth was contrary to their philosophy. The elves believed in the wisdom of being neither rich nor poor. They saw no advantage in amassing an empire whose vast population depended on continued economic and geographic growth. The elves saw this philosophy as self-defeating. They had too much respect for themselves and the world around them, as well as its inhabitants, to be engaged in what they believed to be the foolish pursuit of wealth and power. Their reverence toward one another was expressed daily in the way they conducted their lives, including the manner in which they spoke to each other. Terms such as "most honored one," or "most wise" were used regularly in everyday conversation.

A nation of hunters and gatherers, they lived in harmony with the land. They shared nature's bounty with the multitudes of herbivores they considered to be their brothers of the forest. The respect and loyalty of the more gentle animals was reinforced by the elves' uncanny ability to communicate with them telepathically. This alliance proved to be mutually beneficial, in that elves and animals kept each other informed as to the whereabouts of dangerous carnivores, as well as the evil trolls.

In the early summer of 1564, an historic meeting of the ruling body of the elf nation was called. The six oldest and wisest elves formed the governing committee, known as the Circle of Elders. Their regularly scheduled meetings were held to discuss and review matters of security and food supply, as well as all other matters pertaining to the well-being of the elf community.

On this day, however, a discussion was held on the formation of a new tradition: the quest. The meeting was called to order by Olaf the Sage, the senior elder. As the five others took their seats at the ancient circular table, Gudmund, the minister of security, asked to address the group. "Most honored brothers, I have received word from our scouts, and from our brothers of the forest. There have been no signs of our enemies for weeks. Our last troll sightings reported them to be heading toward the human village at the edge of the forest. I will continue to order more reconnaissance; however, I believe we are safe for the moment."

"I have bad feelings about this Gudmund," Olaf said. "We have always had sporadic sightings--this is highly irregular. Please double your patrols. My instincts are telling me that we are to expect trouble very soon."

"Consider it done, wise one. I have one other matter of some urgency to report. I have been informed that the foraging party has returned, minus one member. Rongee has somehow become separated from the group, and all efforts to locate the adolescent have proved futile. A search party is being formed as we speak."

"Good," Olaf replied. "I hope the young one comes to no harm, but for now you have done all that you can. Are there any other matters that demand our attention at this time?"

Thord the Lawgiver asked to be recognized. "My learned brethren, I believe it's time we did something about these ignorant and vulgar humans. Not only do they have no respect for the sanctity of the forest we share with them, they also have no respect for each other. They are a warring race. Lives are taken indiscriminately every day. Their greed and lust for power will surely bring about their eventual destruction, and possibly our own as well. They must be taught...."

Suddenly, a voice called from outside the chamber. Pallig the Sentry was requesting permission to enter and address the circle.

"Rongee has returned!" With a note of disbelief in his voice, the sentry announced that the young one had been among humans.

"Come forth now," Olaf commanded. "What has happened?"

A small voice came from behind the astounded Pallig. "If I may be allowed, wise one." Rongee stepped out from behind the sentry and bowed deeply. Dirty and bedraggled, his clothes riddled with thorns, the boy addressed the elders.

"Most honored members of the Circle, I am afraid I was foolish, and became enchanted with the wonders of the forest. I had forgotten about the rule of gathering by group. I know not how long or how far I had become separated from the others when I thought I heard some-one sobbing. The cries were slight and off in the distance. Thinking one of my brothers might be hurt, I walked toward the sound, and became even farther separated from my group. Soon, I came upon a female human child. She was sobbing violently, for she was bound to a tree and could not free herself. She begged me to release her before the trolls returned. While still in shock at the sight of this poor child, I heard deep gurgling noises coming from the wood behind me. I feared for my life as well as that of the child, for the noise was rapidly coming closer. I severed her bonds, grabbed her hand, and we ran through the briars and underbrush, toward the human village. We again heard the angry snarling and gurgling noises close behind us, when the trolls re-turned to find her gone. We did not look back. We ran until we could run no more. Suddenly, I was seized violently by my neck! I was being held aloft by a human woodsman, his ax at the ready.

" 'What have you done to my daughter, you vile creature? Speak now, before I off your head!'

" 'Wait! Father! This little man saved me from the trolls! If not for him, I would have been their next meal. Father, the evil ones are close. We must flee, please let him go.'

"At that moment," Rongee continued, "two giant trolls charged out of the underbrush. The very earth trembled under their raven-ous rush. The woodsman put me down and faced them. He remained calm, and threw his ax. His aim was true, for the ax found its mark deep in the forehead of the evil one. It let out an ear-piercing squeal and fell dead. Before the woodsman could remove the second ax from his belt, the other troll retreated back into the underbrush, screaming in panic. The woodsman embraced his child, and then spoke to me.

"'Thank you for rescuing my only child, little one. You are very brave. I fear I have almost made a terrible mistake, but I know not of your kind, and thought only of my daughter's safety.'

"'No harm done, honored sir. The child is safe, and you have slain our common enemy. I must go back now, but know this, honored sir. Your race need not fear the woodland elves. We are at peace with all but the trolls. I bid you long life and farewell.'"

The elders, astonished at young Rongee's adventure, did not reprimand him for being careless and becoming separated from his group. Instead they commended the youngster for his courage in a life-threatening situation, and for showing such compassion for someone not of his race.

Olaf rose from his chair and embraced the boy. "We are all very proud of you, Rongee. Your actions have expressed what all elves strive to be. Go to your family now and get some much-needed rest."

As soon as Pallig and the boy bowed out of the chamber, Solvi the Scholar spoke up. "If I may make a suggestion to my fellow elders, I have an idea that may be worth your consideration."

Olaf waved his arm in a motion that was to grant Solvi the floor. "The learned scholar's ideas are always worth our consideration," he said.

Solvi bowed in acceptance of the compliment before he spoke. "I have given Thord's complaint about the humans some thought, and several points have become clear to me. First, I agree that the unenlightened ways of the human race have become a situation that demands our attention. If we do nothing, the safety of our entire nation could be in jeopardy. However, news of young Rongee's heroic and benevolent actions today will become known to the humans. This will have a positive effect. The humans are not stupid; they are ignorant. The blight of ignorance can be eradicated with the introduction of knowledge. I believe if we inform and protect our youth with the knowledge and power of the ancients, they can venture forth into the world of humans safely. If we instruct our young to engage in deeds that illustrate our benevolent society, the humans will, in time, absorb our beliefs and learn from them. If we show them kindness, they will learn compassion. If we show them truth, they will learn the value of honesty. If we show them tolerance, they will become aware of the pointlessness of violence. In return, our young will learn the ways of the human world: their culture, religious beliefs, family structure, and so on. Upon their return, they will impart to us what they have learned. This will promote understanding between our races, so that one day we may live in harmony instead of fear and suspicion."

Although Thord maintained a degree of distrust toward humans, he could not go against the elves' natural propensity to reach out to those less fortunate than themselves. It was common knowledge among elves that humans were less fortunate--not only in how they were forced to live in those times, but in terms of intellect and wisdom, the elves' advantage was measurable.

And so, a vote was taken, and by majority rule, a new mandate was written into the ancient doctrine of elf culture. It was now written that upon the occasion of his sixteenth birthday, every male elf would be given a great feast to celebrate his ascension to maturity. At precisely midnight on the eve of this feast, the young one would be presented to the Circle of Elders for instruction. At this time he would be endowed by the elders with special tools and privileged knowledge that would ensure the successful completion of his quest.

There were, however, only three successful quests before tragedy befell the elf nation. The peaceful woodland elves were taken by surprise, and their population decimated in the great troll war of 1566. A once-thriving nation of more than six thousand elves was reduced to fewer than five hundred. The rest were either cannibalized or enslaved.

The intrepid survivors escaped to the coast, where they procured a great sailing ship and escaped to the new world, but not before enduring hardships heretofore unknown to them.

The stormy Atlantic was only the first test on a journey that lasted twelve years. The refugees traversed the entire North American continent before settling in the great Redwood Forest of northern California, where they live to this day.

Book One

Nelkie Comes of Age

Chapter One

"Please help us," Nelkie begged. "Bartholomew is hurt! He may be dying! Please open the door!" The young elf pounded on the deep fissures of the bark that concealed the secret door to the Passage Tree. Realizing that he could pound his tiny fist all day against the trunk of this mighty redwood to no avail, he tried desperately to scream louder.

"Coobik! Please open the door!"

Hearing Nelkie's muffled screams, Coobik cautiously opened the door to investigate. With his broadsword at the ready, he faced the youngster.

"How did you get outside, boy? You're in real trouble now." Coobik the Watcher was livid, for he knew he must have been duped. The warrior, charged with guarding the door to the entrance of the elf dominion, tricked by a sixteen-year-old boy! The elders would not take this lightly, he thought.

Just then, Bindar the Gatherer approached. He had returned from his foraging duties and did not understand the odd scene before him. Elves never congregated anywhere near the Passage Tree. This was strictly forbidden, for security reasons. The entrance to their secret kingdom would not remain concealed for very long if there were any activity other than the careful comings and goings involved in their daily lives. It was obvious to Bindar that this behavior was dangerous, as well as foolish. He would tell them so. Before he could voice his objections, Coobik ushered him inside.

"There's been an accident, Bindar. You must attend my post until I return. Keep a vigilant watch. If I do not return in twenty minutes, bolt the door and inform the elders of this emergency."

"Yes, of course," replied Bindar. "Go! I will keep watch here."

Coobik turned to the still-sobbing boy. "Take me to Bartholomew at once!"

Nelkie ran off in the direction where his friend lay, with Coobik at his heels.

Presently, they heard a female voice.

"Hurry! Over here! Straight ahead."

They arrived to find a mature doe licking Bartholomew's wound.

"He is unconscious and has lost a great deal of blood. You must get him help soon or he may die."

Coobik knelt and scooped the boy into his arms. "Thank you, Lilly. I'm sure these boys would have come to much greater harm, had it not been for your kind help."

The gentle doe focused her soft caring eyes on the older elf and made no audible sound, but they both heard her say, "We will always look out for our little brothers of the forest, as you do for us. Be well, my friend."

Coobik responded, "I will have Bindar leave you something special by the heart stones after nightfall." He then turned and sharply commanded Nelkie to return with him immediately.

As they approached the Passage Tree, Bindar's pudgy face popped around the door. "Gracious me!" he cried. "How bad is the boy?" They hurried inside. Coobik laid Bartholomew on the soft ground before he answered.

"Very bad. Broken leg. Lost a lot of blood. Go as fast as you can to the infirmary, Bindar, and bring the doctor. From there summon his parents--and I'm afraid Daido must be informed." Coobik next turned an angry look at Nelkie. "You stay here, boy. You have a lot to explain."

The gatherer was making his way to the manual elevator as fast as he could. Coobik called to him. "Get Balthazar down here too. He should be in the Toy Factory. Nelkie's father should know that his son is in trouble." Bindar nodded and then disappeared into the conveyance.

Nelkie was slowly gaining control of himself. He had stopped shaking and had finally caught his breath. For the first time in his young life, he felt great sadness and confusion. He was almost overcome with grief. The self-confidence that was so much a part of his personality had been shattered. Nelkie wished he could start this day over. He told himself that if he lived three hundred years, he would never have a worse birthday.

Chapter Two

Earlier that morning....

Nelkie was valiantly fighting off a fire-breathing dragon that was easily twenty times his size. The deadly spiked tail lashed out at the elf with whip-like speed.

Using the superior agility and reaction time that all young elves possess, Nelkie somersaulted over the beast's tail, landing flat-footed on an outcropping of rock.

A series of leaps and bounds, and Nelkie had gained advantage. He was now looking down on his adversary from the rocks above. In one motion, he drew his mighty sword, and leaped down onto the monster's neck. He raised his weapon to strike the fatal blow into the dragon's vital artery. Before the sword could pierce the spiny armor, Nelkie was blinded by a sudden flash of light. The light was overpowering. Nelkie became disoriented and lost his balance. He was falling.

He opened his eyes and rolled to his left. The light abated. No dragon. No rocks. Only the glorious golden sunrise streaming through the one foot-by-one foot window in his treetop bedroom.

The elf rose from his bed, his little heart still pumping with the pulsating adrenalin of battle. Stretching to his full height of twenty-seven inches, he shook off the night's adventure, and tried to refocus on the events of the new day. Then he remembered. He would wake up in this room only one more time before he would embark on the greatest adventure of his young life. He spoke aloud, as if to confirm his destiny. "Today is May sixth, my sixteenth birthday. Tomorrow I will leave the Great Redwood Forest, and set out on my quest into the world of humans!"

He removed his nightshirt, and got a clean tunic from the chest. Full-grown at sixteen, he was impishly good-looking. His alert blue eyes sharply contrasted with the vast mop of fiery red, very curly hair. Nelkie's hair was so thick and full that it nearly covered his pointed ears. His mother had told him that she was surprised his hearing, (which was extremely sharp, even for an elf) was not affected by all that hair. She was fond of saying that Nelkie could hear snow falling.

Nelkie's home was hidden deep in the Great Redwood Forest, in the Pacific Northwestern United States. His entire race lived hundreds of feet above the ground, inside the massive redwoods. Although they referred to themselves as American elves, they emigrated here from Scandinavia, after the Great Troll War, more than six hundred years ago.

Secure in their treetop home for generations, they continued to make toys for the children of the world. Very near the top of the expansive canopy was the relay station where the elves welcomed Santa, and refilled his sleigh every Christmas Eve.

It was now time for Nelkie to make his mark. His name would be entered with honor into the Great Book of Deeds. The gallant execution of his duties would be recorded to inspire future generations. At least that was how Nelkie pictured it. He was driven by an abundance of overconfidence, and was certain that he was ready to take on the biggest challenge of his life.

The smell of fresh cornbread began to float under his nose. Nelkie's favorite. He knew his mother had baked this treat as a special birthday present. Breakfast was beckoning. With his hands and feet against the outside of the loft ladder, he slid down into the living area in the blink of an eye. His mother, Anitra, called from the kitchen. "Nelkie, Balthazar, breakfast is ready. Come and sit while your tea is still hot." Balthazar entered the kitchen behind his son. He put his arm around the boy's shoulder and squeezed.

"A grand birthday morning to you, Son. How does it feel to start your first day as a mature elf?"

"I'm really excited, Father, but I don't think I feel any older or wiser. Maybe tonight, when I'm presented to the Circle of Elders, I will feel more mature."

"That you will, Son. It will be a night you will remember for hundreds of years."

Anitra leaned between them to set their tea on the table. As Nelkie looked up, he caught his mother trying to disguise her tear-stained face with a broad smile. He quickly looked away, not wanting to cause her any further discomfort.

"Good morning, Son," she said, unable to commit fully to crying, or smiling. "Happy Birthday, Nelkie. This day has come too soon. You were a toddler not so long ago, and by this time tomorrow you will be leaving us. It is a happy day for you, but a sad one for your parents. I know this is the most important event in the life of every male elf, but it is the saddest of days for his mother." Tears began to flow freely from eyes that were as green as a spring meadow. Nelkie rose and gave his mother a gentle hug.

"Don't worry, Mother. I won't be gone long, and I will return with gifts of wonder for you and Father."

"Oh!" she exclaimed. "Gifts! I was so caught up in my emotions that I almost forgot." She reached into the pocket of her apron and offered Nelkie a small box adorned with a bright red bow. "Your father and I had this made especially for you."

"We wanted to give you something unique on this day. Your mother and I chose something we know you will cherish all your life."

Nelkie carefully removed the bow and opened the box, revealing a gleaming gold ring. In its center was a large amber stone, flanked by two darker-colored stones.

"Father, this is the most beautiful thing I will ever own! Thank you--and thank you, Mother." Nelkie slid the ring on his finger and promised never to remove it.

"We knew you would like it, Son," his father said. "I should tell you that this is no ordinary ring. It was hand crafted by Ragnar, master jeweler and alchemist to the Circle of Elders. This ring is the first item you have ever owned that contains the power of the Ancients. It also contains the very essence of your mother and me, so our spirits will travel with you."

Anitra said, "We hope it will bring you comfort when you are far from home. In a small way, we will be with you on your journey."

At that moment, the family breakfast was interrupted by a loud knock on the front door. Balthazar answered with the customary "Enter, and join us in peace."

A female juvenile of ten years marched into the room in a military manner, and answered, "And may peace be with all of you." Her innocent face was framed by a large volume of very straight baby-fine light-brown hair. Her dark eyes shone with the excitement of the moment. In her fragile-looking thin arms she clutched a large rolled-up parchment embellished with an official-looking blue ribbon. She removed the ribbon, announced herself, and read the ceremonial document.

"Nelkie, son of Balthazar and Anitra, I am Thora, first page to the Circle of Elders. I bring you the warmest of birthday greetings from Daido the Sage, presiding First Elder, and fellow members of the Circle. Your presence, and that of your parents, is required this evening at seven o'clock in the Great Hall. Your birthday feast will be attended by all our brothers of the forest. There will be music, magic, and merrymaking. At precisely midnight, you will be summoned to appear at the Inner Chamber of the Circle of Elders. You will receive counseling, instruction, and gifts from the elders to help you in the successful completion of your quest. We look forward to this evening's feast, and to your presentation to this distinguished body. In keeping with the wisdom and traditions of the Ancients, this is the word of the Circle of Elders." She rolled the parchment back into its original shape, and retied the ribbon. "I present to you this scroll, to be placed with honor into your family archives." She bid them congratulations, and with her official duties executed proficiently, she bowed and backed out of the doorway.

"Wow! That was fantastic," Nelkie said. He was holding his parchment reverently, and grinning from one pointed ear to the other.

Balthazar interrupted Nelkie's euphoria, only to add more. He took a final sip of tea, stood, and faced his son. "You do not have to report to The Toy Factory today, Son. It is customary for the honored elf to have the day of his sixteenth birthday work-free. I have many projects to oversee, however, so I must be off. Enjoy your day, Son. I will see you before tonight's banquet." Balthazar put on his hat and kissed his wife goodbye. "See you for lunch, dear."

Once her husband left, Anitra asked her son what his plans were for the day.

"I thought I would go down to see Bart. You know he's had an awful cold. Maybe if he feels better, we'll swing over to the game room for a while."

"All right," his mother answered. "But remember, young elves are not to go out into the forest in daylight. Tonight you will receive your instructions from the elders, and tomorrow you will be fully prepared for the challenges of the forest."

"Yes, Momma--I know, I know. I'll probably have lunch at Bart's. I'll be home long before the feast."

"Have fun, Nelkie, but please be good. Remember, today is not a day for you to make mischief."

"Mischief? Me? Mother, how can you say that?"

As if she were looking for help from above, Anitra's eyes rolled skyward. "Nelkie, I love you dearly, but I wish you would learn to honor the elf ways more."

Nelkie flashed an impish grin and said, "I will try, Mother."

He left to go down one level in the great redwood. Bart's living quarters were directly below his own. He knocked at the entryway. Bart's mom Sigrid waved him in.

"Happy birthday, Nelkie. Are you ready for your big event?"

"Sure. I've *been* ready. You know, my apprenticeship is going very well," Nelkie pontificated. "I will be a master toy maker like my father in no time, but a mature elf needs to make his mark. We need to break from the day-to-day sameness of life in the treetops, and embrace the adventure that awaits us on the ground."

Sigred smiled to herself in acknowledgement of the ignorance of youth. She thought these statements foolish from one who had never set foot upon the ground. She chose to keep her thoughts to herself, and welcomed her son's best friend. "Bartholomew is in his room; go right in."

"Thank you, ma'am." Nelkie entered his friend's room to find Bart fully dressed.

"Glad to see you're feeling better, my friend," he said.

"Hi, Nelkie. Come on in." Nelkie asked if his friend if he had to report to his apprenticeship today.

"No sir. My father says my engineering studies can wait one more day, until I'm completely over my cold. Are you nervous about to-night?" he asked.

"Don't think so. I'm excited, and very anxious to speak with the elders. Some of our friends have told me stories about what goes on once a young elf enters the Inner Chamber, but they're just guessing. I mean, after all, Bart, I'm the eldest of our group of friends. It's not like any of them have ever been there."

"Yes, of course you're right, but tell me what you've heard. I want to know, just in case any of it is true, because I'm next in line to be presented--you know, I'm only two months behind you."

"Well," Nelkie began, "young Bindar said his father told him that Daido the Wise performs amazing feats of magic and wonder. Things you and I have never seen before, and that can only be explained as supernatural. However, the Bindar I know is not one who will let the truth stand in the way of a good story."

"Are you saying he lies?"

"Lies? No. Exaggerates? Yes. I have also heard that all the elders, in turn, pass on their individual wisdom to the young voyager, and that makes a lot of sense. I just can't wait to find out for myself what the truth is. I've been waiting for so long for my quest to begin, I just can't stand waiting any longer. I want to be out in the forest. I want to be free to do whatever I want. I want to find out if what I've heard is true. Especially things like elves being able to converse with wild animals, and if they are truly endowed with the power of the ancients, which can enable them to levitate objects with their minds, and even render themselves invisible. It sure beats making toys. I really need to get out there. Say, I just got an idea." Nelkie leaned closer to his friend. He lowered his voice so Bart's mother could not hear. "You know, Bart, we are almost adult elves now--certainly I am. I don't think that rule about young elves staying inside during daylight hours applies to me. After all, I'm sixteen today, and I'm a pretty smart elf. I can take care of myself. That rule is probably meant for babies who are not yet experienced enough to venture outside."

"I don't know," Bart said. "My parents always say that any elf that disobeys could meet with grave consequences. Rule Number One for young elves states that no elf shall go through the passage tree into the forest in daylight, until after his presentation to the Circle of Elders, upon his sixteenth birthday."

"You sound just like my mother, Bart. C'mon, let's be realistic. The facts are that I *am* sixteen and I *will* be presented tonight. And for that matter, you are practically an adult yourself. Today is a perfect day for us get a little peek at what awaits us. No one will even be looking for us until lunchtime. We could sneak out and be back long before we're missed."

Bartholomew seriously considered his friend's point of view before he spoke. "Hmm, you could be right, Nelkie. I too have wanted to see what this tree looks like from the ground for a very long time. I think I'm bright enough to handle a little innocent field trip--and besides, according to the ancients, I will be an adult in only two months. What difference could it make if I go out today, or two months from now?"

"Exactly my point, my friend. Although there is as they say, a fly in the ointment. We have to figure out how to get past old Coobik, and that won't be easy."

"You're right. No one goes in or out of the Passage Tree without his knowledge. All movement is recorded in his log, not to mention that he's a half-human giant who carries a broadsword! Not someone I want angry at me, pal. I think we need some kind of diversion Nelkie. If the watcher's attention was elsewhere, maybe one of us could sneak out."

"That's it!" Nelkie said, jumping to his feet.

"Shh!" Bart cautioned. "Not so loud. *What's* it?"

"Don't you see? It's obvious! No one has ever tried to sneak *out* of here before. He's watching for someone trying to break in! He won't suspect a thing."

The two mischievous elves began planning their escape to adventure. Foolishly, they gave no thought to the dangers that lay ahead, and this would prove to be their undoing.

A short time had passed when Sigred announced she had to go to the storage area. "I must get some supplies for my kitchen," she said. "Maybe I'll visit with Anitra for a little while. Will I see you boys for lunch?"

"Yes, Mama, we'll be here." When she was gone, they went

over their plan. After a while they were quite sure that each of them knew his part in the grand scheme perfectly. They stood, shook hands, and smiled at each other. They felt confident that they would fool the watcher, have their adventure, and return safely. This was not to be.

Chapter Three

The two friends made their way through the canopy, passing entrances and exits for different elf functions along the way. They passed The Toy Factory, Food and Grain Storage, and the Emergency Evacuation Tree. Nelkie and Bart continued along the treetops until they arrived at The Passage Tree, with Bart leading the way.

Most of the young elves, including Bart, looked up to Nelkie as a natural leader. It was usually Nelkie who initiated their activities when the young ones were unsupervised. Now and again Nelkie's interpretation of what would be fun or adventurous would lead to problems with their parents. Despite the occasional troublesome result, the boys willingly followed Nelkie's lead because his confidence inspired them, and his schemes and adventures were always fun.

This adventure, however, was quite a different scenario, and Nelkie was smart enough to recognize that fact. His best friend was an engineering apprentice, studying under his father, a mechanical genius. Aud the Senior Engineer was in charge of maintaining and repairing the elevator system that transported elves from the treetops to ground level. Nelkie knew that through his studies, Bart had gained much more than a working knowledge of the system. For this reason, the role of leader clearly belonged to his friend.

Bartholomew opened the door and motioned his friend in. "Step right in, Nelkie, and don't worry. My father has taught me how and why this machine works, and I am fully qualified to operate it." They scampered into the wooden box that was large enough to hold five adult elves. Nelkie closed the half-door safety gate behind them. Once inside, Nelkie reinforced his faith in his friend. "I hope you know I wouldn't let just anybody hold my life in their hands, Bart. We're more than two hundred thirty feet from the ground…that's a long way down."

"I appreciate your trust, my friend--and fear not, you are in capable hands. I helped my father lubricate all the pulleys only yesterday. Here, I'll show you how it works. Once I release this lever, the elevator goes into freefall. You have to work the brake levers very carefully or the ropes can knot up and jam, or heat up and ignite."

"Oh, I feel much better now, Bart! Heat up and ignite. I especially like that part!"

"Relax, Nelkie. It's like the humans are fond of saying--it's a piece of cake." Bart's bony fingers grasped the brake lever, and for a split second Nelkie thought gravity had abandoned him. Nelkie had never ridden the elevator before and felt like his stomach was about to hit him in the chin. While Nelkie's knuckles were turning white in their death grip around the safety bar, Bartholomew calmly worked the brake levers and maintained their descent at a reasonable rate of speed. As Bart stopped at ground level with hardly a bump, Nelkie's grip and fears relaxed. He let out a deep breath and congratulated his friend. "Great job, Bart! All right, phase two. Step back into the corner, and I'll let myself out. You know what to do next. Good luck, pal."

"Thanks. You, too."

Nelkie exited the elevator, and for the first time experienced the earth-scented, darkened chamber that led to the outside world. His eyes were drawn to the only light in the room, which came from a small oil lamp on Coobik's podium. The watcher looked up from his post to see who was there. Mildly surprised to see an immature elf walking toward him, he put down his quill and stood up. "Well, young one, what brings you all the way down here?"

"Good morning, Coobik. I'm Nelkie, I believe you know my

father, Balthazar the Master Toy Maker."

Coobik knew this boy was not yet allowed into the forest. He carried no pouch for provisions, and had no other gear that would confirm his mission status.

"What's your purpose here, Son?"

Nelkie would not allow himself to be intimidated by the giant warrior, for fear of having his grand plan exposed before he could even get outside. He swallowed hard and recited his well-rehearsed speech. "Well sir, today is my sixteenth birthday, and I thought maybe you would let me just peek out the Passage Tree door, just for a moment." As Nelkie spoke, Bartholomew silently exited the elevator and hid among the shadows. "I was hoping that since I'm scheduled to exit tomorrow, you might just let me poke my head out for a minute today. I'm just so excited about leaving on my quest tomorrow, I was hoping you would be kind enough to let me see what awaits outside this door."

While Nelkie engaged the older elf in conversation, Bart crept slowly along the heavily shadowed wall. His heart was pounding with excitement as he drew closer to the door.

"I don't know, Son. This is very unusual. You're asking me to almost break the rules."

"I would *never* suggest that you break any rules, Wise One. Couldn't you just allow me to have my head outside this tree for only a moment? I would really like to see what the forest path looks like. I've only seen the forest from my window far above here, and I've been told that everything on the forest floor is gigantic!"

Coobik felt the young elf's excitement and understood his impatience and curiosity.

"All right, my boy. But only for a moment, and I will have to enter this into my log."

"Thank you so much!"

They both moved toward the concealed door. Bartholomew waited until their backs were turned, and snuck behind Coobik's podium.

The warrior elf unbolted the secret door and slowly pulled it open just a crack. As Coobik scanned the area, Nelkie became enchanted by the musky fragrance of the forest floor.

"Keep your legs and feet inside, Son."

"Yes, sir! I will, sir!" Nelkie slowly moved his head out into the wondrous woodland. "Wow! Look at those flowers! They're almost as tall as me!"

Coobik laughed to himself, and turned his attention to his log-book. While Coobik was busy writing, he was completely unaware that Bartholomew had crept along the shadows and slipped out the door.

Once outside, Bart ran around the trunk of the giant tree. When he was sure he was far enough from the door, he looked up. He was dumbstruck at the sheer height of the tree. He now knew for sure that no one on the ground would ever see any of the tiny windows, which were more than a hundred feet above. He waited for his friend and amused himself by taking in all the sights, sounds, and smells of the forest at ground level.

Back inside the great redwood, Nelkie graciously thanked Coobik for bending the rules.

"I better go back up now. Thank you again, very much."

"You're welcome, Son, and I'll see you tonight."

"Yes, sir." Nelkie walked over to the wall, but only pretended to enter the elevator. He took up his friend's former position and waited.

Presently, as the boys expected, the elevator door opened and out stepped the most roly-poly elf Nelkie knew, with his party of four close behind. He was the father of one of Nelkie's friends. Bindar was at least twice as round as any other elf. Nelkie figured this was prob-ably because he was a gatherer. Every day at this time, Bindar would leave with a large empty sack over his shoulder. He would return sev-eral hours later with as many nuts and berries as he could carry. Nelkie guessed that for every nut Bindar put in his sack, he put two in his mouth. He was a very fat elf.

Nelkie positioned himself very quickly and quietly behind Bindar. The corpulent elf's body shielded him from the unsuspecting Coobik.

"Morning, Coobik. I'll see if I can find some of your favorite blackberries this morning."

"Thanks, Bindar. You folks can let yourselves out while I make my entry here."

"Okay. See you in a couple of hours."

Coobik waved, but never looked up. As the group marched out the door, Nelkie carefully kept in step. He crouched over and made sure he kept Bindar and his gatherers between himself and the watcher, who was not watching anyway. When they were all out the door, the last in line turned to shut the door behind them. Nelkie sprang off in the opposite direction, bounding out of their line of sight. He ran around behind the tree to find his friend still staring upward. When Bindar had waddled out of earshot with the others close behind, he grabbed his friend and said, "We did it, Bart! We fooled 'em. We're outside!" Nelkie followed Bart's upward gaze and was just as taken as his friend. "This must be the biggest living thing in the whole world," he said.

"I think you're right. I can't see even halfway up this thing!" Bart agreed.

Let's have a look around. Maybe we'll see a fox or a rabbit."

"Okay, but let's be careful not to forget where this tree is. You know, there are so many of them, and they all look pretty much the same."

Nelkie looked around and noticed two large boulders leaning against one another. Together, they formed the shape of a ten-foot-tall heart. "All we have to do is remember where those big rocks are," he said pointing.

"Right."

So they set off on their first adventure ever, without a care in the world...least of all, how they were going to get back inside. They danced around the forest, eating fresh berries right off the bush.

"Do you smell that?" Bart asked

"Yes. Honeysuckle," Nelkie answered. The vine towered over their heads. The very air was filled with its sweet perfume. They had never experienced anything like this. They played and danced, and ate for over an hour.

"We should probably think about going back, Nelkie. I'll race you!" Nelkie started after him, but stopped suddenly. He thought he heard something.

"Wait, Bart!" he cried. Then he heard it again.

"Tell your friend to stop! Tell him to stop now! He is in danger. Quickly, now!"

The origin of the voice was a mystery to Nelkie. It was as if the voice was coming from inside his head! He yelled to his friend. "Bart! Stop! Trouble!"

Bart slowed his pace, and turned to look quizzically at his friend. He heard Nelkie's voice, but could not make out the words.

It was then that Nelkie saw her. A beautiful mature doe. She was standing only a few feet to his right. Their eyes met, and the voice inside his head spoke again.

"You must stop him *now*! He is in great danger!"

All at once Nelkie realized that the female voice he heard in his head belonged to the doe, and she was warning him. He shook his head and turned his attention to Bart. "Stop now!" he screamed.

Bart had slowed to a trot. He didn't understand why all of a sudden, Nelkie would not follow. "Why is he yelling?" he asked himself. Just then, with no warning, Bartholomew felt the most intense pain shooting through his left leg. He went down, screaming for Nelkie's help.

Nelkie was frozen with fear. Something terrible had happened to his friend, but he had no idea what. He turned to see the doe walking toward him.

"I tried to warn you," she said. "I think your friend is caught in a bear trap. They are set all along this area. Now go, little elf, and help your friend, before he bleeds to death."

Nelkie was so upset that he was literally shaking with fear. For the first time in his life he was experiencing bone-chilling fear. Under any other circumstances, he would have been astounded that a wild animal could communicate with him using only her mind, but his preoccupation with his friend's agonizing cries for help allowed him to think of nothing else. Gingerly, he passed through the tall flora. He called Bart's name while trying to keep one eye on his feet, and one eye searching. Finally he stumbled onto Bart's tormented little form. The boy was sobbing uncontrollably. Both of his tiny hands were pulling desperately at the steel jaws clamped unmercifully to his leg. Nelkie fell to his knees beside his friend, his heart racing. He was crying, shaking, and scared half to death. He didn't know what to do. There was blood everywhere. He had never seen one of these traps. He felt helpless. In desperation, Nelkie tried pulling on the steel jaws, but all that did was make Bart cry out in agony.

Just then he heard the voice again. It was a calm and soothing voice. Nelkie looked up to see the doe standing over the two of them.

"Stand aside, young one, and I will help you." Nelkie bolted immediately. With the boy clear, the doe reared up on her hind legs, and with all her weight on her front hooves she came down on the trap's release. The jaws sprang open, and Bart screamed again.

"You must get help right away. I will stay with him until you return."

"Thank you, thank you," Nelkie blubbered through his tears.

He ran off frantically searching for the two heart-shaped rocks. There! Off to the Left! Everything was blurry. He could barely see out of his tear-soaked eyes. With his lungs burning, gasping for air, he reached the Passage Tree. At first he couldn't find the door, for it was well concealed within the tree's bark. He began screaming as loudly as he could, "Coobik, let me in! It's Nelkie, please let me in!

Chapter Four

Coobik was beside himself. His initial rage at Nelkie had simmered down to mere anger. It came to him that he was actually angrier with himself than he was with Nelkie. His pride was hurt, and he began to question his own credibility. How could an immature boy perpetrate a successful scam against an experienced warrior? The watcher knew he had to figure out why this debacle had occurred, and how to prevent its reoccurrence. Maybe the mundane sameness of his daily routine had affected his ability to stay alert. He had encountered only minor problems for a very long time. He thought back. The last time things were shaken up at all was about forty years ago. A forest fire had been encroaching on the tiny elf kingdom. There was an air of panic in the forest. Animals large and small were fleeing by the Passage Tree in great numbers, warning the elves of the impending danger. Luckily, humans had beaten back the flames a few short miles from their domain. Since then the humdrum of his daily duties may have lulled this once-valiant warrior into a false sense of security. He decided that he would speak to the elders about changing his routine. He felt that if he could go on regular hunting and reconnaissance forays, his keen sense of awareness would return.

While Coobik was considering all this, and making his log entries, Nelkie sat by his friend, trying not to think the worst. Bartholomew had not yet regained consciousness. His breathing looked more even, Nelkie thought. *I hope the doctor gets here soon. If Bart should die, it will be my fault.*

Presently, the medical crew arrived, led by the chief physician, Malachi. He had been administering medical aid to his fellow elves for nearly two hundred years, and he had seen this kind of injury before. As his two apprentices assembled a small stretcher, he carefully checked the boy for any other problems beside the obvious one. Satisfied, he directed his subordinates to transport the patient to the infirmary.

"His parents are to meet us there," he said.

Coobik put down his quill, and asked if the boy would be all right.

"Yes. He is lucky that you got him back here right away. Luckier still that the trap did not sever his leg. Such an occurrence is not uncommon. We must act swiftly now. I will send you word of the boy's condition."

"Thank you, Malachi."

The doctor led his two stretcher bearers to the elevator entrance. Balthazar, still in his shop apron, stood holding the door open. The physician saw the concerned look on his face and remarked, "He will be fine, Balthazar. In a few hours he will not even be in any pain."

"That's wonderful. Thank you." They passed each other and then Balthazar found his son sitting down, with his back to the wall and his head down. Nelkie had heard his father's voice, but was too ashamed to look at him. He had expected the worst possible reaction, and thus was somewhat calmed by Balthazar's first question.

"Nelkie, are you hurt, Son?"

"No, Father, but I am afraid I have embarrassed you and Mother greatly today. I have done some things that were very wrong. I talked Bart into coming with me. He didn't think it was a good idea, and reminded me of Rule Number One, but I couldn't wait to go out, and I didn't think anything would go wrong."

The young elf looked up, and was startled to see Daido the Elder standing next to his father. Nelkie began to shake with fear. He thought the senior elder would now inform him of his terrible punishment for his unspeakable deeds.

Daido's presence was commanding. Power and authority seemed to emanate from him. At almost four feet tall, he stood more than a foot taller than Nelkie's father. His craggy face and stormy grey eyes had a mesmerizing effect on all his brethren. He spoke softly, but with authority. His voice was very deep, with great resonance.

"Do not fear me, Son. I am here only to gather all the facts pertaining to this incident, and report my findings to the elders for review. Now, if you will, take your time and tell me how all of this has come about."

Feeling only slightly less frightened, Nelkie told the elder how he and Bart conceived and carried out a plan to fool Coobik. He swore he never meant to put himself or his friend in any danger. "I guess my curiosity overwhelmed my common sense. I should have known better."

Instead of showing anger or disappointment in the young one Daido praised the boy for his honesty and sincerity. "Acknowledging one's mistake is the first step toward rectifying that mistake. Your only failure here was not thinking your plan all the way through. Had your thought process gone one step farther, you would have realized the possibility of danger from unknown sources. At which point, I believe you and Bartholomew would have abandoned your plan as a bad idea."

That being said, Daido instructed the boy to get some rest. "I will send word to you after I have conferred with the Circle of Elders. There is a valuable lesson to be learned from this unfortunate experience, Nelkie. I hope that in the future, you will be more conscious of the danger in a hastily conceived plan. Now I must take my leave to convene with the elders."

Daido withdrew silently. Balthazar put his arm around his son's shoulders. "Come. You have had too much excitement for one day. After you have gotten some rest, we'll check on your friend."

"Thank you, Father. I have exhausted myself both physically and emotionally, and I need to lie down in my own bed. Before I do, I want you to know that I understand what the wise one said. I *have* learned a valuable lesson."

"That's all anyone can ask, Son." They entered the elevator together. As Balthazar operated the ropes, they ascended in silence, each reflecting on the events of the day.

Chapter Five

D aido took his seat at the aged oak table, and called the special
session to order. "I am sure you are all aware of the events that
took place outside the Passage Tree this morning. I have asked for
this meeting in order for all of us to become fully informed of these
events, and to find a solution to any circumstances created thereby."
The senior elder went on to report the situation as it was explained
to him by Coobik and Nelkie. "Coobik has been granted permission
to address this meeting, and will arrive momentarily. The floor is
now open for comment."

The high-pitched voice of Wolfstan the Purveyor broke the silence. "My fellow elders, I would like to note that we should count
our blessings. By that, I mean we are lucky the boys did not eat anything poisonous. We are all familiar with the vast array of potentially
lethal vegetation that grows wild throughout our Great Redwood
Forest. Nelkie and Bartholomew have not yet received any instruction concerning the dangers of living off the land. Until today, there
has been no need for this instruction until the youngsters' presentation to the Circle. Obviously, if these boys had ingested any of the
vegetation in question, we would have two very sick young elves
on our hands. Even worse, without knowing what they were eating, they could both have expired before any of us knew they were
missing. I feel it is of paramount importance that we do not wait for
the prospective elf's presentation to impart this vital knowledge. It
should be a mandated course of study for all elves, male and female.

I say this because, if by chance, a disaster stuck--for example, forest fire, emergency evacuation, or even war--at least our young ones would be armed with this information. I would feel much better if I knew that if a separation should occur, our youth would be able to survive until they were reunited with their brethren. I do hereby submit my resolution to the Circle for consideration." With his point well made, Wolfstan took his seat.

Daido then addressed the elders. "Wolfstan has brought an important issue to our attention. I now call for a vote. By show of hands, who supports the introduction of a wild vegetation study into the current curriculum?"

The elders were all of one mind on this subject, and so the motion was carried without dissent.

Hanibal rose to address the group. "As security is my function within this body, I am duty-bound to raise this point with my esteemed fellow elders. I believe what we have here is a serious breach of security. This occurrence could have had ramifications that would directly affect the safety and security we all rely on."

Hanibal's statement was loudly interrupted as the watcher angrily stormed into the chamber. "Hanibal is right! This episode should be dealt with firmly. Those boys ignored Rule Number One, and should be punished!"

Suddenly mindful of his whereabouts, the warrior apologized, bowed deeply, and corrected himself. "Your honored servant requests permission to enter this chamber, and address the wise ones."

"Enter in peace," Daido answered.

"And peace be with all of you," the watcher respectfully returned.

Daido rose and motioned Coobik to a chair. "Now Coobik, my loyal friend and protector," he continued, "I was going to warn you about your agitated human side gaining dominance over your elf half. I see that you have caught yourself, and I compliment you on your self-control. I can only imagine how difficult it is for you to remain objective when half your blood is boiling. Now, on to more important issues. We must understand fully what has happened and why, and learn from this experience. I now open the floor for discussion."

Falco the Keeper of Laws was next to speak. "I am in agreement with Hanibal. This is a security breach--even if it is an inverted one, we must be sure that this remains a one-time event. I believe we should interpret this as a warning. The next question that must be asked is this. Even though Nelkie and Bartholomew have come of age, are they mature enough emotionally, intellectually, and spiritually to be presented to this body at this time? Perhaps we should consider postponement of their quest."

At this point Coobik stood, still trying to subdue his human side, which was screaming for retribution. "If I may address my most-esteemed elders, I am the one against whom this scheme was perpetrated. This ruse was premeditated and clandestine. With that understood, I believe quest postponement for *both* Nelkie and Bartholomew is simply not sufficient punishment. I say their actions are inexcusable. In all honesty, I believe the possibility of banishment should be considered."

Daido leaped to his feet, his calm grey eyes showing the slightest telltale signs of anger and disappointment. "I would like to remind the watcher that this meeting has convened to fix the problem, not the blame. We should all be careful not to mete out severe punishment for something that may not have been more than an infraction. Banishment is our most strict form of punishment, and is implemented only when the elf in question is found guilty of betrayal, or treason. Justice is to be delivered with wisdom and fairness. Let us not forget that the young do not always do the right thing. Foolishness is a by-product of youth. I should also remind our guardian that these proceedings are conducted in accordance with the rules of decorum set forth by the ancients, and adherence to those rules is mandatory. Outbursts of anger or ill-temper will not be tolerated!"

"As always, the insight and good judgment of the senior elder prevails." The watcher made his reply while staring at the floor in embarrassment. Daido's statement had made Coobik realize that his need for revenge against the boys was rooted in his belief that the boys had humiliated him. The watcher's perception of this situation was that he had been shown to be an incompetent fool in the eyes of those who trusted him with their lives. The manifestation of his human emotions resulted in his lashing out in anger. For this, he sincerely apologized. Daido nodded in acceptance, and asked if anyone else had anything to add.

Voltor signaled a request to speak, which was granted. "Most honored members of the Circle, as senior historian, I would like to point out that the boys' presentation is a birthright. We have never denied any young one this honor. I agree with our valiant watcher that what these boys have done is very serious indeed, especially if one considers what may happen in the future, if some form of reprimand is not implemented. I feel that we should take great care in the teaching and disciplining of this generation, for they are like none that have come before. They are more inquisitive, and not just about elf lore and history, but about the world that lies beyond the great forest. They are brighter, and more daring than their predecessors, as evidenced by the events of this morning. Our community has always held the education of our young as a duty. All of us are committed to the acquisition of a higher education. There is, however, only so much we can teach.

"Hundreds of quests have proven to be a successful means for our youth to acquire knowledge and experience that cannot be taught within the confines of our tiny kingdom. If we are to have faith in the Prophecies of the Ancients, which foretell the ascension of a chosen one, a great leader, who will come to power in the twenty-fourth century, and unite our nation with humankind, we must uphold the tradition of the quest. While the possibility still exists of this world eventually achieving a universal peace, we should be vigilant in our pursuit of this goal. If I may move on to the matter of disciplining the boys, I would like to note that a certain amount of trust is involved in our decision: our trust that these boys will not betray their oath of secrecy, and their trust in their own honor and abilities. If we do not foster belief in these virtues, our society will crumble to its very foundation. I would like to go on record as saying that I am in complete agreement with our most senior member in regard to punishment. If we allow these boys to assume the responsibilities of their quest, we will light the path to wisdom and maturity. On the other hand, if we punish them, that light will be extinguished by the winds of disappointment and failure. That is my position, and I will now relinquish the floor."

Daido again addressed his brethren. "Thank you for your intuitiveness, Voltor. You have proved once more that your seat within this Circle is well-deserved. It is also my considered opinion that Nelkie and Bartholomew should not be denied their birthright, and we should continue with our plans to receive Nelkie this midnight. However, there are, as I see it, two separate issues that still need to be resolved. One: How do we prevent a reoccurrence of this debacle? And two: Should some form of discipline be administered? I now open the floor for discussion."

"I have a possible answer," Telrin offered. "I think we can resolve both issues with one solution. By that, I mean both of these boys should be commanded to write a formal apology to Coobik, as well as the general populace. This apology should be posted at the entrance to the Great Hall, where everyone can read it. I believe that having to compose a sincere apology will humble them and thereby resolve the discipline problem. In terms of deterring the possible reoccurrence of this difficulty, I do not think that any adolescent would want to stand before the Circle of Elders in order to explain his wrongdoing. Sufficient incentive to be law-abiding should be provided by the threat of having to face public humiliation as a lawbreaker. I would like to call for a vote on this proposal."

Telrin's suggestion was carried unanimously by a show of hands, after which Daido again stood to address the group. "Coobik has petitioned this body to make a request, which I hope has been tempered by his more rational elf side." The senior elder's comments were met with muted laughter from the Circle, after which Coobik was allowed to speak.

"Most honored elders, I will stand by your decision to allow the boys to advance toward adulthood, even though I am not so sure they are deserving of this privilege. I must now get past this issue and speak to the wise ones on my own behalf. I stand before you humbled by failure. I failed to read Nelkie's deception, the consequence of which was the near death of one of our own. I have given my situation much thought, and have drawn a few conclusions. Firstly, let it be known to all that I do not take my responsibilities lightly. I am honored and indeed privileged to be the one chosen as our first line of defense. Unfortunately I also believe that my perceptions, reflexes, and perhaps even my judgment have been dulled by the absence of physical challenges and regular exercise. I know I can sharpen my skills to their former level if I am permitted to hunt and mount an occasional reconnaissance mission. I beseech you to grant me the privilege of restoring my skills to that of a battle-ready warrior."

"I think I can speak for all of us when I say that we respect your desire for self- betterment," Hanibal said. "I will give you my word, Coobik, that whenever you wish to go out and conquer the forest, I will be honored to man your post myself."

"Thank you, wise one. I esteem your trust, and I will make you proud. If it can be arranged, I would like to set out this afternoon to bag some fresh game for Nelkie's feast tonight."

"Consider it done, brave one. Give me one hour, and I will meet you at your post."

"Thank you, all of you." Coobik continued bowing and thanking as he backed out the door, and out of sight.

Hanibal's grin infected the others as he spoke. "We are more than fortunate to have Coobik as our watcher. He showed his dedication today, and I for one am very proud of him." The others all nodded their heads in collective agreement.

Chapter Six

Malachi's assistants were busy removing Bartholomew's torn clothing, and cleaning his wound. After a short conference with the boy's parents, the doctor assured them Bartholomew would be up and about in a few hours. "Go home and have some tea," he said. "I don't want you to see him right now, because his injury looks much worse than it really is. You can do no good for him here, so go home and try to relax a little. I promise he will walk through your doorway under his own power in a very short while."

The parents left, arm in arm. They were still concerned about their son, but felt better now that they had talked to the good doctor.

Malachi went to his supply cabinet to gather ingredients for his special bone-healing salve. "Let's see...I'll need some stag horn powder, and a small amount of web compound from a giant wood spider. Oh yes, I'll need some evaporating agent and a good amount of aloe." He spread them out on his table, and went to work with his mortar and pestle. "Bee pollen, and then the horn powder," he said aloud. He ground the components carefully, and added the aloe last. When he was pleased with the consistency of the mixture, he brought it over to the boy's bed. Malachi slowly and deliberately showed his apprentices how to properly position and set the bone. Once this procedure was finished, the two assistants began to apply the salve.

"Apply it thicker," the doctor directed. "It should continue at least one inch above and one inch below the actual break." While the two younger elves were busy with their task, Malachi went to the small stone oven that he had fired up earlier. Grasping the stone handle firmly, he raised the door. After peering inside, he informed his helpers of the situation status. "The healing stone is almost white-hot," he said. As soon as you are done applying the salve, we can begin." The younger elves finished up and Malachi picked up the steel tongs that were next to the oven. He removed the small stone, which was about the size of a tablespoon. The doctor then gingerly touched the stone to the salve directly over the break. The wound sizzled with the introduction of heat. Steam rose from Bart's leg as the salve bubbled up around the shattered bone. The boy stirred, but did not wake. Malachi removed the stone after several seconds. He explained to his attentive students that their ancestors had dis-covered that this combination of ingredients, coupled with the heat from this particular stone would produce a chemical reaction. The consequence of this reaction was such that the bone would immedi-ately knit itself back together, and the wound would be cauterized and protected from infection. The rapid cell regeneration promoted by the salve would be complete in less than one hour.

"I will now prepare some of my medicinal hot tea, which when administered will remove all pain from this boy's body." The doctor combined small pieces of selected tree bark, residue from the roots of medicinal plants, as well as some powerful herbs. After blending them into boiling water, he poured the brew into a large mug and let it stand for a moment. "We are now ready to return our patient to the waking world."

Malachi removed his personal blend of smelling salts from his supply cabinet and held them under the boy's nose. Bartholomew in-stantly gagged and sputtered, and then took a very deep breath, his eyes wide with the shock of his sudden awakening. The two assistants quickly grabbed the boy and gently assured him that he was all right.

"Where's Nelkie?" he asked.

Malachi appeared before the boy with his mug of tea. "Your

friend is home resting. He is uninjured. He and Coobik brought you home. Now, drink your tea. We need this in your body to ease your pain. You have also lost a great deal of blood, which is why you are feeling so tired."

The doctor explained how the properties in the tea would help his body to manufacture more blood, to replace what was lost. Bartholomew obediently sipped his tea, while the good doctor busied himself removing the remaining salve from the injured leg. "Observe the power and speed of the healing stone," he declared. As he wiped away the last residue of salve, a collective gasp broke the silence. All that remained of this violent injury was a long pencil-thin jagged line. The wound had closed, but the steel jaws had left their bite mark.

"That purple line on your leg may remain as a scar, Son. I would think it is a small price to pay for such a harrowing adventure."

Bartholomew was feeling the powerful herb concoction working in his body. It was as if medicated vapors were radiating through every cell. "This tea tastes terrible," he said. "But my headache is gone, and I can feel the pain in my leg fading. Thank you, all of you, for saving my life! I was very foolish and careless today. I'm afraid my best friend had the worst birthday of his life because I'm such a clumsy fool."

"A fool is someone who learns nothing from a bad experience," a new deeper voice said. Bart looked up to find the voice belonged to Daido himself. The most senior elder was standing behind the doctor, and had been watching the doctor work his magic. "Welcome home, Son. I'm glad to see you have recovered already. We were all very concerned. Your parents anxiously await your return home."

"Thank you, sir. I feel I owe a great debt to many for my safe return."

"We all owe a debt--or more specifically, a responsibility--to one another," the elder said. "We are all responsible to each other for our health and well-being. We have survived as a race for thousands of years because of this concern that each of us shares. I now see this responsibility growing in you, Bartholomew. My fellow elders and

I look forward to your appearance before the Circle this summer. I must go now, for I have much to prepare for Nelkie's presentation tonight. Be well, Bartholomew." Daido bowed respectfully to the doctor and withdrew.

As the wise one departed, Malachi said, "We are fortunate to have someone of Daido's caliber as our senior elder. A stronger, wiser elf would be impossible to find, in all of the world." The young ones all nodded in agreement.

Malachi then got back to the business at hand by instructing Bart to carefully test the strength of his injured leg. Bart cautiously arose from his bed, slowly putting more weight on the leg. He took a few short steps, and felt the leg would support him.

"It feels a little stiff, but I'm in no pain," he said.

"This is good, this is very good," Malachi assured him. As you continue to walk, the stiffness will wear away, as new blood is pumped to the leg. We are finished here. You may return home, Son."

"Thank you again, Doctor. Will we see you tonight, at the banquet?"

"Wouldn't miss it for all the toys in Balthazar's factory," the doctor said, smiling.

"See you then."

Bart left the infirmary with slow deliberate steps, still not completely trusting his rapidly healing leg. Proceeding through the canopy, he felt his leg growing stronger. His pace returned to normal, facilitated by his anxiousness to see his parents.

Chapter Seven

Nelkie awoke from a fitful rest, still troubled by his morning mis-adventure. He walked over to the washstand and got a clean wash cloth from the shelf. He released the catch on the wall, which allowed fresh rainwater to trickle into a bowl from the small storage barrel outside his window. He scrubbed up, and changed into clean clothes.

Anitra watched her son slowly climb down the ladder from his loft. "Are you still upset about Bartholomew?"

"How did you know, Mother?"

"The only time you don't slide down that ladder is when you are ill, or unhappy. Listen, Son, I think you should go right down and see Bart. You think he's angry, but I think you will find him grateful."

"Grateful! How can you say that? I almost got him killed!"

"No, Nelkie. You may have talked him into disobeying, but it was his choice to join you. He knows that, and he knows you didn't put his foot in that trap. Go now, and sit with your friend. I am sure that both of you will feel much better once you start talking about tonight's festivities."

"Okay, Mother. I will come home in time to change before the feast."

Nelkie hesitated at the entrance to his friend's living quarters. He couldn't help but think that Bart's parents might not let him in. His fears were laid to rest when they both smiled and waved to him from the kitchen. Bart's mother gave Nelkie a hug that literally forced every ounce of air from his lungs.

"Thank you for being a true friend to our son. If you had not gotten help to him when you did, he might have died alone in the forest."

Aud, Bart's father, grabbed Nelkie's hand and shook it vigorously. "Malachi told us that you ran back to get Coobik after Bartholomew got hurt. He said if you had hesitated, Bart would have bled to death. Thank you, Son."

Nelkie felt a little more at ease, but he still felt an apology was necessary. "Sir, I am sorry that I could not prevent the terrible harm that came to my friend today. I feel responsible."

"Nonsense," came the reply. You both made a bad choice to leave the safety of the treetops. We do not hold you responsible for what happened after that. It was an unfortunate accident, and that's all it was. Now go see how Malachi has worked miracles to heal your friend. He is in his room."

"Thank you, sir. I appreciate your not being angry. You know that Bart and I have been best friends since we were babies, and I hope we are still best friends when I am as old as Daido himself."

Nelkie stepped into Bart's room to find his friend concentrating on a maze game.

"How long do you have to be off your feet, Bart?"

Startled, the younger elf looked up, causing the dried pea to fall in a hole on the game board. "Oops! Well, I almost got to the end," he said. Joking, Bart looked at his friend and said, "You know, you're not bringing me an awful lot of good luck today. I'm beginning to wonder if some evil troll has placed a spell on you."

Nelkie gave an uneasy laugh. His friend could see, however, that there was sincere concern in his eyes. Those eyes were still focused on Bart's leg.

"Don't worry," he said, jumping off his bed. "I'm fine. It doesn't even hurt anymore. All that's left is this pretty ugly scar."

"By the ancients, that really is ugly." Nelkie was starting to feel even worse, until he watched his friend dance around the room, pain-free.

"By Bindar's berries!" he gasped. "I've never seen anything as wonderful as this! Your father was right; Malachi really did work a miracle!" All the sad and guilty feelings Nelkie had suffered since the accident melted away, while he watched Bart dance and laugh. They sat and talked about the feast, and Nelkie's big day tomorrow. "I wish I could go with you, my friend. Life in the treetops will never be the same."

"Thanks, Bart. I wish you could come with me. Boy, think of all the possibilities. What an adventure we could have on a double quest!"

"Ah, I think I've had quite enough adventure for one day, thank you."

"Yeah, I know you're right, but still, it sure would be fun, Bart. You know, the really sad part about all this is that even if my quest goes well, you will probably be off on your quest by the time I get back. We will more than likely be on separate paths for several years."

"Yes, I know. When next we meet, our lives will be very different. We will be more experienced in the ways of the world, and hopefully, we will each have gained much wisdom from our separate quests."

Their conversation was halted by a call from the next room. Aud announced that someone was here to see them. "Boys, you had better come in here--this looks like it might be important."

They scampered into the living area, and stopped short. There before them stood Thora, First Page to the Circle of Elders. The boys knew right away that she was there on official business, because she was dressed in her ceremonial robes. She was holding the obligatory rolled parchment. Thora answered the boys' questioning looks with the commencement of her official duties.

"Nelkie, son of Balthazar and Anitra, and Bartholomew son of Aud and Sigrid, the following decree has passed final vote by the Circle of Elders, and has thus become law. The aforementioned young elves are hereby commanded by the elders to draft a formal apology in reference to their defiance of Rule Number One. This apology must be addressed to Coobik the Watcher, as well as all the citizens of our community. Said apology is to be posted at the entrance to the great hall, by no later than 5:00 this evening. This is the word of the elders, in keeping with the creed of the ancients."

Having executed her duties, Thora rolled up the parchment, and presented it to Nelkie. "You are to keep this proclamation for your records." She bowed respectfully, and left the residence.

The boys were dumbfounded. They looked at one another in shock. "Just when I thought our troubles were over," Nelkie said. "I was all excited about the festivities tonight, and now we get blindsided by this."

"I don't know if I can do this," Bart added. "Where do we start? What do we say? To be ordered to write an apology is one thing, but to have to post it where everyone will read it may be more embarrassment then I can bear."

"What other choice do we have, Bart? This is a decree from the entire Circle of Elders. We can't just ignore it."

Aud sat the boys down, and in a warm but serious tone asked them to try to understand that this decree had to do with their understanding of a basic philosophy by which all elves abide. "Our society is a benevolent one," he said. "We are by nature forgiving creatures, but even in our culture, there must be laws. There must be rules. We elves live by the laws set forth centuries ago, by the ancients. These were the very first elders. Their wisdom has prevailed, as illustrated by the fact that our race has not only survived, it has flourished. Our current elders, in their own wisdom, have issued this decree because they know what it will teach you. Let me explain. By putting quill to paper, you will become more conscious of the events that made this apology necessary. You will be forced to think about your actions at length in order to compose this statement. In doing so, true feelings of remorse will surface. The ancients believed that the wheels of forgiveness are set in motion by the engine known as remorse. It is a common wisdom that the truth shall set you free. You will find that when this task is completed, you will not be embarrassed, but relieved and guilt-free. Now I suggest that you both put your heads together and get this done. The afternoon will pass into evening in just a few hours."

"I know you're right, Papa," Bart said.

"We will get started right away, sir," Nelkie added.

"Good. I have a shop meeting to attend, and there is much to do in preparation for the feast. I know you boys will do what is expected of you, and make us all proud. I will see you both this evening. A grand time will be had by all." Confident that the boys now had a better understanding of their situation, he donned his hat and left for work.

An hour and a half later, Bart and Nelkie had edited down their apology to a clear and concise one-page statement. The sincerity shone through, and their remorse was genuine.

"Now it must be posted," Nelkie said.

"I sure hope no one is around when we tack this up," Bart added. "I don't think I could stand the embarrassment of having someone read this over my shoulder."

"Don't worry, Bart; no one will be near the Great Hall until just before the ceremony tonight. Let's get this done, so we can concentrate on the good things that await us this evening."

Chapter Eight

Nelkie and Bart arrived at the entrance to the Great Hall at 4:30. "I'm glad no one is milling about," Bart said. "Let's tack this up on the community board and scoot, before we have to explain anything in person."

Nelkie agreed. He took four of the sharpened wooden pegs from the shelf, and neatly tacked up the document. Just as they stepped back to admire their work, the double doors to the Great Hall flew open, causing both of them to take a step backward.

Coobik the Watcher steamed through the doorway under full power. There was purpose in his step, and the look of someone on a mission in his eyes. When he noticed the boys, he stopped short.

"Well well, what have we here?" Before either of them could answer, they saw the watcher's eyes focus above their heads to the parchment with the heading "Formal Proclamation of Apology." They stood in solemn silence as the watcher read aloud.

> "The following sincere and heartfelt apology is addressed to Coobik the Watcher, and to all our brothers and sisters of the forest as well. We the undersigned do hereby admit our noncompliance and disregard of Rule Number One. We know now, because of the aftereffect of our actions, that this was not just a disobedient act. This was a thoughtless and foolhardy action that resulted in a serious injury, and an immediate disruption in the lives of many of our law-abiding citizens. We are fortunate that our carelessness did not end in tragedy.

We have learned that what one thinks may be "a great idea" may not be so when one thinks it through.

"We sincerely apologize to Coobik for misleading him, and for taking advantage of the kinder, sympathetic side of his character. We would also like to state publicly that our valiant watcher will never again have to face the Circle of Elders to explain any action taken by the undersigned.

"In conclusion, we feel it necessary to extend an ingenuous atonement to the good doctor Malachi, and his assistants, and to all our brothers and sisters who have had their lives disrupted by our imprudent and reckless behavior. We ask for the forgiveness of these good citizens in order for us to move on to become more productive and responsible elves.

"Yours in humble repentance, Nelkie, son of Balthazar and Anitra, and Batholomew, son of Aud and Sigrid.

"Well, by Thor's hammer, if that isn't the most eloquent apology ever," the watcher said. "I must tell you boys," he went on, "not only do I accept your apology; I wish to thank you."

"Thank us?" Nelkie asked. "Why would you want to thank us for what must have been your worst day in twenty years/"

"Well, you see, lads; today's events led me to do quite a bit of soul-searching." The boys noticed a softening in the warrior's eyes, and an earnestness of expression on his face that they had never seen before.

"In the end," Coobik went on, "I felt it of foremost importance to redefine my role with the elders, and they agreed. I have just come from the kitchen, where I delivered six pheasants and a very large boar for tonight's feast. It did my soul good to see that my hunting and archery skills have not evaporated at my podium, and for that, I thank you both."

"It remains gracious of you to accept our apology, brave one," Bart said with a deep bow. Nelkie asked if the watcher would be in attendance this evening.

"Are you kidding? I can't wait to taste some of that roasted boar."

They all shared a good laugh and went their separate ways, each with his own visions of the great feast in his head.

Nelkie arrived shortly afterward at his living quarters, and was greeted by his mother.

"Oh good, you're home. I think you have just enough time to wash up and change. You know your father always likes to be a little early, and since tonight is such a special event for all of us, I'm sure he will come barreling through that door any second now, expecting us to be ready."

"Yes, Mother, I'm sure you're right. I'll be ready in no time. Believe me; no one is more anxious to get to the *fun* part of this day than I am. I feel like when I woke up this morning, it was really three days ago."

At that very moment, as predicted, Balthazar entered the living quarters at a brisk pace. Without stopping, he removed his hat and shop apron, and began to unbutton his tunic. "Anitra, are you and Nelkie ready yet? We don't have a lot of time. You know I hate to be late."

"Don't worry, dear," she said in a calming voice. "We will be ready as soon as you are. Nelkie is getting changed right now, and I just have to brush my hair."

"Okay, very good. We don't want to keep the elders waiting."

Nelkie didn't realize he was standing in front of his bedroom window until he pulled the tunic over his head, opened his eyes, and was staring at the tallest tree in the forest. His first reaction was one of nostalgia. Remembering all the time he spent in classrooms and in the library in the upper reaches of the Fellowship Tree made him smile. It was here that Nelkie's young mind was introduced to the cornerstone of elf society: education. The library housed reference books on all topics of study, as well as a vast amount of literature (fiction, biographies, etc.) authored by humans as well as elves. The elves, as a society, had for centuries passed on to their young an appreciation of great literature, regardless of its origin. Their thirst for knowledge was unquenchable, even though everyone participated in a lifelong study program. Nelkie also felt a strong sense of pride in his race, as he thought back to a special moment in his education. At the age of ten, Nelkie and his class were led into the chamber that held the ancient sacred texts that contained the chronology of his ancestry. He remembered the thrill of being allowed to view original records of the exploits of heroes a thousand years past. His reminiscences of childhood were interrupted by a call from below.

"Nelkie, are you ready yet? It's almost time," his father said.

"On my way down, Father." Nelkie donned his cap, excitement ebbing in his chest, for he knew that every elf in the kingdom would be seated in the Great Hall of the Fellowship Tree, anticipating his arrival.

Chapter Nine

Far below the surface of the forest floor, the palatial Great Hall was the venue for all important community events. As well as being the hall for the send-off birthday bash for every sixteen-year-old male, the Great Hall also hosted every joyous wedding ceremony. This was also where the entire nation gathered to celebrate the life of one who had passed.

Although redwoods are gigantic trees, none has an interior large enough to hold a banquet for hundreds of elves. For this reason, the enterprising forest dwellers dug down. They succeeded in excavating an area throughout the expansive root system, large enough to suit their purpose. A thousand years of arboricultural expertise was put to use during this tremendous task. The elves had to be very careful in their excavation not to disturb any of the feeder roots that were of paramount importance to the health of their giant host. The colossal anchorage roots were just as important, for if they were undermined, or even disturbed, the result could be a catastrophic collapse.

After the excavation was complete, and they were certain that all was secure, the walls were shored up and a wood floor was installed. The construction was completed with the installation of lighting. Several hundred large wall sconces with reflective crystal backing were affixed to the walls of the entire hall. The elves worked for weeks with ropes, pulleys, and a block and tackle to secure overhead beams across the Great Hall, from which they hung scores of oil-fired lamps. The final step was to construct enough tables and benches to seat the entire citizenry in uncrowded comfort.

Tonight, the entire population, save for a small a small security force, gathered to enjoy a bountiful feast. The festivities would also include spirited music, and games of brain and brawn.

The community sat anxiously awaiting the upcoming pageantry. Reflected light on the anchorage roots that lined the walls gave the cavernous banquet hall an otherworldly look. Earthy aromas of soil and ancient wood permeated the Great Hall and reinforced everyone's sense of being one with nature.

All eyes were drawn to the entranceway as Ivar the Crier announced the official start of the evening. "Brothers and sisters of the forest, please stand and receive your Circle of Elders." On cue, the horn section of the orchestra rose to perform the revered anthem of their ancient homeland. As the stirring rhythm of this time-honored hymn began, the elders started their processional to the head table. There were two tables on a raised platform. The head table, reserved for the six elders, was slightly elevated above the table of honor, which was reserved for the honoree and his parents.

The elders entered the hall slowly, in single file, each wearing the brightly colored robes indicative of their station. Ivar announced each of the wise ones as they proceeded down the center aisle. First, Telrin the Minister of Shelter wore the bright-green shades of the forest when it is bathed in sunlight. Hanibal the Chief of Security was robed in stunning emergency red. Wolfstan the Purveyor wore the rustic reddish brown of a bountiful harvest. Next, Falco the Law Keeper's shimmering gold robes were the same shade as the priceless covers that protected the ancient texts. Voltor's expertise of the sciences was reflected in the sky-blue color of his ceremonial garb.

With his crystal-topped staff held high, the last to enter was Daido the Wise, whose resplendent robes incorporated all the colors of his fellow elders, and produced an aura of grace and wisdom that surrounded the senior Eeder.

When Daido took his place at mid-table, he addressed the assembly. "My fellow citizens of the forest, a warm welcome to you all. We have come together tonight to celebrate a milestone in the life of one of our young. As is our tradition, I will now ask all of you to rise and join arms so we may deliver as one the sacred creed of the ancients."

Adhering to ceremonial protocol as written in the ancient texts, the congregation stood, joined their arms together, and recited the creed in unison.

> We are the many that
> Will act as one
> We are the caring who
> Nurture our young
> We are the learned
> Enhanced by the wise
> We are the brave from
> Whom courage shall rise
> We are the teachers who
> Cultivate kindness and goodwill
> As we were in antiquity
> As we are now still!

At the end of the recital, the citizenry took their seats. Ivar's voice again boomed over the crowd. "Behold the power of unity."

At the moment of Ivar's proclamation, all six elders raised their still-entwined arms over their heads. One by one, each elder's robe changed color. Slowly, a wave of change swept across the dais until all six were now garbed in snow-crystal white.

Bartholomew was seated with his parents and his four-year-old sister, Tola.

"Look, look," Tola squealed. "Look at the elders, Bart. Why did that happen? What does this mean?'

"If you look closely, Tola," her brother patiently responded, "you will see that their robes are not pure white, but crystalline white. In other words, all the original colors of the elders' robes have intermingled to become flecks of color within the snow-crystal white they now wear. This symbolizes the unity shared by our leaders. It shows that although they are all individuals, they are all of one mind."

"I think I understand, Bart. They want to show us how well they work together, right?"

"Well, yeah, that's basically it."

"I wanna see it again. When will they do it again, Bart?"

"You will see this happen in two months, when it is my turn to be honored. This is a traditional ceremony. The celebration of every feast begins with the affirmation of unity."

The elders took their seats as Ivar took his cue. The crier's staff thudded as it made contact with the aged oaken floor. As protocol demanded, he made three repetitions with his staff before his singular voice commanded everyone's attention.

"My brethren, I now call your attention to the entrance of this great hall. Please welcome the parents of tonight's honoree, escorted by our second and third pages, Estrid and Gudrid."

Estrid politely took Anitra's arm, and led her down the center aisle, followed by Gudrid, who escorted Balthazar. The proud parents were seated at the table of honor, and exchanged greetings with the elders, now sitting slightly above them.

"And now, on the night before he embarks on his quest, escorted by Thora, First Page to the Circle of Elders, please make welcome Nelkie, son of Balthazar and Anitra."

A collective cheer rose up inside the giant Redwood as Nelkie entered the Great Hall. While Thora escorted him down the aisle, Nelkie smiled broadly, waving to friends and relatives. The first page stopped at the table of honor, where a large throne-like chair awaited her charge. Nelkie, still smiling, thanked the page and bowed.

"You're welcome, and Godspeed on your journey," she answered.

Her duties executed, Thora bowed and withdrew.

Balthazar stood and shook his son's hand, after which Nelkie gave his mother a gentle hug, and took his seat between them.

The crier once again rapped his staff on the hard oak floor. In his clear and resounding voice, Ivar made his last official announcement of the evening. "As decreed by the Circle of Elders, and supported by all citizens of the forest, let the feast begin!"

The orchestra elevated the already festive atmosphere with lively up-tempo music. At once the dance floor became a living entity. Dozens of couples were gyrating and spinning one another, while trying not to collide with several bounding acrobats, strolling jugglers, and magicians. In the midst of all this merriment, the food and drink bearers wound their way around--and sometimes through--the merry-makers to serve the bountiful feast. The deliciously decadent aromas of roasted wild boar and pheasant, cooked to perfection, filled the Great Hall as the diners delighted in food and beverage heaven.

Nelkie looked up from his plate to see his father standing in front of him. He held two large glasses of elf-brewed ale. "I present you, my son, on your sixteenth birthday, your first taste of ale, but enjoy only one tonight. You must have your wits about you at midnight."

Nelkie rose and accepted the brew. Raising the glass, he stood on his temporary throne. "I drink to a long life for a wonderful father, and a dedicated craftsman. I drink also to all of you. May we all live a thousand years!" The assemblage cheered with glasses held high.

Merrymaking was in full swing as the orchestra came alive with the sounds of the drendaga, the age-old folk dance that celebrated life. Legend had it that when a female chose a partner for this dance, it meant the male had lit a candle in her heart. Nelkie smiled when he saw his mother take his father's hand and pull him onto the dance floor. Suddenly, he felt someone take his hand from behind. Startled, he turned to see the lovely Arnora smiling at him.

"Will you dance with me?"

Trying desperately not to stutter or stammer, or in some other way make himself out to be a fool, he simply said, "It will be my honor." Nelkie was finally enjoying his birthday. All the young male elves were constantly talking about Arnora. The youngest daughter of Telrin the Elder was strikingly beautiful. Her cute, slightly turned-up nose and Cupid's-bow lips were delicate, which made her large, expressive green eyes draw you in at first glance. Her hair was the color of morning sunshine, and tumbled over her shoulders in abundant waves. When they faced each other, Nelkie lost himself in her eyes. He was smitten. They seemed to fold into one another as they began the slow, rhythmic steps of the drendaga. Nelkie held his partner close and was mesmerized by the scent of wildflowers. Her scent and her touch were more intoxicating than any ale he would ever taste.

She saw disappointment on his face when the music stopped. "Would you mind getting me a glass of berry punch?" she asked.

"Not at all. Be right back." He returned shortly with a glass for each of them.

"It's so warm in here," she said. "Why don't we go out by the entryway where there's a breeze, and we can talk."

"Good idea," Nelkie answered, and they walked out of the Great Hall together. There was a cool spring breeze blowing softly through the redwood canopy. They watched in silence as the great limbs moved ever so slightly, allowing momentary glimpses of moonlight.

Nelkie was harboring a deep desire to say something clever, or even funny, but he remembered something of an old saying that made him decide not to try: Better to be silent and thought a fool, than to open your mouth and remove all doubt. As he pondered this thought, Arnora broke the silence. "My father says you are the smartest of all the elves your age."

"The wise one flatters me. That is a high compliment from one who sits in the Circle."

"Agreed," she said. "He has seen your work in the Toy Factory, and told me your apprenticeship is going very well. He said your skill level is far beyond the average, given the fact that you have been engaged in study for only a short time. He also told me something else that I found very interesting."

"What was that?"

"He said that only an elf of noteworthy intelligence and more than his share of nerve would ever try to do what you and Bart did this morning."

"Telrin the Elder said that about me?"

"Yes, he did. I am certain," she went on, "that he would never admit this to you, but he is secretly proud of the cunning and courage you exhibited."

Nelkie had a questioning look on his face. "Cunning and courage? I don't understand."

Arnora continued. "He was amused when he told Mother and me about how you fooled old Coobik and got Bart out and then yourself. No youngster has ever tried anything like that before, and you actually got by him! He said you must have nerves of steel."

"My nerves of steel almost got my best friend killed." Her answer was that her father said the important thing to note was that Nelkie never lost his head in a crisis. The fact that he got help, and got his friend back swiftly, was testament to his courage under extreme stress. "He said that your quest among humans should go very well."

"I do hope so. Your father doesn't know that I had help before I ran back for Coobik."

"What kind of help? What do you mean?"

Nelkie told her about the doe, and how calm and helpful she was. Arnora was fascinated. "I have heard rumors about elves communicating with wild animals, but I really thought that's all it was, a rumor."

"It is all true, Arnora. What is most amazing is that no words are spoken. You can hear them speak to you from *inside* your head. They can also hear the thoughts you direct to them. It's a truly fantastic experience, but I was a bit preoccupied at the time, and really couldn't fully appreciate it."

They talked for quite some time, until Bartholomew poked his head out of the entryway. "Better get back in here, kids. It's almost midnight." He popped his head back in and left them standing in the shadowed moonlight. Both of them had never felt so comfortable with someone of the opposite sex. Their first long talk together was an event they would remember fondly for a long time.

He gently took her hand and spoke. "Thank you for asking me to dance. If not for that, I would never have known the pleasure of your company."

"You are more than welcome, Nelkie. I am glad we had a little time to get to know each other before you must leave. I hope the wisdom of the elders will keep you safe, and that you will look for me upon your return." She kissed him softly on his cheek, and Nelkie was thankful they were standing in the shadows, for he could feel his face growing bright red.

As they entered the Great Hall, Nelkie was suddenly swept away by well-wishers and merry-makers. When he gained his equilibrium, he realized Arnora had become one with the crowd. Although he was having fun with many friends and relatives, he knew it would be a very long time before he would gaze into those big green eyes again. In that momentary flicker of sadness, he knew the candle in *his* heart had been ignited also.

A few minutes before midnight, the merriment started to wind down. Balthazar stood at the table of honor and called for everyone's attention. Looking quite regal in his blue and gold robes, he addressed the large group of his fellow elves. "My family and I thank you for honoring my son this evening. It is my belief that he will make us all proud. As you my brothers have elected me council to the Circle of Elders, it is now my privilege to present my son Nelkie to them this night." With his son now at his side, Balthazar raised his glass one final time. He put his free arm around Nelkie's shoulders, and in a voice that resounded all through the Great Hall, spoke to the multitude. "I give you the words of the ancients: *Jidanibry-elem!* Peace and long life to all."

The Great Hall shook with the unanimous response. "Hail Nelkie! Hail the Circle of Elders! Hail the ancients!"

Balthazar finished his last gulp of ale and led his young son out of the hall. Nelkie felt a surge of excitement arising from deep within him. The great honor of being presented to the Circle of Elders was now his. He would now at last, have the secrets of the inner chamber revealed to him. He took a deep breath, squared his shoulders, and followed his father through the never-ending canopy.

Chapter Ten

Together, father and son traversed the secret passages through the eternal canopy. At last, they arrived at the entrance to the stately chamber of the Circle of Elders. Balthazar could not help but notice Nelkie's hesitation. Sensing his son's apprehension, he decided that a little encouragement was in order, but before he could reassure his son, Nelkie spoke up. "Father, I have to tell you that I have looked forward my entire life to this night, but now that it is here, I am fearful. I feel as if there are wild animals fighting to the death in my stomach. So many things have gone terribly wrong today. I'm afraid I may continue to make errors in judgment, ruin the most important day of my life, and cause you great embarrassment."

Balthazar faced the boy and gently placed both his hands on Nelkie's shoulders. "Son, before we go inside, I want you to take a deep breath. I promise you that what you are feeling is to be expected. Every young elf that has stood where you are right now, your father included, has felt exactly the same way you do. The very thought of standing before six of our wisest and most powerful leaders is enough to intimidate any young one. I think you may have compounded your fear with your concerns about being admonished for your misadventure this morning. I can assure you that is over and done. You and Bartholomew have complied with the directives you were given, your eloquent apology has been posted, and there will be no mention of things past. Tonight's focus will be on your future. Right now you have no idea what is expected of you, or what you can expect from the elders. Let me set your mind at ease. The very same elders you are about to meet have sent hundreds of your predecessors into the world of humans. All of these quests were successful, with one exception. Well over two hundred years ago, a youngster named Zaynar did not return from his quest. An investigation revealed that the young one was caught off-guard by a band of Native American warriors. Thinking the elf was some kind of demon, they overwhelmed and executed him. I'm telling you this because even though there were hundreds of quests before and after Zaynar, his demise was taken very seriously by the Circle of Elders. They have vowed to arm every young elf with all the tools he needs to avoid discovery or capture. The elders will not send you into a hostile environment unprotected. I know that when you leave your home tomorrow, you will be confident and excited about the adventure that awaits you."

"Thank you, Father; I do feel a little better now. I guess the thought of being the focus of wrath from those who sit in the Circle is really terrifying. I suppose I should know better, but I guess I still feel a little guilty."

"It's time for you to move past this, Nelkie; I know our leaders have. Now, let us move forward and embrace your future."

They stepped into the dimly lit antechamber to be greeted warmly by Ivar the Crier. "Welcome, my brothers! Welcome to this revered and historic night of nights! Nelkie, son of Balthazar, are you ready to make history?"

"I am, most honored one."

"Then I will proceed." The crier took several steps toward a very ornate door, with hand- tooled hinges, that sealed the archway to the inner chamber. Ivar opened the door slowly, and then stood in the archway. Nelkie was craning his neck to see around the crier, but Ivar blocked all but the amber glow of candlelight. The floor reverberated as the crier rapped his staff three times, stepped to one side, and made his announcement. "To the Circle of the Most Wise, I present

Balthazar, master toymaker and father of our honored trainee."

At that moment, Nelkie's sharp ears made him aware of a very slight fluttering noise off somewhere in the canopy. He turned to look through the open antechamber door. There was a bright golden glow in the upper reaches of the canopy. Nelkie watched as it changed shape. It grew from a large sphere to an elongated shape, not unlike the tail of a comet. Nelkie stared in awestruck silence as he realized the glow wasn't getting bigger, it was coming closer. The strange fluttering noise grew louder. Suddenly the antechamber was flooded with golden light generated from the two-inch wingspan of hundreds upon hundreds of tiny flying creatures. Scores of them swirled above Nelkie's head, creating a spotlight effect on the young elf, while the main body flowed into the elders' chamber, lighting the walkway in front of him. Nelkie was still staring in amazement at the lights above his head, when Balthazar decided to shed a little light of his own on the situation.

"My son, we have been gifted with the presence of our tiny allies."

"Father, they must be the nocturnal forest fairies. I have only heard stories about them, until now! I had no idea they would be here tonight. This is spectacular!"

"It certainly is, Son. But I wonder why they are here. They are curious creatures by nature, but to my knowledge they have never attended a presentation ceremony before. We don't get to see them very often, but they have been our eyes and ears from above on many occasions. The fairies have proved to be valuable allies, especially at night. Look, do you see that one breaking away from the rest? She is heading over to speak with Daido. That's Queen Katherine, their leader."

While Nelkie was taking in all the wondrous sights and sounds around him, Daido stood and addressed the fairy queen. "Queen Katherine, always a pleasure, your majesty. Is it curiosity or business that brings you to us this night?"

"A little bit of both, wise one. As you know, news travels quickly through the forest. We have heard that two of your young had a bad experience this morning. We hope all has turned out well. Word has reached us that there has been a serious injury. If I am to be completely honest, wise one, we have some concern about the uninjured one who is rumored to be departing on his quest. I do not mean to insult this venerable body by appearing to question your wisdom, but as you are well aware, secrecy is vital to our existence, as it is to your own. We can't help but wonder if a young one who has shown such an error in judgment can be trusted to keep our secrets, as well as yours."

"I thank you for coming to me with this matter, my queen, and as always, we appreciate and welcome your concern. We have pledged to work together with all our brothers and sisters of the forest, and your presence here tonight only reinforces your commitment to our common goal. On my word, as senior elder, I assure you that all is well. Bartholomew, the injured one, was well enough to attend our feast tonight. Now, I would like to address the situation concerning Nelkie, who is to leave us tomorrow. I know this youngster is repentant, and is fully aware of his error in judgment. If you would care to look at our community board, at the entrance to the Great Hall, you will see both boys have written a sincere apology. It has been posted for everyone to read. I am sure that any apprehension held by the Court of the Forest Fairies will be alleviated by this document. A special session of the Circle of Elders was convened this afternoon, and it is our concerted opinion that Nelkie will remain true to his oath of secrecy. If you would care to speak with the boy yourself, he stands there, before his father."

"Thank you wise one. Just a word, if I may."

"Of course."

The fairy queen floated gracefully across the room, her miniature vestment trailing behind in golden phosphorescence. As she hovered a mere eighteen inches from the boy's face, his reaction was to stiffen his posture, as a soldier would come to attention in the presence of an officer. He did not, however, avert his gaze. Nelkie's eyes held fast their focus on the eyes of the queen.

"Do you know who I am, Son?"

"It is my honor to be addressed by Queen Katherine, most revered ruler and protector of all nocturnal forest fairies." His bow was low and respectful.

The queen looked deeply into Nelkie's eyes, almost as if she were looking through them into his mind. After a long moment, she seemed satisfied, and returned a regal nod. "I wish you well on your journey, young one, and know that my loyal subordinates will be watching over you."

"You have my deepest gratitude, great queen; I am forever indebted to you and your subjects."

The fairy queen turned her attention to the circular table. "Wise ones, with your permission, we would be pleased to brighten this chamber, as you may find candlelight insufficient to suit your purpose this evening."

Daido answered, "By all means."

With a gesture from their queen, thousands of tiny wings began to pulsate. Like minuscule turbines creating electricity, the fairies brought forth a soft golden glow that illuminated the chamber.

Queen Katherine retreated to her perch high above the chamber, as Daido and Balthazar made eye contact with one another and smiled. Both of them were proud and pleased with what Nelkie had said and done. He seemed to know instinctively that respect and flattery are the best strategies to employ when dealing with fairies, especially their queen.

Daido now turned to Nelkie, who was still standing just inside the archway, with his father. For Nelkie, just to be in the elders' presence, in this chamber, on this night, generated deep feelings of respect, if not awe. He had heard since he was a child that Daido was rumored to be almost four hundred years old, although no one knew for sure.

A.J. PROFETA

The senior elder's carriage was such that nobility radiated from him. His face, weathered from centuries of life's challenges, was framed by a full head of shoulder-length silver hair, and a beard that almost reached his knees. The luster of all that silver hair glimmered in the reflected light. The bell- shaped sleeves of his crystal-white robe draped elegantly from his outstretched arms as he welcomed the father and son. "Enter and join company with your Circle of Elders, and let their combined wisdom enlighten your mind and lift your heart."

Golden light from the wings of hundreds of fairies danced off crystal beaded curtains that flowed down the walls, reflecting a multicolored prism that washed over the entire chamber.

As dictated by protocol, it was now time for Balthazar to formally present his only son to the Circle of Elders, entrusting his progression from adolescence to the care of his respected leaders.

"Most honored members of the Circle, I present my son Nelkie to you for instruction. At this appointed hour, I commit his future into your learned hands. May he have the capacity to learn all you teach, and the wisdom to use what he will learn with integrity."

The elders, knowing that this moment was the height of emotion for every father, tempered Balthazar's departure with compassion. Daido again spoke for the group. "We humbly accept the responsibility and trust that you bequeath this body. When next you see your son, you will know your trust has been well placed."

"I already know this to be true, wise one. With your permission, I will retire to await his farewell with his mother."

Balthazar then bowed to the Circle, and retired from the chamber.

As Nelkie watched his father's departure, feelings of uncertainty washed over him. He had never before felt so alone. He knew he was about to take a giant step upon the path of life, and his nerves were becoming a bit unsettled.

Daido the Wise had handled this moment of transition for hundreds of young males prior to Nelkie. He knew better than to leave the youngster staring at his departing father for more than a few seconds. As if he were Nelkie's grandfather, Daido put his arm around the boy and smiled. "Come, let us leave your childhood behind and embrace the mystical magic that is your heritage." Daido motioned toward the timeworn oak table that had grown dark with age.

The remaining elders were seated in their customary circle. Directly in front of each of the wise ones, about a foot in from the edge, Nelkie observed a small cutout in the shape of a star, approximately two inches in diameter, six in all. His focus was diverted from the table when the five remaining elders rose in response to Daido's motion.

Adhering to the age-old rules of decorum, the senior elder conducted the formal introductions. "Nelkie, son of Balthazar and Anitra, I present to you your Circle of Elders." Upon introduction, each of the wise ones would execute a bow of respect to Nelkie, and then take his seat. "Closest to you is Hanibal our Minister of Security. Moving right is Telrin, our Minister of Shelter. To his right is Wolfstan, our Chief Purveyor. Next is Voltor, our historian, and Dean of Sciences. On the far end we have Falco, our Keeper of Laws."

If someone had asked Nelkie at this point how he felt about himself, he would have said he felt very small, even insignificant. He stood in the shadow of those charged with keeping all elves safe, healthy, and undiscovered by humans--a daunting task at best. Nelkie's introspective thoughts were halted by the voice of the senior elder.

"Nelkie, the quest you are about to undertake carries with it great responsibility. There are many reasons that make this custom necessary. Firstly, it is a rite of passage from childhood to adulthood. It is also a mission which, if successful, will enable you to teach, by your example, some of the wisdoms we embrace in everyday life, which have been all but forgotten by the human race. It is written in our texts that the young one is to perform an act or deed for the greater good of humankind. We should remember, however, that it matters not if only one person is benefitted by this deed, as long as the act itself is noble. We have always believed that by the commission of random acts of kindness, and deeds of noble origin, humans will learn by our example. It is also known that one who has *been* helped is more willing to help others. There has been concern among our elders for centuries that humans believe life is defined by one's personal wealth and material possessions. Often greed will overtake common sense in the pursuit of these possessions. The virtues of honesty, loyalty, and tolerance have been pushed aside for the sake of personal gain. This, along with the lack of respect for Mother Earth, may eventually bring about the demise of all human life, and possibly the destruction of the entire planet. It is now your time, Nelkie, to do your part in this grand agenda. We believe that many small contributions will lead to the accomplishment of a larger goal. You can help us all to gain one more step toward having human feet on the path that will lead to a fellowship of man. There is on record in our archives, a Proclamation of Promise, which states: 'On the occasion of the accomplishment of a global brotherhood of mankind the Nation of Woodland Elves will be compelled to share their knowledge of the powers of the universe, for the benefit of all who share this planet.' We are committed to this endeavor, but only when the time is right. If the power of the ancients should fall into the wrong hands, it could mean a disastrous end for us all. For this reason, I direct your attention to Brother Falco, who will instruct you concerning the laws you must obey. Falco, if you will."

The keeper of laws rose from his chair. The large book in front of him had a thick wooden cover that had been hand-carved centuries ago. "Welcome, Nelkie," he said, and opened the book. "These laws were written many generations ago in our Scandinavian homeland. They were created in order to protect our race from harm, and to ensure harmony among all elves. I know you are familiar with some of them from your required schooling. I am here to make sure that you understand and will comply with these directives." Falco put on a small pair of spectacles. The somber look on the elder's face told Nelkie that what he was about to hear was of the utmost importance. Falco produced an official-looking parchment from the back of the book, and passed it across the table to Nelkie. "This document is our sacred Oath of Secrecy. It is written that no elf shall leave the safety and security of the Great Forest without submission to the requirements within. You will now, before these witnesses, read this document aloud, and sign your name in affirmation."

The young elf obediently took the parchment in his hands. The document was almost fluttering in his nervous grasp. Nelkie gathered himself and began to read. "In order to protect and preserve the peaceful and harmonious lives of all my brothers and sisters of the forest, I Nelkie, son of Balthazar and Anitra, do solemnly swear that I will never reveal the location or even the existence of any elf community. I pledge to uphold this oath even upon threat of death." In a nervously shaking hand, Nelkie signed his name to the bottom of the page. His duty completed, he slid the parchment back across the table.

The law keeper accepted the document and filed it back into the book. "We thank you for your compliance, Nelkie. I would now like to address the reasons why this affirmation is law. You have been taught about our terrible defeat in The Great Troll War, which precipitated our long journey to what is now America. Many of us escaped, but thousands of us did not. This is your history, Nelkie. This is how you became an American Elf.

In the year 1403 AD our Scandinavian ancestors were betrayed. This betrayal came not from an elder or warrior elf, but from a simple foraging elf named Arbathor. Corrupted by greed, Arbathor arranged a pact with the evil trolls. In exchange for gold and jewels, enough to last several lifetimes, he disclosed the location of local elf villages. This nearly caused our extinction. The end result of this treasonous act was the destruction of our homeland, and the enslavement of our race. Under the cover of night, the trolls mounted a massive surprise attack.

The unsuspecting elves were quickly overpowered and captured. For this reason, the Primary Law was created. It states that any elf who willingly discloses the location of any elf community shall be banished forthwith to the Forest of Eternal Woe. In this alternate dimension between earth and sky lies a desolate forest of dead souls, where a fog that never lifts bars the warmth of the sun. Sadness and despair are the only companions that dwell in this place. There will be no forgiveness for betrayal, and no escape…forever.

"A noble elf," Falco continued, "learns to respect the wishes of others. He is conscious of the effect his actions will have upon the feelings of others. To gain honor among his peers, as well as his own self-respect, he will do his best to help the disadvantaged. He will be fair in his judgments, and he will be loyal to those who have placed their trust in him. These are the basic truths that bind us together. Abide by them and your heart will be proud and pure, and your spirit strong and true."

Falco removed his glasses and closed the book. The elder brushed a curl of sandy blond hair from his face, and Nelkie saw that Falco's expression had softened. The elder spoke in a gentle voice, and asked if Nelkie had any questions.

"None, sir, but I would like to assure The Circle that any secrets entrusted to me will remain secrets. On this you have my solemn promise, as well as my signature."

"Very well. I am pleased that you understand the seriousness of your adult responsibilities. You will find that through the acceptance of these responsibilities, your self- reliance will grow, and as you gain experience, wisdom will be its byproduct. My component of your instruction is now concluded. You must now give your attention to Hanibal, who will present you with the first of your gifts."

"Thank you for your time and sage advice, wise one; I am most fortunate to be the beneficiary of your knowledge and experience."

Hanibal stood and motioned to Nelkie. "Come here, Son; I have something for you to take with you." As Nelkie walked around the table, a thought occurred to him. Since this was the first time the young elf was in close proximity to his elders, he noticed things about each of them that were new to him. As he approached the minister of security, he found it fascinating that he had never noticed before that Hanibal was by far the most fit of all his elders. Although he was of average height for an elf (thirty inches), and his ceremonial robes kept the elder's muscularity hidden, Nelkie couldn't help but notice the size of Hanibal's shoulders. Not only were they broader than any of the others, they were the size of softballs. Nelkie, upon noticing the drape of the elder's robe in front, understood that a lifetime of hard physical work produced a flat stomach in spite of Hanibal's advanced age.

Nelkie's level of anticipation rose as Hanibal reached inside his robe and pulled out a small medallion. The young one could hardly contain his excitement, as his eyes focused on the stunning ruby in the center of the medallion. The older elf removed the thick gold chain from around his neck, and placed it over Nelkie's head. Hanibal's expression turned from affable to serious, almost stern.

"Do not remove this medallion for any reason. It may be argued that this tool will be your most important means for survival in a life-threatening situation."

As he tucked the necklace into the boy's tunic, he explained, "I am in charge of your *personal* security as well as that of our community. This little medal holds within it a thousand years of knowledge. It is the manifestation of the true power of our ancestors. It has been tuned to your specific body chemistry, and is activated by your touch and your voice alone. To escape danger, you must press the ruby and say 'I must go.'

"When this is done, you will feel a momentary chill as the molecules that make up who you are will now be rearranged at the speed of thought. The end result, which will be instantaneous, is that your presence will fade into oblivion. As if you were an early morning fog that has been burned off by the sun, you will have rendered yourself invisible to all. However, you must be sure to remember to remain quiet when you are in this state. Although you cannot be seen, you will be heard, and thus give away your position. Now, moving on, to reappear, you must again press the ruby and say 'I must return.' If you have any doubts or questions, Nelkie, now is the time to ask. I join my fellow elders in our united plea. Please do not depart from the Exit Tree to start your quest if you harbor any uncertainties. Your Circle of Elders is here to make sure that you have left nothing to chance in terms of your safe return, upon completion of your quest."

For the first time in his life, Nelkie was truly speechless. To meet one to one with his fabled leaders, and then to be presented with this astonishing medallion, had left him truly awestruck.

Slowly, he collected himself, knowing that all eyes were upon him.

"Most wise Hanibal," he began, "I am deeply humbled by the generosity of my elders. I know this medallion will sufficiently increase my margin of safety. For this I am very grateful, and I assure you that I will never remove it from my neck. Your instructions, sir, were clear and precise, and I therefore have no questions."

"I am pleased, young one, and I have every confidence that you will succeed in the world beyond the great forest. Now, if you will turn your attention to our senior elder, he has another gift for you, which requires further instruction."

Daido stood and thanked Hanibal for the efficient discharging of his duties. The senior elder now cast a benevolent gaze on Nelkie. From out of Nelkie's line of sight, Daido produced a rectangular wooden box, about two feet in length, and very narrow.

"I have a tool to present to you. I call this a tool because through this stick you will learn how to summon the power of the ancients. It will be of great help to you on your journey." With his face beaming as if he were a young father presenting his little boy with his first bike on Christmas morning, Daido beckoned the boy closer. He placed the box on the table and opened it. He then removed an elegantly carved elf-sized walking stick. The knob end had an exquisitely carved design consisting of six stars in a circle. "The design on the knob is to remind you that you may also access the unified knowledge and experience of your Circle of Elders, should your need be genuine. If your request for power is rooted in greed, anger, revenge, or any other negative force, you will find this to be nothing more than an ordinary walking stick." Daido removed the stick from its ornate case, and held it out to Nelkie.

"Thank you, honored sir," he said, his eyes glued to the stick. He ran his small hand along its length. The young elf admired the meticulous workmanship of his new gift, and how this beautiful walking stick felt in his hands. The fact that this was a tool, and could serve him in many other ways, put his curiosity on overload.

"Forgive me, sir, but should I be in need, how will I make it work?"

"Patience, young one. All will be made known to you shortly, but to answer your question simply, you will command this stick with your mind. You will now learn how to channel all that you are, and all that you know, through this stick. We will return to this part of your instruction, but first, Brother Telrin must complete his part of this presentation." The senior elder's arm swept over the table as he spoke, until it stopped in front of the minister of shelter. Telrin took his cue, stood and cleared his throat. Nelkie could not help but notice that he was, by far, the smallest member of the Circle. He wore the full flowing robes that were customary for elders, but Nelkie observed the robes only disguised a very small-boned tiny body. His twenty-three-inch height was capped by a crown of steel-grey incredibly wiry hair. Nelkie knew that despite the elder's diminutive appearance, he possessed great strength and power that came from deep within this little being.

Telrin softly cleared his throat. "Ahem. I bid you good fortune on your quest, Nelkie. As you know, our shelter is my concern. I make sure that our redwood hosts are in good health, and remain structurally sound. Among my other duties, it is my responsibility to inform you that you must always be very careful when choosing a place to sleep. Wherever you make your bed for the night, it should always be a good distance from any well-traveled road, or path through the wood. Before you sleep, you should make sure to use your medallion, lest you are discovered before you wake. If you make your bed upon the ground, he continued, you will find fir boughs to be the most comfortable. Small pine limbs would be a good second choice, as their needles are also very soft.

"In your travels, you may enter one of the big cities that lie beyond the Great Forest. Some of your predecessors have reported to us, upon their return, certain situations which we have endeavored to remedy. For example, you may find yourself needing to gain entry to, or possibly escape from, a place that is locked." Telrin reached into a pocket inside his robe, and produced a key that looked small even in the elder's tiny hand. "I am to present you with this key," he said. "If the need arises for you to open a lock, any lock, except one with a numerical combination, this key will do the job. May I see your stick, please?"

Nelkie held the stick out, knob first, and watched closely. Telrin slid his thumb under the knob, and it popped open. Nelkie leaned over and saw a perfectly carved-out compartment in the handle. Telrin placed the key into its receptacle, and snapped the knob shut. "As long as you have your stick, you will have your key." He smiled and returned the stick to its owner. May the peace of this tranquil forest go with you." The undersized elder bowed to Nelkie, and took his seat.

At this juncture, Daido resumed his role as master of ceremonies. He stood, and politely bowed to Telrin. "Well done, my brother."

The birthday elf looked to the senior elder as he made one more introduction. "Our chief purveyor will now provide you with nutritional information as well as sustenance."

With a polite nod to his fellow elder, Daido took his seat, as Wolfstan stood and spoke to Nelkie. "As you know, it is my responsibility Nelkie, to send you off with nourishment as well as knowledge." It was at this point that Nelkie noticed for the first time that any elf whose responsibilities had anything to do with food was considerably rounder and heavier than the average elf. Bindar the Gatherer was one fine example, and it was now obvious to Nelkie that Wolfstan was as fond of food as the gatherer.

The elder's short pudgy body waddled like a duck's as he strode over to Nelkie's side of the table. He carried with him a provisions pouch, with a shoulder strap. The wide, jolly smile on his face expanded as he informed Nelkie of the pouch's contents.

"Here are some of my favorite raw vegetables, dried fruits, and some nuts for snacks. There is also quite a bit of preserved boar meat, to help you keep up your strength, for your quest may take some time to accomplish. More importantly, you will find a small book to use as a guide. Read this book carefully before you pick anything in the forest to eat, or before you accept any food from strangers. For example, you will find several berries listed here which are poisonous to elves. There are other foods that will make you sick, and weaken you to the point where you become easy prey. You *must* be aware of these things so that you do not fall victim to dangerous beasts, or to humans that may have evil intent."

"Thank you, Wolfstan. I will be sure to read and remember."

"Very good, very good. I will now leave you in the capable hands of our senior elder."

Daido thanked the portly elder, and then turned his attention to the entire group. "My esteemed brethren, if you would all rise and come together for the Enabling Ceremony."

The five seated elders all stood, and one by one placed both hands face down on the circular table. When the fifth and final elder did so, the table began to move. Its massive legs were telescoping downward.

This motion continued until the tabletop was flat on the chamber floor.

Daido spoke to Nelkie while motioning with his staff in the direction of the table/platform. "If you will follow me, Son."

Nelkie obediently fell in step behind the wise one. Once they were standing in the center of the platform, inside the circle of six stars, Daido again addressed his fellow elders.

"We will now proceed with the unification process. We will guide this boy, Nelkie, son of Balthazar and Anitra, into the domain known only to adult elves." The senior elder's focus returned to the young elf, as he instructed Nelkie to hold his walking stick aloft with both hands.

With the excitement of anticipation resonating through his bones, Nelkie obeyed, and waited for the unknown to become known.

One at a time, in a clockwise motion, each elder of the Circle inserted his staff, into the platform. They stood, each with his hands clasped around his staff, their heads bowed in total concentration. Daido completed the circuit by inserting his staff, with its gleaming crystal orb, into its receptacle at the table's center.

At once Nelkie could feel his senses growing more acute. His awareness of all things-- from the fairies fluttering above him, to his place in the universe--was becoming more clear. His mind was being flooded with thoughts that were not his own. Suddenly he became aware of strong vibrations emanating from beneath his feet. As the vibrations gained intensity, the young elf could see the gleaming white orb atop Daido's staff begin to glow. At first the crystal glimmered with all the brilliance of white diamonds. Then as the vibrations in the floor became more pronounced, the orb turned from dazzling white to a brilliant electric blue. There was now a crackling sound coming from the tip of Daido's staff, as if live electricity were being generated in its core.

The face of Daido the Wise was bathed in this electric blue light, his hands tightly grasping his staff, his eyes focused on the orb as he spoke. "Behold the power of the ancients."

The instant that Daido made this proclamation, the orb released what appeared to be a sustained bolt of lightning. Nelkie had seen lighting streak across the evening sky and disappear, but this was very different from anything he had ever seen, or would ever see again. This was a constantly bright fork of energy that buzzed and cracked loudly. It shot out of the orb, and was now connected to the tip of Nelkie's walking stick. It was growing in volume as well as intensity from moment to moment. The young one tightened his grip as his stick vibrated wildly, jolting and jerking back and forth. Nelkie could not control the fingers of fear as they spread their chilling touch along the walls of his stomach. Like a frozen fire, it raged through his insides. Fear! Fear of the unknown. What if something had gone terribly wrong? How would he know? What could he do?

Before he could be consumed by fright, his inner strength rose to the surface. His natural instincts, along with the intelligence he was born with, would not allow him to be overpowered by ignorant fear. He knew deep down, that whatever was happening, he would survive. Something told him that when this event reached its crescendo, not only would he be changed forever, but this change would be for the better, and would define who he would become.

He kept his eyes on the tip of his stick, and watched as the right prong of the bolt streaked over Daido's head and into the tip of Telrin's staff. Nelkie was totally fixated on the surging blue bolt, as it jumped from Telrin's staff to Wolfstan's and from Wolfstan to Falco. This continued until all six elders and Nelkie were connected by the energy force. The crackling sound grew louder, as if live electrical wires had been cut and were now spewing sparks in a whiplike fashion, around the chamber.

The young elf was still trying to mentally grasp what was happening, when the force expanded again. All seven elves were still connected to each other when the force produced a third prong. The energy seemed to be alive. It was intelligent, purposeful. It slowly encircled the youngest and the oldest elves in the chamber. The constantly spiraling surge wove itself around Daido and Nelkie until they were almost blurred from view.

From the corner of his eye Nelkie saw the senior elder open his arms, until they were completely extended. The next thing he knew, both he and the elder were moving, but not of their own volition. They began to rise, and within seconds they had ascended a full six feet above the platform. The fairies were fluttering madly just above their heads, producing even more golden light. The entire chamber was alive with prismatic illumination. Crystal beads reflected every color Nelkie could imagine, and some he would never witness again.

Nelkie's fears vanished as he now began to understand and absorb. This was a transference of power, knowledge, and energy from the ancients to the elders, and then to Nelkie himself.

This event was almost spiritually overwhelming for Nelkie. He was now being raised to a new and fascinating plateau of consciousness. By absorbing the knowledge of the ancients, Nelkie was leaving the mysteries of his childhood behind, and exchanging them for the cumulative wisdom and awareness of the elders. A network that was both intellectual, as well as spiritual enveloped him and gifted him with grace.

After several minutes, the transference reached its peak, and the surge of energy ebbed. The energy force slowly faded to a softer, lighter shade of blue, and then, in an instant, returned to the orb from whence it came. Daido and Nelkie landed lightly, back onto the platform, as if by their own step.

When the force had dissipated, everything seemed to return to normal; everything except Nelkie's emotional state of grace. The experience had made his mind older, stronger, and much more aware. He had undergone a metamorphosis that in every way had made him more proficient.

Daido removed his staff from the platform, as did the others. At once the telescoping legs returned the table to its original position, at which time Daido asked everyone to sit.

Before taking his seat, Daido addressed the young one. "Nelkie, your Circle of Elders welcomes your ascension to adulthood. I feel very strongly, and I am sure that I speak for all of us, that you are to be congratulated for your composure and comportment. There have been many instances, over the centuries that this Circle has convened, where we have seen dozens of young males paralyzed with fear. Some have been terrified to the point of losing consciousness. You have handled these proceedings with grace and aplomb. This is very strong evidence that you will achieve great success on your quest."

"I thank you, wise one, for I am deeply honored by your approval."

"You are welcome. Now, as I come to the end of my responsibilities this evening, I have only one more thing to tell you. The collective knowledge and power of this Circle has been imparted to you. You will find that when the need arises, you will know how to summon this power to aid you. Use it wisely, and it will serve you well."

Nelkie bowed in respect and gratitude. "I am forever in your debt, most honored one. You have my most sacred word that I will be true to the spirit in which this extraordinary gift was given."

Daido thanked all his brethren for the successful execution of their duties, and officially closed the proceedings. "Nelkie, it is late, and you must rest before your departure. You have had a very eventful day, to say the least. Remember that along with the wisdom of the ancients, and the power of this Circle, you also have the trust of family and friends, indeed the entire nation of elves. We know you will make us proud."

"I will do my very best, wise one. I am ready now to accept this challenge, and complete my duties with honor."

"Then you may take your leave, my son. Your parents await your final night at home. I hope to see you upon your return, to congratulate you on your safe and successful journey. Go now and return to us healthy and wise."

Nelkie graciously thanked all the elders again, and holding his walking stick with pride, bowed deeply, and backed out of the chamber.

When Daido was sure that the young adult had passed beyond earshot he turned to his brethren. "This one has always been a handful, my brothers, but I think tonight we all learned what he really is; one of a kind, a singular elf." There was no dissenting opinion among them.

Once he was out in the cool night air, Nelkie danced from limb to limb in the great crown of redwoods. He thought there was a strange light above him that seemed brighter than moonlight. Looking up, he was delighted to see all the fairies had left the chamber, and were swirling above him. The light emitted from these tiny winged creatures made the inner canopy look as if the moon had tripled its light output. A carnival atmosphere ensued as the group whirlpooled through the treetops. When Nelkie arrived at his living quarters, he bowed to the flock, with his arms extended. "Thank you for illuminating my way home. Seeing all of you tonight has brought me much pleasure."

Queen Katherine fluttered away from her subjects, and alighted on Nelkie's shoulder. "I speak for all the forest fairies when I say that we were privileged to attend this evening. Your composure and maturity are reassuring. We wish you great success, and a safe return." She ascended from his shoulder to his cheek and deposited a quick kiss. "For luck," she said, and streaked off to lead her charges out of the canopy. Nelkie watched with a warm heart as their light faded off into the distance. *I wonder where they're going*, he thought, as he opened the door.

Chapter Eleven

Upon his arrival at the tree that was his home, Nelkie burst into the living area, his voice high with excitement. "Mother! Father! Come see what the elders have given me! It's so wonderful! I can disappear, I can open locked doors, I can...." Nelkie stopped short, thinking that he was now supposed to behave in a dignified manner, after his empowerment by the Circle of Elders. His youthful enthusiasm, however, was like a pressure cooker about to explode and blow the lid completely off his dignity.

"Balthazar smiled because he fully understood the awkwardness his son was feeling. Being chronologically still a youth, but spiritually and intellectually an adult affects one like an ill-fitting suit. Balthazar knew that Nelkie would soon sort things out and embrace his new world.

"Take a deep breath, my son, and come and sit beside your mother and me, we want to hear all about it."

Anitra had been sitting in her favorite chair, darning the family footwear. She set her sewing aside to give her complete attention to her son. "I rarely have the opportunity to converse with our elders, Nelkie. I can't wait to hear what they said to you."

"Mother, they know everything about everything. Especially Daido. He has truly mastered the powers of the ancients. I know now what Father meant when he said tonight will be a night that I will remember for hundreds of years."

Nelkie gestured wildly as he told his parents of his rising to join the senior elder in midair, high above the heads of the members of the Circle. He could hardly remain in his chair while telling them of his empowered walking stick, and the key concealed under its knob.

Balthazar smiled because Nelkie's exuberance reminded him of his own presentation to the Circle nearly two hundred years ago. *Ah, to be young*, he thought. Watching his young son, he fondly remembered his own journey into adulthood so long ago. "Nelkie," he interrupted, "This is all wonderful to hear, but it's very late and you must be on your way before the sun is high tomorrow. Anitra, would you please prepare some hot broth to help our son sleep tonight."

The loving mother rose and went to her kitchen. Opening several jars of herbs, she thought, *Now it's my turn to work a little magic.*

She carefully mixed spices, herbs, and a small amount of potion from her grandmother's secret recipe. As she heated and stirred the mixture, she was certain that this broth would put even the most ex-cited young elf to sleep. Once he took a few sips, Nelkie would have no choice but to surrender.

Meanwhile, in the living area, Balthazar was well into a men-tally prepared speech. "Know this, my son: unless fate smiles upon you, your quest will not be easy. Humans are not at all like us. Elves trust one another. We do not lie. We are not jealous. We share all we have with each other. This is the exception rather than the rule with humans."

The young elf listened attentively to his father. He knew his father had lived among humans for almost two years, and his advice was born of firsthand knowledge. Balthazar had helped many people while on his quest, one of whom would have died if not for his quick thinking and courage. Nelkie knew his father's words were true, and his warn-ings should be heeded.

Just then Anitra came into the room with a steaming cup of herb broth. "Drink this while it's hot," she said. "It will give you strength and help you sleep."

"Thank you, Mother; it smells delicious." He sipped the broth, still jabbering about fat Wolfstan, who walked more like a duck than an elf, and Telrin the tiny elder with the biggest head of wiry hair Nelkie had ever seen.

Nelkie had barely finished his broth when his eyelids began to grow very heavy. He did not want to sleep. Sleep would mean that this milestone day had come to an end. Nelkie wanted it to last forever. The broth, however, was in control. His great-grandmother's recipe was carrying him off to sleep, and he was powerless to stop it.

Balthazar carried his groggy son up to bed. He returned to the living area to find his wife in tears.

"He's so young," she said. "If he should need us, if he is hurt, we won't know. I fear he may come to great harm among humans. It is much more dangerous out there now than when you were coming of age."

"I agree," Balthazar replied. "It *is* more dangerous now. The humans have far greater numbers than ever before, but let us not forget, they are not his equal when it comes down to intellect. We both know that even by elf standards, Nelkie is smarter than most. Left to his own devices, I'm sure he will prevail."

Anitra had to concur. Her husband had told her that their son was excelling far beyond their expectations at his apprenticeship. She fondly remembered how six-year-old Nelkie would follow his father to work, pleading with him to "teach me to make toys." The always safety- conscious Balthazar put his young son off. He wanted the boy to be a little older before he started handling sharp chisels and saws. After months of pleading, Nelkie had worn down his father's defenses. The master toymaker could no longer look into his young son's pleading eyes and disappoint him. He sat Nelkie on his lap behind the scroll saw. Balthazar placed a piece of wood on the saw table and instructed his son to place his hands on top of his father's. The master craftsman worked the foot pedals that made the very thin saw blade oscillate, while showing his young son how to work the wood through the blade. It wasn't long at all before Nelkie could operate the scroll saw proficiently without his father's assistance. His skills developed quickly, and by the time he turned ten years of age Nelkie's woodcrafting talents were equal to, or better than some of the experienced crafters under Balthazar's supervision.

Anitra knew her husband was right. In many ways, their son was gifted. Nelkie's quick wit and instinctive ability to analyze and solve problems would give him the upper hand in most situations. She shrugged her shoulders as she reasoned out loud. "Maybe I'm upset because I know he will be leaving in the morning, and I will miss him so."

"I know his absence from the toy factory is going to be hard for me to get used to."

"It would be so much easier if we knew when to expect him back, but we have no way of knowing," she said.

Balthazar told his wife she must try to stop worrying. "You and I must realize that his time has come and we must wish him well, and let him go."

"Yes, of course you're right, my husband," she said, wiping her eyes with her apron. "Let us go to bed, and tomorrow we will send him off with a good meal and all our love."

They climbed quietly into bed and as is customary with elf couples, they curled around one another until they fit together like a pair of stacked spoons. Nothing further was said. They each knew the other was sad, for their only son would be gone before the sun was high.

Chapter Twelve

Two hundred thirty-six feet from the ground, a tiny ribbon of sunlight found its way into Nelkie's little window. The warmth of an ever-brightening spring morning penetrated his eyelids, intruding on dreams of fantastic adventure. He blinked and rolled over instinctively. His mind lurched from neutral into overdrive. Nelkie sat bolt upright, thinking that last night had been just a dream. In an almost automatic reflex, his hand reached for the medallion. It was really there! He threw off the covers, and scrambled to the foot of his bed. His walking stick was still on top of his clothes chest. It was not just a dream. It was all real, and it was all awesome. He hastily put on a clean tunic. The smell of freshly baked cornbread drifted upstairs, and under his nose. Nelkie wondered if there actually was some sort of connection between his nose and his stomach. This almost seemed plausible to him since the second he smelled cornbread, he became very hungry. The elf finished dressing as quickly as he could, and slid down the ladder into the living area. He heard his father's voice booming out of the kitchen.

"Wife! Is the tea ready yet? I hear him coming!"

"Yes, my husband. Sit and I will serve you both."

"Morning, Mother; morning, Father. It sure is a bright sunny day today."

"Good morning, Nelkie," Anitra answered. "Yes, it is a beautiful day. I think if it were raining today I would be even sadder than I am already."

"Don't be sad, Mother. Today is a great day. Today I start my life as an adult."

She started to cry anyway. At that moment, Balthazar drew his son's attention away from his mother. "Son, I know your head has been filled with instructions, warnings, and rules you must obey. However, I would not be a good father if I did not make sure I covered every safeguard I know, to protect you. I want to make only one more point before you leave. Always be aware of your surroundings. Take notice of who and what are in your immediate area. There have been only a few unfortunate elves that have met with dire consequences over the centuries, but in every case there misfortune was the result of either misplaced trust, or a lack of awareness. Be alert and you will be safe. That is the best advice I can give you."

Anitra placed large portions of sausages, pheasant eggs, and hot cornbread in front of both of them and said, "Listen to your father, Nelkie; he spent almost two years on his quest, and he knows much of the human ways."

"I thank you both for being the best parents any elf could hope to have. I promise you that I will not daydream and lose track of what is going on around me. I remember the story of Rongee from school. I am very much aware that if one is distracted, even for a moment, a disastrous situation could develop. To be honest, Father, I am a little scared. I know that humans are giants compared to us. They must be very strong as well. I have to admit that I also have some concerns about the dangerous creatures lurking about in the great forest. I must pass through their domain before I even get to see my first human."

Balthazar saw the concern on his son's face, and tried to reassure him. "You must have faith in your own intellect, my son. You will quickly learn to use the tools given to you by the elders. Your walking stick alone has a thousand uses. You may be small by human standards, but you do have the means to turn that to your advantage, if you only think about it for a while. I am sure that should you encounter evil, you will conquer it. I am also sure that you will recognize a situation where you may do some good. You may even make some humans better people by your example."

"I appreciate your trust in me, Father, and I'll not disappoint you. It's true that I'm a little scared, but I'm more excited about what lies ahead than I am fearful. I am very excited to see humans up close and possibly even converse with some of them, but I'll not be foolish. I want only to experience life beyond the great forest long enough to do what is expected of me. Then I want to come home and finish my apprenticeship. I am very proud when I see the respect from your peers for the expertise and quality of your work. I will never forget that Christmas Eve, when the great man of Christmas himself climbed out of his sleigh to seek you out. Santa told everyone that Balthazar the Master Toymaker keeps alive the tradition of true craftsmanship. Toys that receive the approval of the master will survive for generations. He said it was his honor to deliver your toys to the children of the world. Someday, I too will receive such a compliment because I was taught by the best there ever was."

Balthazar enjoyed these last few moments with his son. All at once, he felt pride, love, and sorrow, for he knew the time had come for Nelkie to leave.

Anitra hugged her son tightly. "My only child," she said. "Come back to us as soon as you can. We will miss you every day until you do. Heed your father's advice and that of the elders. Now go," she said. "I'm starting to cry again."

Nelkie kissed his mother's cheek and told her that he loved her. The he hugged his father and said, "The next time we see each other, I will have an amazing story to tell." He smiled and waved and then bounded out the door. He skillfully skipped from limb to limb, tree to tree in the intertwining canopy of giant redwoods.

At last he arrived at the upper reaches of the Passage Tree. The entrance to the passageway was two hundred eighty-seven feet from the ground. With his walking stick, his medallion, a bulging provisions pouch, and a full belly, he felt ready to take on the world.

Chapter Thirteen

Nelkie worked his way from the outer limbs of the Passage Tree toward its massive trunk. He walked through the passageway to the elevator, and was pleasantly surprised. Thora stood holding the elevator door open, resplendent as usual in her ceremonial robes.

"Good morning, noble wayfarer. It is my honor to escort you down to the exit chamber, and to inform you that our elders send their most sincere wishes for your safe return."

"Thank you, Thora. This is indeed a pleasant surprise."

"You are welcome, brave one," she said, as she set the elevator in motion.

Nelkie's face reddened slightly when he realized that the first page had addressed him as "brave one."

Wow, No one has ever called me that before. It took a moment before he understood that although "brave one" was a term of respect reserved for adult males, he was now considered to be an adult and was to be spoken to as such.

Thora's expertise did not go unnoticed by Nelkie, when she brought the elevator to a smooth stop at ground level. The first page then escorted Nelkie through the chamber to Coobik's podium. As required, she resumed her ceremonial duties.

"Good morning to you, sir. I am to present Nelkie to our most esteemed watcher, to officially record the embarkation of his quest." She turned to face her charge. "Godspeed, brave one, and know that you carry with you the faith and trust of all your brothers and sisters of the forest." She bowed to Nelkie, and then to Coobik, turned on her heel, and disappeared into the elevator.

The watcher greeted the young traveler with a smile. "A very good morning to you, Nelkie. I see that *today* you are officially sanctioned for embarkation."

"I am, brave one. I have plenty of provisions, my trusty walking stick and best of all, the support and approval of our elders."

"Congratulations, Nelkie. You had a bit of a shaky start, but I am very glad to see that all has worked out well. I am honored to make this historic entry in my log." The younger elf waited patiently as the watcher made the following entry:

May 7ᵗʰ 10:04 a.m. Nelkie, son of Balthazar and Anitra, being fully supplied and sanctioned, departed from this post to assume the responsibilities and requirements of his quest.

"And now, my young brother, I will see to it that your path is clear." The watcher marched from his podium to the exit door, and drew his broadsword. With his sword at the ready, the warrior elf unbolted the door with his free hand. Ever so slowly, he opened the door; first only a crack, and then no more than an inch. The watcher's keen eyes surveyed the immediate area, and perceiving no danger, he pulled the door open and stepped outside. "Wait for my signal. I must be sure it is safe before I allow you to exit." Coobik continued his patrol around the trunk of the Exit Tree, constantly scanning the surrounding area. Satisfied, he stood before the doorway and motioned Nelkie forward with his broadsword. "You may proceed, my brother. Upon your return, rap your walking stick three times, then twice, then thrice more. I will then unbolt the door and welcome you home. I bid you farewell, my young brother, and may the path you choose bring you back to us forthwith, healthy and wise."

Nelkie bowed, and returned, "I will do my best, brave one; be well." He stepped out of the Exit Tree and into the filtered sunlight of their beloved forest. He had taken only a few steps when he heard

Coobik slam and bolt the door behind him. The reality of his situation hit him like a dump truck unloading boulders. For the first time in his young life, he was totally alone. This stark realization gave rise to a sudden note of caution. Nelkie checked his surroundings before pushing off in earnest. He turned to give a farewell glance at the Passage Tree. The door had disappeared into the bark as if it was never there. He stared at the now door-less tree, trying to sort out all that he was feeling. He was having thoughts that had never occurred to him before. Every minute of his life thus far had been spent in the company of at least one or two of his fellow elves. Now he could only guess when he would see another elf. Ironic as it was, Nelkie couldn't help but think that this must be what a human convict felt like when he was sent to prison--locked away from the ones he loves, and forced to live in unfamiliar surroundings. The Ironic part was that Nelkie had much the same feelings, but he was *outside*. The awe-inspiring solitude of the Great Forest seemed a bit foreboding. It was beginning to become clear to him that there were many interconnecting facets involved with this quest thing that he had never considered.

"I can't live in fear," he told himself. "Fear of the unknown is foolish. The only way to conquer that fear is to make the unknown become known, and the only way to accomplish that is to push on." Resolute in his conviction, Nelkie pushed off on his walking stick and headed off into the Great Forest. .

He marched along for a few hundred yards and came to a sudden stop. When he approached the heart-shaped rocks, the events of the day before dominated his thinking. Nelkie, in his mind's ear, could still hear the tortured screams of his best friend. He could still see the angry look on the watcher's face.

Nelkie was suddenly pulled from the negativity of the previous day by a very strong feeling that was new to him. He wasn't even sure if this feeling was emotional or physical, or both. He had never quite felt this way before. Whatever this feeling was, it was getting stronger. It was an awareness of some sort. A kind of sixth sense. Yes, he was becoming aware of something, or someone. There was very definitely a new presence in his immediate area. Just when this awareness was reaching the point of causing anxiety, the spell was broken by a familiar voice.

"Is anything wrong, my young friend? You look troubled." Nelkie looked to his left to see Lilly, the doe that had helped him yesterday strolling out from behind the large rocks.

"Wrong? Uh—no, Lilly, I was just thinking about what happened yesterday, and I guess, about how alone I am out here today."

"As long as you are within the boundaries of the Great Forest, Nelkie, you will never be alone. Although it is true that there are great dangers out here in the wild, you will find that you have many allies."

"Allies? What allies?"

"Your allies are the gentler creatures of the forest. Herbivores, mostly. We have long ago made a pact with the elves to keep each other abreast of any dangerous situation, such as the presence of predators. You know it is foolish to try to reason with a mountain lion, or an adult bear. They would eat you as soon as look at you. I would advise you to keep your distance from wolves as well, Animals that hunt prey are of a different temperament. I am quite sure that you will meet new friends among our brothers of the forest, who will be happy to help you in any way they can."

"This is fascinating information, Lilly. I can't thank you enough for telling me. I feel safer already. So, based on what you have told me, I assume you know many of my fellow elves."

"Oh yes. Very well. I see your foraging parties almost every day. That sweet little Bindar always leaves me something to eat over there, by the heart stones. I should also tell you that I owe my very life to the great Daido."

Nelkie sat down on a log and pulled a carrot out of his provisions pouch. "Really? Daido saved your life?"

"I would not be alive today if not for his protection." The doe continued, "One fall afternoon, I was looking for food, not far from here. All of a sudden, I heard a loud crack and almost immediately I felt a searing hot pain in my shoulder. Instinctively, I ran as fast as I could. I didn't know what happened at the time, but a hunter had shot me. I was losing a lot of blood and I grew very weak. All I knew was that there was danger present, and I must flee. It wasn't long before I became very dizzy and fainted. I awoke some time later to find this creature standing over me. His staff was touching my shoulder, but strange as it may sound, I felt no pain. He spoke to me and told me not to move, for it was still not safe. Shortly, two hunters emerged from the underbrush. They were only about ten feet away! I wanted to run, but Daido looked at me and shook his head. I obeyed.

"I heard one hunter say, 'I know I hit her! She's got to be right around here somewhere.'

" 'Maybe she ran off that way,' the other one answered. Then they wandered off away from us. Daido then explained to me that he had healed my wound. He then said that he had rendered himself invisible. He told me that because his staff was touching me, I too was hidden from the hunter's eyes. We were both under the power of his staff, and could still see each other. I owe my life to Daido. Since that day, many years ago, I have made my home as close to the elves as possible. I watch for Bindar and the others when they are foraging and do whatever I can to help them. They, in turn, see to it that I have food during the harshest of winters. We have forged a strong bond over the years, from which we have all benefited."

"No wonder you were so quick to help Bartholomew and me when we got into trouble. We were fortunate to have help so close at hand."

"As I have been. Well, I'm feeling a little thirsty; I think I'll walk down to the creek and get a drink. It was nice to see you again, Nelkie, and I wish you good luck on your journey."

"Thanks. Hey, how far is the creek from here?"

"Oh, about a mile or so--why?"

"Hold on a second. I want to try something. Daido presented me with this walking stick last night and I've been aching to try it out. I have been told that I can use it to channel great power. Let's see. I think it would be nice for you to have a pool to drink from right here."

Nelkie walked a few paces to where there was a slight depression in the ground. He placed one end of his stick into the depression and closed his eyes. A look of intense concentration came over his face. He opened his eyes and focused on the tip of the stick. He simply said, "Water." The stick became the elf equivalent of ground-penetrating radar. Nelkie focused his concentration through the walking stick and into the ground. In his mind's eye, he could see a gently flowing underground stream. The elf deepened his concentration into an almost trance-like state. His intense focus zeroed in on the depression that lay at his feet. When he spoke, his voice was authoritative and confident. "The spring comes forth." There was a bubbling, churning sound coming from the earth as it yielded to his will. Slowly at first, only a few droplets of water broke the earth's surface, a few inches from Nelkie's stick. Within seconds the droplets turned into a babbling fountain that filled the twelve-foot-wide depression in the ground with cool, fresh spring water.

Nelkie smiled with pride and withdrew his stick. He was elated that the first time he called upon his stick to use his newly granted power, it produced the desired effect quickly and flawlessly.

Lilly had seen the magical gifts the elves possessed before, but was nevertheless amazed by the power of this neophyte elf. She walked to the edge of the pond and drank her fill. When she was finished, she looked up at Nelkie and once again her soft and gentle voice infiltrated his head.

"Nelkie, that was wonderful! And the water is so cool!"

"The water is cool," he said, "because it comes from an underground spring. This pool will be continually fed by that spring. If you should come here to drink ten years from now, there will be water. I can't tell you how I know this, but I am certain that it is so."

"Maybe that stick of yours has the ability to expand your mind, as well as your physical powers," the doe replied.

"You're exactly right. I can tell you that using this stick affects me mentally, physically, and even spiritually. It is a supremely exhilarating experience."

"Well, thank you very much. Now I don't have to walk very far at all to quench my thirst. That was very kind of you."

"Not at all, Lilly. It was the least I could do for a friend. Well, I would love to stay awhile longer, but I have a long journey ahead and I really must be going. Be well, and I hope to see you upon my return."

"Stay safe, my little friend, and thank you again."

Nelkie bowed to the doe, waved, and strode off into the forest.

Chapter Fourteen

Now that Nelkie had taken the first steps of his journey and left his home behind, his concentration was on what lay ahead. His accomplishment with the drinking pool had assured him that he could use his new tools with confidence. He marched on to meet his future with his head held high. The never-ending forest, which at first seemed intimidating, now spread its limbs like a mother's arms to welcome him.

This was a time of discovery for Nelkie. Around every curve of the forest path, he saw, heard, or smelled something for the first time. His keen mind absorbed a tremendous amount of information within only a few miles from home.

The elf trekked along the forest path for more than an hour with all of his senses on overload. The fresh clean aroma of evergreen, Mother Nature's air freshener, welcomed him to her unspoiled pristine home. A soft spring breeze flowing through the canopy created ever-changing patterns of golden sunshine along his path. His super-sensitive ears were receiving multitudes of sound from the woodland orchestra. Small birds sang above him; squirrels scratched tree trunks beside him as they raced up and down. Like all elves, Nelkie was naturally sure-footed, with exceptional balance. This evolutionary trait allowed his race to travel through the vast canopy as easily as humans did on the ground. Nelkie was actually somewhat out of his element. He was surprised to find that walking on the ground took some getting used to. It was a new experience for him to be walking on a surface that was constantly changing and much more uneven than tree limbs. Looking up, instead of where he was walking, Nelkie stepped on a small stone that slid the along the ground, causing him to lose his balance. This had never happened to him before, and he found himself suddenly on his butt, laughing like a child in a funhouse.

While continuing to move on, he pulled a small leather bag out of his pouch and poured out some pine nuts. Hiking happily along, savoring his snack, the young elf busied himself by trying to identify different species of trees and shrubs. *Surprising*, he thought, *how much of this I remember from school.*

The awesome size of everything that grew in the forest was what fascinated him the most. Nelkie was used to living in the treetops, where his surroundings were scaled down to elf-sized. Now, out in the world, he was truly dwarfed by the vast vegetation. Even the bushes that would be considered small by human standards towered over his head. There were wildflowers growing here and there, some small and delicate, some large and flashy-looking. Nelkie was not surprised to see blossoms as big as his entire face.

What *did* surprise him was his first encounter with a bumblebee. Not only was this annoying creature as big around as his clenched fist, but the horrendous buzzing it generated assaulted Nelkie's sensitive ears, requiring a hasty departure from the area.

At one point he stopped, certain that he had heard something un-familiar. It was a very slight sound, so the elf strained to focus his acute hearing. A very soft chomping noise seemed to be coming from the ground near Nelkie's feet. Finally, his eyes came to rest on a caterpil-lar making lunch out of a maple leaf. He sat down to watch. *Curious-looking fella*, he thought. *Kind of looks like a worm wearing a sweater.* Nelkie sat spellbound watching how much and how fast the caterpillar could eat. In about four minutes the furry little creature devoured the entire leaf, which was at least five times its size. *Well, I guess this show is over*, he told himself. *I should be moving along anyway.* Much to his surprise, the position of the sun was telling him that he had hiked right through his lunch. It was now late afternoon and he was getting hungry. Rather than remain stationary, he chose to walk and eat. The curiosity and anticipation about what lay ahead was too strong for him to waste any time sitting, so he reached into his pouch and munched on some dried boar meat while moving ever forward.

It wasn't long before the light began to fade and Nelkie's thoughts centered on his first night alone in the great forest. He had been hiking eastward along a well-traveled deer path, when he remembered his instructions from the elders. Nelkie stepped off the path to look for a safe place to bed down for the night. About twenty yards off the path he came upon a fir tree that was surrounded by vine-encased shrubs. "This is perfect," he said aloud. "I can snap off a few fir boughs for my bed, and have some security being enclosed by shrubbery." Almost instinctively, the elf knew what to do. Recalling his early schooling in the structure and growth patterns of different species, he set about arranging small branches upside-down to create his bedding. Nelkie had been taught that the ends of evergreen branches, because of their weight, tend to curve downward. "So, if I turn them over," he told himself, "they will curve upward, cocooning me in Mother Nature's arms." He lay on his back with his provisions pouch under his head and stared through the canopy at a clear sky, dotted with billions of stars. Though he was thrilled with nature's magnificent beauty, fatigue began to overtake him. Nelkie rolled over on his side and was just about to drift off, when the nocturnal voices of the forest invaded his peace and tranquility. Not too far from his position he heard movement through the underbrush. An owl hooted somewhere above him. Then he thought he heard a grunt-- *Or was that a growl?* Knowing that there was no one around to warn him of any impending danger, he grew fearful. Darkness had settled over the forest, making his surroundings seem even more ominous. Something screeched overhead, and Nelkie sat bolt upright. Whatever it was had moved on, leaving the elf visibly shaken. Fear and uncertainty were ruling his thoughts. *Do predators attack in the dark? Should I stay awake all night, and sleep tomorrow? But then I would have to travel through the forest in the dark because I slept all day.* Frustrated and fearful, the elf lay back down, trying to understand his feelings, and what to do about them.

The only time he had ever been alone in the dark was when he was in his room high above the forest floor, safe from any threat. This situation was not something he had thought about, and he continued to grow uneasy. Before he allowed himself to become terrified, the voice of reason somehow rose above his fear. He pressed his medallion and said, "I must go," and told himself that he was an adult now, and adults are not afraid of noises in the night. *I will not live in fear. I can call upon the powers of the ancients should I have to face a perilous situation. I am not without tools and I am not without skills.* He curled himself up in a ball, and drifted off to sleep, dreaming of a girl with hair the color of sunshine.

The elf had fallen into such a deep and restful sleep that he did not wake when he was visited by a battalion of nocturnal forest fairies. He stirred only slightly when dozens upon dozens of the tiny creatures worked together to cover the youngster with a blanket of insulating fir. As Lilly had told him, he would never be alone in the forest.

Chapter Fifteen

A screeching blue jay sounded reveille shortly after dawn. Nelkie was catapulted back to consciousness. He was wide awake, but slightly disoriented. It took a few seconds before he got his bearings. Once he realized he was not in his bedroom loft, but out in the forest, he sat upright. Pushing off his soft-needled blanket added some confusion to his rude awakening. *How did that get here? I don't remember pulling anything over me.* He dismissed the blanket mystery, thinking he must have gotten cold during the night and pulled a limb out of his bedding.

The blue jay screeched again as it flapped over his head. *I wonder what he's so angry about. He sure is starting off his day with a bad attitude. Well, I have more to worry about right now. For one thing I'm hungry and have more important things to do.*

A quick security check of the area revealed no threat to his safety, so he pressed his medallion and said, "I must return." He reached into his provisions pouch and pulled out a chunk of cornbread and a few berries. A few gulps of water from his boar-skin canteen, and he was ready to continue his journey. Gathering up his few belongings, the elf set out to find the path he left the night before.

It was another gorgeous spring day, and Nelkie's pace was quick and energetic. He couldn't wait to see what kind of adventure the new day would bring.

Most of the morning was uneventful. Nelkie kept moving, concentrating on covering as much ground as possible. He tried to imagine what his first encounter with a human would be like. *What if this person is not what he seems to be? Will I be able to recognize deception or dishonesty?* The elf put his doubts and questions aside for the present, because he understood there was no other choice but to deal with each situation as it arose.

It was almost midday when Nelkie crested an almost vertical hill that had taken him two hours to climb. The hill was so steep that for the first time since leaving home he actually had to use his walking stick. When he reached the summit, his legs were burning with fatigue and he was almost out of breath. Even his arms ached from constantly using his stick to gain leverage. Nelkie glanced back down the hill. *By Bindar's berries, this hill would scare a mountain goat.*

The hill came to a slight plateau, and Nelkie, eager to go down the other side, scrambled across the top. He stopped, absolutely awestruck at the beauty that lay before him. The plateau sloped gently downward, opening into a vista of such astounding beauty that the young elf felt as if he were in the presence of God. The great forest had yielded to a glade that went on for several hundred yards. A carpet of bright orange and green covered the ground from the foot of the plateau across the length and breadth of the glade. The contrast of green stems and brilliant orange blossoms from the millions of wild California poppies was a sight Nelkie would hold in reverence for his entire life. *Whatever fate comes to pass on the far side of this forest matters not, for I have been privileged to behold beauty of such a singular nature.* Nelkie sat on the ground at the edge of the plateau for more than an hour, silently absorbing the spiritual splendor of being one with nature.

Eventually, he felt the continuing call of his quest, and he knew the time had come to leave this sacred place. When he looked beyond the glade, the great forest appeared to be a world without end. The enormity of the great forest was staggering. *It really looks as if there is no end to this woodland. It could be weeks before I even get close to human habitation. I must pace myself and make sure I'm getting enough rest, and nutrition to keep a high level of strength and energy.* He set off down the plateau with intention of being across the open glade, and into the safety of the wood before late afternoon. Wading through countless waves of chest-high flowers was surreal. In order to navigate through the proliferation of flora, Nelkie had to perform a sort of upright-but-swimming motion. The fragrant fun went on for several hours until the elf had crossed the glade and could once again walk among the trees. He had never before had such a good time alone.

As the days wore on, Nelkie grew accustomed to everyday life in the great forest. Being constantly accompanied by the scampering of small animals abated any feelings of loneliness. The wonders of nature at its unspoiled best were revealed to him with the discovery of every meadow, stream, and glen he would come upon.

Like all young elves, Nelkie had spent most of his life anticipating and preparing for his quest. Now that he was on his mission, he was already having experiences far beyond anything his young mind had envisioned. The sheer vastness of the great forest had become a metaphor for Nelkie's quest. He had no idea how deep the forest was, or when he would emerge from its depths into a land populated by creatures he had never seen.

He sat down to contemplate his situation, and to take in some nourishment. Nelkie was beginning to understand the difference between the childish excitement young elves felt when looking forward to this day, and the challenge of being alone and facing life in the wild.

While he was chomping on a carrot, Nelkie's thoughts were interrupted by a feeling that something was not right. He refocused his thoughts on the immediate area. At first he couldn't put his finger on it, but he knew something was off. Then it struck him. It was conspicuously quiet. There were no small animals around, not even squirrels. He could hear birds, but they were off somewhere in the canopy, not fluttering through the trees as they had been all morning. Nelkie wondered if he was the only thing breathing for hundreds of yards around, and if so, *why*.

He stood in the strangely silent forest, looking and listening. After a long moment, the elf detected a very slight, muffled sound. He couldn't quite identify its origin. *What is that?*

Once he had taken a few steps, a strange awareness came over him. It was that odd feeling he experienced the day before, when Lilly had walked into his immediate area. Nelkie felt the presence of another being. While he was trying to understand the uncanny emotional tingle he was feeling, he heard something. At first he thought it was a slight whimper. Yes, it was some small animal in distress. Cautiously, he tip-toed toward the sound. Only a few yards from where his sixth sense began to tingle, he came upon a fallen tree. Slowly drawing closer, he saw the tree was hollow and something inside was moving.

"Hello--are you all right in there?" He spoke softly in a gentle tone, not wanting to scare whoever was inside. Momentarily, the whimpering grew louder as a small, black, fuzzy form emerged from the log. It was adorably cute. If this had been almost any other animal, Nelkie would have picked it up and cuddled it. Instead, he froze. His heart and stomach were doing flip-flops. Fight or flight adrenaline was pumping through his body with the force of a fire hose. The three-month-old black bear cub was now outside the log, and making more noise than before. The elf's first reaction was to look beyond the cub for its mother. As he looked up, the air around him seemed to shatter from the savage, predatory roar behind him. The angry mother was only fifty or sixty yards away, and on a dead run. Nelkie bolted from the cub as fast as he could. Over his shoulder he could see the bear gaining ground fast. He jerked the medallion out of his tunic and screamed, "I must go!" Nelkie slowed down, then stopped and stood perfectly still. The bear hesitated only a moment before resuming her charge. She was still headed directly for him. Adrenaline-laced thoughts sped through Nelkie's brain like a launched torpedo. *How can this be? She can't see me; why is she still charging? How does she know I'm still here?* He turned and ran for all he was worth. The snarling bear was still gaining. Nelkie spotted a hemlock tree. With no other choice, he leaped into the low-hanging branches, climbing as fast as he knew how. The bear was relentless. She reached the tree only seconds behind him. She only hesitated for an instant before starting up after the terrified elf. Up he went, higher and higher, the bear now almost within striking distance. Nelkie was running out of limbs. There was nowhere else to go. His heart felt like it was about to pound its way out of his chest. Still, the bear advanced. Nelkie could climb no farther. He was trapped. The threatening bear was now only four feet away. Nelkie stood on the highest limb that would hold him. With one arm around what was left of the trunk, he held the other out, pointing his stick at the oncoming beast. Shaking with fear, he tried desperately to concentrate and focus his energy. He stared into the face of death and shouted, "Fire!" In a blinding flash of light, a ball of fire spit from his stick and exploded smack on the bear's nose. She staggered, but wouldn't give up. Claws extended, she swiped in vain at the nothingness where the flame had attacked her. Again, in desperation, Nelkie shouted. "Fire!" Again the fireball exploded into his attacker's nose. She howled in pain, and retreated. With her fur singed and her nose stinging, she apparently had had enough. She climbed down and ran off to her still-whimpering cub. Together, they lumbered out of Nelkie's line of sight. He breathed a very deep sigh of relief. Holding up his walking stick, he scrutinized it, as if he expected some enlightenment from the stick as to what had just occurred. *Wow! How did that happen? I just thought "fire," and there it was. Maybe this is what Daido meant when he said I would learn how to channel the powers of the ancients through my stick, but I don't have a clue how I made this happen.*

Nelkie decided that the mysteries of the stick would probably become clear to him with his continued use of this tool. He turned his attention back to why the bear was still chasing him even though she could not see him. Still panting and shaking in the top of the hemlock, it dawned on him how the bear knew where he was. Then it came to him. *She followed me with her nose! My medallion is a miraculous device, but it can do nothing about my scent.*

Still forty feet up in the hemlock, Nelkie was in no hurry to come down. Panting and shaking with fear, he thought long and hard about the life-threatening situation he had just survived. He had come to the realization that although his walking stick and medallion were very useful "tools," as the elders called them, they would not necessarily be the answer to every problem he encountered. He must always keep his wits about him, and learn to expect the unexpected.

After he had sufficiently calmed himself, Nelkie climbed back down. Physically drained, he was also hungry and very thirsty. He pressed his medallion, returned to visibility, and took several long gulps from his water jug. Rummaging through his provisions pouch, he produced a meal of mostly raw vegetables, and the last of his cornbread.

Once he had eaten, Nelkie found his emotional state had more or less returned to normal. Convinced that his foot race with the bear was as dangerous as things were going to get today, he strengthened his resolve and once again set out to continue his quest.

Chapter Sixteen

Nelkie walked at a brisk pace for several hours, feasting his senses on the natural beauty of his beloved forest. He was enchanted with surroundings that were always beautiful to look at, often fragrant or tasty, and occasionally even musical. Feelings of kinship with nature were undeniable. Every woodland elf, for more than a thousand years, had been soothed to the depths of his soul by the peace and serenity of the forest world. Nelkie was no exception. He was in his sanctuary. His spirituality had awakened.

The birth of these sacred feelings paved the way to a new self-perception. The emotional exposure of these passions was creating a pathway toward giving him a clearer understanding of who he was.

As Nelkie traveled on, he came upon a stream that flowed through a tranquil glen. He followed the stream until he approached a waterfall at the far side of the glen. A large flat rock proved to be an adequate bench. He would rest here while continuing his self-reflection. The gently flowing water seemed to help clarify his thoughts, as he pondered his future.

The perception that in a day or two he should be nearing the forest's edge provoked an abundance of mixed emotions. He wanted to explore the woodland, and learn more about his brothers and sisters that lived here. Nelkie was very much at home, and at peace. Spiritual stimulation was a totally unfamiliar experience for the elf. So profoundly was he moved, that he briefly considered putting off the continuation of his quest. The thought of staying to absorb the rapture of the Great Forest was an enticing temptation, but in the end, his better judgment won out, and he headed east, into the rising sun, marching ever closer to a world dominated by humans.

Nelkie found the next few days to be uneventful. He befriended a variety of new creatures along the way, but for the most part, he spent the daylight hours hiking through the vast forest. By the time dusk would arrive, fatigue would force him to stop, enjoy a light supper, and turn in for the night. Well-rested at dawn, he would begin his regimen again, with eager anticipation.

The miles between the elf and his home were mounting with every day he put behind him. The tranquility of the forest was soothing. He felt more in tune with the animals, as well as with his developing sixth sense. It now only took him a moment to pinpoint his focus on whatever life form was approaching. When any warm-blooded creature crossed within fifty feet of the elf, he knew exactly where it was, and how many of these beings were advancing into his area. He could not discern, however, whether the advancing life form was animal, human, or elf. Comprehending his developing skills helped him to regain some confidence, which was understandably shaken by a five-hundred-pound bear. Periodically, the vivid picture of that charging bear would replay in his mind, reminding him to remain vigilant.

After a long day's march, Nelkie had curled up in a bed of pine boughs. He had almost drifted off to sleep when the now-familiar sixth sense started to tingle. Jumping to his feet, Nelkie grabbed his walking stick and focused his concentration on the underbrush twenty feet away. He knew by instinct that there were two creatures approaching, but this time the warning felt noticeably different. His senses were not ringing like a fire alarm. It was more of a mild enlightenment of a new presence. Danger was not an issue. The elf had learned that if he was at risk, his initial warning system would have gone off more violently.

Presently, he had only to solve the mystery involving the identity of his approaching company.

He stood up, pointing his stick at the underbrush. Mustering up his best authoritative adult voice, he commanded: "All right, I know you two are out there. Come out and show yourselves. Come out now, or I'll come in after you." There was some rustling in the lower bushes, and some low groaning, and then they emerged.

Two chubby raccoons waddled out of the underbrush. "See! Now you really did it! You got him angry. We'll be lucky if he doesn't turn us into bugs!"

"Me? You're the one who wanted to spy on him. I wanted to leave him alone."

Nelkie couldn't help but laugh. What a sight these two were. They lumbered out of the bushes, their heads low to the ground in embarrassment, each blaming the other for their supposed misfortune. It was obvious these creatures were frightened. Nelkie thought it was almost humorous that his twenty-seven-inch presence should appear threatening to anyone. He thought it was ironic that they were frightened. Though they were a non-aggressive species, the elf knew these two could easily claw him to pieces, especially given the fact that each raccoon was almost half his size. The gentle cognizance of his sixth sense, however, assured him these animals were docile. He lowered his staff, and greeted them warmly. "I apologize for threatening you, but I couldn't very well go to sleep without knowing who was out there."

In a shy, almost imperceptible inner voice, the portly male answered. "That's okay. We were just looking for something to eat, and heard you making your bed. Word had reached us that one of the magical creatures that live deep in the woodland was near. We have never seen an elf, and were just curious. We didn't mean to disturb you, honest."

The female wouldn't let up her tirade. "Stop sniveling, you old fool, and take your punishment. If you weren't so fat and clumsy, we wouldn't be in all this trouble."

"Fat! Me? Well, you're not exactly skinny, you know."

"Stop it, you two. Nobody is going to punish anyone." He reached into his pouch and pulled out a handful of berries. Holding out the offering to them, he said, "Are you guys always this cranky when you're hungry? And why do you think I want to harm you?"

The male advanced cautiously. Standing on his hind legs he carefully examined the berries with his front paws. "Uh, thank you for your kindness. We have heard the elves have strange powers, and can command the forces of nature at their whim. We were afraid you would be angry at being disturbed and would turn those powers against us. Oh—here, Betty, there's enough for both of us."

Betty took a few berries, and like her mate, inspected her food closely before she ate it. "Beezel has always been much too curious," she said. "One day I'm sure his curiosity will be the death of both of us."

"Well, you have nothing to fear from the woodland elves," Nelkie assured them. "You should know it is true that we are a gifted race, and have the power to manipulate the world around us, but we are forbidden to use these powers in a negative or abusive manner. We live in harmony with nature, and all those with whom we share this world. All we wish to do is to promote tolerance and brotherhood among all species. Now I would love to tell you all about our history and culture, but I'm afraid it's getting late. I must get some rest so I can be on my way shortly after dawn. I have a long way to go, and much to do before I can return home. It's been nice meeting you, but if you will excuse me, I would like to retire now."

"Of course, by all means," Beezel said. "Come on, Betty; let us leave this good elf in peace."

"Okay, okay," Betty replied. "Thank you for the berries, and good luck to you." She then waddled over to her mate, and picked up right where she left off when they first came out of the bushes. "Aren't you coming? You always dawdle so. I don't know how I've put up with you all this time."

"Put up with me? I'm the one who has to put up with your constant complaining. And another thing...." Beezel's inner voice trailed off as they melted into the night.

The elf laughed to himself. *The argument with no end. There they go, together forever in their blissful crankiness.* He curled up in his bed and let sleep overtake him.

While the young elf enjoyed a deep and restful sleep, Queen Katherine appeared, along with legions of her faithful subjects. True to her bond with the Circle of Elders, Katherine and her followers kept a silent vigil while perched above the little traveler. The nocturnal forest fairies remained until the first light of dawn began to filter through the canopy. Nelkie began to stir, which was their signal to return to the safety of the upper canopy, now that their charge was delivered unhurt to another dawn.

The warm spring sun shone through the forest canopy, announcing its cloudless glory. The radiant light penetrated Nelkie's eyelids. Gently awakened by nature's alarm clock, he sat up and rubbed the sleep from his eyes. He took a deep breath. The clean morning air signaled a fresh start to the new day. Nelkie set out along the forest path, excited to see what new discoveries the day would bring. His lighthearted mood was further enhanced by the cheerful birdsong that seemed to spread throughout the forest. The squirrels always made him smile as he watched them scurrying up, down, and around the tree trunks as if they were on a life or death mission.

It was inevitable, however, that these emotions would give way to excited anticipation. His curiosity about the human world, and what type of good deeds he would be able to accomplish, were his driving forces, and he had no choice but to push on.

It was late morning before Nelkie stopped to rest. A fallen tree provided a place for him to sit and take a drink. After washing down several mouthfuls of nuts with a few more swigs from his water jug, Nelkie felt re-energized and ready to continue his trek.

The experience of having to defend his life for the first time had accelerated Nelkie's maturation. Remembering his father's advice about keeping his wits about him, and using his intelligence to prevail, boosted his self-confidence. He was no longer the cocky youngster, flying about the treetops with reckless abandon. Nelkie had become an accomplished woodsman, who could back off a bloodthirsty bear without help from anyone. He was self- assured, not cocky.

Morning faded into afternoon and Nelkie kept moving ever forward. He had traveled a great distance so far, and he was determined to put several miles more behind him before he turned in for the night, but suddenly, he had to stop. At first the elf was not sure why he stopped, but then, he felt that something was amiss. He thought, *The last time I had this feeling, that angry bear caught me off guard.* Determined to not be caught unawares again, he surveyed the area, carefully trying to sniff out any trouble. The birdsong that had accompanied him for hours was gone. So were any other signs of life. The only sound his sensitive ears could pick up was the occasional rustling of leaves in the light breeze.

As suddenly as a lightning strike, Nelkie was overwhelmed with feelings of urgency. His senses were telling him--no, screaming at him--that someone or something was coming closer. His instincts told him to focus in on a clump of underbrush, some sixty-odd yards away. Every hair on his body knew that trouble was about to emerge from that thicket. The exploding intensity of his sixth sense was almost more than he could physically withstand. The ringing in his ears had escalated to an alarming gong-like warning. He felt the presence of three…four…no, *six of them!* Nelkie tightened his grip on his stick, and tried to prepare for the worst. Finally, his ears tuned in to the snarling and threatening growls. The elf stood his ground.

Chapter Seventeen

One by one, the six timber wolves slinked out of the underbrush. Nelkie could almost feel their hunger. They inched closer, baring their fangs, threatening. The predators started to fan out around him. They were trying to encircle him, to block his escape. Their heads low to the ground, the pack had formed a semicircle in front of him.

I can't let them close the circle--if they surround me, I'm finished! Nelkie would not allow himself to panic. *Think! There must be a way out!* His nimble mind was weighing options at the speed of light. He knew that even with his stick, fighting off six full-grown wolves would be impossible. *Wait! My stick! My stick is not a club, it's a tool. I must concentrate.*

Nelkie raised his stick above his head, but before he could summon its power, he was distracted by a seventh presence. It was coming up behind him with blazing speed. Knowing it would be certain death if he took his eyes off the wolves, he tried to stand sideways to catch a quick glance at the oncoming intruder. He saw the form of a large stag gracefully sprinting toward him with tremendous speed. Perceiving this not to be a threat, he quickly turned back to the wolves. They were closing in.

Nelkie focused his concentration inward. Summoning his empowered knowledge, he began to make great swirling motions with both arms extended above his head. His stick began to quiver as the elf intensified his single-mindedness. As his concentration peaked he felt an eruption of inner power rising, growing, building. Physically trembling, he felt a voice that was not his own reverberate through the forest as he roared the word "Wind."

Still gesturing wildly, he again thundered out *Wiiinnndddd!* At once, leaves and small sticks began to swirl in the air directly in front of the pack. The velocity of the whirlwind increased rapidly, and larger debris swirled into a growing funnel. The wolves cautiously hesitated. At that moment, the stag came to a sudden halt, just inches from where the elf was standing. For a brief moment, Nelkie stood in awe of the sheer size of this magnificent animal. He was surely over two hundred pounds. The ten points of his antlers formed a majestic crown on this tall, muscular beast.

The stag lowered his head, and Nelkie heard a booming voice say, "Hurry! I am here to help! Grab hold, and climb on!" Nelkie looked back at the wolves. He knew his wind barrier would not keep them at bay for much longer. They were already edging their way into it, testing it to see if they could penetrate unharmed.

Without further hesitation, the elf seized one of the massive antlers, and swung a leg over the huge beast's neck. In the blink of an eye, the stag was up and away. He seemed to achieve maximum speed immediately. At first, because he was frightened and unfamiliar with the proper way to ride, Nelkie bounced and flopped about like a flag on a windy day. As the beast sprinted away, he felt the elf bounding and jolting up and down, and was concerned he might fall off. "Rock back and forth with the rhythm of my gait, little one. Move with my motion, not against it, and you will not bounce." Nelkie followed his liberator's advice, and found his seat. He was exhilarated. His body was now in perfect tandem with the animal's powerful muscles, as they pumped and propelled them far from danger. They dodged branches and jumped over fallen logs, all at breakneck speed. Riding on the stag's back had jacked up the magnitude of Nelkie's sensory stimulation to the point where it transcended all else. His eyes watered from the speed at which this animal cut through the air. He heard nothing but the deafening sound of air rushing past his sensitive ears.

He grasped the felt-like surface of the antlers, and together they flew through the air with every graceful leap and bound. The stag's musky, earthy smell enveloped Nelkie, as he became one with his brother.

The elf wanted to stay in this moment forever, but he knew he must force his way back from this euphoric state. He must know if they were still being pursued. Glancing over his shoulder, he saw the wolves had breached his wind barricade, but were far behind. The stag continued to lope along with grace and ease for more than a mile. The next time the elf looked back, he knew the wolves would have to go hungry a little longer. They were nowhere in sight, and his internal alarm was silent. He leaned closer to the animal's ear and spoke. "I think we're safe now. Thank you, thank you for saving my life."

The gallant stag slowed to a bouncy trot, with the elf bobbing and jiggling uncontrollably. Nelkie's insides didn't unscramble until his ride came to a complete halt. In less than five minutes Nelkie's emotions had run their entire spectrum, and left him breathless and shaking. The stag, however, was not even slightly winded. The strength and stamina this animal displayed were almost beyond comprehension. The elf needed a few moments to gear down from the extreme sensory overload.

"By the power of the ancients, that was one wild ride! I can't thank you enough. If you hadn't come along when you did--well, I don't even want to think about what might have happened."

"You are very welcome. I am always glad to help, especially when I see someone facing odds like that alone. My name is Rajah--and what may I call you?"

"I am called Nelkie, and you may call me friend for life. You put yourself at great risk to help a stranger, and for that I will always be in your debt."

Rajah walked over to a small brook, and Nelkie climbed down onto a large flat rock. "No debt is owed, my little friend. I am sure you would not turn your back on someone in need; nor can I. Anytime I can do anything to disappoint those wolves, I will. You know, they do not belong here, and I want to send them back where they came from. There has never been a wolf sighting here, until this year."

"So where did they come from?"

"I think they have drifted down from the north. It may be that there is less competition for prey in *our* forest. Anyway, this was not my first encounter with them; there used to be eight of them."

"What happened to the other two?"

"About a month ago, they cornered me with my back to some large boulders; I had to fight my way out. I was quick enough to gore one of them, and toss him into the pack. I reared up and stomped another's skull, while his friends were trying to regroup. Once I had broken through their circle, I escaped. Those flesh-eating fiends will never make a meal out of me, and I will also do whatever I can to keep the smaller creatures of this forest from falling victim to those slobbering savages."

Nelkie saw extreme anger flashing in the eyes of this majestic beast, and was taken aback. Cautiously, he offered a word of advice to his new champion. "My friend, I was raised to believe that prolonged anger is a destructive emotion. In my society, anger exists, but we have learned to defuse it through negotiation, and if necessary, arbitration. Beware of your rage, brave one, for anger can be the mother of mistakes. An enraged mind does not often make rational decisions. Your survival is important, Rajah. If our brothers of the forest are to continue receiving the benefit of your strength and courage, you must not act on negative emotion."

"I know there is wisdom in what you say, Nelkie, but there is no negotiating with wolves. Don't worry. I'm angry, not foolish. I only wish I could do more. I am young and strong now, but it saddens me to think that the day will come when I am too old or tired to protect the innocent, and the helpless. If I should die in mortal combat, who will take my place?"

If ever there was a true friend of the forest, surely it is this noble beast, Nelkie thought. *Maybe I can find a way to give Rajah some advantage that will enable him to continue his crusade with even more success. I believe this demands significant consideration.*

Rajah lowered his massive antlers and said, "Climb aboard, my friend, and allow me to make your journey a little less tiring, at least for today. You still have a great distance to cover, so you might as well ride while you can."

"Thank you. I will not be fool enough to walk, when I can ride, and have fun as well!"

Nelkie climbed on, and Rajah carried him along with no trouble at all. They talked for hours, each enjoying the other's company. A strong bond was forming between them, forged by mutual respect. Among other things, they discussed each other's plans for the future.

Rajah told Nelkie that he must soon find a mate. "You see, I too have recently come of age. It is time I started a family of my own. I would especially like to have a son. I would enjoy teaching him the ways of the forest, and telling him of my adventures, and maybe when he comes of age, he too will protect the less fortunate. What about you? Do you ever think about starting a family of your own?"

"Not really. My thought process right now doesn't go that far into the future. I have a mission to complete first, but there is someone special waiting for my return."

Nelkie told his new friend about all the excitement of his last night at home. "There was a grand feast, with music and merriment until midnight, and then I was presented to the Circle of Elders to be empowered for my quest. The elders' performance of their ancient skills was truly awe-inspiring. I was moved beyond explanation, but I must admit that sometimes, when I lie down at night, I remember that special dance I enjoyed so much with Arnora. I can shut my eyes and almost smell the wildflowers in her hair."

"Sounds to me like she is very special," Rajah said.

"Yes, she is, but I cannot allow my mind to get all tangled up in romantic daydreams. I have more important things to think about. Arnora will be there when I return, but I must return with honor."

"Yes, and speaking of your journey, I should tell you that you are no more than a day or two at most from the edge of the forest. I will keep you company tonight, if you like, but tomorrow we must go our separate ways. I must go back deeper into the forest, and you must seek out humans beyond this woodland. From this point forward you must be vigilant. You could encounter humans at any time."

As the afternoon wore on, the two travelers grew hungry. Rajah spotted a yew bush, and strolled over to enjoy one of his favorite foods. Nelkie climbed off his friend's broad back to stretch his legs. A search of his pouch produced a few tasty plant roots, and there were still a couple of handfuls of pine nuts left. While Rajah enjoyed the tender new shoots of the yew, Nelkie's thoughts were centered on a review of the day. *What a day this has been! I could not even imagine such an adventure, and I'm still on the first leg of my journey. I wonder what lies ahead.*

The chewy plant root satisfied his hunger, and the pine nuts were a tasty dessert. A few swallows of cool water, and the elf was good to go. Once they finished eating, Rajah informed his friend that there was only a little more than an hour of light left. "Why don't you hop back on, so we can cover a little more ground before dark?" The stag once again lowered his head, and the elf gratefully climbed up.

As the sun gradually descended in the western sky, the two travelers moved on, ever closing the gap between them and civilization. As nightfall approached, they came upon a small meadow, rich with tall grass.

"This is a good place to make our bed for the night," Rajah said. Nelkie agreed, and climbed down. They walked through the tall grass, looking for a soft spot to bed down. When they found a spot to their liking, they stopped and the great beast carefully lowered himself into a prone position. "Ahh, this grass is nice and soft."

Nelkie sat cross-legged, facing Rajah. "You know, I wish you could continue on my quest with me, but I guess that's impossible. It's too bad, Rajah; we would have great adventures together."

The stag yawned before he could answer. "We have had a great adventure, Nelkie, and don't worry; we will see each other again. I'll be watching for you, and who knows, maybe your return will stir up some excitement in these woods, and we'll be off and running again."

"That would be great," the elf answered, "and I'm sure I'll be looking for you as well. If nothing else, I'll have a heck of a story to tell."

"I know you will, my little friend, but for now we had better get some rest. You don't have to put your head on the hard ground. If you would like, you can lean on me--at least I'm not cold and rough." Nelkie accepted his friend's offer and laid his head on the stag's broad back. The stag's warm fur and rhythmic breathing were lulling him off to sleep when Nelkie's inner consciousness perceived movement in his immediate surroundings. His sixth sense was telling him the movement was benign, but extensive. There appeared to be a large cloud of life forms entering his space. He looked up and smiled at the golden blanket of a thousand forest fairies performing their nightly ritual. He gently nudged his friend. "Look," he said, pointing toward the canopy. They both were wrapped in the protective glow generated by the flock of tiny sentinels. A calm and blissful sense that the forest was at peace enveloped both of them. Nelkie observed a familiar form break ranks, and gracefully flutter to the ground. Out of respect, the two travelers stood to greet her majesty. The stag bowed his enormous antlers before he spoke. "Queen Katherine. So good to see your grace. I would conclude that your presence this close to the forest's edge has something to do with my young friend here."

"Quite so, my dear Rajah, and as always, I am pleased to see you remain healthy and strong. It is because we are so close to the edge of the forest that I have come to offer a word of caution to Nelkie." She turned to face the elf. "I congratulate you on your progress so far, young one. The woodland is all abuzz with reports of your recent exploits with the dreaded wolves. Well done! It is now my duty to inform you that my subjects and I have reached our limit, in terms of travel. We can go no farther without risking discovery and capture. This will be the last night we will be able to stand our watch over you."

"I'm not sure I understand, your majesty. Are you telling me that you and your subjects have been with me all this time?"

"Only at night, when you would be most vulnerable."

"I am very grateful, my queen, but I had no idea of your presence, and no one had mentioned anything to me about this before I left."

"There was no need for you to know. Now, brave one, we will assume our watch in the canopy above you, and allow you and the noble Rajah to get some much-needed sleep. Rest well, for the best of your adventure awaits you on the morrow."

"Thank you, your grace, and good night."

"Good night Nelkie, and good luck to you." The queen dashed off to join her subjects perched high above the forest floor, while Rajah and Nelkie settled in for a rest that was both peaceful and secure.

Chapter Eighteen

Dawn was creeping slowly over the mist-covered meadow. Nelkie stirred, and then opened his eyes. The elf sat up to find his friend already awake. "How long have you been up?" he asked, through a yawn.

"Not long." Rajah stood, stretched, and shook his massive head, as if to shake the lingering sleep from his brain.

"Did you sleep well, big fella?"

"Yes. Very well, and you?"

"Like a baby."

Nelkie didn't tell his friend that he had been considering a way to reward his gallant rescue. The answer had come to him overnight through a vivid dream. When it came to him, the solution was obvious. It was just as obvious that what Nelkie wanted to do would be far beyond the reach of his powers alone. He would need help. Nelkie remembered Daido telling him that he had the ability to call on the Circle of Elders, should he be in need. Now was as good a time as any to put this ability to the test.

"You are as brave as you are benevolent, my friend, and benevolence is something all elves understand. Now, if you will indulge me, I will endeavor to do something for you."

"I need no reward. To know that the two of us are removed from harm is reward enough for me."

"I appreciate your unselfishness, Rajah, but my intentions are to give you a gift that will benefit all the woodland creatures."

"I'm not sure I understand--what kind of gift are you talking about?"

"Stand still, and trust in the benevolent power of elves." Nelkie raised his staff above the stag's massive antlers, his free arm stretched across the beast's back. With closed eyes, he focused inward. He envisioned the elders together in their chamber, and telepathically sent them a request for assistance. Centering his concentration deeper and deeper, he called forth the ancient empowerment. From the depths of his soul the discharge of raw power worked its way through his core. When Nelkie felt his stick begin to oscillate, he called upon the Circle to boost his power even farther. A filmy aura of transparent scarlet appeared and began to envelop both the stag and the elf. It floated around them like smoke, as Nelkie thrust both arms skyward. "May the benevolent and mighty power of the Circle of Elders enhance and protect this stouthearted defender of the forest." As Nelkie spoke, the aura widened and its color intensified. It flowed from scarlet to purple, and then into an iridescent rainbow. With the appearance of the rainbow, Nelkie could feel the presence of the elders. He knew somehow that Daido and the others were working with him.

Suddenly an eruption of brilliant blue crystals fired from his stick and completely encircled Rajah. The elf held on to the violently jolting stick, as the crystals swirled around the stag's legs, back, and antlers.

Rajah stood motionless, frozen with astonishment. The swirling crystals seemed to be transferring some form of electrical charge into his legs. The stag felt his strength increasing, but there was more, much more. There were intense feelings pulsing through his entire body. Feelings he didn't understand.

Nelkie, now half-entranced, was holding on to his staff with both hands. Without warning, the swirling crystals shot toward the canopy, and as suddenly as they had appeared, were sucked back into Nelkie's still-vibrating stick. Immediately the multi-colored aura disappeared, and Nelkie collapsed on the ground.

Confused and greatly concerned, Rajah hurried over to his fallen friend, gently nudging him with his nose. "Nelkie! Are you all right? Say something! What just happened?

The elf slowly rose to his feet. He pulled a stuck pinecone from his mop of curly hair, and tossed it aside. "Whew! That was almost more than I could handle." Still a little shaky, Nelkie continued. "I'm kind of new at this, and I'm not always sure what to expect. I was warned that the use of large amounts of this knowledge and power at one time can be physically draining, but I'm okay, just a little tired. What about you? Do you feel any different?"

The stag thought for a moment, taking stock of himself. "Yes, I do feel different, very different. I feel…well, aware, I guess would be the best way to put it."

"Aware is what you are, Rajah. Right now you are more aware than any other animal in the world."

"What do you mean, Nelkie? What has happened to me?"

"I will explain. It occurred to me that living this close to the edge of the forest, the greatest threat to you is not from within the forest, but from outside. I'm sure you have had some experience or knowledge of hunters. You now have no reason to fear them, and I will tell you why. The new awareness you feel is a gift the elders have given you, through me. Your senses are now so acute that a hunter who has you in his rifle crosshairs will no longer be a threat to you. Your senses are so sharp that even though you do not see, hear, or smell the hunter, it will be impossible for him to bring you down."

"I don't understand, Nelkie. How can that be?"

The elf went on to explain that as soon as the rifle was fired, Rajah would feel the disturbance in the air as the bullet was passing through it. Instantly knowing from which direction the projectile was coming would give him time to step out of its path. "Also," he continued, "if you should, let's say, come upon a snake, and it strikes at your leg, it will miss."

"It's not that I don't believe you Nelkie, and I don't want to sound ungrateful, at all, but honestly, you're not making a lot of sense. A snake will strike if it feels threatened. Most snake bites happen because the victim doesn't even know the snake is there, and almost steps on it. No one can react fast enough to get out of the way in time. We're talking about less time than it takes to blink!"

"Precisely," the elf answered. "Your reflexes have been enhanced a thousandfold. Just as you will feel the bullet piecing the air three hundred yards away, you will feel the air around you disturbed as the snake moves its head to strike. The difference here is that your reaction is strictly a reflex. Your thought process is not involved in the decision. In other words, you're right, there is not enough time, even if you saw the snake, for your brain to recognize it and send a message to your legs to move out of the way. The snake is too fast. You would surely be bitten. What will happen now is much simpler and much quicker. Your body will feel the disturbance in the air, and instinctively move you out of harm's way. Your brain won't be involved until you notice that you've suddenly jumped aside, and *then* you will see the snake, and know why."

"Now I understand. This is a miraculous gift, Nelkie. I am forever in your debt."

"Nonsense," came the reply. "This enhancement may be a reward for all you have done, but in the long run, it will benefit many, not just yourself. With this new power, your life expectancy will probably double. Being the noble animal that you are, the amount of good you will do will also double. Many of the woodland's weaker creatures will be safer because of your natural tendency to be protective. It makes me feel pleased, and very proud to be a part of this."

"I too am proud," Rajah said. "To be chosen to receive such a gift from a race as wise and virtuous as the woodland elves is an honor that one can only hope to live up to."

They were both feeling a little ill at ease, because they knew what must happen next. Neither of them wanted to be the one to initiate their farewell.

Rajah took it upon himself to get things moving. "Look, Nelkie, we should probably say our goodbyes here. I thank you and your elders for their benefaction. You have my word of honor that I will use this gift to protect others. You told me yesterday that I may call you friend for life. I would be honored if you would do so as well. I hope time passes quickly until we speak again."

Nelkie stoked the noble beast's neck. "Our time together has been too short, my friend. Be well."

"Good luck to you, Nelkie."

In order to keep their departure from becoming awkward, and knowing there was nothing more to say, the two friends simply turned, and walked off in opposite directions. Neither one would look back.

When Nelkie reached the edge of the meadow, he came upon a welcome sight. His stomach was beginning to growl for its breakfast, and there it stood. A large flowering cherry tree was just starting to show its pink buds. To elves, the early spring buds of a particular type of flowering cherry were as sweet as candy. To make sure he was right, he pulled out the little book given him at his presentation, and referenced the species. Elated with the positive result, he picked a handful and devoured them. *They really are good!* The happy elf enjoyed his breakfast banquet, and stashed a dozen more sweet buds in his pouch. His belly full, he was now ready to set about the business of the day.

He walked on, still feeling a little melancholy about leaving his new friend behind, but he told himself not to dwell on what had happened, but to focus on what was about to happen. Nelkie picked up his pace, ever alert to his surroundings.

The sun was not cooperating on this cool morning, and refused to show its face. The misty morning had evolved into a boring, gray day. *I can't imagine anything exciting happening on a cloudy day, but after all that went on yesterday, I think a boring gray day may not be such a bad idea.*

He journeyed for several hours, and was starting to feel a few pangs of hunger. He really wanted a big chunk of cornbread, but he told himself that was only because he had already eaten the last of it. Instead, he contented himself with a few more cherry buds, and moved on.

By midafternoon, Nelkie's legs were fatigued. He decided to sit awhile and rest. In the stillness of the forest, he thought he heard a strange sound off in the distance. He turned his head and tried to concentrate on which direction the sound was coming from. Sure enough, his keen ears picked up the sound again. It was still too far off for Nelkie to identify, but whatever this sound was, it felt strangely out of place in the forest. The sound was slightly clearer now, as it got closer. It sounded strange to him because the sound was new to his ears. The sound was human.

His inner sense began to tingle. He could now make out voices. Men shouting something. Just to be safe, he touched his medallion. Until he could properly assess his situation, it would be better for him to see without being seen. Gingerly, he moved toward the voices. His sixth sense was going off like a fire alarm. Nelkie was overflowing with excited anticipation.

Suddenly, he saw him. A man, in a red plaid shirt. He looked very frightened. The man was running as fast as he could. Loud voices were exploding behind him.

"Slater! Stop! Stop, or we'll shoot!

Nelkie ducked behind some underbrush, even though no one could see him. He recognized what the two pursuers were pointing at the first man. He had seen pictures of hand guns in school. This was not good. Nelkie was sure the man in the plaid shirt needed help, and he needed it now. The men brandishing pistols were about twenty-five yards behind, and gaining. They were approaching a stand of trees heavily laden with vines. Nelkie saw his chance.

He called on his practiced ability to focus inward, instantaneously. With the continued use of his power, Nelkie had become more comfortable and more confident in his proficiency. There was no lag time between "need" and "deed."

He raised his stick, pointed it at the cluster of vines, and commanded, "Burst forth and grow." With the speed of thought, his stick responded. The mass of vines exploded with split- second growth. Faster than the eye could explain to the mind, the mound of vines sprouted upward and interwove themselves into an impenetrable barrier between the hunters and the hunted. The two men were running so fast, they had no hope of avoiding the natural web that barred their way. They fell into the mass of vines and became hopelessly entangled. It took them several minutes to free themselves from Nelkie's obstacle. The elf was smiling, still hidden and feeling quite proud of himself, while he eavesdropped on his victims.

"What the hell happened here, Tom? I swear, I didn't even see these vines until it was too late. It's almost as if they jumped up and attacked us, as stupid as that sounds."

"I don't understand either, Rob. Maybe one of us stepped on a loose piece of brush, and all this junk was connected to it."

Tom Backer finally got to his feet, and while pulling the last piece of brush from inside his shirt, offered a hand up to his partner. "Damn, Rob, that was like stepping on the wrong end of a rake and having the handle hit you smack in the face!"

Rob Petersen pulled himself up, with Tom's help, and said, "Well, regardless of what happened here, or why, we'll never catch Slater now. It looks like the slippery poacher got away again. I can't believe this guy's luck!"

Nelkie, who was listening intently, searched his mind in vain, for the meaning of the word "poacher." The illegal taking of game animals was not something that existed in elf culture.

Tom was slowly shaking his head. "You know, Rob, when we came across another raccoon caught in one of Slater's traps, I was almost mad enough to shoot him right there."

"Yeah, I know. That poor little critter probably suffered quite some time before it bled to death. That man is no more than a wildlife assassin. I really want to put him away."

"Well there's not much we can do right now; he knows these woods as well as the animals. I'll bet he's a mile away by now. Let's head back to the field office and file another report. Man, this is frustrating. That creep has been getting away with this for years, and he's gotten away again."

A cold chill came over Nelkie when he realized the full gravity of the situation. As suddenly as he became involved, there was a complete reversal of what appeared to be right and wrong. He had made a terrible mistake. He moved closer to the two men. They were both dressed identically. Nelkie read the patch on Tom's shoulder. "State of California Game Warden."

The elf's stomach turned upside down. He felt sick. *Oh no--these good men were only trying to protect the innocent animals of this forest, and now I've helped an evil man to escape! This Slater person probably set the trap that almost cost Bart his life!*

Guilt weighed heavily on Nelkie's conscience. The same overpowering, all-consuming guilt he felt over his misadventure with his best friend had returned full force. Nelkie had made a serious error in judgment and as a result, an evil man remained free to continue in his evil pursuits. He watched the two disappointed wardens walk slowly away. He heard them pledge to each other that they would catch this Slater person, if it was the last act of their lives. Nelkie touched his

medallion and returned to visibility. He sat down on a rock to contemplate his grief.

For the first time since he left home, Nelkie's confidence had been
severely shaken. *Just when everything was going great, this happens. Am I
inept? Is my reasoning flawed?* The elf went over the entire episode in his
mind, before his self-doubt crippled his judgment. *What if, as it appeared, Slater was an innocent man being pursued by criminals? If I had waited
to gain more information, a blameless person could have gotten killed. Now, because I acted, a guilty man escaped, But no one got hurt.* Nelkie remembered
the great Daido telling him that realizing one has made a mistake is the
first step toward rectifying that mistake. *Okay, I made a mistake. What can
I do to rectify that mistake?*

The answer was obvious. He must find Slater and somehow bring
about his incarceration. A tall order, but Nelkie felt determined and he
knew that he could summon help. He turned his back toward civilization and headed into the woodland, determined to make things right.
Knowing that Slater had already gained valuable time, Nelkie trudged
off in the direction he last saw the man in the red plaid shirt. *"Slater
must be one clever human to be able to avoid capture over a period of years--
this won't be easy.* Nelkie decided he could use some help. He needed
someone with keener eyes than his own, or at least someone with a
better vantage point than his twenty-seven inches above ground level.

Presently, he came upon a small clearing. Once he reached its center where he had an unobstructed view of the sky, he looked up and
took a few deep breaths. He had a basic idea of what he wanted to do,
but no idea if it would work. He called for help.

Holding his stick with two hands, as if it were a baseball bat, he
raised it over his head and tried his best to focus his thoughts. The elf's
inner power responded. His body became charged with energy, and in
turn so did his stick. As his staff quivered and shook, Nelkie shouted
at the sky, calling for the creature he knew could assist him. "Help me.
Help me now. Evil lurks among you. Help me seek him out and I will

rid you of this threat forever." Nelkie's concentration level reached a trance-like state. The stick had begun to emit a low-pitched whir, almost a whistle. The sound intensified, building ever louder. As the volume increased, so did the pitch. It was higher, and going higher still. With a final shrill burst of sound, the unmistakable screeching of a large bird of prey cast skyward.

Within seconds, a dark figure streaked across the sky, its wings folded back. His stick fell silent. The elf looked up to see the dark projectile heading toward him unfold its wings and alight at his feet.

The red-tailed hawk addressed the elf respectfully. "I have heard your request for help, wise one. What is this evil of which you speak?"

Nelkie explained to the hawk about the escaped poacher. "If he is not caught, more helpless children of the forest will become victims of his greed. I am sure he is not too far ahead, but I don't know in which direction he made his escape. It is urgent that I know his location. Can you inform me of his exact whereabouts?"

The large hawk was instantly airborne. He circled overhead, fascinating Nelkie with the sheer breadth of his magnificent wingspan. "Don't worry," the hawk cried. "Your poacher will not escape the eyes of this hunter. I will return shortly." With a few strong thrusts of his powerful wings, the hawk disappeared into the shaded canopy.

Nelkie sat down to contemplate his next move. Should he capture this evil human and try to deliver him to the wardens? Or would justice be served if he rendered this man as helpless as a mouse, and allowed the larger predators to mete out his punishment? He tried to discern what Daido, in his wisdom, would deem an appropriate solution. *In what way would all beings, both human and non-human, be served best?*

Nelkie was still pondering his options when the hawk returned.

"The one you seek is not too far afield--I would say, a little more than a mile away, by human standards. He may have already met with the justice you wish for him, but that is for you to decide. Come, I will point the way." The swift hawk flew from tree to tree, waiting for the elf to catch up. Nelkie tried his best, but his short legs were no match for a pair of wings that could fly at the speed of an archer's arrow.

After a short while, Nelkie looked up to see the hawk perched on a tree limb, gesturing with one wing. "There lies your villain," he said. "If it were my choice, I would leave him to his fate. I have done as you asked. I will go now and let you do what you will with this wretch."

"Thank you, my friend. Your quick assistance is gratefully appreciated." Nelkie bowed in reverent gratitude.

"Any time you are in need of these keen eyes, wise one, do not hesitate. I am proud to help a brother of the forest."

With their business concluded, the hawk soared off, his graceful silhouette shrinking into the afternoon sky, until he was gone.

Nelkie now turned his attention to the problem at hand. A dozen or so yards from him, Slater lay motionless. The elf cautiously moved closer. Now he understood why the hawk would have left him. The poacher's leg was almost crushed by the steel jaws of one of his own traps. The poetic justice of this scene was fair enough for Nelkie's winged friend.

Upon closer examination, Nelkie found the man to also have a broken collarbone. He surmised that in his panicked run to escape his pursuers, Slater had become oblivious to the location of his own traps. He was probably running at full speed when he became snagged. Unable to break his fall, Slater fell hard on his shoulder, causing the collarbone to break clean. The poacher was now helpless. Because of the broken collarbone, he was unable to roll over, let alone release himself from the steel jaws. He had passed out from loss of blood, and was going into shock.

Nelkie had to make a decision, and he had to make it now. If he delayed too much longer, this man would surely die. *Some would say you reap what you sow,* he thought. *I am sure many would not fault me for saying you got what you deserve, and I should leave you to die alone in these woods.* The elf knew that this was not a decision he could live with. It was contrary to all he was taught, and all he had become. Elves were dedicated to enriching life, not destroying it. Nelkie could not help but feel pity for this man. Even though he knew Slater never had a conscience, and had been greedy and self-serving all his life, Nelkie could not let him die.

Suddenly, he felt a tingling sensation on his ring finger. He turned his palm over to look at the ring his parents had given him. A very slight vapory haze had encircled the center stone, like the halo around the moon on a wintery night. Nelkie remembered his father's words. "This ring contains the very essence of your mother, and me, so our spirit will travel with you." Nelkie knew he had made the right decision, and his parents approved.

Nelkie's confidence was growing, and with the resolve that the forces of good were on his side, he set about the task of saving Slater from his self-imposed doom. His idea was an ambitious one. The point, as Nelkie saw it, was to find a way to get the poacher to voluntarily change his ways. He felt that he would achieve the quickest and most profound solution by striking fear into the heart of this hapless human. Fear for his life would be the surest way to motivate Slater into turning over a new leaf. The next question was, how does a barely two-foot-tall elf intimidate a 250-pound human?

Nelkie knew the power of the ancients resided within his elders, and they in turn, could, if they felt the cause was just, impart that power to him. Confident that his plan although unorthodox, was ethical, and that the end justified the means, he petitioned the elders for their assistance. He moved closer to the unconscious poacher and concentrated on sending a mental image to the elders.

"I ask your help, wise ones, to turn this soul from evil. I summon the powers of The Circle of Elders for guidance and strength." With his arms outstretched and his mind in total concentration, Nelkie's consciousness traveled from the forest floor to the fabled inner chamber of his elders. The earnestness of his plea for their support was met with universal acceptance. His leaders joined together to consolidate and magnify their energy. The two thousand years of combined experience and practice in the use of these extraordinary powers enabled them to send the young one the assistance he required, through the metaphysical antennae provided by Nelkie's walking stick.

Nelkie received his answer in the form of energy. He felt a whirl-pool of electricity boosting his strength level, lifting him physically as well as spiritually. With the assimilation of this ancient power, the elf implemented his formidable plan.

An enormous surge of energy had entered his body through every pore. Nelkie's body began to levitate. As he rose above the forest floor, he felt every muscle heaving, expanding. He was gaining girth. He was growing! His chest became broader, thicker. His legs grew longer, more muscular. The process did not come to a halt until Nelkie's newly formed presence achieved a height of nearly nine feet. The creature he had become now floated nearly ten feet above the ground, with a foreboding presence that would strike fear into the heart of the bravest of men. His size was not all that had changed. What once was a thick mop of curly red hair had morphed into ghostly strands of white that fell straight past his shoulders. Nelkie's youthful, radiant complexion had become ashen and hard. Even the boyish blue eyes had turned grey and cold as steel.

The giant pointed his now twelve-foot-long stick at the motionless form below him. "Awaken!" The voice that boomed out of Nelkie's throat was that of some baritone demon whose powerful resonance startled even the elf. "Awaken," he bellowed again, as the stick expelled a blast of smoke-like vapor into Slater's face. "Awaken and meet your destiny, Slater." The voice of Armageddon seemed to gain even more power as it echoed off the huge tree trunks.

Slater's return to consciousness was ushered in by an icy dagger of fear plunging directly into his heart. Soul-wrenching terror fell like a curtain over the poacher's pain-soaked eyes as he beheld the titan suspended above him.

The giant spoke. "Slater! You are minutes from death's door. By all accounts you deserve this fate you have cast upon yourself. Hear me now, before it is too late. I have been sent here to offer you one chance at redemption; however, there are strict conditions."

Slater's pain-wracked body was trembling with fear. "Anything! Anything! Just tell me what you want! Please help me, please!" He was sobbing uncontrollably, partly from the pain of his wound, and partly because he had never known such fear.

The giant continued. "I have the power to free you. I also have the power to heal you, right here and right now. Before I do this and save your unworthy skin, you must swear by your immortal soul to do two things."

"Anything, please, just don't let me die!" The poacher's voice was choked with emotion; he was alone and frightened, and he could feel his life slipping away.

"You must swear to me now," the giant thundered, "that you will go from here to turn yourself in to the authorities, to pay for the wrongs you have committed."

"I promise. I swear, you have my word. What else must I do?"

"You must also pledge to dedicate the rest of your life to the preservation of all living things in this vast woodland. Swear this oath now, and I will let you live."

"Yes, yes, of course, I swear. Please save me--I don't want to die out here alone."

"Before I set you free, I must tell you that I will know if you do not keep your word. If this be the case, it will be my mission to hunt you down and force you to face consequences far more torturous than you confront today." The last sentence was spoken with such reverberating timbre that Slater recoiled into a fetal position, shuddering with fear.

The giant swung his mighty staff in a whipping motion at the trap's release. At once there was a flash of bright light, and a crashing sound as loud as a thunderclap. The steel jaws sprang open. With his staff now pointing to Slater's mangled leg, the giant slowly descended to the ground. He then touched the leg with the tip of his stick, and simply said, "Heal!" Within seconds, the wound closed, and all traces of the injury disappeared. When the stick touched the shattered collarbone, Slater could feel rapid movement under his skin, as the bone fragments knitted themselves whole again. In less than a minute, the giant had rendered Slater healthy, and pain-free.

The poacher was on his knees, with tears streaming into his tangled, dirty beard. "Oh God! Thank you, whoever you are. I swear, I'll do what you ask. I will surrender to the game warden today, *now!*"

Still on his knees, as if he were a caveman witnessing fire for the first time, Slater stared with wonder through a flow of tears. "I don't understand who or what you are, or how you can perform such miracles. All I know is that I would have died out here alone, if you hadn't helped me. No one has ever helped me. Not once in my life. You won't have to hunt me down; I will keep my word."

Nelkie decided that a mystical exit would reinforce Slater's resolve. He pointed his staff at the poacher, and spoke once more with the voice of a demon. "Go now, human, and do not be fool enough to think you can lie your way out of your oath. I *will* be watching."

The giant turned his back to Slater, touched his medallion, and vanished into thin air.

Nelkie now stood a mere fifteen feet away, concealed in his cloak of invisibility. Before he returned to his normal self, he wanted to observe the poacher's behavior a little longer. If Slater were not true to his word, Nelkie could not resume his quest until he had dealt with this problem to his satisfaction.

Physically strengthened, but emotionally exhausted, the poacher first managed to get himself on all fours. With severe unsteadiness, he slowly forced himself to stand. "Oh my God! What was that thing?

Does it live here in the forest? How did it know my name?"

Nelkie, meanwhile, was trying to suppress his laughter at being referred to as an "it." The elf listened to Slater's blubbering, which assured him that he had put enough fear into this man's heart to last a lifetime. *Now, if fear motivates this criminal to mend his ways, then I have corrected my error, and no one was hurt in the processs.* Nelkie thought there was a good chance that this self-serving man with no conscience would make the right choice. It didn't matter to Nelkie that his methods were unconventional to say the least, as long as they produced the desired effect. His elders, however, were taking notes. Daido had shared his insight with the other members of the Circle that there was "something different" about this young elf. Elves had never before solved any type of problem by being confrontational. In spite of that fact, the elders' decision to compound the young one's power with their own was unanimous. They recognized the wisdom that had begun to flower in the young one. They may not have agreed initially with Nelkie's tactics, but in the end, the suffering inflicted on their brothers had stopped, and the perpetrator was repenting. For this, Nelkie had gained their respect.

The poacher continued his self-conversation, trying to make sense of his otherworldly experience. He examined his torn pant leg. It was still covered with his blood. Slater pulled back the shredded material to expose his bare leg. There was no gash or cut of any kind, not even a bruise. "How could this be? What kind of voodoo is this? I gotta get to the field office and turn myself in for my own protection, before that thing comes back to kill me!" The now- reformed poacher took off at a run, still not understanding how he could.

Satisfied that he had completed a difficult task, Nelkie set about returning to his normal size. He fixed his attention inward, and engrossed himself in the mental picture of the inner chamber of his leaders. "My humble gratitude, wise ones, for your combined strength and assistance. My responsibility has concluded satisfactorily. I now wish to continue my journey into the human world. With your help, I will reinstate my customary appearance, and resume my quest."

Nelkie folded the giant's massive arms across his chest, bowed his head, and closed his eyes. A comforting warmth surrounded the elf, as the elders made their presence known. Their combined power enveloped Nelkie, wrapping him in benevolent grace. The transition was swift, as Nelkie's body gently returned to its normal size. The elf found himself sitting with his back to a pine tree when the metamorphosis was complete. The extended use of all his inner power had left him bone- and brain-tired. Both demanded rest. Relying on his medallion to keep him unseen, he leaned back against the trunk, bowed his head, and immediately fell into a deep and restful sleep.

Chapter Nineteen

The poacher charged through the game warden's field office door, screaming about a giant with the voice of God. He was moving much too fast to keep his balance once inside and tumbled to the floor, a human pinwheel of arms and legs. Assistant Warden Rob Petersen recognized Slater right away. He didn't understand what the poacher was screaming about, but he knew he wanted to get a set of cuffs on him as fast as he could. Scrambling to get his long legs out from under his desk, he smashed his right knee. "Oww," he cried out, now limping toward the sprawling Slater.

Tom Backer came out of the adjoining room to see what all the commotion was about. "What's going on here, Rob?" The first thing Tom saw was Rob reaching for his handcuffs with his right hand, while trying to catch his balance on the desk with his left. Then he saw Slater on the floor and rushed over to try to help Rob subdue their surprise prisoner. The two wardens seemed to have an awful time handcuffing a willing prisoner. Finally, with Slater's help, they succeeded. They sat him in a chair and looked at each other, Tom spoke first. "Is it just me, or have we been tripping all over this guy for two days now?"

"No, it's not you," came the reply. "This guy's a jinx."

Their confused conversation was interrupted by Slater's continued tirade.

"Hey! You guys better lock me up! I'll sign a confession. I've trapped bear, deer, and small game for years; there, I admit it. Now lock me up before that guy comes back and kills me!"

"What guy? Who's going to kill you?"

"I don't know who he is, but he's about ten feet tall, and he looks like the angel of death!"

"Angel of death?" Tom asked, with a bewildered look.

"Yes," the poacher continued. "His skin, his face, he looked like he was dead, I swear, I'm telling the truth! He floated in the air above me and he said he'd kill me if I didn't turn myself in. It's all true, I swear. If you don't believe me, look at my leg. I stepped into one of my own traps when you guys were chasing me. He touched my leg and the wound healed, it was magic!"

The two wardens were positive their prisoner had flipped out completely, but still, they had to look at his leg. The right leg of Slater's jeans was in shreds, and blood-soaked.

"It would appear there should be several nasty gashes here from that trap, but there is no trace of even a small cut," Rob reported.

"See! I told ya," Slater answered. "I told ya, he touched me with that magic stick, and it healed!"

"Oh boy," Tom said, reaching for the telephone. "Hello? EMTs? I need an ambulance and a straitjacket right away. Yes I said a strait-jacket." Tom turned away from Slater and covered the mouthpiece. "This is Warden Tom Backer. I'm calling from our field office. We have a poacher in custody who's claiming he was threatened by a ten-foot-tall angel of death with magic powers! *Now* do you understand why I need a straitjacket for this whacko? Get here quickly, will ya? This guy is completely crackers!"

The emergency medical technicians arrived before dark. They administered a strong sedative, and restrained the poacher on a gurney. While they were loading him into the ambulance, Slater was still screaming about lightning bolts freeing him from the jaws of death.

Tom and Rob were shaking their heads in unison as the ambulance sped off to the nearest hospital.

"Poor cuss," Tom said. "I don't know what happened to him out there, but it sure sent him into fantasyland."

"I agree," answered Rob. "But what do you make of his leg?"

"I don't know, but one thing's for sure. It wasn't healed by magic."

Book Two

Heroes and Villains

Chapter 20

July 24, 1976. Flushing, Queens, New York City. Sixteen-year-old Albert Parker walked out of his bedroom to once again find his alcoholic father passed out on the couch. The teenager was relieved. When his father was not drunk, he was antagonistic, and when he *was* drunk, he was abusive. Lonnie Parker hadn't worked in two years, and stopped looking six months ago, when he started his current bender. The only time there was any peace in their home was when the "old man" was unconscious. It was 11:00 a.m., and Albert's mother was out working the second of her three jobs. Since she was the only breadwinner, the poor woman had to work sixteen hours a day, six days a week, just to keep a roof over their heads. Liz Parker accepted the challenge of raising her teenage son alone. She adored Albert, and tried to instill in him a strong sense of responsibility. His father set a poor example, which made Liz double her efforts to convince her son to aspire toward higher education. "You don't want to wind up like your father. He went from one unskilled job to another, never making enough for us to live on. Finally, the booze won out, and he just gave up. Stay in school, Albert, and get a degree. Make your mother proud."

Before her son was out of grade school, Liz had passed on her love of classic books to Albert. After reading *Tom Sawyer*, *Treasure Island*, and *The Hobbit*, he developed a passion for books that would remain with him for his entire life. In middle school, Albert became a fan of O. Henry, and when his mother found out he loved "surprise endings," she introduced him to the tales of Guy de Maupassant. He devoured them, as well as everything written by Sir Arthur Conan Doyle. Albert was smart, but stubborn. He had to go his own way.

Against his mother's wishes, Albert quit school to help out with expenses. He told his mom it was only temporary. Once things got better, he would return to school. He lied.

Albert Parker discovered at thirteen that he could take care of himself. When two older toughs tried to bully him out of his lunch money, he fought back. Albert was genetically blessed with "fast hands," and the instincts of a natural athlete, which to his surprise, left his attackers battered and bleeding in short order. It wasn't long before everyone knew who the toughest kid on the block was. By the time he was sixteen Albert was helping out his mother with money he had earned by being the lookout on various neighborhood burglaries. He had built a reputation for being tough under pressure, and for being someone who knew when to keep his mouth shut. The local bad guys took notice, and Albert knew that bigger and better things were coming. The money would start rolling in pretty soon. He would save what he could, until he had enough to move his mom and himself out of the run-down projects on Roosevelt Avenue. Albert had no problem spiriting his mother away and leaving his drunken father to fend for himself. After all, it was the old man's fault they were forced to live in substandard housing, and barely had enough to eat. Not to mention that his mother was working herself into an early grave.

Albert walked out of his apartment building, into a front yard strewn with beer cans. He stepped over the broken gate that had been on the ground for six months, kicked a torn bag of garbage into the gutter, and headed down Prince Street.

His friend Paco was standing in front of the Riviera Bar and Grill, smoking a Marlboro. "What's happenin', Parker?" he said through a veil of blue smoke.

"Not much. Ya seen the fat man yet?"

"Yeah, he's inside, havin' his breakfast beer."

The "fat man" was one Harvey Blydel, a 300-pound cab driver who controlled a network of local thugs, thieves, and felons. Harvey knew what was ripe for the taking, and who had the nerve to take it. He made a comfortable living setting up store burglaries in Flushing and Elmhurst. Local "smash and grab" artists would break in, steal what they could in three minutes or less, and sell their plunder to Harvey. Harvey, in turn, would fence the loot with connections on Long Island, for a considerable profit. Albert was making a hundred dollars per job, big bucks for a teenager in 1976, and Harvey Blydel always had another prospect waiting. Sometimes they would steal merchandise (tools, clothes, even bicycles); other times, they might only rifle the cash register. Albert had made six hundred dollars in the last month, three hundred of which he gave to his mother. He was looking for more.

Blydel was washing down his pastrami and eggs with a Budweiser when Albert approached the last booth in the barroom. "Hey kid, ya wanna sammitch?"

"Nah, thanks. I need work. Anythin' shakin'?"

Harvey looked down the length of the room, and then, certain they were alone, leaned closer to the boy. "Yeah. I already talked to your buddy Paco. You guys are ta meet up with Eddy Donnelley tonight. He'll pick you up at 2:00 a.m. right behind the taxi stand on Roosevelt Avenue. We got a stereo store in Elmhurst. Corner of 76th St. Sliding metal gates with cheap locks. Donnelley's already got the bolt cutters. Real simple. They get the word from you, Eddy cuts the locks off, Paco throws a milk crate through the window, grab what you can, jump in the van, and go. I'll meet you at Eddie's place, tomorrow at 10:00."

"Count me in, Mr. Blydel. Two a.m., taxi stand. I'll be there."

"Good. I'll have your hundred tomorrow mornin'."

Albert left the bar, firmed up plans with Paco, and then strolled down Prince Street. With nothing better to do, he thought he'd cross over Northern Boulevard, and see if anybody was hanging out at the King and Queen Billiards. As he approached the front door of the pool hall, he noticed a crowd forming just a few doors down. All at once, the double doors to Dudley's Gym and Boxing Club flew open. Dozens of young fighters, and assorted hangers-on were swarming around the heavyweight champion of the world, as he made his way to a waiting limo. Mohammed Ali hastily signed a few autographs, and then waved to his fans, before speeding off. Albert was flabbergasted. He had never seen a celebrity up close before, and this just seemed surreal. The crowd was slowly filing back into the gym. Albert stopped one of them and asked, "Hey, what on earth was Ali doing at a rundown boxing club in Flushing?"

A shirtless and muscular black kid, only a few years Albert's senior, shot him an annoyed look. "If I were you, junior, I wouldn't come around here calling Ben Dudley's gym "rundown," that is, if I wanted to keep my teeth. Ben's trained four world champions, and he's a class act, with a lotta friends, so you better think before ya go runnin' your mouth."

"Sorry, I just wanted to know what was goin' on"

"Well, mista big stuff, the owner of this 'run-down gym' just happened to be the assistant team trainer when the Champ won his gold at the Olympics. They're old friends, and whenever the Champ's in town, he pays his respects, something a punk like you would know nothin' about."

"Hey, you better back off, Bozo; I don't take that kinda talk from nobody!"

"Oh whut, you gonna lump me up, punk? I don't think so, but if you wanna try, you're welcome to come inside and put the gloves on. I don't fight no punks on the street."

Albert had never lost a street fight, and was fearless. He felt this kid had disrespected him, so he jumped at the chance to teach him a lesson. "Yeah? Let's go, big mouth; you're overdue for an attitude adjustment."

Albert followed his antagonist through the front door, into an atmosphere that captivated his senses, as well as his curiosity. So much
was going on all at once, that Albert stopped to take it all in. The smell
of sweat was almost overwhelming. Sounds generated by more than
fifty men deeply engaged in various forms of intense exercise had a
hypnotic effect on the teenager. The place had a pulse, and it drew
Albert in. The bone-crushing thud one fighter produced by slamming
a five-punch combination into a heavy bag made Albert shudder. At
the same time, he could hear the sound of leather hitting leather, leather hitting flesh, while the ratta-tat-tat of someone working a speed bag
provided a back beat to this strange urban opera. Above it all, trainers
were screaming instructions to the fighters sparring in two regulation
rings. Albert Parker, meet adrenaline.

They walked over to the ring at the far end of the gym, seeing two
exhausted fighters climbing through the ropes. A silver-haired black
man of about seventy years of age was holding the lower rope open
with his foot. "Good workout, boys. Robbie, I want you to work on
your defense more, and Mike, good combinations, but I want you to
work the body more. Wear your opponent down. You're good, Mike,
but you can't knock everybody out in the first round. Now, hit the
showers; I'll see you guys tomorrow."

The trainer turned from the former combatants when he noticed
Albert walking toward him with one of the regulars. "What's happenin', Leon? Who ya got with ya?"

"Just some local punk that needs to be taught some respect, Ben.
Can we use this ring for a few minutes?"

"Yeah, but go easy on the kid, and make sure he's got headgear, and
a mouthpiece."

"I don't need no headgear. It ain't gonna take long for me to take
loudmouth Leon here apart," Albert protested.

"Look, kid, I don't know who you think you are, and I couldn't care less, but we got rules here. No headgear, no mouthpiece, no fight. Now, I already know you're a fool, because you're about to climb into the ring with Leon Rawlings, this year's lightweight Golden Glove champion. If you think I'm going to leave myself open for a lawsuit after Leon scrambles your brain, you had better think again. No headgear, no fight. My advice would be for you to walk outta here while you *can* still think, but if you're dumb enough to go through with this after what I've told you--here." Ben Dudley shoved the headgear into Albert's stomach, turned, and walked away. Before Albert could react, Dudley was already yelling something about "hooking off the jab" at another fighter in the far ring.

"Got second thoughts, punk?"

Albert looked up to see Rawlings, with gloves and headgear already on, bobbing up and down in the ring above him.

"You don't scare me, Leeeon, I'm gonna hand you your head, as soon as I get this stuff on."

Leon just grinned through his mouthpiece as one of the other trainers laced up Albert's gloves. The trainer held the ropes open, and asked, "Who's your next of kin, kid?" While laughing at Albert's foolhardiness, he stepped down to watch the fight.

Albert lunged at his bouncing opponent, throwing a roundhouse right. Rawlings blocked the punch with his left, and answered with a hard right cross. Albert backpedaled, but didn't fall. Before Albert could steady himself, Leon was on him like a swarm of bees. In the space of about four seconds, the Golden Glove champ showed Albert *why* he was the champ. A lightning- fast double jab to Albert's nose disoriented him, and when the champ delivered a right to the body, and a hook to the head, Albert went down, sliding across the canvas on his back like a hockey puck.

Enraged, Albert got up, and ran across the ring, arms flailing. The champ sidestepped his windmilling opponent, and then, with expertly delivered precision, unloaded a five-punch combination that again put Albert on his back. Battered and bleeding, Albert struggled to get to his feet. Rawlings was still bobbing up and down like a human pogo stick, with barely a bead of sweat on his forehead. "Had enough yet, punk?'

Albert looked Rawlings in the eye and spit his defiant reply through swollen lips. "I'm just gettin' warmed up, turkey." Being the street fighter he was, Albert again charged across the ring at his opponent, but this time he faked a wild right. When Rawlings brought his hands up to block, Albert delivered a vicious left hook to the ribs, which brought Rawlings hands back down to protect his body. It was now Albert Parker's turn to show the champ why he had respect on the street. Albert had quick hands, but he also had a quick mind. The second Rawlings' guard dropped, Albert seized his opportunity, and unloaded a powerful hook to the champ's temple, sending him stumbling sideways. Seeing his adversary hurt, Albert moved in for the kill, but he was outclassed. The champ shook the cobwebs from his brain before the flailing Parker could reach him. Rawlings waited till the last second, then bobbed to his right. His clumsy adversary couldn't stop his wild charge and stumbled into the ropes. When Albert bounced off the ropes, and turned around, Rawlings greeted him with a vicious uppercut, sending the teenager to the canvas for the third time. Albert's world was spinning. Everything was blurry, he couldn't focus, but yet some driving force inside him made him try to get up. He got to his knees, and fell over. Crawling and clawing to his knees again Albert heard Rawlings voice off in the distance. "All right, kid. You've had enough. I don't want to beat you to death; that's it."

Rawlings pulled off his headgear and started walking toward his corner. Albert wouldn't give up. He forced himself upright, and started after Rawlings. "Hey, I ain't done with you yet! Come back here!" All bravado and guts, Albert's staggered charge was pointless. Still dazed, he couldn't even walk in a straight line. He was spent, but he kept coming. Rawlings stood at the far side of the ring, with his hands on his hips, staring in amazement. *I don't believe this guy. He just don't know how to quit!* The champ was impressed. This was one tough kid. He had to respect his guts. The Golden Glove champ knew he had an unfair advantage before they ever stepped into the ring, and honestly thought the kid would have second thoughts, when he found out he was facing a champion. Albert never hesitated, never showed any fear. He just charged ahead, and now was mounting one last stumbling attack. Rawlings walked over to his exhausted opponent, and as Albert drew back his right, Leon wrapped him in a bear hug.

"Look, kid, it's over. You got no more gas in your tank. You're tough, kid, very tough, but you can't win this one on guts. I ain't gonna hit you no more. Let it go, kid; ya got nothing more to prove."

At that moment, Ben Dudley, who had seen the whole bout, entered the ring and separated the fighters. He stood between them and put one arm around Albert. "C'mon, tough guy," he said. "It's over. Come with me. We'll get Mickey to clean you up a little, and then we can talk. I got a deal for you, if you're interested. If you're as smart as you are tough, you'll listen. Hey, Mickey! Get this kid some soap and water."

As Dudley was helping Albert through the ropes, Rawlings yelled over. "Ya showed some real guts, kid; I'm proud of ya. Whut's yer name, anyway?"

"Albert Parker, and you ain't so bad yerself."

Fifteen minutes later, a very swollen Albert Parker was sitting across the desk from the legendary trainer. "Look, kid, you can't fight worth a damn, but ya got plenty of heart. I gotta respect that. I can see some raw talent in you. If you're willin' to work, I can teach you 'the sweet science.' I'm not sayin' you could be a champ; I'm sayin' if ya work hard you might make a livin' in the ring. It's better than workin' for that loser Blydel. Don't look so surprised, kid. This is my neighborhood too. I know who's doin' what to whom, and if you keep up what *you're* doin', ya gonna wind up in jail, or dead. Now, I said I'd train you, and I'll do it for free, but there are rules and conditions."

"Like whut?"

"First, we don't even start until you bring me written proof that you either went back to school, or ya got a full-time job. No job, no deal. Second, you do what I tell ya in this gym. You train hard. A hundred percent all the time. I don't train no slackers. That's it."

"I gotta think about it." Albert got up and headed for the door. He put his hand on the knob, stopped, and turned to face the trainer. "Thanks, Mr. Dudley. I appreciate you takin' an interest in me; I just gotta think on it."

Ben Dudley didn't look up. He picked up the phone and said, "Don't think on it too long; my door won't be open forever." He started dialing. Albert walked out.

Paco was still standing in front of the Riviera, hanging all over a girl named Maria. He looked up to see Albert's swollen face, and stopped talking, mid-sentence.

"Hey man, what happened to you? You get into a hassle with the fat man?"

"Shuddup, Paco. I ran into a door, all right? I'll see ya at 2:00 a.m."

As Albert walked away, he overheard Paco say to Maria, "Man, I ain't never seen no door lump nobody up like that!"

Albert Parker had to think. He was approaching one of life's crossroads. On one hand, he felt great about his experience in the gym. Through all the pain and swelling, he still wanted to go back in there. He had gained the respect of a Golden Glove champion, and gotten noticed by a world-class trainer. *I fight pretty good now. Maybe if I was trained by Ben Dudley, I could be a champ some day.*

On the other hand, his mother needed help, and Blydel provided easy money…so far. He walked for hours with no destination. He strolled past a supermarket with a help wanted sign in the window. *Whut kinda money am I gonna make baggin' oranges? But maybe Ben was right. Somethin' could go wrong on one of Blydel's jobs, I get popped, and now*

Mom's got no help from nobody.

Albert wound up walking several miles to find himself in Flushing Meadow Park, staring up at the Unisphere. He was beat-up and tired. *The only thing that doesn't hurt is my hair. God, that Rawlings can hit!* It wasn't long before he succumbed to his extreme fatigue. Albert curled up on a park bench and fell into a sleep deep enough to qualify as a coma. He slept undisturbed for hours.

When Albert finally woke, it was dark. The first thing his eyes focused on was the illuminated Unisphere. He was cold, and tried to sit up. Every muscle in his body protested adamantly. Suddenly, panic set in. He looked at his watch. It was 2:45. *Well, maybe this is the way it should be. My decision has been made for me. Yeah, I'll take that job at the supermarket tomorrow. Look out, Rawlings; you ain't gonna be so lucky in the rematch, now that I got a trainer.*

He dragged himself out to the street and hailed a passing cab. The driver had the radio tuned to the news, and Albert had to shout his address over the babble. He settled back into the seat, only to hear something that made his blood run cold.

"This just in to newsradio eighty eight. There has been a police shooting in Elmhurst, Queens, just minutes ago. Off duty police sergeant Angel Perez shot and killed a suspect breaking into the stereo store below his apartment. The suspect, tentatively identified as Paco Velez of Flushing, turned, brandishing a gun. The officer fired twice, hitting the suspect in the chest. He was pronounced dead at the scene."

Albert's whole body quivered. He felt as if all the blood had run out of his body. He felt empty. Until this moment, Albert, like most sixteen-year-olds, thought himself invincible. He understood the possibility of arrest, but not once did he ever consider that his life could come to a violent end. The shocking reality of Paco's demise was the epiphany Albert needed to turn his life around.

Chapter 21

Albert hated his supermarket job. It took him sixty hours to make what Blydel would pay him for two nights' work. Life was hard, but the shock of reality brought on by Paco's death taught him a valuable lesson. *Chasing shopping carts in the rain, and baggin' groceries ain't exactly fun, but no one ever got shot or even arrested for doing an honest day's work!*

Albert refused to dwell on the negatives in his life. Instead, his concentration was centered on the positive: boxing. When he wasn't working, he was training. He was out of bed by 5:00 and in the gym by 5:30. He was a supermarket slave from 8:00 till 6:00 Monday through Saturday, with Sundays off.

Although Albert was thrilled that Ben Dudley had shown an interest in training him, it didn't happen at all the way Albert thought it would. The feisty teenager thought he would be back in the ring right away, probably sparring with someone a little less talented than Leon Rawlings—not so.

"First we get your skinny butt in shape, and then we'll see if you can learn to box," Ben told him. Albert raised no protest. His "fast hands" and superior hand-eye coordination allowed him to master the speed bag almost immediately. Albert also enjoyed working the heavy bag. *It really feels like you're layin' inta somebody*, he would think. Of all the exercises on his training program, the only one Albert hated was jumping rope. He had two reasons for this aversion. One, he just couldn't seem to get the hang of it, and every time he would get tangled up and trip, he would have to put up with the taunts from the other young fighters, and two, it made him feel like a sissy.

His opinion changed radically one morning, when he watched 240-pound Jamal Worthy workout for twenty minutes with a jump rope. The big man jumped, skipped, hopped, and even danced with that rope. His motion was graceful, even elegant. The heavyweight was as light on his feet as a twelve-year-old schoolgirl. All of a sudden, Albert didn't think this was a "sissy thing" at all. He wanted to learn from the master.

"Hey man, I ain't never seen nobody dance like that with a rope. What's the trick to it?"

Worthy had his face buried in a towel. He looked up at the youngster and smiled a wide, toothless grin. "Well, firstly, young'un, can't nobody do this while they lookin' at their feet." He threw the rope to Albert. "I saw you over there, tanglefoot. Look, it's all timin'. Keep your head up." The good-natured heavyweight spent a few minutes showing Albert a few pointers. It wasn't long before it began to click for him, and Albert began to skip faster and faster, while the rope made a loud whirring sound, telling him that he had finally gotten the hang of it. "Thanks, Jamal. I don't think I would have figured this out by myself."

"No problem, young blood; but listen, let me give you a little more advice. Having fast hands is great, but it ain't enough. Ya gotsta have fast feet too. Like the man says, 'float like a butterfly, sting like a bee.' Any fighter that can do both is gonna be a winner."

"Thanks, Jamal."

In the months that followed, Ben Dudley taught Albert "the sweet science" punch by punch. The jab, the right cross, the uppercut, and what was to become Albert's signature punch, the hook. After many months of workouts, and hitting a bag that couldn't hit back, Ben finally let Albert back into the ring. He was going to spar three rounds with another neighborhood kid of about the same skill level, or so everyone thought.

Albert wasted no time. As soon as he had touched gloves with Angel Torres, and the bell sounded, he was on him. Angel was a slow starter and tried to feel Albert out in the first round. Parker would have none of it. He waded in with a quick double jab, followed by a right to the body and a left to the temple. Torres was on his back, with his mouthpiece hanging out sideways. It was over.

Ben Dudley was watching from Albert's corner. His years of experience training world- class athletes told him this kid was special. He saw something beyond Albert's natural athletic agility and superior coordination. This kid had an inbred killer instinct, born of survival on the mean streets of Flushing. When he saw his opponent was stunned, Albert Parker didn't hesitate. Instead, he would move in for the kill, immobilizing his adversary before he could recover. Dudley knew this was one of the many key elements that define a world champion, and Albert came by it naturally.

"Good combination, Albert, but don't let this one go to your head. Tomorrow I'm gonna let you go a few rounds with Randall Peachtree. We'll see how you do against someone who can counterpunch, and has excellent defensive skills."

After helping his opponent up, Albert turned to the trainer, spat his mouthpiece into his glove, and smiled. "Bring him on, Ben, and we'll see if he can counterpunch a windmill."

"Hit the showers, wise guy."

On the following day, Albert put on a repeat performance in the ring. In forty-five seconds of the first round, a confused and beaten Randall Peachtree found himself on the canvas with his headgear turned sideways over his nose. At the clang of the bell, the counter-puncher was easily overpowered by an octopus in boxing gloves. The speed and accuracy of Albert Parker's eight-punch combination left Peachtree no opportunity to counterpunch, let alone protect himself against the onslaught.

Ben Dudley could feel electricity permeating the air in his gym. Albert had drawn a crowd. There was a buzz amongst the other fighters, as they watched "the new kid" make short work of a more experienced fighter. The excitement Albert generated was contagious. This kid had the fastest hands, and the best left hook Dudley had seen in twenty years. He allowed himself to think he just might be training a future champion.

Joe Bertoli, one of the other trainers, held the ropes open for the still-smiling Albert. "Good round, kid. I swear your arms were goin' like a pair of pistons on a steam train. Ya got some great speed. I think I'm gonna call you 'Piston Parker' from now on. Yeah, I like that. Albert 'Piston" Parker.'" And so, with that dubbing, Albert received a name that would become famous, and stick with him for his entire life.

Chapter 22

Albert's teen years sped by at a staggering pace. He had become a perpetual-motion machine. Not only did his boxing skills develop quickly, with Ben's tutelage, but the confidence he gained in the gym manifested itself throughout the rest of his personal life. He enrolled in night school and earned a high school equivalency diploma. Albert's work life improved by leaps and bounds as well. His boss took notice of Albert's work ethic, and it wasn't long before he left the shopping cart chase behind, and was promoted to stock boy, in the dairy department. Within a year, he became the assistant manager.

Soon after his promotion, Albert met Lisa Venturini. She was walking through his department and saw him pricing a case of butter.

"Excuse me, sir, but can you tell me where I can find soy milk?"

Albert turned toward the melodious voice and was momentarily stunned. She was far and away the most beautiful girl he had ever seen. Her face was framed by wave upon wave of almost blue-black hair, which tumbled abundantly past her shoulders. Albert's first thought was that he had seen hair that color only on Chinese people. As their eyes met, he started to answer her question, but became severely distracted by eyes as deep and as blue as the Mediterranean.

"Uhh, sorry, what did you say?"

"Soy milk. I'm lactose intolerant, but I like my coffee light. I need to find the soy milk."

"Right. Okay, soy milk is right over here in the next dairy case." He walked over and handed her a half gallon. "Is this okay?"

"Perfect. Thanks for your help."

"No problem. Making pretty girls smile is the best part of my job; come back and see me again soon."

She smiled over her shoulder as she walked away and said, "Maybe I'll do that."

As she left the dairy department, Albert wanted to kick himself for not asking her name, but somehow he knew he would get another chance.

Liz Parker was thrilled with her son's progress. She never knew what Albert had been involved with in his former street life, but she sensed, as every mother can, that her son was headed down a crooked path. Now, only two years after learning of Paco's death, Albert had moved them into a two-bedroom apartment in Bayside, and bought them a car! It didn't matter that it was a fifteen-year-old Buick, with 78,000 miles on it, because it gave Liz and her son an independence that they had never known before. They had left the "old man" behind, and began a new and wonderful life.

Another part of that new and wonderful life was that for the first time ever, Albert was able to secure health care for himself and his mother through union benefits. He had made an appointment with a local doctor for a physical, and upon entering the reception area, was both surprised and delighted to be greeted by a young raven-haired beauty.

She followed a smile of recognition with a friendly greeting. "Hi! How are things in the dairy department?"

"Homogenized, pasteurized, and mostly boring," he said, returning her smile. "Glad to see your name tag...now I don't have to call you Ms. Soy Milk. How ya doin'?"

She laughed and said, "Still lactose intolerant, but fine. Are you here to see Dr. Weinberger?"

"Yeah. I have a 9:30 appointment."

She gave him some forms to fill out, and was called away.

After his examination, Albert stopped at the receptionist's desk and summoned the courage to ask for a date. Lisa happily agreed. When he hit the street, Albert felt that his life couldn't get much better. He had a date with a beautiful girl, he was making decent money at the supermarket, and he had yet to know defeat as an up-and-coming fighter. What more could anyone ask for?

As time went by, Ben Dudley spent more and more time with his protégé. His training regimen became more focused, and more technical. Albert kept a training log religiously. There were notations made about everything from his gym workouts and strict training diet to the amount of sleep he was getting. It was all beginning to pay off. Albert, at twenty-one, had matured into a full-fledged middleweight. He began to rack up a number of wins in the amateur rankings. All the while, Ben was fine-tuning Albert's natural talent, and crafting a personal fighting style that would precipitate a first place finish at the annual Golden Gloves competition, held at New York's Madison Square Garden.

By this time he and Lisa had married, and she had become his biggest fan. She attended all his fights from the first row. Before each bout she would stop in his dressing room, give him a "kiss for luck," and say "Knock 'em out and make us rich, golden boy." After each victory, Albert would bask in the glory of Lisa's admiration. Knowing how proud she was of him only added to his determination to succeed.

Albert's stunning upset win over "Irish" Kevin Regan, in the Golden Gloves final, was indeed a triumph. Regan was the defending champion, and was 64-0 in amateur competition. Albert was given all he could handle in the first two rounds. Wading in off a relentless jab, Regan pummeled Albert with three- and four-punch combinations. The reigning champ continued to pound his challenger mercilessly

for the next four rounds. Dudley would plead with his fighter between rounds to concentrate on defense. Albert was way behind on
points, and was taking a beating. He was still on his feet, but the punishment he absorbed had slowed his reaction time. Regan was continually beating him to the punch. Albert had never fought anyone
that had faster hands than his own. Regan's speed and accuracy kept
Albert from getting inside to unleash his power punches. Confusion
and frustration began to show on his battered face. Albert had never
been seriously hurt before, either in the ring or in the street, but
this time things were different. Regan was too fast for him, and the
punches seemed to be coming from every direction. Sensing his opponent's bafflement in the final round, Regan got cocky. Thinking
victory was only one punch away, he played to the crowd. Showing
off, Regan wound up his right in an exaggerated windmill fashion.
Albert saw his opening and seized the opportunity. Bleeding from
his nose and mouth, and running out of gas, Albert reached deep
inside himself and threw a savage hook into Regan's ribs. When the
surprised champ brought his hands down to protect his body, Albert
delivered a textbook left hook to the temple. Regan was out cold,
before he hit the canvas. Albert "Piston" Parker had won his first
major title, and scores of new fans, on sheer guts. His boxing skills
were impressive, but there was a deeper, more profound reason for
Albert's growing fan base. He had shown, in very dramatic fashion,
that he possessed the heart of a champion. Sports fans love to cheer
for and share in the triumph of the underdog. The emotional climax
of a last-second knockout, delivered from a fighter that appears to
have been beaten, is what legends are made of. No one knew this
better than Ben Dudley.

After all the excitement and celebration had ebbed, Albert settled
back into his training routine. He was pounding the heavy bag as if it

could hit back when Ben walked over. "Hey, champ; stop in my office after your workout. We have a few things to discuss."

"Sure, Ben."

When Albert had cleaned up, he strode into Ben's office. He was carrying a fat paperback novel that was too big to fit in his pocket. After placing the book on Ben's desk, he pulled up a chair. "You wanted to talk to me?"

"Yeah. Whatcha readin'?"

"Dumas. *Three Musketeers*. Tough read. It's not American English, but it's a great book."

"Yeah, I saw the movie. Lotsa sword fights. Look, I wanted to tell you that everybody here is really proud of you, kid. You come a long way."

"Thanks, Ben."

"But that's not why I asked you to stop by. It's time we talked seriously about your future. You still got a lot to learn, but I think you can go far in this game. I want you to have a few more amateur fights. If you keep doing well, I think we should talk about turning pro."

Albert jumped to his feet, pumping his fist in the air. "All right, yeah! That's what I'm talkin' about!"

"Now don't go getting' all excited here yet. Like I said, you still got a lot to learn. For one thing, Mr. Piston, you're gettin' hit too much. You might win a few fights by bein' able to take more punches than your opponent, but you'll wind up dopey, and not knowin' what day it is before you turn twenty-five. I don't want to see you end up like that, kid. Listen to me: work harder on defense, and learn to work the body more. Like the saying goes, 'Work the body and the head will fall.' If you can learn to do all that well, you'll have a shot at becoming a champion."

"Not only *can* I do it, but I *will* do it. You just watch me."

"Okay, champ. That's all I needed to hear. Now you better get off to work before they fire you for being late again."

"I'm already gone, boss…and Ben, thanks for having faith in me."
"Yeah, yeah. Get outta here."

Over the next six months, Albert honed his skills to near perfection. He was dedicated to achieving success and worked hard day and night. In the end, his amateur record stood at 36-0, with 33 knockouts. Ben Dudley became Albert's full-time trainer and through his connections, found his protégé an honest manager. Under Ben's tutelage, Albert's debut fight as a professional ended in a first-round knockout. He followed this stunning start with a string of six more knockouts, all before the seventh round. Albert "Piston" Parker was on his way, and the boxing world took notice. As he worked his way up in the rankings, he began to fight in larger venues and the money began to pour in with every victory. His fan base grew and he got more and more press coverage. The fact that Albert came off as gracious and humble during interviews only added to his now-expanding popularity. Boxing insiders, as well as the public, wanted to know more about the young upstart from Flushing.

By the time he turned twenty-three, Albert was ranked the number nine middleweight in the world. He was certain he would never again have to work in a supermarket. Ben closed a deal on a larger, more modern gym in LA, and they moved their base of operations to sunny California. Albert bought his mother a comfortable three-bedroom home in the suburbs, and continued to march upward in the rankings. He was still undefeated.

Financial independence was almost within reach, but because Albert had known the hopelessness of poverty, he was frugal. He and Lisa moved in with his mother, so Albert could continue to save for their future. His trust and love for Lisa were unconditional, evidenced by the fact that all their accounts were held jointly. With his wife looking after their money, Albert could concentrate on furthering his career, free from financial complications.

All seemed to be going well, until one evening when Albert returned home from training. His mother was in the kitchen, busy preparing dinner.

"Hi, Ma; where's Lisa?"

When Liz turned from the stove, Albert knew right away she wasn't happy. "Albert, please sit down. We need to talk."

"Is somethin' wrong, Ma?"

"Look, I want you to understand that I love Lisa, and I know she has made you very happy, but I think you and she should have a sit-down talk before things get out of control."

"Whut things?"

"Money, Albert. You need to talk to her about her excessive spending. Lisa is out clothes shopping again as we speak."

"Aw, don't worry, Ma; I'm makin' big money now, and I don't see how a few fancy dresses are gonna put us in the poor house. She came from nothin' too, ya know, and she's been good to me. She deserves nice things."

"You don't understand. Look, I don't expect you to recognize names like Gucci and Versace, but if your wife keeps buying five hundred dollar handbags and two thousand dollar dresses, it will only be a matter of time before we are all in trouble. If, God forbid, you should ever get hurt in the ring and your career comes to an abrupt end, we won't be able to manage your debt. Albert, she charged a diamond bracelet last week that must have cost three thousand dollars! It's true you're doing very well right now, but you are *not* rich. Please tell me you'll talk to her."

"All right, all right. I'll talk to her, I promise. Don't worry, Ma. I'm gonna be champ someday, and then I'm gonna by you an island!"

"I don't need an island, Albert; I just need a roof over my head, food in the fridge, and my baby boy to be happy and healthy."

"I've never been happier, Ma, and you just ask Bobo Brazinski how healthy I am. If you remember, he had to be carried out of the ring in the sixth."

Liz let it pass, but she was still very worried that her son had really no idea how bad his wife's spending had become. She didn't want to stick her nose into her son's personal finances, but she knew Albert was too consumed by ambition to be distracted by a spendthrift wife. Liz Parker resolved to keep an eye on her daughter-in-law's spending.

Albert's life was rocketing by. Between his demanding workout schedule, and the frequency of his fights, it wasn't long before he had completely forgotten his mother's warning. As the big bucks continued to roll in, Albert became more confident that he would become a world champion, and thus become financially independent. Lisa, however, had different ideas. She was spending their money as fast as Albert could make it.

Within a year of his move to California, "Piston" Parker had battled his way to become the number two contender in the world. After a grueling session with his sparring partner, Albert climbed out of the ring as Ben approached. "Got big news, champ. Clean up and come to my office."

Twenty minutes later, Albert was sitting in his trainer's office. Billy Parsons, Albert's manager, was also in attendance. Billy spoke first. "Albert, I just got off the phone with Pug Bartlett. He wants to promote a fight between you and La Mont Taylor, the number one contender, but that's not the good part. The winner is guaranteed a shot at the title. Coco Rivera has already agreed to fight the winner in Las Vegas, June tenth."

"Bring 'em on, Billy! You're lookin' at the new middleweight champion of the world!" Albert knew he was about to realize a dream that had been almost eight years in the making. This was the best day of his life so far, with a much better one on the way.

Billy Parsons eyed his fighter's youthful exuberance and offered a word of caution. "Don't put the cart before the horse, Piston. You still have to get past Taylor. I almost didn't take this fight because you've only faced one other lefty, and if you remember, he gave you trouble. A victory over La Mont Taylor is not a foregone conclusion."

"Ah, don't worry, Billy. I can take 'em. I'll spar with nothin' but good southpaws until the fight. It's in the bag."

Chapter 23

After the contracts for the Taylor fight were signed, Albert had six weeks to prepare for the bout. Ben thought his fighter had more than a good chance to win it, but only if his offense was relentless. At the first of several strategy sessions, Ben laid out the foundation of their fight plan.

"Look, Piston, I don't have to tell you this guy's reputation for being tough is well- deserved. We've watched his fight films. Taylor is twenty eight and one, with twenty six KOs, and as you saw, four of those KOs came after he was knocked down at least once. Mickey McGinnis had him down twice and still lost it in the tenth on a TKO. La Mont Taylor is no pushover, Albert. You're gonna hafta use everything in your toolbox to win this one."

"Yeah, I know he's a tough guy, Ben. I'll just have to bore in and unload my best stuff."

"No, Albert. Not this time. That's what his camp expects you to do, and you can bet that he's already training to keep you away with that long reach of his."

"Are you telling me *not* to try to knock him out?"

"That's *exactly* what I'm telling you. We hafta counter their strategy with our own. More titles are won with brains than with brawn, Piston. You gotta outbox Taylor. I want you to go inta this one expecting to go twelve. Of course, as always, if you see an opportunity to end it early, go for it. But let it happen, be patient, don't *look* for it. Taylor is a clubber that can take a punch. I don't want you to go toe ta toe with this guy. Be smart and play this one to go the distance. The closer we get to the later rounds, the better chance you have to win it on points. Get inside, work quick combinations to the body, and get out. Wear 'em down, champ. By the eighth or ninth, he'll be ready to go. You stick to this fight plan and we'll be in Vegas in June."

"Okay, boss. I don't like it, but I know you've never steered me wrong. I'll do what you say."

"Good. Now I'm gonna start you off tomorrow with Jimmy Ruiz. He's a southpaw from LA, and a pretty tough kid. I want you to work on those combinations, and on gettin' in and out clean, okay?"

"No problem."

But there was a problem. Albert hadn't fought a lefty in over a year, and he ended that one in the first round. His opponent was over-matched. Now, against the scrappy Ruiz, his attempts to get inside were clumsy and badly timed. He was fighting someone who was facing the wrong way, and as a result, Albert found himself continually getting his feet tangled up with Ruiz. His sparring partner, who had fought mostly right-handed adversaries, was used to this. He had learned to capitalize on their confusion. Once Albert stumbled, Ruiz would pop him with quick two- and three-punch combinations, disorienting him even more. It was beginning to look like the young upstart was taking Albert to school, when finally, some of Ben's direction, shouted from Albert's corner, got through to him.

"No, no! Get outta there! Circle left, away from his power. Yeah, that's it. Now jab, jab."

Albert thought he finished his sparring session with a good showing, but it wasn't good enough for Ben Dudley.

"That was terrible! If you try to fight Taylor like that, he'll bust you up!"

For the next month Ben harped continuously on Albert's defense and footwork. As the big fight loomed closer, the constant drilling from his trainer produced positive results. Albert had sparred dozens of rounds with six different up-and-coming southpaws, and made short work of all of them. He was ready.

Lisa Parker turned every head in attendance when she walked into her husband's dressing room. She looked every bit the sultry movie siren in her white fox jacket, dripping in diamonds, with her raven hair perfectly coiffed in a magnificent crown of curls. Her presence alone gave Albert even more incentive to win.

"Hi, baby. You look great. Wish me luck."

"You don't need luck, honey. You're gonna knock 'emem out and make us rich."

"You're damn right I am!" Albert hopped off the massage table and smacked his gloves together. "I'm ready. Gimme a kiss for luck, anyway." She planted one on her husband's lips and said, "Go get 'em, champ." Lisa nodded politely to Ben and left the room.

Ben Dudley was holding Albert's robe open. "Okay, Piston, it's time. How da ya feel?'

"I'm good, Ben; let's go get this guy."

"Remember, don't rush it. We trained to go twelve. Stick to the plan, Albert."

"Don't worry, I got it. Quick in and out. I'm gonna take him apart piece by piece."

"That's what I wanna hear. *Now* let's go get this guy."

Albert walked out into the hallway surrounded by his handlers. As soon as they entered the arena, the raucous crowd erupted. The blaring bedlam of thousands of fight fans was deafening. Hundreds of camera flashes exploded in rapid succession, firing off like tracer bullets in a war zone. Albert, with his head down and his hood up, started the slow trot down the center aisle. Ben had both hands on his fighter's shoulders, while trotting right behind. Security people lined both sides of the aisle to keep back slappers and well wishers at bay. "Doc" Devlin, Albert's cut man, held the ropes open as the entourage approached. Albert "Piston" Parker ducked into the ring, dancing around his corner, throwing short rights and lefts. He glanced over to his opponent's corner to see Taylor glaring at him, pointing and giving him a thumbs down. Albert just smiled back while thinking, *Enjoy the moment while you still can, Taylor, 'cause I'm about to stick that thumb where the sun don't shine.*

In short order, the two combatants were staring each other down in the center of the ring, as the referee was giving his instructions. When the bell sounded to start the bout, no one, not even Ben Dudley, was prepared for what they were about to witness.

Albert shot across the ring like a man possessed. He faked a lead right, and then jabbed with his left. He followed up with a quick right to the body and a hard right uppercut that sent Taylor reeling. It was only six seconds into the fight and the crowd was already on its feet.

Taylor backpedaled half a dozen steps, desperately trying to clear his head. His reputation for being able to take a punch had evaporated. La Mont Taylor had never taken a punch from anyone who could hit as hard as this kid from Flushing. Albert moved in for the kill. A right-hand lead landed on Taylor's nose. La Mont brought both his forearms up beside his head "peek-a-boo style" to protect himself. Albert then unloaded a crushing left hook to the body. Taylor grimaced and instinctively brought both hands back down to protect his rib cage. Once again Albert's two-punch hook to the body, hook to the unprotected head combination paid big dividends. The force of Albert's second hook hit Taylor like it had been gathering steam from Cleveland. He went down face first, arms spread out on the canvas, and didn't stir until the referee counted to nine. Twenty-five hundred fans exploded into pandemonium when Taylor was counted out. Shouts of "Pis-ton, Pis-ton, Pis-ton," filled the arena. Seventy-seven-year-old Ben Dudley bounded over the ropes to envelop his fighter in a bear hug, his eyes filled with tears. "You did it, Piston! Good God, you really did it!" Seconds later Lisa joined them. The uproar from the fans was so all encompassing, she was yelling, "I love you, champ," and couldn't hear her own voice. The ring was filling up with dignitaries and former champions congratulating Albert and Ben, as well as a few Hollywood types and several hangers-on.

The bell clanged over the din, as the ring announcer barked into his microphone. "Referee Joe Johnson stops the fight at forty-eight seconds of the first round. The winner, by knockout, and still undefeated..... Albert 'Piston' Parker!" The picture of Johnson holding Albert's hand high in victory was in every newspaper's sports section the following day, along with the story of his stunning upset of the number one contender.

Albert's stellar performance, along with his humble "nice guy" image, propelled him into superstardom. He became the media's darling overnight, and was in high demand on the talk show circuit. All of this positive exposure increased Albert's popularity and intensified the hype over his upcoming title fight. Boxing fans were in love with this kid from the poor side of town, who battled his way to the top of the boxing world.

The promoters took advantage of Albert's newly found celebrity and arranged a whirlwind coast-to-coast publicity tour. Ticket sales for the closed circuit coverage of the fight broke all existing records by a wide margin.

After all his commitments were fulfilled, Albert desperately needed to take a break. He took Lisa to Hawaii for two weeks, where he thought they could just relax and enjoy each other's company, but that was not to be. Albert had become famous, even in paradise. While Lisa was in her glory, basking in her husband's celebrity, and soaking up all the media attention, Albert was beginning to tire. All he really wanted was to be alone with his beautiful wife, and work on a tan. He had been in constant motion for a long time and he needed time to relax, and prepare for the biggest fight of his life. Lisa was oblivious to this and kept dragging him out dancing, or to all-night parties. Albert did not get the solitude or the rest he so deeply needed. He returned to his training camp tired and confused.

Chapter 24

Albert and Lisa returned to California on Friday April 2nd. On Saturday, Albert checked in with Ben, and promised to start training in earnest on Monday morning. During their conversation, Ben was sure that something was bothering his fighter. In many ways, Ben and Albert shared a father-son relationship. Albert loved and respected Ben for taking him under his wing and lighting the pathway that was to lead him out of his former life. He admired his trainer's wisdom and Albert was in awe of Ben's accumulated knowledge of the fight game. Ben, in turn, admired Albert for having the guts and determination to turn his life around. In only a few years, they had grown closer than many biological fathers and sons. It was because of this strong bond that Ben was compelled to ask Albert what was bothering him.

"Whatsamatter, Piston? Dincha like Hawaii?"

"Hawaii was great, Ben, but…uh, I dunno. I think Lisa and I might not be in the same place right now, and I'm a little worried."

"Whaddaya mean?"

Well, I thought we'd be able to spend some time alone on vacation. Ya know, lie on the beach and just enjoy each other's company."

"Yeah, and?"

"Well, it seemed to me that all she wanted to do was party every night, and rub elbows with the rich and famous crowd. That's not me, Ben. I've worked real hard for a long time to try to build a secure life for Lisa and me, and to provide for my mom, in her old age. I really don't care to go out drinkin' every night with movie people."

Ben made every effort not to let on how deeply he was concerned. The old trainer had been around the fight game for more than fifty years and he had seen it all before, many times. A young fighter achieves some success. As he advances in the rankings, he marries a bombshell trophy wife who becomes drunk with celebrity. She spends his money as if she was printing it herself, and then, when the fighter's career goes south, she moves on. Many of these women make contacts and connections along the way through their first husband's fame. The fighter winds up broke, or punchy, or both. Meanwhile, his ex winds up married to a movie star, or a big-shot politician.

Albert was approaching the pinnacle of his career and Ben did *not* want anything to affect his fighter's concentration. After all the work and dedication, Ben would rather die than see Albert's dreams shattered like so many hopefuls before him.

"Don't worry, Piston. Every marriage has its bumps. Hell, me an' Pearl divorced in '74, remarried each other in '79, and almost divorced again in '83. We finally settled down and somehow learned to deal with one another, because we realized in spite of all the bumps along the way, we belonged together. Give it some time. You're still newlyweds. She'll come around; you'll see."

"Yeah, maybe you're right, Ben. She's not a bad person. I think she just kinda got swept up in all this."

"Sure."

Albert smiled at Ben and said, "All right, look, I'll see ya bright and early on Monday morning. We got two months to figure out how we're gonna send Rivera back to Panama without his belt!"

"Now you're talkin', champ!"

Feeling better after talking to Ben, Albert stopped at a florist on the way home and bought Lisa a dozen roses.

Chapter 25

Albert loved his little house on Mariposa Drive. It was cozy without being small, and it had a good-sized yard with a pool. As he wheeled the Cadillac into the driveway, he knew he'd find Lisa out by the pool, and his mom enjoying her afternoon nap on the living room couch. He parked the car at the end of the driveway and strolled through the garden gate into the pool/patio area. Lisa was stretched out on a chaise, her bikini-clad brown body glistening with tanning oil in the late-afternoon sun.

"How lucky am I, that I get to come home to the most beautiful girl in California?"

"Only in California?" she replied.

He laughed and handed her the roses. "These are for you, baby."

"Oh--thank you, Albert; how sweet."

"Hey, look, I was thinkin', since I have to start trainin' again on Monday, why don't we go to Ernesto's tonight? We both love the food, and parmigiana ain't gonna happen for me again till sometime in June."

"Sounds great, honey. Just give me a few minutes to freshen up."

Before they left for dinner, Albert poked his head into the living room. Sure enough, Liz was curled up on the couch. He decided to let her sleep and scribbled off a note, to let her know where they went.

As always, Ernesto himself greeted the Parkers, and ushered them to his best table. Being a huge fight fan, he was delighted to have this top contender and his gorgeous wife frequent his restaurant. He also enjoyed the benefit of increased business when people like "Piston"

Parker hung out at Ernesto's.

They thoroughly enjoyed their meal and lingered over an exquisite bottle of Chianti until almost 9:00. Albert was so relaxed and contented to have an enjoyable evening with his wife that he didn't even mind signing autographs for the handful of fans that occasionally interrupted their dinner.

It was almost 9:40 when he pulled Lisa's Mercedes into their driveway. The couple went in through the front door to find Albert's mother still curled up on the couch.

"You better wake her up, Albert. She'll be up all night if you don't." Lisa dropped her jacket on a chair and headed toward the bathroom, while Albert knelt down next to the couch and kissed his mom on the cheek. She felt cold, and didn't respond.

"Mom?" Gently, he shook her shoulder. "C'mon, Mom, ya gotta get up for a while." Still no response. A chill came over him as he shook her shoulder again, this time more intently. "Lisa! Somethin's wrong! She won't wake up!"

"What?" Lisa came out of the bathroom to find Albert shaking both of his mother's shoulders, his voice cracked with emotion. "Mom! Wake up! Please!"

Lisa rushed over and grabbed her mother-in-law's wrist. She could find no pulse. She answered Albert's pleading look by pulling a make-up mirror from her purse. She held it under Liz's nose for about twenty seconds. The mirror stayed clear. She looked at her husband and said, "You'd better call 911; I don't think she's breathing."

"Oh, God! Oh, God--no!"

Paramedics arrived within six minutes. They tried to revive her, but it was too late. Liz Parker had passed away.

An autopsy was performed, and it was determined that Liz had died from a brain aneurism. The coroner explained to her grief-stricken son that a vein had ruptured in his mother's brain, causing her demise. The doctor went on to inform Albert that usually, the only warning sign would be a severe headache, and most people would attribute that to stress, or tension. "Sometimes, there is no headache," he said. "The vein just bursts, and unfortunately, it is almost always fatal." The doctor wasn't positive, but he estimated the time of death between 6:00 and 9:30 p.m.

Upon receiving this news, Albert was overcome with guilt. Although it was not true, Albert believed if he had awakened his mother when he first came home, she would still be alive.

After the funeral, Albert returned to his training schedule. He was consumed by guilt, and his grief was unbearable. These powerful emotions evolved into full-blown anger, which he directed toward his unfortunate sparring partners. In a two-week time frame, Albert had disposed of four sparring partners, one of which wound up in a hospital. Ben was having trouble lining up replacements. The word was out. Parker was out of his head, and no one would have anything to do with him.

Ben tried talking to his fighter. He was more than concerned, not just about the upcoming title fight, but about the state of Albert's mental health. He tried the father-son approach, but Albert was inconsolable. When June arrived, Albert was in the best physical shape of his life. He had trained like a man obsessed, and his physique broadcast the fantastic proof. He was literally ripped with definition.

The fight was now only days away, and Billy Parsons had a one-on-one with Ben Dudley.

"Well, what do you think, Ben? Does our boy have a chance?"

"Billy, if he could win it on sheer strength and stamina, the fight would already be his. But to tell ya the truth, the kid ain't been right in his head since his ma died."

"I noticed some changes in his personality, but I just chalked it up to pre-fight jitters."

"Nah, it's more than that, Billy. He aint the same 'Piston.' He's been trainin' like he wants to beat Rivera to death. I don't think he can trade with a guy who's 62-1, with 58 KOs."

"Can't you talk to him, Ben?"

"I tried. All he does is 'yeah, yeah' me, and then he goes ahead and clubs another sparring partner into submission in two or three rounds."

"Well, the promoters have millions tied up in this fight. We'll just have to go through with it, and hope he wises up."

When the big night arrived, Albert was warming up in his dressing room under Ben's watchful eye. Every three minutes or so, Albert would stare at the dressing room door, but for the first time since they were dating, Lisa didn't show. Ben sensed the anger and disappointment building up in his fighter, and tried to calm him.

"Maybe she's caught in traffic. Don't worry, champ; I'm sure she'll be ringside when the bell rings."

"I dunno, Ben. I got a bad feelin'. She's been actin' funny lately. Things ain't been good."

"Look, champ, ya gotta focus. This is the biggest night of your life. You can't let anything distract you. If you do, you give Rivera the advantage."

"I know, I know, Ben. Don't worry, I'm gonna take him apart."

Coco Rivera had been at the very top of his profession for more than four years, and had successfully defended his title five times. Parker never took into consideration that while he was studying Rivera's fight films, his opponent was doing the same. Coco made a mental note of the fact that eight out of ten times, Albert's signature double hook came immediately after a double jab. Rivera made a few adjustments to his fight plan, knowing that if he could execute quickly and effectively, he could catch Parker off guard, and out-hook the hooker.

After the introductions were made, Albert looked out to ringside and saw Lisa's empty seat. As he waited anxiously for the bell, his emotions went haywire. All the anger, guilt, grief, and disappointment of the last two months were about to explode into pure rage. Rivera was the devil. Rivera killed his mother. Rivera stole his wife. Albert was going to beat this guy into a bloody pulp. He was going to make him pay for all the pain and sadness.

The bell sounded and Albert lunged across the ring. Piston's right-hand lead caught Rivera by surprise, but when Albert followed with a double jab, Coco was ready. As Albert's second jab was on its way, Rivera fired a rib-crushing left hook, followed in a split second by a hook to Albert's head, with everything Coco could put behind it.

Albert fell to the floor, a victim of his own signature combination. Rivera was jumping up and down, hands raised high over his head, as the referee counted "Piston" Parker out. The fight was over in twenty-four seconds of the first round.

Chapter 26

For the first time in his career, Albert woke up on his back, surrounded by doctors, his trainer, cut man, and his manager. As soon as the doctor gave the okay, his handlers helped him up. Rivera came over, gave the obligatory half-hug, and danced away.

Albert stood in the center of the ring and suffered the humiliation of knowing the whole world was listening to the ring announcer bellow out that he had been KOed in twenty-four seconds. Albert hung his head as the announcer continued, "And *still* middleweight champion of the world…Coco Rivera!"

Over the next several weeks, Albert sunk into a deep depression. He had come home from the fight to an empty house. Lisa was gone, and so was her Mercedes. Her closets and dressers were empty, and as Albert was to find out later, so was his bank account.

The love of his life turned out to be nothing more than a gold digger. Lisa didn't think her husband could beat Rivera. She realized this goose was *not* going to lay any more golden eggs, so she left to seek her fortune elsewhere.

Albert had never before felt so alone. His beloved mother was dead, his wife had deserted him, and his career was in the toilet.

The one person that stuck by him was Ben Dudley. He promised Albert that if he listened and followed Ben's advice, as he had in the beginning, he could get his career back on track. "One defeat does *not* mean your career is over. Even the great Ali didn't win every fight. I got Billy workin' on a rematch with Taylor. It'll be a good payday, and once you get by him again, we'll see about another crack at Rivera. Coco will jump at it, because it will be a huge purse, and he thinks you'll be an easy win. If you're willin' to really knuckle down and follow my instructions to the letter, I know how we can beat Rivera. You can still be middleweight champ; it's just gonna take a lot more work. Whadaya say, Piston?"

Albert never looked up. "Okay, Ben. Anything you say. I know I can trust you."

Ben was worried that Albert's heart wasn't in it, and he was right. Parker trained every day, but the hunger just wasn't there. La Mont Taylor knocked Albert out in the fifth round of their rematch. Shortly after that, Albert "Piston" Parker disappeared.

His emotional and physical decline began to gain momentum only two days after the rematch, when a depressed and defeated Albert Parker walked into a neighborhood bar, with the sole intention of getting himself blind drunk.

Like millions of emotionally exhausted and clinically depressed people before him, Albert sought relief from his heartbreak and hopelessness with alcohol. When he wrapped himself in the blanket of intoxication, he could, at least temporarily, escape his pain. The daily agony of his life would fade into the shadows of alcoholic oblivion.

Lisa had maxed out every credit card they had, to the tune of more than $200,000. Albert paid his debts in full with the purse from his last fight. There wasn't much left. He let the bank foreclose on the house on Mariposa, and he walked away, and kept walking.

Now homeless, he wandered aimlessly along the California coast. It wasn't long before he took to always having a pint of bourbon in his pocket. When his money ran out, he subsisted by doing odd jobs, and sleeping in parks, or on the beach. Year after year, Albert faded deeper and deeper into the fog of alcoholism. When he wasn't handing out flyers on some street corner, or raking someone's yard, he was a no-madic drifter, a vagrant, tramping around in the same alcoholic stupor that had eventually killed his father. His life had deteriorated to the point where he would spend his last handful of change on bourbon instead of food. He had become malnourished and sickly.

Early one evening, after receiving $25 from an elderly widow for cleaning up her yard, Albert rushed to the liquor store. A short time later, Albert was sitting alone on a park bench, clutching the brown bag that held both his dinner and his best friend: Jack Daniels.

The former number one middleweight contender had been re-duced to a bewildered drunk, staggering out from between two parked cars, into the path of an oncoming Lincoln Continental.

Congressman Pat Walsh slammed on his brakes, but it was too late. He had swerved to try to avoid hitting the stumbling rag man, but opposing traffic allowed him only a few inches to maneuver. He clipped the pedestrian with the Lincoln's right front fender. In what seemed almost to be a surreal slow-motion sequence, the unfortu-nate vagrant cartwheeled back toward the sidewalk. His upper body spun into a parked car, bouncing the poor man back into the street and onto his back.

As soon as he could bring the car to a complete stop, Pat lunged into the street and over to the motionless form, spotlighted by the Lincoln's headlights. While Pat was trying to find a pulse, a police car pulled up behind him. The officer hurried over and saw the shocked look on the Congressman's face. "Don't worry, sir, I saw him walk out in front of you. It wasn't your fault. That stumblebum didn't even look."

Pat gave the cop an angry look. "I'm Congressman Walsh, Officer, and I'm not looking to avoid responsibility here. Now get on your ra-dio and get this man an ambulance immediately; he barely has a pulse." The cop obediently ran back to his patrol car.

Pat turned his attention back to the victim. Lying in the street, in close proximity to the unconscious Albert was a dog-eared copy of Ivanhoe, by Sir Walter Scott. The Congressman had seen something fly away from the victim, when his body slammed into the parked car; now he knew what it was. *I don't imagine that there are too many drunks that read classic literature. I wonder who this guy really....Oh my God.* While putting the book back in the man's trench coat pocket, Pat looked at his face for the first time. Pat Walsh had been an avid fight fan since his teens, and his recognition of the accident victim was instantaneous. There was more than enough light, between the street lamp and the Lincoln's headlights, to make a positive identification. Pat knew right away that this man lying in the street, unconscious, in tattered clothes and stinking of booze, was a former world-class prizefighter.

The Congressman followed the ambulance to the hospital. After giving a full report to the police, he waited patiently for word on the patient's condition. A good forty minutes passed before he looked up to see a doctor walking toward him. "Congressman Walsh?" Pat nodded. "I'm Dr. Weinberger. Mr. Parker is pretty banged up, but he'll recover. He has three broken ribs, his left arm is broken, and he has several cuts and bruises."

"Is he conscious, Doctor?"

"Barely."

"May I speak with him?"

"Yes, but please be brief."

"Certainly." Pat entered the room and witnessed a man at the very rock bottom of his life. "Mr. Parker, I'm the man that hit you. My name is Pat Walsh, and I'm a US Congressman. I want to help you get your life back, if you will let me. We'll talk more when you're in better shape. I'll be back in a few days."

Pat returned as promised, but was not given a warm welcome.

"Look, Congressman Whatever-your-name-is, if you're lookin' for me to let you off the hook, don't worry, your political future is not in jeopardy. Nobody gives a damn about a drunken has-been."

"You're wrong on that one, Piston. *I* care."

Albert hadn't been called "Piston" since he left the fight game. The Congressman had caught him off guard.

"What? You know who I am...or maybe I should say who I used to be?"

"Sure I do. What fight fan wouldn't? It was inspiring to watch a tough kid battle his way out of a crime-riddled ghetto, all the way to the number one contender in the world. I saw the first Taylor fight from ringside. You were amazing. People still talk about that great double-hook power combination of yours. All the sports writers said there was no stopping Albert "Piston" Parker. I thought you were a shoo-in for the title."

"Yeah, so did I. Funny, how that worked out."

"Look, Mr. Parker, I don't know what terrible circumstances caused such a dramatic turnaround in your life, and frankly, it's none of my business. However, I have personally seen you accomplish great things. This tells me that you had to be smart, dedicated, and hard-working, as well as talented. If there is anything worse than a wasted life, it's a wasted life that belonged to someone who was gifted with a superior talent. That would be you, Mr. Parker, and that's why I'm here."

"So what's your game, Congressman? Did you come here to preach to me about the demons of drink, or do you just want an autograph, or what?"

"Neither, Mr. Parker. Look, I know for you to rise as far as you did in the fight game, you had to be a pretty tough guy. That doesn't go away; it's still in there, deep inside you. If you can reach inside and bring that tough guy back, I have a proposition for you. I'm going to start my campaign for the US Senate in a few months, and among other things I am going to need is more personal security. If you're willing to enter a rehab program, Mr. Parker, I will pay for it. If you successfully complete this requirement, I will have a full-time position waiting for you as my personal driver/ bodyguard."

Albert was stunned. He had spent the last ten years of his life in an alcohol-induced fog. He had no friends or relatives and his life had no direction, or purpose. The former world-class prizefighter had lost forty pounds, and his health was failing. The accident was a wake-up call. Somehow Albert knew that if he didn't accept the Congressman's generous offer, he would probably be dead within a year. All the emotion he had kept buried deep inside for all those years erupted en masse, causing his entire body to shudder, as if the dam of passion had finally burst from internal pressure, releasing gut-wrenching tears of heartbreak and hopelessness. He raised tear-soaked eyes to his would-be benefactor and simply said, "Help me, help me please; I can't pull out of this alone." Pat Walsh embraced the troubled ex-fighter and answered his cry for help.

"It's okay, champ. I *will* help you, and together we *will* get you past this. If you can bring yourself to trust me, in time you will see that it is not too late for you. I know you have the potential to defeat your demons, and lead a life that is far more satisfying and productive than you now know."

Albert Parker had reached another of life's crossroads. He had to make a decision that would seal his fate, one way or the other. Ten years of alcohol abuse was killing him, and yet the physical need for it was gnawing at him like the incessant pain from an infected tooth. He was sick. He didn't know if he could trust his own judgment, and for the first time in his life, he was truly filled with fear. It was this fear, a fear of being manipulated, or of being used for someone else's gain, that caused him to blurt out unfair accusations at the Congressman. "You tell me to trust you, when every person I've ever trusted, with only two exceptions, has used me, ripped me off, and deserted me. I'm not stupid, Congressman. I know every good politician has to be very convincing, if he's gonna get anywhere with his career. My street education is telling me that if your publicity people play up the angle that you brought a former celebrity back from the jaws of death, the voters will love you and you'll win by a landslide."

"Mr. Parker, if the circumstances were different, I would be insulted, but I do understand where you're coming from and you have more than enough reason to be suspicious." Pat took a card from his pocket and placed it on the table. "My offer stands. You don't have to take me up on it. It's your call, Piston." Pat opened the door to leave, but turned to face Albert once more. "I was sorry to hear about the passing of Ben Dudley, I know he was one of your two exceptions. I would assume that your mom was the other, and now you've lost them both. I am truly sorry. You can call that number at any time, if you change your mind." Pat closed the door silently, and was gone.

Chapter 27

Albert walked out of the hospital, into the bright California sunshine. He had gone through two nightmarish weeks of detox and healing, both emotional and physical. Neither process was anywhere near completion, but he felt better than he had in years. He was clear-headed, and this was the first day in a decade that his body was free of toxins. His ribs would still take some time to heal, and every time he coughed, or God forbid, sneezed, he would be in agony. His arm would remain in a cast for several weeks, but at least most of the blue-black bruises on his face had faded. Standing on the street corner, Albert took a deep breath and surveyed his surroundings. Directly across the street was a row of stores. He scanned the storefronts. Dolly's Dress Shop, the Puppy Palace, Morning Glory Coffee Shop, and The Captain's Keg Wines and Liquors. Albert reached into the pocket of his tattered trench coat and came up with $1.87, and Congressman Walsh's business card. His first reaction, born out of habit, was that he didn't even have enough for a half pint of bourbon. Coffee was the only other choice.

Albert had never noticed, or cared how passers-by perceived him. He had been embedded in his own self-pity, and his cognizance and reasoning had been drowned in a waterfall of bourbon. Things were about to change. Albert Parker was going to make a self- assessment, brought on by a five-year-old boy. As he sipped his coffee at a small table on the sidewalk, a young mother passed by, with her little boy in tow. "Mommy, Mommy, look at the dirty man!" The young woman pulled the boy along, reprimanding him without ever looking up. For Albert, the youngster had brought about an epiphany. The one-time successful sports hero looked down at his oil-stained jeans and his torn sneakers with shame and embarrassment. A five-year-old had shown him how far he had let himself go. Albert pulled the card from his pocket and walked to the phone booth on the corner, and made the call that would change his life forever.

Pat Walsh pulled up in front of the hospital and picked Albert up within twenty minutes of the phone call. The ex-fighter climbed into the front seat, his mind tortured and confused by an avalanche of emotion. All in the same moment, he was scared, unsure, ashamed, and desperately alone. As he slid in beside the Congressman, feelings of gratitude, indebtedness, and even hope swirled among the growing emotional melee.

"Thank you Mr. Walsh, for helping me. I have nowhere else to go. I have no family, no friends, no...people."

"No thanks are necessary, Albert; you made the right choice... and call me Pat. I took the liberty of already enrolling you at New Beginnings, so there would be no red tape delays, if and when you called. I want you to know that there are no strings attached to my job offer, other than you are required to complete the program and remain clean and sober. New Beginnings is a strictly a voluntary center; no one is going to babysit you, and you are free to leave whenever you wish. I know you can do this, Albert, and I'll do whatever I can to help you, but in the end, the only one that can conquer your demons is you."

Pat drove through the center's main gate and parked in front of a sign that said "Admissions." Albert let out a nervous laugh, and Pat asked what was so funny. "Not funny," Albert replied, "Ironic. We go in through a door that says 'Admissions,' and I know I will have to 'Admit' to myself, and probably a bunch of other people here, that this is my last chance to get some sort of a normal life back."

"Piston, I believe that to be a very perceptive observation, and a sign that you are already on the right track. I knew you were tough enough to get through this; now I know you're *smart* enough. C'mon, let's get you signed in."

The New Beginnings program lasted four months. Albert's medical records were reviewed, and his physical condition re-examined in detail. He was put on a healthy diet, specific to his nutritional needs. Daily workouts in the center's gym brought his body back into superb condition in a matter of weeks. The combination of good food and vigorous exercise strengthened his spirit, as well as his body. Albert went through intensive counseling, both in group as well as one-on-one. It was extremely hard for this tough guy to open up and bare his soul to a total stranger. Tough kids from the street as well as professional fighters will never show weakness. They both learn early on that once your weakness is exposed, it will be exploited, and you will end up on the ground. Albert had been under tremendous pressure while training for a title fight. To lose his mother, lose the fight, and find out that the only woman he had ever loved was only after his money, all in the span of only one month, was more than he could bear. He just gave up on life. After weeks of counseling, it all came to a head one evening, and Albert broke down and cried like a four-year-old. Albert Parker had never cried before. Not even when he was alone. The emotional release was a milestone in his rehabilitation. Sharing his pain with an understanding counselor removed the tremendous weight that was keeping him from moving forward with his life. For Albert, New Beginnings had been true to its name. The staff had walked him out of clinical depression as well as his dependency on alcohol and had showed him the way to *his* new beginning. He completed the program and when Pat picked him up, there was bounce in his step and a sparkle in his eye. His gratitude toward Pat manifested itself in a loyal friendship that would last a lifetime. There was nothing Albert wouldn't do for Patrick Henry Walsh.

During the next few months, Albert learned the Congressman's schedule, and became his shadow. Pat never had to look over his shoulder; Albert always had his back. The ex-fighter's admiration for his employer grew as he got to know him better. Albert found out that he was only one of hundreds of people, organizations, or causes that Pat Walsh helped personally. He was a humanitarian, a philanthropist, as well as an honest man.

It wasn't long after Albert assumed his duties that the Congressman mounted his campaign for the US Senate. It was at an outdoor fund raising event, held in a park in DC, that Albert proved Pat's trust in his abilities was well-deserved. The Senate hopeful was delivering a speech, and had the crowd pretty fired up. Albert was strolling through the throng, scrutinizing everyone he saw. Something caught his attention. At first he wasn't sure what was off about this guy, but quickly he realized that this man was the only one in the crowd wearing a long-sleeved shirt. It was August.

The man in the long-sleeved checkered shirt was moving slowly, almost methodically closer to the stage. Acting on instinct, Albert quickly wove a path through the crowd. Just as he got within an arm's length, the suspect started to reach behind his back, his right hand moving as if it were going under his shirt. Albert seized the man's wrist, forcing it into the middle of his back. In the same moment, the bodyguard gained a firm grip on the suspect's collar, rendering him immobile. "I'll break your arm in a heartbeat if you even think of resisting."

The man in the checkered shirt was caught completely off guard, and offered no resistance. Albert's next thought was to find someone in authority, and hand his prisoner off, when he heard a voice from his past say, "Hang on to him, Piston."

Albert cocked his head in the direction of the vaguely familiar voice.

"Frank?" A suit-jacketed arm reached around the ex-fighter, and pulled a pistol out from under the checkered shirt.

"Good catch, Albert. I saw this guy moving up to the front a little too quickly. I went after him, but you were closer and got to him first. Nice work."

The last time Albert saw Frank Martini, he was wearing a blue patrolman's uniform, and was keeping the fighter's adoring fans from swallowing him alive as he entered the arena.

"Frank, I can't believe it! Damn, it's good to see you!"

Martini produced a pair of handcuffs and took possession of the prisoner. Together he and Albert steered him out of the crowd. "Good to see you too, Piston. Especially right now. What are you doin' here, anyway?"

"Long story, Frank. In short, I'm working for Congressman Walsh, and I'm glad to see you're still working crowd control."

"I am, but I made lieutenant. Now I'm *in charge* of crowd control." Frank handed their prisoner to a couple of uniforms, after which, the two old acquaintances shook hands and promised to keep in touch.

As Martini melted back into the crowd, Albert looked up at the stage. Pat had seen the whole episode and when their eyes met, he nodded his approval. At that moment, Pat Walsh knew that the chance he took hiring Albert was a smart move.

Albert went back to his duties feeling like he had just won the middleweight title.

Chapter 28

Nelkie awoke from a sound sleep with a sticky face. The first thing he beheld was a long tongue and large dark brown eyes, protruding from a mound of orange fluff. The red fox pup had picked up Nelkie's scent in passing, and curiosity had gotten the better of him. His nose had led him to the elf's invisible presence, and now the pup was trying to figure out, by way of taste, who or what he had come across.

It took Nelkie only a moment to realize what was going on, and he couldn't help laughing uncontrollably as the fox continued the ticklish onslaught. "Hey, c'mon, let me up," he blurted out between fits of laughter.

At the sound of Nelkie's voice, the pup was startled, and even more confused. He yelped, turned tail and disappeared into the underbrush. "Aw, too bad I frightened him; I would have enjoyed playing with the cute little guy, if he didn't run off. Oh well, it's time I moved on myself."

Nelkie rummaged through his rapidly diminishing food supply and came up with enough scraps to abate his morning hunger. As he gathered his possessions and prepared to set off, he noticed there was still a soft glow emanating from the ring his parents had given him. Strong feelings of self-esteem washed over him, knowing his parents approved of his actions regarding the poacher. His confidence had been bolstered by the fact that he had successfully resolved his first challenge involving humans.

Nelkie understood, as Daido the Elder had told him, that learning from one's mistakes was a stepping stone to maturity. Although his blunder had caused Slater to escape initially, Nelkie's actions thereafter produced a more than satisfactory conclusion. As Nelkie saw it, if not for his involvement in the chase, only one of two things could have happened. Slater could have eluded the wardens, and ended up bleeding to death in one of his own traps, or he could have been caught and sent to prison. The elf was certain that his solution produced the best result in the end. Andrew Slater had just been through the most awe-inspiring event of his life and Nelkie was sure that the poacher would never return to his former ways.

As the day wore on, his excitement began to ebb. All signs pointed to his arrival in the human-dominated part of the world within a day or so. Driven by the anticipation of what wonders awaited him, his pace was quick and purposeful. The clean, fresh spring breeze brought sweet smells of the forest to the elf, energizing him, moving him forward. Nelkie had never felt more alive.

Before he was aware of it, the late afternoon began to yawn into evening, and Nelkie observed the great forest starting to thin out. More of the sky became visible through the formerly dense canopy. He became cognizant of signs of human existence as he neared the outer edge of their domain.

These must be footpaths, he thought, approaching an area that intersected his own untraveled path. He thought the pathway was too wide to be made by deer, and kneeled down to look for more signs. "Ahah," he said out loud, as if he was Robinson Crusoe discovering Friday's footprint in the sand. "Bootprints! Several humans have traveled this path, and not too long ago!" He followed the imprints to a much wider trail that revealed small tire tracks. Following the tire marks for several minutes led to the discovery of a large pond. Nelkie figured out that whatever small vehicle this was, it had turned around and backed up to the edge of the pond. Along the pond's periphery there were traces of a blue granular substance. Nelkie theorized that someone had driven a small vehicle to the edge of the pond and dumped or deposited this granular substance into the water. Upon closer examination, he saw that the pond water was exceptionally clear, and free of pond lilies, or any other form of choking vegetation. *Whatever this grainy stuff is,* he thought, *it must be beneficial to the water.* He bent down and brought a handful of pond water to his nose. It was odorless. He wet his lips. Detecting no foul taste, he sipped a little more. It tasted as fresh as rainwater. The elf happily refilled his water pouch and headed down another well-traveled path. He viewed his pond discovery as an encouraging sign. Obviously *some* humans were making an effort to preserve their fragile environment. Surely these were good people.

Only a few minutes had passed when Nelkie perceived a change in the weather. The clear spring evening had become overcast. The light breeze that drifted across the pond only minutes ago was now growing into a gusty wind. The distant rumbling of thunder did not diminish his hopeful anticipation. Even as the rain approached, he was certain that this evening was the advent of a great adventure, which was positive in nature.

Presently, it began to drizzle and Nelkie felt an urgency to seek shelter. He scanned the thinning trees in his immediate area, without any positive result. By chance, the elf looked up. "What's this?" he said aloud. "By Bindar's basket: a stroke of elfin luck!" Nelkie's eyes came to rest on a tree house that was about twelve feet above his head. He walked around the back side of the tree, and discovered a handmade wooden ladder leading to an open doorway. His first thoughts questioned why anyone would want to build a house *outside* a tree, but he dismissed them as unimportant, and scurried up the ladder. The elf curled up in a corner of his temporary home just as it began to pour. He was safe and dry, and using his provisions pouch for a pillow, he let the rhythm of the rain lull him into a deep sleep.

Unknown to the peacefully sleeping elf, only a few miles from where he lay, events were taking place that were to shape his quest, as well as his life, in ways he could never imagine. The forces of good and evil were staging for a clash that would shake Nelkie's world, and all who dwelled within it. Nelkie was about to plunge head first into the darkest depths of the human saga. A creature that had known only kindness, brotherhood, and the peace of living in harmony with the earth was now to be confronted with blind ambition, deceit, and even murder.

Chapter 29

The fifty-foot-long tanker truck made its way off the exit ramp. Emblazoned on the tractor's doors were crossed American flags with the words "Walsh Trucking" in patriotic red, white, and blue. A shadowy figure of a driver was all that was visible through the smoked windows. The big rig rumbled through the small town of Buena Montana, California. On the outskirts of town, the driver downshifted and turned onto an old logger's road. The truck slowed, belching out thick, black diesel smoke from its twin stacks.

The soft light of early evening reflected off the spotlessly clean tanker as it approached the edge of the great redwood forest. For half an hour, the big rig snaked its way along the narrow logging trail, until the driver turned onto a dirt road. The long-abandoned and untraveled road ended at a small clearing, barely large enough to turn the truck around. As soon as the driver positioned his rig to head out the way he came in, he shut it down and exited the cab. He was clad in black jeans and a dark, hooded sweatshirt that concealed his face. He hurried along beside the trailer, overtly adjusting the signs that read "DANGER, CORROSIVE CHEMICALS." The dark figure reached under the trailer and turned a small valve wheel. The sound of escaping liquid broke the tranquil silence.

Fifty feet away, facing the truck broadside, a small man with a video camera was recording as thousands of gallons of toxic waste spewed onto the pristine forest floor.

Exactly one week after the toxic crime against nature, a large political event was being held in the state capitol of Sacramento. The California Democratic Party was honoring a man whom many considered to be a great American, the senior senator of the state of California, Patrick Henry Walsh III. In the grand ballroom of the four-star Hotel Californian, over a thousand people paid five hundred dollars a plate to see their beloved Senator Walsh receive the cherished John F. Kennedy Humanitarian Award.

The junior senator, Wilfredo Guzman, acting as master of ceremonies, quieted the audience. "My fellow Democrats, it is my extreme honor to present this well-deserved award to my mentor and friend. Senator Walsh comes from a long line of distinguished public servants. His father, as many of you know, was a five-term US Senator and, of course, Patrick Henry Walsh I was the much-revered California Supreme Court Justice for many years. My friend Pat III continued his family's tradition of patriotism and public service. Back-to-back tours in Viet Nam resulted in a Purple Heart, as well as a Bronze Star, for bravery under fire. Pat left the Army a captain, and continued to serve his country as the youngest Congressman in the state of California, before being elected to the US Senate in 1990. He has fought throughout his career to keep our country strong, and to educate our youth. That is what this evening is all about. The Walsh family has always been active in civic and philanthropic endeavors. Pat Walsh I donated the maternity ward at Mercy General in 1937. Pat II, among other generous deeds, created the Inner-City Scholarship fund in 1953. Deserving students from all backgrounds and races still receive help from this fund today, which brings us back to the current Patrick Walsh. Pat III conceived, financed, and directs Youthsport USA, a non-profit organization that not only provides sports equipment to America's young, but a place to use it as well. This organization also fights the growing danger of violent gangs, by providing an open social atmosphere and an alternative place for our youth to congregate. For his selfless dedication and his genuine concern for America's youth, it is my honored privilege to present this year's John F. Kennedy Humanitarian Award to Senator Patrick Henry Walsh III. Come on up here, Pat!"

The audience exploded with applause as the fifty-two-year-old statesman approached the podium. At six foot four and two hundred fifteen pounds, the senator was a man with an unforgettable physical presence. A full head of wavy salt and pepper hair only added to this image. He greeted the younger man with a warm smile and a firm handshake. "Thank you, Will…that was very, ah, embarrassing." While the audience laughed, Wilfredo passed a wooden plaque into Walsh's left hand, and said, "You're welcome," and then sat down.

The senior senator addressed the crowd. "Thank you all very, very much. This is truly a great honor, and all this good publicity in an election year doesn't hurt either." Again the audience laughed and applauded.

He looked at the plaque, and then out to a thousand admiring faces. "Seriously, friends, I'm really not very good at this sort of thing, so I'll try to keep it short." Looking at the award again, he said, "I won't bore you by reading this lengthy inscription, although it is very gracious. What I will bore you with, however, are the ever-growing needs of our nation's youth. The children of America are besieged daily by all the worst possible temptations. The horrors of drug addiction are romanticized. The false or misplaced loyalties of gang affiliation are legitimized. The respect for the rights and property of others is being vaporized. Those of us who were raised to believe in the virtues of kindness, honesty, and respect should be righteously outraged that our young may be led astray by misinformation, misguided peers, or ill-gotten gains. I urge you to join me in the creation of a vanguard to instill the true meaning of the virtues we all hold sacred into the hearts and minds of our young. With your help, we can help thousands of children to attain the courage, wisdom, and self-reliance they will need to face the challenges that await them. Thank you again for this wonderful award, and remember, Youthsport begins with YOU! Thank you."

The audience rose to give the senator a standing ovation. Their applause was thunderous. He waved and flashed his famous warm smile, while he headed out of the hall. He was met at the elevator by his secretary, Anne Clark. As she spoke, he shook his head, pointing to his ear. The tribute coming from the ballroom was so loud that it overpowered her small voice completely. Pat pushed the "down" button, and the elevator door opened. He pressed the "L" button and the doors closed, quieting the din.

She tried again. "Very moving speech, Senator. I'm sure you inspired many of your constituents to support your efforts. I'm afraid there are several items on your desk that need your attention, before you fly back to Washington tomorrow."

"That's okay," he answered. "I was going back to the office to drop this plaque off and make a few phone calls. What have you left for me there?"

As the elevator doors parted, revealing the plush hotel lobby, Anne fumbled through a dog-eared memo pad. "Let's see, Bobby Bergman dropped off the rough draft of your speech for the League of Women Voters on Wednesday, You can review that on the plane. I typed the contract renewal with Chem-Tech for Walsh Trucking--that requires your signature." She was now almost at a jog, trying to keep up with the senator's long strides. Undaunted, she kept reading. "Your letter to Senator Scott guaranteeing him your support for the crime bill also needs your signature. There's a letter from your son, a request from the Sierra Club for you to speak at their annual meeting, and your wedding anniversary is Friday... twenty-six years, sir."

The two of them hurried across the sidewalk to a waiting town car. A distinguished- looking gentleman in his fifties held the back door open. At first glance, the chauffeur looked every bit the English manservant type. His prematurely white beard was close-cropped, and his perfectly tailored suit, with its sharply creased trousers, only added to his professional persona. However, upon closer examination, one might notice something slightly amiss. One look at this man's face would tell you that his name probably wasn't Jeeves. It was obvious that his nose had been broken more than once, and that there was a prominent build-up of scar tissue above each eyebrow. Although the man was smiling broadly, something behind those penetrating slate-grey eyes suggested that this man had been somewhere that most men would never dare to go.

Anne greeted the chauffeur first with a smile and a friendly "Hi Albert," before scrambling into the back seat, barely avoiding being steamrolled by the ever-locomotive senator.

Pat's greeting was apologetic. "Sorry to keep you waiting so long, Piston; you know how these things can go on and on."

"No problem, Pat; I've just been gnawing on the steering wheel for the past two hours." They all laughed, as Albert shut the door firmly, and got behind the wheel. The big Lincoln roared to life and while Albert pulled away, Anne decided she would join the chauffeur in a good-natured razzing of their boss. Since his earliest days as a Congressman, Pat's two closest and most trusted employees were Anne Clark and Albert Parker. When the three of them were alone together, they often traded friendly barbs.

"Hey, Albert, don't feel bad; I've been waiting for him in the hall-way, watching the waiters carry trays of prime rib past me. I know the hired help is never allowed to dine with the mucky-mucks, but this was torture!"

"Yeah, I know, it's a dirty job, but someone's got to...."

"All right, I get it," Pat said, holding up both his hands in mock anger. "I *am* sorry, guys, so let me make it up to you. Anne, why don't you come to the office with us, and while I'm upstairs, you can join Albert for dinner at Rutha's, in the lobby. Order whatever you want and put it on the corporate card. I'll join you for an after-dinner drink when I'm done."

Anne leaned a little closer to the driver and almost giggled. "Isn't it amazing what laying a little guilt trip on the boss can get you?"

"That's what I'm talkin' about," Albert answered.

After parking in the underground garage, the threesome strolled over to the elevator, still wisecracking with one another. Pat was crying poverty, while the other two were complaining about working for a slave driver. It was all in good fun.

The elevator doors opened at the lobby, flooding the small space with the enticing aromas of garlic and basil. They both thanked the senator and Anne took Albert's arm, saying, "Whatever else we order, I simply must have some garlic bread." The doors closed and Pat continued up to his office. He was reading the kudos on his plaque when the elevator bumped to a stop at his floor. While pulling his keys out of his pocket, he stopped short when he noticed the lights were still on in his office. *Strange,* he thought. *Anne would never leave the lights on.* He tried the door. It was unlocked. *Maybe Anne left in such a hurry, she just forgot to lock up. I have been running her a little ragged lately.* He grabbed the doorknob to his private office and walked in. A look of astonishment—then outrage--came over his face.

A small, dark man sat in Pat's chair. His muddy shoes were propped up on the desk, soiling the official papers to be signed. A low, raspy voice croaked out of the little man's mouth. "Good evening, Senator. How was the award banquet?"

In spite of his indignation, Pat remained cool and sized up the intruder. The raspy voice disguised some kind of accent. Pat couldn't put his finger on it. From his dark complexion, he guessed the trespasser was Middle Eastern, maybe from Iraq or Syria. Calmly, but firmly, the senator told the little man to get his feet off the desk. "Who are you, and what are you doing here?" he demanded. "Don't you know it's a federal offense to break into the office of a United States senator?"

"Relax, Patty boy. The door was open."

"Okay, that's it!" Pat made a move toward the smaller man, fully intending to pick him up by his neck and toss him into the hall.

"Not so fast, Senator Do-good, or I'll blow a hole in your five-hundred-dollar dinner!" The man produced a large handgun from under his jacket and pointed it at the senator's stomach. Pat stopped short. He knew, at that range, the little Arab couldn't miss with his eyes closed.

"What do you want from me...money?"

"Relax, big guy. I'm just the messenger." He reached into his jacket, still pointing the pistol at Pat, and tossed a small package at him. The senator caught the parcel in his right hand. It was wrapped in plain brown paper. Nothing was on the outside of the package except Pat's name in black magic marker.

"What's this?" he asked.

"It's something you'll study carefully, if you have a brain in that million-dollar head. I'll give you a couple of days to consider how your career and family fortune can nose dive as a result of what's on that DVD; then, maybe we can have another little chat." The dark little man purposely kicked all of Pat's papers off the desk as he got up. Moving around the desk, he slowly advanced toward the door. The Arab's eyes never left the senator's midsection. The long barrel of his hand gun was rock-steady. The senator felt sure that whatever sleazy business this little man was involved in, he had probably used that gun more than a few times with deadly consequences.

The arrogant little man backed slowly out of the private office. He slithered around the door frame so that the last thing out the door was the barrel of his gun.

Pat hesitated for a few seconds, and then followed. The intruder had already cleared the reception area. Pat cautiously opened the door to the hallway. No one there. The little man had vanished in mere seconds and had done so soundlessly.

The senator looked down at the parcel in his hand. "Well, let's see what this is all about," he said aloud. He unwrapped the package and walked over to the DVD player in the bookcase opposite his desk. Pat's first thought was that he might have angered some Arab politicians with his strong opinions about America's foreign policy. He was not at all prepared for the scene that now played before him. To his complete surprise, the scene began with one of his brand-new diesel trucks pulling a tank trailer into a pristine forest meadow. Although the video was obviously recorded by an amateur under poor conditions (a bouncing picture from an unsteady camera operator in failing light), the important details of the footage were unmistakable. As the big rig turned around in the clearing, the camera zoomed in on the crossed American flags painted on the cab door. The Walsh Trucking logo filled the small screen.

"What on earth is going on here?" he shouted at the image. The next thing he saw was the driver alighting from the cab and straightening the signs on the trailer. His hooded sweatshirt hid the features of his face from the camera. Pat's eyes narrowed with disbelief when the driver opened the valve and a frothy yellow liquid plunged to the ground. Before the screen went black, Pat heard a raspy foreign-sounding voice say, "You're busted, Senator," followed by laughter that sounded sinister, almost foreboding.

Pat sat down behind his desk and buried his head in his hands for several minutes before picking up the phone. He dialed Albert's cell, which was answered on the first ring. "Hey, Piston, slight change of plans. When you guys are finished with dinner, would you come up for a few minutes? I need to show you something."

"Right away, boss." He had a quizzical look on his face as he put the phone down.

"What's up?" Anne asked

"Dunno, somethin' ain't right. We'd better finish up and find out; he didn't sound happy."

The two loyal employees finished their meal and were in their boss's office within minutes. The look on Pat's face told them there was serious trouble brewing. Anne spoke first. "What's happened? You look worried."

"I'm afraid I have a crisis on my hands, and worse, it seems the problem originates on my own land up north."

Before anyone could ask any questions, Pat pointed the remote and clicked. Once again, the Walsh logo filled the screen. Pat let them view the video in its entirety before clicking it off. Albert was still staring at the blank screen with an almost confused expression, when Pat broke the silence. "I believe the voice you hear at the end belongs to the rat-like creature that was sitting with his feet on my desk when I arrived. Obviously, I'm being set up for blackmail, but I don't know if this frame-up is political or just common criminal greed."

Albert asked, "Are you saying you don't know if you're being blackmailed into changing your political views, or if someone is after your personal wealth?"

"Exactly. What I do know is that the seedy little man that ambushed me tonight is not the boss. He admitted to being just the messenger."

"Ambushed! Whadda ya mean, ambushed?" Albert cried.

"Well, he did have a rather large gun."

"Wait a minute," Ann interrupted. "How did he get in? I know I locked the door before I left!"

"I don't know, Anne, maybe he picked the lock, but that's not important. I need to find out who this guy is, and who he's working for."

Albert's eyes widened. "Damn! I shudda been here!"

"No, Piston. It's far better that I was alone with him. No one got hurt. Listen, guys, I showed you all of this just in case something weird should happen in the next few days. At least you can give the authorities a start. I think I recognize that meadow in the video. It may be part of my family's property up north. If I remember correctly, it's off an old logging trail at the edge of the forest."

"Look, Pat, this is getting pretty deep," Anne said. "You had better get R.J. on this right away, before anything else happens."

"Yes, of course," Pat answered. "I just wanted to brief you both first. Now, where did I put his private number?"

"*You* didn't put it anyplace. *I* put it on your list of contacts, on your cell," Anne said.

"Right."

R.J. Abbott had been a loyal friend and a member of the senator's "inner circle" for more than two decades. After fifteen years with the FBI, he founded his own private security and investigation firm, R.J. Abbott International. By working long hours and giving his clients personal and confidential service, his professional reputation became well-regarded by wealthy and well-connected clients. His worldwide client base included captains of industry and European royalty, as well as several high-profile show business people, and one US senator.

Pat located the number in his contacts and called. As usual, it was answered before the second ring. "Abbott."

"R.J., it's Pat Walsh. I'm afraid I have a serious problem."

"What's happened, Pat?"

"Someone broke into my Sacramento office. He left me a very incriminating video. No demands have been made yet, but I'm sure someone is going to try to blackmail me." Pat went on to explain what was on the DVD.

"Yeah, it's blackmail, all right. Look, Pat, leave everything just as it is and I'll take the first flight out I can get."

"Thanks, R.J.--anything else?"

"Yes. Try to keep as close to your regular schedule as possible. We don't want whoever is behind this to think you called in any help."

"Okay, will do; and thanks again, R.J."

"No problem, Pat, and try not to worry. I'll talk to you soon... bye."

Pat put the phone back in his pocket and looked at Albert. "Piston, I feel better already. R.J. will be out here as soon as he can get a flight."

"Anything I can do, Pat?" his secretary asked.

"No, R.J. said just to keep to our normal routine, but thanks for asking."

"Okay, boss, why don't we take Anne home and head up to the country. It sure has been a long day."

"You bet, Albert. I could use some of that woodland peace and quiet to soothe my soul. There's not too much that will ruin your day faster than having someone point a pistol at you."

"I shoulda been here," Albert lamented again.

"Piston, I appreciate your dedication, but believe me, it's better that you weren't here. Even the fastest fists are no match for a bullet. This calls for R.J.'s expertise. I know he'll get these guys. Now let's go home."

The big Lincoln swallowed up mile after mile of highway. Albert always enjoyed taking the senator home to his beloved forest. His entire family loved being close to nature and always found peace at their ancestral home.

For thousands of years, the majestic redwood forest stood unspoiled in northern California, the only place on earth where these giant trees could flourish. Some of these colossal trees would top out at a height of over three hundred fifty feet. Before commercial logging began in the 1850s there were over two million acres of pristine redwood forestland. By the 1960s, logging had consumed nearly 90% of all the original redwoods.

Patrick Henry Walsh I, through hard work and wise investments, had made his fortune in the roaring twenties. A naturalist and conservationist, before the terms were ever coined, he was more than concerned about the rapidly disappearing redwoods. His knowledge of the law was extensive, so he knew any legal action would take years to produce a law to protect the forest. So, he did the next best thing. He bought over a thousand acres and established what would become the Walsh family compound.

Albert wheeled the limo onto the only paved road to encroach on the forest. It was nearly two miles long and barely wide enough for two cars to pass one another. The road ended at two massive stone pillars supporting wrought-iron gates that were ten feet tall. The gates were closed.

"What's this about?" Pat asked, as they pulled up.

"I took the liberty of calling ahead to have the gates closed," the chauffeur answered. "In light of all that's happened, I wanted to make sure the Mrs. was safe. I know the security cameras have the grounds pretty well covered, but there's no sense in making it easy to get in."

"I know you're right, Albert, and thank you, but I really can't stand my grandfather's gate. I don't have the heart to take it down, but it looks like the entrance to a prison when it's closed like that."

"I agree," Albert said, reaching for the remote control on his visor. "It shoots your 'open door' policy all to pieces, but in this case, better safe than sorry."

"As usual, you are on task, Piston--thank you."

The gates swung inward and Albert piloted the Lincoln along the half-mile driveway to the main house. Pat never considered himself the owner of this home, which was one of the largest log homes in the country. He saw himself as more of a conservator of the compound, preserving it for the next generation. The home itself, built from the native trees that were cleared for the roadway, had grown immensely since his grandfather's day, as had the size of the estate. Pat II had purchased an additional thousand acres, and Pat III added several hundred more. Each generation contributed additions to the original home as well. In its present incarnation, this magnificent home boasted a dozen bedrooms, each with private bath. The industrial-sized, commercially equipped kitchen could support a staff large enough to serve a state dinner for visiting dignitaries. Vaulted ceilings and hand-hewn natural timbers adorned a dining room that could seat forty guests. The main house also contained many formal and informal entertaining areas. These included a billiard room, complete with a fully stocked bar, and a small theater. Guests could also avail themselves of the pool and cabana area, as well as the senator's workout center, which housed a complete Nautilus circuit, steam room, and large whirlpool bath.

The senator had his own suite of offices in the north wing, which included a library and a computer room. There were several outbuildings, garages, guest houses, and stables as well.

Albert eased the limo to a stop in front of the main entrance.

"I'll say good night now, Albert. You can put the car in for tonight." Pat slid over to the door and got out.

"'Nite, Pat. See ya in the mornin', and Pat…you know R.J. is gonna find this guy, right?"

"Right."

Barbara Walsh greeted her husband in the foyer. At forty-nine, she was still physically stunning. Regular exercise and a sensible diet had kept her slim enough to fit into her wedding gown, twenty-six years later. She handed him a glass with two fingers of Glenmorangie on the rocks, as was his routine. He responded, as always, by curling his arm around her waist, gazing lovingly into her green eyes and calling her by his favorite pet name. "How's my Babette this evening?" he asked, while affectionately caressing her neck.

"Much better, now that you're home. I just got in a half hour ago myself. They shared the obligatory "hello kiss," and he asked, "How's your mother?"

"Well, she gave us quite a scare, but Dr. Ormond prescribed some antibiotics, and said she'll be up and around in a day or two. My dad has assumed command of the household and all is well on the Western front."

"Great. I would have liked you to be at the dinner, but I'm glad you got to see your folks and that your mom's okay." They walked to the living room and sat on the couch.

"How 'bout you? Tough day?"

"No," he lied. "Just another day at the office," he said, smiling.

She knew right away that he was keeping something from her. The senator broke eye contact when he answered the question and his body language became almost defensive. "Look, honey, I know something's bothering you; I can always tell. You don't have to give me all the details, but I would rather you were honest with me and tell me what you can. I'm a big girl. Maybe I can help."

"I'm sorry, Babs, I should know that I can't fool you. You know me too well. I am concerned about a developing problem, but it would do me no good to discuss it with you until I have all the facts. I do appreciate your concern, but for now, I would like to put my problems behind me and just enjoy my nightcap, and your company."

She wrapped both her arms around his free arm and put her head on his shoulder. "Okay, Senator, I can live with that." Suddenly, she sat up. "Oh, before I forget, Tommy called for you. I think he wanted to congratulate you on your award. You should call him tomorrow."

"I'll call first thing in the morning. I'll bet that by some strange coincidence, he will just happen to be low on cash," he said, in mock annoyance.

She smiled at him, knowing he was probably right, but she also said he shouldn't complain. "He made the dean's list again this semester," she reminded him.

"I know, and of course I'll send him a check as soon as I find out how much he needs. He's a good kid, and I'm very proud of him."

"Okay. Now that we have all of the current business settled, Senator, let's get some shuteye."

"Sounds good to me; it has been a very long day."

Saturday morning, Pat was up by six-thirty, as usual. After a forty-minute workout and a shower, he headed for the kitchen. Rosalinda, the cook, knew the senator's schedule and habits well enough to have his special Saturday morning breakfast on the table when he arrived. Three eggs, over easy; bacon, white toast, and plenty of coffee. There were four newspapers next to his plate. "Señora, you are almost too efficient. What would I do without you?"

"Thank you, Señor Walsh. Enjoy your breakfast." She busied herself in the pantry, while Pat dug in. He loved bacon, but allowed himself only four strips, and only on Saturday. As he chomped on his bacon, Barbara flitted through the kitchen, car keys jingling in her hand. In one sweep, she gave her husband a peck on his cheek, announced she was off to run some errands, and was out the door.

Just then Albert strode into the kitchen. At fifty years old, he still possessed the gait and posture of a professional athlete. "'Mornin', Pat. 'Mornin', Rosie. Any coffee brewin'?"

Rosalinda bustled out of the pantry. "Sit, Señor Alberto. I will make you some eggs."

Albert held up his hands. "No thank you, Rosie. Just coffee, thanks."

She put a cup in front of him, but before she returned to her duties she said, "You should eat, Señor. You are too skinny," and she was gone.

"So, Senator, you certainly look bright-eyed and bushy-tailed."

"Yeah, I feel good this morning. I had a great workout. Now I just have to call my son, and wait to hear from R.J."

"Okay, boss. I'll let you conduct your business. If you need me, I'll be down at the cottage."

"Thanks, Piston. I'll talk to you in a little while."

Pat picked up the phone and dialed cross-country to the small apartment his son shared with a fraternity brother named Robert. The phone was answered so quickly that the senator wasn't sure he had heard it ring. "Hello, Tommy?"

A nervous-sounding voice on the other end replied, "No, this is Robert."

"Hi, Robert. This is Senator Walsh. Is Tommy there?"

"Uh no sir, but I'm glad you called. I'm a little worried."

Pat's stomach went queasy. An icy fear crept over him, but he stayed calm. "What's wrong, Robert?"

"Well, sir, he was supposed to meet me for racquetball yesterday at four o'clock, but he never showed. I wasn't really worried until I got up this morning. He never came home last night! I called around, but no one has seen him. It's after eleven a.m. out here, and nobody has seen T.J. for almost twenty-four hours!"

Pat felt physically ill. His stomach was in knots. His voice however, remained calm. "All right, Robert, I'm sure there's a reasonable explanation for his whereabouts. Let me make a few calls of my own. In the meantime, if you should hear from him, tell him his father is not happy, and to call home right away."

"Yes, sir. I'm sorry; I didn't mean to alarm you, but I thought you should know."

"I'm sure he'll show up soon, but in any case, there's no need for an apology; you did the right thing."

"Thank you, Senator. I'll be sure to let you know the moment I hear something. Goodbye, sir."

Pat hung up and looked at his watch. *R.J. is probably at my office by now. I should fill him in.*

Just then, the phone rang. Startled, Pat quickly answered. "Hello?"

His worst fears were realized when a gravelly voice with a Middle Eastern accent replied, "Good morning, Senator Do-good. How's Tommy?"

Pat's normally well-kept temper exploded. "Listen, you sick little dwarf, if any harm comes to my son, I'll hunt you down myself and shoot you like a rabid dog!"

The Arab remained cool and unfazed by the threat. He mocked the senator's stature and trivialized Pat's attempt at intimidation.

"I wouldn't go down that road, your grace. I don't think you would want to find out how far out of your league you are by watching the bodies pile up around you. Now here's what you *will* do. Get in your Jeep and come down to the meadow in the video. In case you're unfamiliar with your own property, it's a hundred yards off the old logging road, at the edge of the forest. Do it now, and come alone." The phone went dead.

Pat headed for the garage at a dead run. Albert saw his friend start the Jeep and peel out of the garage. He flagged him down. Pat slammed on the brakes, knowing that if he didn't stop, Albert would surely follow in one of the other cars. "I don't have time to explain now," he said. "I'll be back in a little while to fill you in. Stay here!" The senator sped off, while Albert felt a sickly feeling growing in his stomach. He didn't like it, but he would wait.

Pat accelerated out of the compound with the Jeep's wheels spewing clouds of dust behind him. He turned onto the old logging road at breakneck speed. Bouncing and bumping the Jeep along the winding road, he nearly lost control. At last, he came to the meadow. Desperately scanning the area, he could see no one. He brought the Jeep to a halt at the center of the meadow and switched it off. Pat got out, certain that he could feel someone watching his every move. Suddenly, he sensed movement in the trees nearby.

The small, dark intruder from Pat's office walked slowly out of the woods. He held a small pair of binoculars in his left hand and the now-familiar long-barreled hand gun in his right. He was still wearing that sneering grin. "Good response time, Patty-boy. My employer would like you to consider this proposal." The little man put the binoculars down softly and produced a manila envelope from under his jacket. He tossed it at the senator's feet. "Pick it up and take it home. You will hear from me again in a few days." The dark man did a slow visual inspection of the surrounding area. When he was sure they were still alone, he spoke again. "So there may be no doubt in your mind as to what is going on here, I will explain it but once. It will cost you a fortune to try to disprove what is on that video, if it's even possible. The American people will never believe that their ultra-rich senator was *not* trying to save hundreds of thousands of dollars in disposal fees by illegally dumping toxic waste in a remote corner of his own land. It would *not* be hard for the American public, or the rest of the world for that matter, to believe that one more rich politician has succumbed to greed. I would also caution you that if you do not find the terms of the contract in that envelope agreeable, your son's remains will never be found. Now pick that up and go."

Pat was so filled with rage that he wanted to tear this little man's ugly head from his shoulders with his bare hands, but he could not allow anger to cloud his judgment. *God knows where they're holding Tommy. Even if I could get that gun away from him, I could be putting my son's life at risk.* Powerless to do anything else, he picked up the envelope and got back in the Jeep. Driving slowly out of the meadow, he passed a stand of 100-foot-tall hemlock trees that were already turning brown from the toxic waste dumped over their root systems. Looking at the dying trees, he couldn't help but wonder if he would ever see Tommy alive again.

The dark man watched the senator depart and carefully followed his progress through the binoculars. When Pat was far enough away, the Arab retreated to the edge of the woods and began removing several evergreen boughs that concealed his motorcycle. He pulled a white jogging suit from the saddlebag and after removing his dark jacket and black jeans, he tossed them into the woods and put on the jogging suit. In case anyone had seen him drive onto the property, he wanted to look completely different driving out. After donning a white helmet with a smoked face shield, he fired up the bike and headed for the highway at a moderate rate of speed. Once he made it down the entrance ramp and blended into traffic, his escape was complete.

Pat returned to the compound to find Albert pacing back and forth in front of the garage. The ex-fighter got into the Jeep and they continued on to the main house.

"I've got big trouble, Al. They've taken Tommy."

"Who?"

"Don't know yet; but by God, I'll find out."

The two men strode into Pat's private study and shut the door.

The senator opened the envelope and spread its contents out across the desk.

"Looks pretty much like standard legal forms for sale of property," Albert noted.

"Yes, so far," Pat agreed. "Let's see if we can find where the nuts and bolts of this proposal are." His eyes quickly cut through the mumbo-jumbo of legal clap-trap. "Party of the first part, heretofore referred to as blah, blah, blah, etc., ah…here's the bombshell." He read on for a few moments and then looked up at Albert, enraged. "No big surprise here, Piston. Just plain greed. Money. That's all this is about. These people, whoever they are, want to clear-cut the entire property, because the lumber alone is worth millions."

Albert was reading over the senator's shoulder and pointed out some of the details. "It says here they want you to sell two thousand acres of prime forest land, for what amounts to a minimal cash down payment and a very small percentage of the profit from the lumber sales. This is outrageous! That amounts to pennies on the dollar, in terms of value, not that you would *ever* sell, at *any* price!"

"Nor would any of my heirs," Pat added. "What's even worse is that once they own the land, and the forest has been decimated, they are free to develop it any way they wish. Who knows what kind of monstrosities they will build here!" Pat's face was crimson with anger. "These madmen want to destroy a forest that was thriving before this continent was discovered! They would gladly demolish an entire ecosystem, and induce the extinction of several endangered species, not to mention depriving future generations of the beauty and wonder of this sacred place. All in the name of greed!" Pat flopped down in his chair, totally disgusted.

Albert felt terrible. He wanted to help his friend, but he had no idea where to start. "Pat, these people are trying to commit a crime against humanity. It's a shame that they can even *attempt* this, but what can we do?"

"I don't know, Piston; I'd better get a hold of R.J. This thing has mushroomed out of control, and I can't afford to take the slightest chance until I know that Tommy is safe." The senator dialed his office and R.J. answered.

"Senator Walsh's office."

"R.J., it's Pat. I'm afraid the unthinkable has happened. Tommy has been kidnapped."

"Damn! I'm sorry, Pat. There's no way anyone could have seen this coming. Listen, try to stay calm. I know it looks very bad right now, but believe me, I've been down this road before, several times, and I know my way. I'll dispatch two of my best men to Ithaca right away. They will go over that college town from top to bottom. I've got about another hour here; then, I'll shoot up to your place. I've made some progress."

"You mean you might have some *good* news for me?"

"We have some good footage of your intruder from the surveillance camera here. I'm running a make on him now."

"That is good news. All right, I'll let you wrap up and we'll see you when you can get here."

"Affirmative. Try not to worry; I'll have all my best people on this until we catch these guys."

The senator hung up the phone and released a deep breath. He was still very upset. He looked at Albert and shook his head. "Look, I have to go out for a while and think. Maybe I'll take the Jeep into town."

"Sure, Pat. I'll hang around and keep an eye on things," Albert replied.

"Good. Thank you. I would like you here when R.J. arrives. You know how much I value your input."

"Wild horses couldn't keep me away. If there's anything you need, Pat, I'm here."

"Thanks; I'll see you in an hour or two."

Chapter 30

Pat went out to the Jeep and headed slowly down the access road toward town. The senator's head was filled with very troubling thoughts about Tommy. While the Jeep rolled past some of the most serene and unspoiled land in the country, Pat's mind was being tortured by the worrisome probabilities that awaited his only son.

He meandered along the forest's edge, lost in thought. When they first found out Barbara was going to have a boy, she insisted that the "Patrick Henry Walsh" tradition was to end with her husband. "I'm sorry honey, I love you," she said, "but Patrick Henry Walsh IV just sounds too pompous." After much discussion and debate, Barbara acquiesced to continuing the patriotic theme and they agreed on Thomas Jefferson Walsh. From infancy, he was called Tommy by his parents, but of course his friends shortened that to T.J.

Like most of the Walsh men, Tommy was headstrong. Pat was afraid that his son would more than likely attempt to escape his captors. Even more cause for concern was the fact that Tommy had studied martial arts for more than eight years and held a black belt in two separate disciplines. The senator dared not consider the consequences, should his son choose to stand and fight. Thoughts of that nature made him come to the decision that he must do whatever was necessary to put an end to this situation as soon as possible. He decided that unless R.J. showed up with an infallible plan to get Tommy back unharmed, he would give in. He would sell his beloved family treasure to get his son back. There was never any question that his love for his son far outweighed his love of the land.

With his decision made, Pat felt only slight relief. There was still a chance for things to go sour. He elected to head home and inform Albert of his decision, and then try to figure out a way to tell Barbara.

After turning the Jeep around, Pat noticed a figure walking out of the woods. He recognized the man in the green work clothes as Pete Baxter, his superintendent. It was Pete's job to manage the grounds and keep them free of destructive forces, whether they were natural or manmade. His duties extended hundreds of acres into the forest. This was a full-time job, for which he was paid well. He was also provided with a house for his family that was rent-free. The house was close enough to town so that the Baxters didn't have to live like hermits. Pete loved his job and loved the fact that he could walk out his door and be at work. Only a few yards from the house was a large barn outfitted with everything from all-terrain vehicles and myriad farm equipment to firefighting gear and first aid supplies for injured animals. Pete was well- qualified for his position, having degrees in arbor culture and botany. He also held a certification in ecological land management. Pete Baxter considered it a privilege to work for a man who was so dedicated to keeping the forest in pristine condition.

Pete spotted the senator's Jeep and started waving enthusiastically. Pat pulled over to find out what Pete was so excited about.

"Good morning, Senator. I've got great news!"

Pat got out of the Jeep and shook and shook his employee's hand. "Mornin', Pete. How's Mary, and that cute little boy of yours?"

"Very well, sir, thank you. I believe I'm about to improve your day. You know that mystery poacher we've been trying to catch for the past six years?"

"Yes, of course. Talk about a thorn in your side. The closest we've ever come to him was finding some innocent animal in one of his traps. He always seemed to know where we were waiting for him to show up. Don't tell me you finally caught him?"

"I wish I could claim the glory, enator, but it seems he turned him-self in. His name is Andrew Slater, and he freely admitted to poaching on your property, as well as the adjacent federally owned land."

"This is great news, Pete, but why would a man who has eluded capture for six years suddenly turn himself in? I can't help but find that a little strange, don't you?"

"You want to hear 'strange,' listen to this. I got a courtesy call from the game warden this morning. Evidently, this Slater guy came scream-ing into their office a few days ago, demanding to be arrested. He was spouting some nonsense about a ten-foot-tall demon or something, that threatened to kill him if he didn't surrender to the authorities!"

In spite of all his troubles, Pat couldn't help but laugh. "A ten-foot-tall demon, huh? That goes beyond strange, Pete. Where is this lunatic now? In a hospital, I hope?"

"Oh yes, sir. They took him away in a net. I spoke to Tom Jordan this morning, and he told me about his conversation with Slater's doctors."

"The guy is obviously off his rocker," Pat concluded.

"I certainly thought as much, but here's the really weird part. The doctor says he's calmed down since he was admitted, and hasn't men-tioned the demon again at all. It's almost as if Slater knows that stick-ing to the demon story assures him permanent residency in a rubber room. However, he did draw a detailed map of all his traps, including the one he says he was caught in. He told the doctor to pass the map on to the game warden, but, get this, he said, 'You guys can think I'm crazy, but when you find traces of *my* blood in that trap, I would like you to explain why I'm not injured!'"

"You're right, Pete. This is nothing if not strange."

"There's more, Senator. The guy passed all the psychological test-ing, with average responses. According to that, he's as normal as you or I!"

"Except for the demon thing, of course," Pat said, still amused. "If he's not crazy, then I must be."

"One more thing," Pete went on. "When he was formally charged with several counts of poaching and I-don't-know-what-else, guess what he said? 'Thank you!' He actually thanked the DA for pressing charges! Go figure that one."

"I wouldn't even try. At least we know that he's locked up and we won't find any more animals caught in those awful steel traps."

As the lighter conversation faded, Pat was reminded of his current and much more serious problem. After careful consideration, the senator decided that the right thing to do was to tell Pete the bad news. "Listen, Pete, I really hate to ruin your day, especially after you brightened up mine, but I'm afraid I must. You have been a loyal and trusted employee of this family for twelve years now, and you have a right to know."

"What is it, Senator? What's wrong?"

"I'm not going to beat around the bush, Pete. I'm just going to give it to you straight. I'm sick over this, but I have no choice. Due to a situation that appears to be far beyond my control, I'm being pressured--no, forced--to sell this land."

"What? This forest has been Walsh family land for three generations! You always said it would remain so as long as there was a Walsh left to protect it!"

It broke Pat's heart to hear the astonishment and disappointment in Pete's voice. "You have a right to be upset, and I really can't blame you." Pat swore to his employee that he had no other option. "You must understand, Pete, that for me to make a decision to give up something that means as much to me as this Shangri-la, this heaven on earth," Pat said, spreading his arms open to illustrate his point, "I must be faced with a life-or-death situation."

Pete knew his employer well enough to understand that what he was being told was the absolute truth. The enormity of the senator's problem could have international implications, and Pete understood that as well. "I'm very sorry, Senator. This has been quite a shock. Is there anything I can do to help?"

"No, I'm afraid not. Look, Pete, it will probably take a good amount of time for the deal to be finalized. I promise you, I will speak to some people I know in the Department of the Interior. They owe me a favor, to say the least. I hate to uproot your family, but I'm sure I'll find you something agreeable. Until then, I hope you won't hold this against me, and stay on as long as you are needed."

"You know I will. Maybe we'll both get lucky and this problem will work its way out."

"There's a small possibility of that happening, Pete, but I don't want to give you any false hope."

They said their goodbyes, and Pete strolled up to the barn. Pat turned the Jeep toward the main house. He sped up the dusty trail with a great sadness welling up inside him. For the first time in his life, Patrick Henry Walsh felt like a beaten man. As he approached the gate, a solitary tear rolled down the big man's face.

Chapter 31

Billy was just seven years old, the first time he saw him. It was an event that would shape his entire life, right up to and including his tumultuous retirement years.

Early one Sunday morning, Billy ran out to his tree house with a box of doughnuts and a quart of milk. He was going to have a grown-up breakfast in his own little house. It had rained the night before and the ladder was still wet. He climbed the ladder slowly, careful not to drop his breakfast. It was when he reached the very top rung of the ladder that he saw him. The little boy was so shocked that he dropped everything and nearly lost his balance. When the carton of milk careened off the ladder and hit the ground with a plop, the little form on the floor of the tree house stirred and awoke. Billy stared in disbelief at a creature he thought only existed in fairy tales! There before his eyes was a boy much older than himself, but less than three feet tall!

Billy was staring curiously, but quietly at the trespasser's large pointed ears, when the strange being jumped to his feet, clearly startled. What happened next made Billy absolutely sure that magic does indeed exist in this modern world.

As Billy climbed slowly into the narrow doorway, he noticed his surprised little stowaway clutching a necklace. The little boy approached the creature with cautious plodding steps, but when he was almost close enough to touch him, the visitor said, "I must go," and in the blink of an eye, he was gone. Vanished!

Billy was stunned, to say the least, but more than that, he was terribly disappointed. He wanted to know who, or what was in his tree house.

"Wait! Come back! I won't hurt you, I promise."

A small voice answered from the corner of the room. "How do I know I can trust you? I have been told that humans will lie."

"I'm only seven years old. I don't want to hurt anybody. Honest, mister, I just want to be your friend. Billy's young mind was running at full speed. He had to think of something to say quickly, before this magical creature disappeared forever. "Look, if I promise to keep my hands in my pockets, will you come back? Pleeeease?"

The small voice answered, "I must return," and just as suddenly as the creature disappeared, he reappeared at the far end of the room. Billy was transfixed. Here, right before him was a fairy tale come to life. Even the clothing on this tiny person was straight out of one of Billy's storybooks. The child stared at Nelkie's stocking cap, bright-red tunic, green leggings, and ankle-length shoes that were turned upward at the toe. Billy had his suspicions about what this magical little person might be, but he had to ask to be sure. "Who are you? *What* are you?"

"I am Nelkie, son of Balthazar the Master Toymaker. I am an American elf."

"You're an elf? You mean elf, like the ones that work for Santa?"

"Precisely!"

"But I thought you guys lived up at the North Pole! What are you doin' way down here? Are you lost?"

"I am not lost, I am on a quest. Many of my brother elves *do* reside at the North Pole, although you would never be able to find them. Many others have emigrated around the globe centuries ago."

"Oh. Uh, what's a quest, and what's a ema, emmag…."

Nelkie's mouth bowed into a broad smile. The pure innocence of this human child had melted his heart. Compared to his first encounter with a human, the elf was enjoying this fateful meeting. This juvenile's perception of the world was not yet clouded by the temptations that would lead someone like Andrew Slater down a crooked path. The child merely wanted to get to know and understand Nelkie. The elf hoped that as this boy child grew into manhood he retained the honesty that was already evident in his personality. Nelkie was happy to answer the boy's questions.

"A quest is a mission," he answered. "A task I have been given by my elders, and one that I must accomplish with honor. To emigrate, my curious friend, means to leave one's homeland, and make a new home in another place. Now, I would like to know who you are. What is your name?"

"I'm Billy Baxter and this is my tree house."

"This is where you live?"

"Well, not really. That's where I live," he said, pointing out the window to a large house in a clearing about a hundred yards away. "My dad built this tree house for me so I could have a little house of my own. Pretty cool, huh?"

"This is a very sound structure, Billy. Your father is a very good carpenter."

"My dad is very good at a lot of things. He knows all about trees, flowers, and all the animals in the forest. That's his job. He looks after everything that lives in the forest. The senator told me that my dad is his most valued employee."

"Who is the senator?" Nelkie asked.

"He is a very rich, very important man. He owns the whole forest!"

"How can anyone own the whole forest? The forest is for everyone to share and enjoy."

"Yes, it is, and I think that's why he pays my dad. My dad makes sure any hunters are reported. He also looks after sick trees and makes sure all the streams and ponds have clean water in them."

"That sounds to me like a very important job. Your father must be a very important man as well."

"Oh yes, very important. Look, Nelkie, I was just going to have breakfast, but I dropped the food when I saw you. Are you hungry?"

"I am, Billy."

"Well, wait here a second. I'll go back down and get the milk and doughnuts."

Nelkie realized that he was dealing with a child that posed no threat to him. At the onset of their meeting, he could take no chances. Nelkie was caught off guard and child or not, this human was more than twice his size. Now he felt that he could relax, share a meal with the boy, and get to know him.

Billy returned with the food. He took two plastic cups off the shelf and poured them each some milk. The boy put two doughnuts on a paper towel, next to each cup.

Nelkie looked at the doughnuts and then at his host. "What are these?" he asked.

"Chocolate-covered doughnuts," was the reply. Billy took a big bite and a large slug of milk, which left a white moustache over his smile.

While the younger boy ate, Nelkie opened his pouch and pulled out a small book. With a very serious look on his face, he thumbed through the pages, all the while mumbling to himself. "Chocolate, chocolate. Let me see here." He found what he was looking for right after "chives." "I don't mean to sound ungrateful, Billy, but I cannot eat chocolate. It will make me sick."

Nelkie thought it wise not to tell Billy that according to the book given to him by Wolfstan the Elder, chocolate is deadly to elves. One bite would produce sudden and certain death. Nelkie was no longer hungry.

The little boy felt badly. His new friend could not share his breakfast and Billy would feel guilty eating in front of him. "Hey, Nelkie, I have an idea. I'll run back to the house and get you some real food. We call this stuff 'junk food.' It tastes great, but it's really not very good for you. It'll make you fat. What kind of food do elves like?"

"I'm very fond of cornbread, fruit, and nuts," Nelkie answered. "I have not tasted meat for more than a week."

"No problem. We got all that stuff. I'll just be a few minutes." Billy hurried down the ladder and dashed across the yard.

Once he was in the kitchen, he stopped and listened carefully. *No sign that Mom and Dad are up yet. Good.* He set about his task. In the cupboard, he found a box of zip lock bags. He grabbed half a dozen and started foraging for his friend. Billy found his first pay dirt in the breadbox. "Here we are, corn muffins," he said aloud, and dug three out of the package. He put the muffins in a plastic bag and sealed it. Next, he rummaged through the cabinets, while carefully balancing on a chair. The boy came across a plastic bowl with a snap-on lid. Inside he found his second "prize," trail mix. "Oh boy! Nuts, raisins, and seeds. Nelkie will probably love this stuff." Into another plastic bag it went.

Now he moved on quickly to the refrigerator. *Gotta find some meat.* He opened another plastic container to find last night's spaghetti sauce. "Meatballs!" he said triumphantly. "That's meat, and really good meat." Billy got a fork and stabbed three of them, one at a time and managed to navigate them into another bag, even though they were dripping with tomato sauce. He put away the remaining evidence and scampered out the kitchen door.

The little boy ran as fast as he could back to the tree house, hoping his new friend hadn't gotten scared and run away. He called to Nelkie when he reached the ladder. "Are you still up there, Nelkie? I got some food."

"Yes," the elf answered. "Please come up."

Billy came through the small doorway to find Nelkie sipping a cup of milk. "Look! I got you everything you wanted, even meat!"

Nelkie's eyes lit up as he looked at the supply of food. His expression changed, however, when his eyes came to rest on the bag of meatballs. Nelkie stared curiously at them, and then back at Billy. "What are those?" he asked

"Meatballs!"

"Meat-balls," Nelkie repeated, still looking a little confused. "Forgive me, Billy, but I have never seen round meat. What kind of animal was that?"

Billy thought hard for a minute. He wanted to be sure he had the correct answer to such a serious question. "Uh, I think it's cow meat," he said, with a little uncertainty in his voice.

"Cow meat?" Nelkie replied. "I don't know, Billy; I don't think that's for me."

Billy Baxter couldn't believe his ears. Surely there was no living creature on earth that would not just love his mom's meatballs! "Listen, Nelkie, I'm tellin' you--they are delicious! Just try one and if you don't like it, I'll take them back."

Nelkie was not having any luck looking up meatballs in his little book. He decided that he would try a small bite. If they were not listed in his book, they probably weren't dangerous, just odd. "All right," he said. "I'll try a small piece, but what is that red-colored thing all over them?"

"Tomato sauce," Billy answered. "We usually eat this stuff heated up, but I eat cold meatball sandwiches all the time. Now here," Billy said, holding out a chunk of meatball on a fork. Nelkie took a small bite and chewed slowly.

Suddenly, the elf began to smile. Something new and wonderfully delicious had touched his taste buds. "I have never tasted anything so good," he said. "May I have some more?"

Billy slid the plastic bag across the table and said, "See? I told ya. They're great! Here, take the rest of 'em."

In no time at all, Nelkie devoured two whole meatballs. "Wow! You were right, Billy. Meat-balls are great, even if they are cow meat."

It was turning out to be a great day. Nelkie had discovered a new delicacy, and Billy had been befriended by a magical creature that until today had not existed in his world.

Nelkie crammed the remaining food into his pouch. He thanked his new friend for his kindness, after which they talked for more than an hour. Billy was spellbound as Nelkie explained his quest and told of his adventures with the wild animals of the great forest. It warmed Nelkie's heart to watch the little boy's excited face, when he told him tales of bloodthirsty wolves and a gallant stag named Rajah.

Suddenly, Nelkie's sixth sense alerted him to the presence of an intruder. "Someone approaches," he said.

Billy looked questioningly at the elf. "What?"

"Someone approaches the tree house." The elf rose to his full height. "I will stay with you, Billy, but I must not be seen." With that statement made, Nelkie touched his medallion, spoke the required words, and promptly disappeared.

"Billy? Are you up there?" a man's voice called.

"Yes, Dad. I'm just having some breakfast."

"Well, okay, but I want you back in the house in ten minutes. It's almost time to get ready for church."

"Okay, Dad, ten minutes." Billy's eyes were darting around the room, as if he thought he could see the undetectable elf if only he could focus hard enough. "Nelkie? Are you still here? That was just my dad."

Nelkie voiced the phrase "I must return," and as quickly as he had vanished, he was back.

"Boy! That really is a great trick, Nelkie. I wish I could learn to do that."

"First of all, Billy, that is no trick. What you see, or rather, don't see, is ancient knowledge, gifted to me by my elders. Of course, you must understand that most grown-ups don't believe that elves are real. I'm quite sure, my young friend, that no one outside of this room will ever believe that you even *saw* an elf, let alone witnessed his ability to disappear and reappear."

"Well, I know what I saw you do," Billy insisted, "and if nobody believes me, I still know what I saw."

"Yes, you do," the elf agreed. "You are one of the very few who have caught an elf off guard. You even have firsthand knowledge of my mission. As I explained before, I am to find something I can do for humans to improve their life situation."

"I know one human you could help with his life," Billy said.

"Who might this person be? Remember, one person, or the whole race, it makes no difference. If I can help, I will."

The little boy's expression became very serious. The transformation made him look much older than his mere seven years. "It's my dad," he said, with tears beginning to well up in his innocent eyes. "I heard Mom and Dad talking last night. It was late and I guess they didn't hear me get up to go to the bathroom. They thought I was still asleep. Anyway, Dad sounded very sad. He said he saw the senator yesterday and he had very bad news. I didn't understand all of what they talked about, but I understood the bad news part. Dad said the senator was being forced to sell the forest. I heard him tell Mom that it won't be long before they cut it all down and build some housing development for rich people."

At first, the gravity of what Nelkie heard didn't sink in, perhaps because the news was coming from a seven-year-old, who may have misinterpreted the facts. *But what if he is right?* Suddenly it hit him like a pail of water thrown in his face! "Cut it down! They can't cut it down!" Nelkie's mind was awash with visions of hundreds of his fellow elves forced out of their beloved homes. He thought of all his friends in the forest. They would all be forced to seek food and shelter somewhere else, if there was somewhere else! Many of them would surely die. His heart grew heavy when he thought of Lilly, the beautiful doe, who looked out for the elves, and they for her. Now it looked like they were all going to be refugees from the Great Redwood Forest.

Nelkie felt fear growing inside of him. It was the same sickly chill he felt when he discovered his best friend caught in a bear trap. It felt as if ice was forming around his heart, freezing him, making him unable to act. The thought of so many innocent souls torn from their homes, and their beloved forest clear-cut, was almost more than he could bear. Nelkie soon realized that he must snap out of this panic he felt. He had to gather his wits and get to the source of this terrible situation. His great and honorable quest to help humans would have to wait. He had to help his own kind first. Little did he know that at that moment, the fates of many humans, as well as those of all the forest dwellers, were becoming significantly intertwined.

"Look, Billy, I can't make you any promises because I don't have all the facts yet, but I will do whatever I can to help."

"Will you talk to the senator and tell him not to sell?"

"I don't know yet what I'll do, but I promise you I will use all the power I can summon from the elders to make sure the forest remains as it is today."

"I can help you, Nelkie. Just tell me what to do."

"First I need to know where the senator lives. I must go to his house and see what I can learn."

"That's easy," the boy replied. "Do you remember passing a duck pond, a little way back in the woods?"

"Yes. Back about a mile or so. If memory serves me, there was a stand of weeping willows at one end of that pond."

"Yeah, that's it. If you walk around behind those willows, you'll see a path. My dad and I have hiked up to the main house that way. It takes about a half hour."

"Good. I'll go at once. Try not to worry, Billy. I'll find out what I can. I promise I will get back to you in no more than a few days."

"Will you shake on it?" Billy asked, offering the elf his hand.

"Of course, my friend," Nelkie said, taking the boy's hand and shaking it with conviction. "My father told me long ago that an elf is only as good as his word. You have my word, Billy, that you will hear my voice again. Now, you had better go back to your house and get ready for church. Your mother and father are expecting you."

"Yeah, I know," Billy said, staring at the floor. "I really want to go with you, Nelkie. I know I can help you."

"I'm sure you could too," Nelkie agreed, "but I'm not sure it would be safe. Besides, your parents would miss you. I would like to keep you out of trouble, in case I need your help later on."

"Okay, Nelkie. I'll go to church, but I won't like it. See you in a couple of days." The seven-year-old carefully climbed down the ladder and ran across the back yard.

Nelkie waited until Billy had gone into the house. He touched the stone in his necklace, spoke the required phrase, and started down the ladder, invisible to the world.

Chapter 32

The warm spring sun was rising higher in the sky. Nelkie looked up and figured that if Billy's directions were correct, he could expect to have the senator's house in sight by noon.

He marched along at a quick pace. His mission had taken a new direction and now there was a sense of urgency driving him to obtain information as soon as possible. He could not formulate a plan of action, other than to remain invisible and get close enough to the humans to actually *hear* them. Maybe the facts would become clear to him through their conversation.

After a short while he arrived at the duck pond. *Ah, there are the willows.* Quickly, he made his way around the pond until he came to a well-traveled path. "This must be it," he said aloud. Nelkie started up the path filled with nervous anticipation. Although the elf was much smaller than his seven-year-old friend and had much shorter strides, he came upon a clearing in only about twenty minutes.

As the woods thinned before him, Nelkie could see a large bright-green lawn straight ahead. Silently, he walked out of the woods and stopped. The sight of the senator's enormous log home was spectacular. He stood motionless for a long moment, taking it all in.

Between Nelkie and the house was an Olympic-sized swimming pool surrounded by a flagstone patio. At the far end of the pool there was a building that was open in the center, except for the roof that connected changing rooms at either end. As he walked by the open area, Nelkie tried to make sense of the complete kitchen and fireplace.

He thought maybe the humans held some kind of religious feast here that had something to do with fire and water.

Beyond the pool, Nelkie was only about twenty-five yards from a patio area at the back of the house. As he drew nearer, he remembered his father's warning always to be aware of his surroundings. He stopped to visually survey the patio area.

The custom-cut stone patio was about twenty feet wide and forty feet long. A green canopy extended from the house to cover almost half the area. Just outside the perimeter stood a twelve-foot tall hand-carved totem pole. The elaborate piece of Native American art was a gift from a grateful tribe that the senator helped to receive federal recognition. Nelkie was studying the house when he noticed movement behind the windows. He was trying to focus on the two figures inside when his sixth sense warned him that someone was entering his immediate area. His ears then picked up a kind of jingling noise. Nelkie turned in the direction of the intrusion.

At that moment, a full-grown black Great Dane came trotting around the corner of the house, his license and ID tags jingling away. Nelkie held his breath. This dog was almost as big as Lily the doe, and could easily tear him to shreds. The elf was frozen in his tracks, desperately hoping this monster would just wander away.

Nature betrayed him. A light spring breeze carried Nelkie's scent to the dog's sensitive nose. The second the Great Dane was aware of the new scent, he began to snarl. Nelkie had only a second or two to make a decision. He turned and leaped onto the totem pole.

Now that he had made a noise, the dog knew *exactly* where he was. Nelkie scrambled up the totem pole with one hand clutching his walking stick and the other pulling him higher. The dog was now in a frenzy. He had reached the pole and was alternately snarling and barking. The brute tried in vain to climb up after his prey. Nelkie had made it to the top of the pole and was straddled across its uppermost head. The black beast was on its hind legs, jumping and biting at Nelkie's scent. The totem pole was starting to move under the huge dog's weight. Nelkie hung on as the pole began to teeter.

Suddenly, the back door opened and a woman in a tennis dress ran across the patio, yelling at the dog. "Samson! Get down! Are you crazy? What on Earth are you after?" she said, grabbing the dog's collar.

The dog would not relent. He was reacting like a hungry shark that smelled blood. After about twenty seconds, the one hundred twenty pound woman knew she was not going to win a tug-of-war with a 160-pound Great Dane. She turned to call for help, but Pat and Albert were already on the patio.

In his best loud and authoritative voice, Pat commanded his dog. "Samson! Down!"

Hearing his master's voice, the huge animal obeyed. He was still looking up at the pole, but now he was only whimpering.

"I'll take him down to the kennel, Mrs.," Albert said. He took a firm grip on Samson's collar and walked him toward the fenced in area south of the house. The big dog did not go willingly. He was still crying and looking backward over his shoulder, but he allowed Albert to lead him away.

Pat and his wife stood on the patio, staring blankly at the totem pole, as if they were waiting for it to explain what had just happened. Barbara spoke first. "I don't understand. Samson has been walking past that thing for six years and never gave it a glance. Today, he decides to attack it?"

"I wish I could give you an explanation, Barb, but I don't get it either. Anyway, we have bigger fish to fry. Come inside. We have to talk." Pat held open the screen door and then followed his wife inside.

As soon as Nelkie felt he could climb down without being heard, he carefully descended. Albert came around the corner of the house as Nelkie was crossing the patio. He opened the door and went in, with Nelkie almost on his heels. Once inside the family room, Nelkie stopped to quickly survey the room and its occupants. He figured out who the senator was, and the woman in the tennis dress must be his wife. He guessed correctly that the man he followed into the house was an employee.

There was a third man in the room, dressed in casual clothes. Nelkie figured that if he could remain undiscovered, he would find out who the third man was, and possibly a lot more.

All three men looked more than a little uncomfortable when Barbara initiated conversation. She directed her remarks to her husband. "Pat, I know something is terribly wrong. I knew when R.J. arrived looking so stone-faced, and the three of you sequestered yourselves in the study for two hours. Now are you going to tell me what's wrong, or do I have to guess?"

"I'm sorry, Barb. I was really hoping I would tell you about this in the *past* tense, but I became aware of this problem only last night and I haven't been able to get to the bottom of it yet. Things have escalated quickly, and I need to bring you into the loop."

Nelkie thanked his elfin luck. It appeared that his timing could not have been better. From his vantage point near the door he could sit on the floor and see, as well as hear, everyone in the room.

Pat continued. "I'm afraid we have a couple of very serious problems." The senator explained to his wife about finding his office door open at 9:00 p.m., after leaving Anne and Albert in the lobby. "While they were having dinner, I was being confronted by an armed thug who left me the DVD you're about to watch." Pat nodded to Albert, who started the video.

Every eye in the room, including Nelkie's, was focused on the TV, as the tanker truck turned around in the meadow.

"Hey, what's going on here?" Barbara asked. "Isn't that one of the new fleet of trucks you bought to service the chemical waste hauling contract?"

"The very same," Pat answered. "I'm afraid this is where it gets ugly."

Barbara watched in horror as the dark figure opened the release valve and emptied thousands of gallons of toxic chemical waste onto the unspoiled forest floor. She looked at her husband and then at Albert, her expression one of anger and confusion. "How could this be?" she asked. "None of our drivers would commit such a heinous act! Don't we require a background check and references before we hire for these positions?"

"Yes, our company requires a minimum of five years hazmat experience, along with a clean license, and references. *That guy* is not a Walsh trucker. We found out the truck was hijacked about five miles from the chemical plant. There was a staged accident. Our driver stopped to help, and was jumped by four men. Three of them abducted our driver and held him until they could make this video, and ditch the truck. He was released the next day, unharmed. Unfortunately he couldn't give much help to the police. All his abductors wore masks and spoke very little."

"What do these people want, Pat?"

"You'd better sit down, Babs; I'm afraid it only gets worse from here." The senator could not think of any gentle way to break the news of Tommy's kidnapping, so he made it short and to the point. He narrated the scene in the meadow, where the Arab informed him that their son was being held captive. Barbara Walsh was used to dealing with political and business problems of international scope, but this had caught her off guard and unprepared. She felt blindsided. Normally, whenever she was faced with a difficult problem, Barbara's "deal with it" personality would quickly and efficiently analyze the problem and come up with viable options. This time it was different. This time, it was her son. Her brain blasted into overdrive, trying to find an immediate answer to a problem that did not have one. "Oh God, what do we do now? Have you spoken to the FBI or the Secret Service? Who has jurisdiction here?"

"Okay, slow down. One thing at a time. I called R.J. last night, as soon as that little thug left the building. I didn't think it was a good idea to have FBI and Secret Service people stepping all over one another, and turning our home into some kind of crime-fighting carnival. We need to keep things calm here, so we can think this out and make rational decisions. Now, that being said, R.J. has been on this from the get-go. He has several of his best men looking for Tommy as we speak." Pat took a deep breath and then went on to tell his wife of his decision to sell. "I must fly back to Washington tomorrow, and I imagine whoever is behind this will contact me there." Nodding to the investigator across the room, he continued to bring Barbara up to speed on the developments. "R.J. will continue to concentrate on finding out where Tommy is being held. If he cannot be found by the time I have to sign the contracts and go through with the sale, he is to back off. We all agree that Tommy's safe return is the only objective here."

"Of course I agree with you, Pat, and I understand now that you didn't say anything about Tommy last night because you didn't have all the facts yet." Her voice was beginning to crack with emotion as she got up from the couch and walked toward the fireplace. She needed to turn her back to the men in the room. Her eyes were welling up, and she did not want them to know she might be losing her composure. There was, however, one male in the room who witnessed her momentary breakdown.

Nelkie had remained seated on a corner of the raised hearth, safely isolated from the group. Or so he thought. As Barbara approached the fireplace, the elf was taken by surprise. He dared not move for fear of making a noise and being discovered, but this woman was coming right at him. If she didn't stop within the next three feet, she would step on him! Nelkie held his breath as Barbara came to a halt directly over him. He knew he was invisible to everyone in the room, but Barbara was directly over him, looking down with tear-soaked eyes. He was starting to think, *Maybe she can see me,* when a single tear rolled off her face, and splashed down on Nelkie's cheek. That one tear brought with it an ocean of pain and fear, washing over Nelkie's heart with the force of a hurricane. The sympathy that poured out of the elf for these good people had elevated his quest from something he was assigned to do to something he was now *compelled* to do.

From the moment the elf saw toxic chemicals being dumped deliberately in his beloved forest, Nelkie was in a state of shock. This act was an abomination! The human equivalent of what he was feeling would be that of a priest watching his church burn to the ground. It was a sacrilege! Anger was an emotion new to Nelkie, and he did not like it. Instinctively, he knew this was a negative and destructive force, and he fought to get past it. When Barbara broke down, overcome with fear for her son's life, Nelkie's eyes welled up with tears of compassion. *So this is what the wise ones warned me about. There are evil ones who will destroy all that is good in order to achieve their unprincipled goals. I must remain calm and gather all the facts. I need more information to formulate a plan to defeat these evil ones, whoever they may be.*

Barbara had calmed herself to the point where she could speak without losing her composure, but she was clearly still upset and visibly shaken. She agreed with her husband that they had no choice but to concede to the demands imposed on them, unless Tommy could be safely extracted. "R.J., wouldn't the people behind this plot be exposed, once the deal is finalized? Won't we know who they are?"

"I wish it were that simple, Barb. Whoever is behind this is no dope. It would appear that this person knows something of politics and the law. We all know that the tide of public opinion can turn with the commission of one disagreeable act, or in some cases, just the suspicion of wrongdoing. Even though Pat's current approval rating is in the upper eighties, if that video goes public, he will be crucified. Americans will hold Pat responsible for the illegal dumping. In the meantime, it will take years to sort through the holding companies, limited partnerships, and dummy corporations, which in turn generate mountains of paperwork and legal mumbo-jumbo. By the time we find out who actually bought the land, the mastermind of this plot will be living somewhere out of our reach, happily counting his millions from the sale of all that redwood."

Albert spoke while he was setting up the surveillance footage from the federal building. "These people, whoever they are, are professional thugs and swindlers if nothing else. Is there anything we can do, R.J.?"

"Yes, Albert. We are not completely in the dark. The surveillance video revealed a clear close-up of the Arab fleeing the building. I called some people I know at Interpol, and they have given me a positive ID on this guy. His name is Mohammad Abdul Salaam. He is an Iraqi national and a freelance terrorist. Salaam holds no allegiance to any country. Strictly mercenary. He will work for anyone who will pay his price. According to my sources, he's known in the trade as 'the stiletto,' and is suspected of being involved in, or responsible for, at least half a dozen assassinations. He's a ruthless character, this one. I have several agents trying to ferret him out, as we speak. I believe he is the one who can, and will, eventually lead us to Tommy."

Nelkie sat motionless on the floor, quietly absorbing all that he saw and heard. He started this day with the intention of trying to help someone keep his job. The challenge seemed simple enough to rectify, given enough information. Certainly there was no danger involved. Now, less than two hours later, he had stumbled onto an extortion plot and a kidnapping. Up until this very moment, Nelkie always thought that he would skip through his quest. The knowledge the elders had given him would protect him. He would put in the required time, impart some elfin wisdom to the humans, and get back to his life in the treetops. Nelkie, like all young elves, had led a sheltered and protected life. He was raised in a society where no one stole, no one envied, and no one ever experienced despondency. Greed, ambition, violence, sorrow, and suffering were just words. He understood their meaning, but now it was the *depth* of that meaning that had become evident on the faces of Barbara and Pat Walsh. When one can actually see people enduring pain and suffering, the effect can be contagious.

Now he understood that life in the world of humans was not at all that simple. There was no doubt that the next decision Nelkie made could place his quest, and even his life, in grave danger. However, his heart ached for these good people who were being forced into submission. His eyes welled up with sympathetic tears when he watched Barbara Walsh try to fight off the fear that she might never see her only son alive again. The good senator, who had just received an award for *his* selflessness, was trying to console her. The elf saw in these humans the same virtues he learned from his parents and from the wisdom of his elders. Surely these were humans of exceptional character. He could not stand by and watch these people suffer. Although he was not yet sure how, he knew he could help them, and so the decision was made. Now the elf set about creating a plan of action. *Somehow, I must find out where the senator's son is being held. Once I know that, I'm sure I can successfully affect his escape. More than that, I must find out who has hired this Salaam person, and expose him and this evil plot. All this must be accomplished with great haste, before the evil ones turn the world as I know it upside down!*

Chapter 33

Emil Stanfield exited the squash court at the Downtown Sportsman's Club. He had perpetrated another punishing victory over his lawyer, Phil Morton. As usual, he was gloating. "You're gonna have to play harder than that, if you want to win, Phil. A four-point total over three games is pretty bad, even for you!"

Phil was so exhausted he could hardly walk. The truth was he *had* played as hard as he knew how. His face was beet-red. His headband was so heavy with sweat; it had started to sink down over his eyebrows. "It wouldn't have been so one-sided if you didn't play like an obsessed madman," Phil complained.

"I've told you before, Counselor, for all intents and purposes, our friendship is over when we walk onto this court. It doesn't resume again until we walk off. I play to win, in sports and in life. Winning at a competitive sport, to me, is the equivalent of getting into a bar brawl in a rough-and-tumble biker bar. I feel good after I kick some butt."

Phil Morton really wanted to tell his boss what he thought of him. He dreamed of saying, "Emil, you're a ruthless, greedy, self-important man without a hint of a conscience," but Phil Morton was not ready to kiss a quarter of a million dollars in annual legal fees good-bye… at least not yet. This was the case with most of Stanfield's associates. They were all willing to put up with his merciless and unforgiving business practices because he made them money. More often than not, big money.

Emil Stanfield was a shrewd businessman, who built his financial empire over a foundation of small businesses he either bought and sold for huge profits, or crushed out of competition through price wars or frivolous lawsuits that his competition could not afford. The word "compassion" was not in his vocabulary.

Stanfield was out of the shower and almost fully dressed by 7:20 a.m. He loved starting his day with an early-morning conquest. It charged him up. It reassured him of his power over the average man. This morning in particular, he was exceptionally wired. He had a 9:00 a.m. appointment in his office with the owner of High Sierra Log Homes. The cold and unyielding hand of Emil Stanfield was about close around the neck of yet another unsuspecting CEO.

Through the network of corporate spies he kept on retainer, Stanfield was able to find out that the Chief Executive Officer, Percy Lambert, had been involved in a tragic hunting accident six years ago. Lambert had taken his office manager, Donald Ferris, on a hunting trip. They had mistakenly wandered onto privately owned land. According to the police report, Ferris claimed sole responsibility for the sorrowful catastrophe that followed.

While unaware that he was trespassing, Ferris committed the most foolish, and sadly, one of the most common mistakes made by inexperienced hunters. Seeing movement in a thick clump of bushes, Ferris fired his rifle in a kneejerk reaction, without any visual confirmation of his target.

The two hunters didn't know that three young boys were playing hide and seek, only fifty yards from their parents' weekend cabin. They were horrified when they came around behind the underbrush to find the lifeless body of a nine-year-old boy.

Ferris pled guilty to criminally negligent homicide. He got off lightly, considering the nature of his crime. He had no criminal record, not so much as a speeding ticket. Ferris was a model citizen and a deacon of his church. He received a five-year sentence.

Stanfield's investigators thought it a little more than odd that having done his time, Ferris was hired back by Lambert at a much higher position. Right out of prison, Ferris assumed the post of district manager for Sierra Homes at three times his previous salary. This did not sit well with the investigative staff, so they dug deeper.

It wasn't long before they located Ferris's former cellmate, who told them what they suspected all along. In a jailhouse confession, Ferris admitted that it was Lambert who fired the fatal shot. The bad publicity would have ruined Lambert's business and Percy was not someone who could survive in jail. He cut a deal with his young office manager. In return for taking the fall for his boss, Donald Ferris would be richly rewarded.

With time off for good behavior, Ferris was out on probation in three and a half years. At only thirty-eight, he had many years ahead of him in which to enjoy his boss's generosity. After Stanfield's efficient staff waved a check for $30,000 in front of Ferris's former cellmate, he agreed to sign a witnessed affidavit, detailing the jailhouse confession. This signed and sworn document was in Emil Stanfield's pocket as he strode gleefully out of his private elevator. He poured himself a mug of black coffee and sat down behind his large and imposing oak desk. Smiling, he sat back and waited for the 9:00 fly to enter his web.

At 9:04, Stanfield's secretary announced Percy Lambert. Lambert walked into the private office suite with a broad smile and an outstretched hand. "Good morning, Mr. Stanfield. It's a pleasure to finally meet you." Lambert mistakenly thought that since his business was doing so well and had recently expanded into the midwestern states, that Stanfield was about to offer either a generous buy-out, or a very profitable merger. He was dead wrong. Percy Lambert was smiling at the most brutally calculating, evil man he would ever meet.

Stanfield ignored the offered handshake and stared coldly into the eyes of his prey. "Let's skip the small talk and get right down to it, shall we?" He tossed the affidavit across the desk. "I think you should read this before anything else is said."

Lambert's expression had changed instantly from one of warm friendship to confused disappointment. He opened the envelope and began to read. Within a few moments, all the color drained from his face. He began to sweat.

"What does this mean? Why did you give this to me? It's all a pack of lies, you know. Someone must be trying to make me look bad... none of this is true."

Now Stanfield was smiling. He could tell by Lambert's shaky voice and defensive body language that it was time to move in for the kill.

"Maybe they are all lies," he said. "Hopefully, no one will ever know."

"What on earth is that supposed to mean?"

"I am happy to explain," he said, tossing another stack of papers across the desk. "It means, you will sign these contracts by noon tomorrow, or you will see your face on CNN tomorrow night--and not in a flattering light, I might add."

Lambert was shaking so badly he had to put the contract down on the desk, in order to read it. "Why, this is ridiculous! You're offering me twenty cents on the dollar! My company is worth millions! I don't have to sit here and take this!"

"Percy, Percy," Stanfield said, still smiling. "I don't think you fully understand what I've been telling you. I am a well-connected man, and I've documented everything here. This is no schoolboy threat. If these contracts are not signed by you and on my desk by noon tomorrow, I will fax that affidavit to a friend, who is a senior vice president at C.N.N. You will be national news by 11:00 p.m., and a household name by Wednesday morning. The way I figure, your sales will start slipping immediately and in six months, you'll be bankrupt. On the other hand, look at the bright side. Sign the contracts and you will still garner several hundred thousand dollars. With a little hard work and the right investments, you may be able to regain your fortune." Stanfield knew Lambert's only choice was to give in to his terms. If he did not, the news story would effectively assassinate his character as well as his business. Emil Stanfield reveled in the crushing victory, as he ended his oratory by mocking, then dismissing the helpless Lambert. "I will guarantee you that once the sale is final, your *good name* will be kept scandal- free. It's your call, Percy. Noon tomorrow, or *news* tomorrow night. Now take those contracts and get out!"

Percy Lambert got up and silently left the suite in an extreme state of shock. Twenty minutes ago, he was anticipating the deal of a lifetime, and now his entire life had collapsed like the proverbial house of cards.

Emil Stanfield had successfully beaten another power broker into woeful submission. He sat back, and lit a cigar in celebration.

The pieces of his plan were all falling into place. Once the senator yielded his forest land, the redwood sales would bring in millions, and he could build log homes out of what was left. His newly formed Rocky Mountain Resorts Company would begin building a playground for the ultra-rich, as soon as the land was cleared. His lifelong goal of becoming a billionaire was at last within his grasp, and the beauty of it all was that the goal would be reached at the expense of Patrick Henry Walsh III! *God, this is sweet. After thirty years, I'm finally gonna get even with that spoiled rich kid.* He put his feet up on the desk and calmly blew smoke rings at the ceiling.

Just then, his secretary's voice jarred him back to his present reality. "Mr. Stanfield, Mr. Morton is here to see you."

"Send him right in."

Phil Morton lumbered in, still looking like he was out of breath. "Emil, we have to talk about your growing empire."

"Why, Phil? What's the problem?"

"Well, first of all, here are the pertinent papers on your latest acquisition. You are now the proud owner of the Handy Houseman Handyman Service. We have franchised business in thirty-four states, and we are growing. Speaking of growing, you now own so many corporations that own companies that sell franchises, that have limited partnerships, and so on, that your financial portfolio has become an auditor's nightmare!"

"What are you driving at, Phil? Get to the point--I'm a busy man, and I don't have time for trivialities. That's what I pay you for."

"All I'm trying to say is that the way you have insisted I set up your affairs is extremely complicated. There are a lot of easier ways to do this, you know. If I ever had to prove in court that you owned all this, it would take the rest of my life!"

"That's the way I like it."

"Now wait a minute, Emil. I've worked for you for more than twenty years, and as far as I know, we haven't broken any laws; yet. It's been my experience, however, that a set-up like yours is usually designed to hide something. I have to ask you now, are any of these companies you own involved in anything illegal?"

"Of course not, you fool! Look, Phil, I've made you a very wealthy man. Is this how you show me your gratitude? It's because you work for me that you drive that hundred-thousand-dollar car home to your two-million-dollar house! You're supposed to be a hotshot lawyer; do you see anything illegal?"

"Well, no, but I don't know if I have all the information I should have to be sure."

"You know all you need to know. Just do your job, and everything will go on just as it has for all these years. Make sure your associates get all my taxes paid, and get me as many write-offs as possible. Especially the high-profile charitable contributions. I want my public image to be one of a philanthropist, not someone trying to avoid giving his money back to Uncle Sam in taxes."

"Okay, you're the boss. I'll do it your way, but you should know that it's costing you three or four times as much to keep track of things, under the current system."

"Yeah, yeah. Just do it and let me worry about the cost, okay?"

"All right, fine. Look, I have to file your lawsuit against Cookie's Take-Out Restaurants today. Do you plan on owning that chain also?"

"No. I plan on bankrupting Cookie's with legal fees, over the next couple of years. That will give my own chain of take-out stores a bigger chunk of the market," he said, with pride.

"Nice strategy," Morton answered, with more than a note of sarcasm. "I'll let you know how it goes." Phil picked up his briefcase and walked out, wondering what kind of man would go out of his way to bankrupt a family business. Cookie's started as one mom-and-pop barbeque stand, thirty years ago. They now had twenty stores in three states. If Emil Stanfield had his way, "Mom and Pop" would be in their seventies and on welfare. Morton could not help questioning the wisdom of working for such an obsessed and heartless man.

Stanfield was on the phone as soon as Morton left. He dialed the Arab's cell. "Salaam, move the package to location two this evening. Get back to me as soon as it is secure."

"Consider it done."

Emil hung up, very pleased with how his day was going. *Now let's see...Senator Pat should be flying back to Washington about now. I think I'll let him stew another day or two before I have Salaam pay him another little visit. Anything I can do to prolong the pain just tickles me to death.* A bellowing baritone laugh that could have belonged to the devil himself echoed through the office suite, as Emil Stanfield got on with the day's work.

Chapter 34

The meeting in the Walsh family room was winding down. R.J. announced his departure. "I really should be going. I have field agents to check in with and a million other details to attend to. Pat, you have my private number. You know I'm available at any hour, even if you only have a question, so please don't hesitate to call. Barb, I know this is very scary, but believe me, I *know* they won't hurt Tommy and risk blowing the whole deal. This buys us a little more time and increases our chances of finding your son."

"Thank you, R.J. I have every confidence that you and your agency will do everything possible to bring Tommy home. Pat and I trust your judgment implicitly. We know you're doing the best you can, and we can ask no more than that."

All four of them walked out to R.J.'s Land Rover. After several goodbyes and thank yous, R.J. climbed in, waved and headed for the main gate. Pat turned to face his wife. He saw the stress etched across Barbara's face and made a suggestion. "Ya know, Babs, I think a long walk would do us a whole lotta good."

"I agree. We can do nothing for now but wait. We have always done our best thinking when surrounded by the peace and serenity of the woodland. Let's go." She took her husband's hand in hers and they started off down their favorite trail. Pat called to Albert over his shoulder. "Hold down the fort, Piston. We'll be back in an hour or two."

"Will do. I think I'm gonna curl up with a good book. I'll be down at the cabin if you need me." Pat waved as the couple melted into the lush greenery.

Nelkie had waited until everyone was outside before he even attempted to move. He thought if it was safe enough, he really wanted to explore the house. Nelkie felt that he might learn more about the Walsh family by observing their home. The pictures on the walls, photos, and personal memorabilia scattered throughout the house would help him understand more about who Pat and Barbara Walsh really were.

Several photographs on the mantle showed the Walsh's with their kids, in various stages of childhood. Nelkie took special note of the photos of Tommy and committed them to memory. Along the wall, above a buffet table, were pictures of Pat and Barbara with dozens of heads of state, two Popes and the last four Presidents of the United States.

I guess little Billy was right when he said the senator was a very important man, Nelkie mused. *It would appear he is well-known and respected by rulers the world over!*

While the elf could still hear the humans talking outside, he strolled down the main hallway, remaining invisible for his own security. The first room he came upon was the library. Nelkie was familiar with many of the books and was impressed with the eclectic collection. The Walsh library housed everything from Grimm's Fairy tales to John Grisham, Charles Dickens to Charles Schultz. Many were signed first editions. Nelkie wished he could spend a few hours thumbing through some of these treasures, but alas, there were more important things awaiting his attention.

The elf walked across the hall and slowly, silently, opened a door. He stood in the doorway of a game room, evaluating and interpreting what he saw. He recognized the pool and ping-pong tables as vehicles for human recreation, but the room contained many large items that were new to him. After carefully shutting the door, he walked over to one of these machines to investigate. It appeared to be some kind of game, but the playing surface was far above Nelkie's head. He pulled over a chair and climbed up to have a look. At this time, the energy projected from Nelkie's medallion manifested itself in the immediate disappearance of the chair he was standing on. Although momentarily stunned at this, he realized that there were many things he had yet to learn about his newly gained abilities. He knew now that when in a state of invisibility, anything he touched would disappear from view as well. He would soon become aware that this applied to everything up to and including objects as large as a full-sized Lincoln Town Car! Nelkie shrugged his shoulders and made a mental note. Since he was alone in the room, the fact that everything he touched temporarily disappeared didn't seem important right now.

Standing over the game, he could now clearly see colorful illustrations of jugglers and circus clowns on the playing area. There were five shiny steel balls in a channel to his right. While leaning over the machine to get a closer look, Nelkie absentmindedly touched the playing area to steady his balance and accidentally hit the "on" button.

Without warning, bells started ringing on the tote board in front of him, spinning numbers wildly, while making an alarming "thugga thugga" sound that pounded painfully into the elf's sensitive ears.

At the same moment, Albert was about to enter the library across the hall. The activation of the pinball machine shattered the stillness of the empty house like a mirror falling off the wall. The ex-fighter was physically jolted by the loud breach of the peace. He ducked as if to avoid an invisible punch. Steadying himself against the wall, he turned his attention to the game room.

Nelkie, also stunned by the sudden explosion of noise, thrust himself backward, hoping that if he got off the machine, the noise would stop. This movement was pure reflex and affected his balance. The chair went out from under him, and the elf fell back onto the playing surface of the adjacent pool table. Falling backward, with nothing to grasp, or to break his fall, Nelkie smacked his head on the hard slate tabletop with such force that he blacked out.

Albert had opened the door to the game room not knowing what to expect. The ex-fighter stood in the doorway in a state of total confusion. He was a street-smart-no-nonsense-guy. What he saw was not supposed to happen in his logical-thinking, black-or-white-world.

The ex-fighter had been standing in the game room doorway when a chair near one of the pinball machines seemed to fall over backward, all by itself. An instant later, there was a slight thud coming from the vicinity of the pool table. Suddenly, to Albert's utter astonishment, the entire pool table vanished! A quick, but thorough observation of the room convinced him that he was alone…or was he? While he was trying to figure out how or why an eight-foot pool table could just disappear, Albert thought he heard a groan. *That sounded like it came from where the pool table was.* He walked over to investigate, and promptly walked mid-stride into the pool table. "Whut the?" Thrusting his hands out in front of him, as if he were a blind man, Albert felt the cushion, and hand over hand, walked around the table, all the while feeling it, but not *seeing* it. "Oh, this is just too weird," he said aloud. Not knowing why, he ran his hands across the playing surface and was almost startled out of his shoes! His hands touched what he thought was a baby, or maybe a small child, but at the same instant, Albert's hands, arms, and entire body disappeared! Terrified, he jumped back, letting go of the tiny form on the table. In less time than it took to blink, his body became visible again. "My God, what's goin' on here?" He looked around the empty game room as if he expected an answer to come from the walls. The confused chauffeur inched closer to the unseen pool table. He touched, let go, and retouched the little body several times like he was trying to lift a hot dish out of a microwave oven. Each time he watched himself vanish and then reappear in a nanosecond. Albert was at a total loss for an explanation. He felt like he had fallen through a tear in the fabric of reality and landed in a void where nothing made any sense. *Is this whut it's like when you really lose it? When you actually go nuts for real? Nah....If I was really crazy, I wouldn't be worried about it, I'd just be crazy. Well then, if I'm not crazy, this must really be happenin' and there must be an explanation for it!*

Another faint groan came from the tabletop. Determined to get to the bottom of the situation, he seized the tiny body, lifted it into a seated position, and held it in a bear hug from behind.

Nelkie was slowly returning to consciousness and found himself at a severe disadvantage. He was immobilized--and worse, he couldn't see who or what had this hold on him. His arms were pinned against his body, preventing him from reaching his medallion, which he thought might be a bad idea anyway. The irony of the situation was most annoying. To be blind and immobile as a result of using a tool that was designed to protect him was very frustrating. He had no way of knowing who was holding him captive, or what possibility there was for escape. Right now, his only hope was to try to talk his way out of this situation.

"Let me go!"

"Not a chance, pallie-- not until you tell me who you are, what you're doing in the senator's house, and whut's up with the disappearing act!"

"My name is Nelkie. I am the son of Balthazar the Master Toymaker. I am an American elf."

"Yeah, yeah; and I'm Rosie, the Queen of Corona. Come off it, half-pint. Are you a midget, or whut? Is this some kind of publicity stunt? 'Cause if it is, your timin' couldn't be worse. C'mon, out with it, little guy; whut's goin' on here?"

"If you let me go, I will render myself visible and be happy to answer all that you ask. You don't have to feel threatened; I will not hurt you. You have my word."

"Threatened? You gotta be kiddin'. Nobody your size is gonna make me feel threatened unless he's holdin' a gun on me."

"Then why won't you let me go? Don't you think it would be better if you could see who you're dealing with?"

"Okay, okay…but don't try anything funny." Albert let go of the elf and stood between Nelkie and the door, with his arms folded across his chest. Nelkie spoke the required phrase and reappeared, still seated on the pool table. Albert never expected to see a youngster with a huge mop of red hair, pointed ears, and very odd clothing. Stunned as he was, he showed no emotion and maintained his authoritarian air.

"Okay, short stuff, start talking. What are you, a circus clown? How did you get in the house?"

"I followed you in, after you led that four-legged monster away from the totem pole. Thank you for that. I thought my quest was about to come to a violent end after he chased me up there."

"So! It was you that set Samson off! At least *that* makes sense. All right, now, before I lose what few marbles I have left, start talking. You can start by explaining the costume. What did you do, run away from the circus?"

"I didn't run away from anywhere. I am here on a quest. I am here to help."

"Help who?"

"Billy Baxter's father, the senator, his missing son, all of you," the elf said, matter-of-factly.

"Forgive me, half-pint, but how is a midget gonna help the senator?"

"I am not a midget. I told you, I am an American elf. I have been empowered by the Circle of Elders, and I am prepared to help find and rescue Senator Walsh's son.

"Look, sonny, I don't know who you think you're dealing with here, but let me clue you in. I'm a former world-class prizefighter, and a former drunk. I'm a pretty rough customer, and I don't believe in elves, or Santa Claus. So, you had better come up with a better story real quick, or I'll hand your young butt over to the Secret Service. Those boys don't think too fondly of anyone entering the home of a United States senator, without being asked. Now, let's have the truth."

Nelkie hopped off the table, shaking his head. "I have told you the truth. You humans certainly are strange creatures. I stand before you, in the flesh, and yet, you still deny my existence!"

"It's not your existence I deny, it's your story.

"Okay, let me try something else that may convince you." Nelkie picked up his walking stick that had rolled under the pinball machine. Albert barely gave it a second look. What appeared to him to be a three-foot-long broom handle with a doorknob on top of it did not present a threat.

The elf held out his stick in the direction of the now *visible* pool table. He reached out with his free hand, making a grasping motion. Albert chuckled to himself as he watched a look of extreme concentration come over Nelkie's face. He was sure this was a put-on.

Suddenly, Albert heard the familiar clacking sound of billiard balls hitting one another. His attention now drawn to the pool table, Albert saw the balls rise out of each pocket, and then float over the middle of the table, and start to spin in a circular motion with such speed that they seemed to form one large ball. He stole a quick look at Nelkie, whose arms were now spinning wildly about his head. The look on the elf's face was intensely serious. Albert began to feel a little unnerved, and turned his gaze back to the spinning billiard balls. As he did so, the cue ball became separated from the pack. The white ball rotated around the pack, looking much like a planetary mobile, with the moon spinning around a model of the Earth. The difference was that only Nelkie's will held everything suspended above the table.

Before Albert could say anything, the elf brought the entire spinning mass to rest on the table. The balls were arranged as if they had been racked, with the cue ball at the opposite end of the table. As Albert took a step closer, Nelkie mentally set the cue ball in motion and sent the racked balls flying around the table at a dizzying rate of speed. Albert stood open-mouthed as every ball on the table, except the cue ball, found a pocket.

"I gotta admit, little guy, that was quite a trick, but it still don't prove nothin'. You're a pretty good magician, or illusionist, or whatever, but that's all. A trick is not gonna make me believe in elves or Santa Claus; I wasn't born yesterday."

Nelkie looked the ex-fighter in the eye and realized he was going about this the wrong way. This guy was convinced that Nelkie was no more than a sub-sized human magician. "Can I ask you a question Mr....Ah...?"

"Parker, Albert Parker, and you better make it a good one, shorty, cause you're about one minute from bein' arrested."

"I understand, Mr. Parker. Let me ask you this. Can you remember a Christmas when you were young, perhaps six or seven years old, when you may have discovered a present under your tree that no one could explain?"

"What do you mean?"

"Think back. Think real hard, Mr. Parker. Maybe you wished for a scooter or a sled, and there it was on Christmas morning, only your parents didn't buy it for you."

Albert didn't see the point in all this, but he couldn't help remembering the good Christmases, before his father became an alcoholic. All of a sudden, Albert's eyes widened with recognition. "Wait a minute! Nah, that can't be possible; there's gotta be a logical explanation."

"Please tell me about it," Nelkie asked. "I know you remember something."

Albert shrugged his shoulders. "Well, there was this *one* Christmas. I must have been seven or eight; anyway I already knew there was no Santa Claus."

"I see; please go on."

"I asked my dad for this big wooden ferry boat I saw in the toy store window. It had wooden cars you could push up a ramp onto the boat. It was a cool toy. Anyway, I was very happy to find it under the tree. When I thanked my dad, he said "you're welcome," but he had a strange look on his face. I do remember hearing him ask my mom later that night, if she had bought the ferry boat. She said she thought he did. I was just so happy to get it, I kinda forgot all about the mystery. I don't know if they ever figured out where it came from."

"I can tell you," Nelkie said, very self-assured. "It came from the great man of Christmas himself."

"Oh, right, I believe that. And I believe in fairies and flying dragons too. C'mon, what did you say your name was, Nellie?"

"Listen to me for a minute or two," Nelkie said. His tone was more of a command than a request. "You humans do not have all the facts, and the ones you *do* have are distorted and have lost their true meaning over the centuries. On my honor as an elf on a sacred quest, I will now try to give you the truth. All myths and legends have their origins in truth. Most of the stories you heard as a child have their roots steeped in ancient history. Have you ever asked yourself, how can it be possible that there are tales of flying dragons from ancient cultures on either side of the planet? It was impossible for these cultures to have communicated with each other that far in the distant past, and yet the legends survive. Why? Because they are based in truth. There *were* dragons in ancient times, and there may still be a few that have survived to this day. I myself have seen and spoken with nocturnal forest fairies not more than two weeks ago, but I can't expect you to believe me, just because I said so. I can however, straighten out the Santa myth for you. First of all, Santa does not deliver all the toys to all the children, all over the world. Sure, he does leave many toys for the very poor children, whose parents can't afford to buy any, but in most cases, he leaves only one or two. Those are the ones that the parents either couldn't find in stores, or toys they didn't know the child wanted. If you are good, Santa does his best to reward you."

At this point Albert was rolling his eyes, and had about all he could take of fairies, dragons, and Santa Claus. He was about to say so, when Nelkie said, "I guarantee that your ferry boat had a design burnt into the underside. There are several designs, all having to do with stars.

The type of star design denotes where the toy was made."

"Wait a minute, little guy. You're startin' to scare me a little. I don't know how you knew that, but there was a design on the bottom of the boat. I remember it very clearly."

"Did it look like this?" Nelkie said, holding out the handle of his walking stick.

"Good God, Nellie, that's exactly it! Six stars in a circle! I can close my eyes and see it on the ferry boat!"

"Your ferry boat was made less than a two-week walk from where we stand. Six stars in a circle is the mark of my race, the American elf, and my name is NELKIE, not Nellie."

"All right, Nelkie it is."

Albert took a long hard look at this less-than-three-foot-tall being and was still confused. He would never take the slightest chance concerning the safety of the senator and his family, but there was something about this creature. Something he couldn't put his finger on, something in the back of his head told Albert that he just might be for real. "Look, Nelkie, I have no idea how you make things disappear, or how you did that thing with the pool balls. Most of all I can't figure out how you could know about the six stars in a circle. God help me, but I actually want to believe that you are an elf on some sort of mission, but everything I know is telling me that this is impossible!"

"That's because you do not *know* what you think you know. You believe what you have been told, and you accept that as the truth. That is all I am asking you to do. Believe what I'm telling you is true, and I will prove it to you in a short period of time. I pose no threat to you or the senator. I am here to help you, Mr. Parker, and you would be wise to accept that help; it will prove to be in your best interest."

"How's that?"

"Let me explain *my* situation to you. I am faced with a very difficult task that I am not sure I can accomplish alone. You and I have a common interest and I believe if we can work together, we can attain a common goal. If you will give me a few minutes, I will do my best to make it all clear to you."

"Go ahead, little guy. I can't wait to hear this," Albert said, with more than a note of sarcasm.

"First of all, I can fully understand your skepticism. It is the nature of your race. However, as I said before, all human myths and legends have some basis in truth. It is true that stories become exaggerated by being told again and again over the centuries, but the question to consider is: Why did these stories come into existence in the first place? In most cases, it's because a human saw something that he didn't understand and it frightened him. Dragons would be a good example. As for my origin, my ancestors, known as woodland elves, emigrated here from Scandinavia more than six hundred years ago. After living in North America for several centuries, we became known as American elves. We are *not* human, but a separate species and we are *real*," Nelkie said, pulling on his pointed ears to illustrate his meaning. "Mr. Parker, I assure you, we are a peaceful race, and want only to live in harmony with nature. The reason I am here before you today is because I am bound by ancient tradition. Our elders have always been concerned with the way in which the human race controls the earth. The constant pursuit of wealth and power has corrupted many of your race and put the future of this fragile planet in jeopardy. In their wisdom, the elders have chosen to show by example that what really promotes a successful society is the adherence to and the understanding of virtue. Honesty, trust, loyalty, generosity, tolerance--and of course, love--will elevate mankind far beyond the petty gratifications of wealth and power. I was sent here, as were many others before me, to show someone a kindness and possibly improve their life situation. The hope here is that those shown kindness will share it with others. Together, we can change the world for the better, one person at a time."

Albert's disbelieving attitude was starting to soften. Although he was still struggling with accepting the existence of elves as authentic, he fully understood what Nelkie was saying about loyalty. Albert Parker was nothing if not loyal. Another fact that was making him more receptive was the unmistakable intellect possessed by this tiny creature. Clearly this was a very intelligent being, but there also was a genuine sincerity about Nelkie that was disarming.

"Look, Nelkie, so far, I'm impressed with your little speech. It's all very noble and all that, but in *my* world, I am charged with the protection of this family from any possible threat to their safety. I need to know, right now, how you know about Billy Baxter, and why are you poking around in this house?"

"Fair enough. I sought shelter from the overnight storm and fell asleep in Billy's tree house. I had forgotten to use my medallion and was discovered by the child. After much discussion, he told me that his father will lose his job because the senator must sell the property. Up to this point, Mr. Parker, my quest seemed to be a simple task. Help out some unfortunate human, show him a kindness, and hope he learned something from it. Then I would be free to return to my life in the treetops, where I would really rather be. Now all of that has changed. We are in crisis. Not just you and the Walshes, but my entire race as well!"

"What on earth are you talking about?"

"When I followed you into the family room, I saw the videos and heard the conversation. I know all the details, and it is indeed a sad state of affairs. Please try to understand that I was raised in a society that knows nothing of greed, lies, or deceit. Given that fact, it fills me with a great sadness to witness the cruelty one human can force upon another." Nelkie's voice was cracked with emotion and Albert couldn't help but notice the tears welling up in the eyes of the elf. He believed the poignancy displayed by this diminutive creature was genuine. The bodyguard's street-wise skepticism was wavering.

"It doesn't matter," Nelkie went on, "that those who are suffering are not of my race. No one should be victimized. This is predatory behavior and with or without your help, I will not rest until those responsible are brought to justice. It is the great hope of my elders to one day co-exist in harmony with humans. You and I, Mr. Parker, now have the opportunity to prove this is possible."

"I don't know. You present a good case, Nelkie, but really, this seems all too fantastic. It might help me to believe you if I knew you had some other reason for getting involved in this mess. I mean, the fact that you come from a race of good guys who just want to help doesn't really cut it. I learned a long time ago that there's no such thing as a free lunch. There must be more to it than that."

"Oh, but there is, Mr. Parker; much more. You see, as a result of the senator's problem, our fates have become desperately intertwined. You must understand that if the evil ones get their way and the forest is clear cut, my entire nation will become refugees. Hundreds of my brothers of the forest, as we call them, will also become homeless or starve to death due to the unavailability of food. We cannot allow this to happen! Please Mr. Parker, trust in the wisdom of the elders and work with me to stop this evil."

"I don't believe I'm saying this, but…okay, I'm gonna go against my better judgment and go with my gut instinct. I'm willing to at least explore the possibility of us working together. If in the end, Tommy is home safe because you and I put our heads together, that's all that matters; but make no mistake, little guy, I'm still skeptical. You are not supposed to exist in my world, and that's enough to throw a dark shadow over everything."

"But, as you humans are fond of saying, 'the end justifies the means,' and that's good enough for me."

"Okay, so where do we start?"

"I'll get to that point in a few minutes, but first I need to know more about you. I surmised that you work for the senator in some capacity, but I sense there is more to your relationship than that."

"You bet there is," Albert said, with conviction. He then went on to explain why he and Pat had been the best of friends for decades. "Senator Pat Walsh is one of the finest people on this planet. He helped me to regain enough confidence in myself to climb out of the depths of depression and alcoholism. Not only has he helped me become clean and sober, but he showed me by example how to win the respect and admiration of others. He did all of this without making me feel like I was accepting charity. He gave me a hand up, not a handout."

Albert went on to narrate his short but distinguished prizefighting career, complete with a display of shadow boxing. He demonstrated his famous double hook combination with genuine pride. His tone became more serious when he spoke of the demons of drink. He mentioned the accident, even though he had no recollection of it. When he described how Pat followed the ambulance to the hospital, instead of going home and leaving the details to the police, Albert became a little choked with emotion. He finished his monologue with overtones of respect, if not reverence, for the best friend he had ever known. "I saw a lot of the ugly side of people in the fight game, Nelkie. Brutality, greed, people's lives being ruined for the financial gain of others. Pat Walsh is the exact opposite of these people."

"It does my heart good to hear of such a man, Mr. Parker, and it makes my mission more gratifying if I can help someone who is worthy."

"You'll never find someone more worthy…and call me Albert. So now the question is: What *can* we do to help? You got any ideas?"

"I know we are in deep need of more information," the elf answered. "I believe the man called R. J. is right. If we can find the Iraqi, he will in time lead us to Tommy."

"It does make sense," Albert agreed. "But where do we start to look?"

"I think the senator's office would be a good place to start," Nelkie theorized.

"I don't know, Nelkie. R. J. is one of the best in the business; it's not likely that he would leave any stone unturned."

"It wouldn't hurt to check; and besides the office, where else *could* we look?"

Suddenly, Albert had a revelation. "The meadow, Nelkie. The clearing where the dumping took place! Let's look there first."

"Great idea, Albert! I agree. Can we go now?"

"Yes. Just let me leave Pat a note. I'll say I went for a ride and I'll be back in a little while. Then we can go down to the barn and get some transportation."

"Okay," Nelkie said, "but I must render myself invisible. I'm sure you understand that if anyone else discovers me, it will only hinder our investigation."

"Hey, your secret's safe with me, little guy. I don't want to *even try* to explain you to anybody. It would probably get me a one-way ticket to the loony bin."

Albert's attempt at humor was lost on Nelkie, but at least the elf was sure they could work together to achieve a common goal.

After leaving a hastily scribbled note, they went out through the family room, with Albert holding the door open for his invisible friend. They walked down to the barn and Albert slid back the massive door. Nelkie was impressed with the variety of vehicles available. Parked next to the senator's limo was a Jeep. Next to that was Barbara's Escalade. In the back of the barn were several vintage sports cars, along with half a dozen motorcycles.

"Let's take one of the trail bikes," Albert said. "It will be faster if we cut through the woods." He pushed one of the bikes outside and asked Nelkie if he had ever ridden one.

"I have never been on any kind of a vehicle with a motor."

"Don't worry, Nelkie. It's fun. Trust me, you'll love it." Albert straddled the machine and fired it up. The sudden extreme noise forced Nelkie several steps backward, with both hands covering his sensitive ears.

"C'mon, little buddy," Albert yelled over his shoulder. "Grab my arm and swing a leg over the seat. You can put your feet on those little pegs down there."

Albert almost dumped the bike over when Nelkie took hold of his arm and vaulted onto the seat.

"Whoa, baby! Maybe we should rethink this!"

"I'm sorry, Albert. I'm still new at this and I don't always remember there are ramifications involved."

"Ramifications! This is not a ramification, this is a problem. How am I supposed to drive?"

"I apologize. As you saw inside the house, when I render myself invisible, everything I touch also disappears."

"Damn. I can't believe this."

"What's so hard to believe? Look down. You humans are a strange race indeed."

Albert looked down. He could feel the bike vibrating between his legs, but his eyes were telling him it wasn't there! His hand was on the throttle, which responded normally when Albert revved up the motor, but he could see neither the bike, nor his own hands! Albert decided not to try to explain that "I can't believe this" was just an expression, and shouted over the bike's idling motor. "Let me ask you something. If you let go of my shirt, will I be visible?"

"You will be, but not the vehicle. I'm still touching it, but we have a bigger problem."

"What now?"

"My feet do not reach the pegs. I will have to hold on to you."

"I gotta tell you, Nelkie. This is a little unsettling."

"Trust me; you'll get used to it." The elf enjoyed using Albert's own words to make light of the situation.

"Okay, okay. Hold on and we'll give it a shot."

Albert slowly let out the clutch and pulled away from the barn. He rolled down the drive at a snail's pace, until he felt more comfortable driving the bike that wasn't there. Gradually, he gained enough confidence to shift gears and he cautiously piloted the bike off the road and onto the trail that would take them to the meadow. As they passed a stand of mature beech trees, two hikers emerged from the woods, about twenty yards from the trail. Hearing the noisy trail bike, one of the hikers complained to the other.

"Ya know, they shouldn't allow motorcycles out here, Randy. It spoils the peace and…Randy?"

Randy stood motionless and wide-eyed, pointing to the other trail. The hiker's eyes followed his friend's finger until they focused on a sight neither of them could comprehend. All that was visible to them was a large rooster tail of trail dust being kicked high into the air by the bike's back tire! They both heard the bike shift gears, but there was nothing in front of the constantly gushing trail dust!

"Randy! Did you see that?" his friend said, overstating the obvious.

"No! And neither did you!"

"Oh come on, I know you saw what I saw."

"Look, Tim, if you try to explain what you just saw to anyone, they will have you hauled off to the funny farm in a butterfly net!"

"But what if it was some kind of alien spacecraft from another world?"

"Shut up, Tim."

Chapter 35

Albert was pleasantly surprised at how well he adapted to driving the invisible trail bike. When they got within a quarter mile of the meadow, Nelkie tapped him on the shoulder. "Stop here."

"What? We're not there yet"

"Stop now! I'll explain, but you must shut this machine off!"

"Okay, okay. Keep your shirt on!"

"Why would I want to take my shirt off now?" Nelkie said in a confused tone.

"Oh, brother! Never mind."

Albert pulled a few feet off the trail and cut the motor. "Now, what's the emergency?" he asked impatiently.

"There are two men in the meadow. I think we should go the rest of the way on foot. Maybe, if we can get close enough to hear them, we can find out who they are."

"Yeah, all right, but how on earth did you know they're out there?"

"I can feel their presence."

"Say what?"

"The elders have gifted me with a kind of sixth sense that warns me of the presence of others. The power of this gift, and several others the elders have provided me with, have been growing intensely with continued use. Only a week ago I could tell when a living being entered *my* immediate area. Now I am aware that *I* am entering someone else's dominion."

They got off the bike and as Albert came back into full view, he shook his head in mock disbelief. "Boy, you're just overflowin' with weird little tricks, ain't ya?"

"It is not a trick. It is a gift, and a valuable tool to help me accomplish my mission safely."

"Hey, I'm sorry. Don't be so sensitive. I really didn't mean to poke fun at you."

"No apology necessary," Nelkie assured him. "We have a lot to learn about each other. I am confident that as we get to know one another better, we will work out our differences. Now, we should move on to more important things. I think we should both remain invisible so we can get close enough to hear what's going on."

"I agree. I see what you mean now, about it being a tool. We would be crazy not to take advantage of this 'gift' of yours. So how 'bout if I hoist you up on my shoulders? Would that work?"

"Yes. As long as I am touching you, no one will see us."

"Okay, let's do it."

Albert held out his arms in the direction of the little voice. Nelkie grabbed hold and Albert deposited the elf on his shoulders. Nelkie sat comfortably atop his mobile guide, while Albert walked carefully toward the meadow.

Within a few minutes, they could see a four-wheel-drive pick-up truck parked near the center of the meadow. Two men in work clothes were on their hands and knees, meticulously observing something on the ground.

"We must get closer," Nelkie whispered. "Be very careful. Remember they can't see us, but they can hear us."

"No problem."

Albert moved gingerly through the meadow grass until they were within earshot. The two spies tuned in to the conversation, as one man sent the other to get something from the truck.

"I got the plaster kit, Marty; where do you want to start?"

"Over here, Joe," was the reply. "I think we'll get the best cast of this tire tread right about here. If we're lucky, we might be able to trace our guy from the tread on his motorcycle tires."

"Yeah, *if* this motorcycle belonged to our Iraqi, and *if* it's got an oddball tread design that we can trace. Pretty 'iffy,' Marty."

"Yeah, I know, but we can't afford to miss any possible lead. We're talking about a kid's life here, Joe."

"Well, while you're doing that, I'm gonna have another look around. I'll follow these tracks back to where he must have hidden the bike. You never know. He could have dropped something, or left some kind of clue behind that might help."

The invisible confederates watched in total silence from only about twelve feet away. Each of them wished that he could speak to the other, but dared not break the silence. They both figured out that the two men were field agents working for R.J. Abbott.

Ever so slowly, Albert put one foot in front of the other and carefully followed the agent named Joe to the tree line at the edge of the meadow.

"Hey, Marty! I found something!" Joe had come upon the scattered evergreen branches the Iraqi had used to conceal his motorcycle. More importantly, he found the discarded pants and jacket.

Marty left his plaster mold to set, and joined his partner. "Nice goin', Joe! I wish our suspect was dumb enough to drop his wallet, but this might help."

Joe handed the black denim jacket and pants to Marty. "Kind of ordinary," Joe said.

"Well maybe the lab will turn up something we can use," Marty replied.

Nelkie and Albert quietly observed as the two field agents combed the immediate area in a very precise and orderly manner. They even examined each evergreen branch individually. Convinced there was nothing more to be uncovered, they began to pack up.

"Let's get this stuff over to the lab, Joe," Marty urged.

"Be right with you. Just let me get these clothes into a plastic bag and then we can get out of here."

When Albert was sure the truck was far enough away, he put Nelkie down. "Ahh, here I am," he said looking at his bright red shirt. "Do you think you could become visible for awhile there, little guy? It would be nice if I could see who I was talking to."

Nelkie complied. "I think they covered this area efficiently enough," the elf said. "But there is somewhere they did not look."

"Well, I must have missed it too. What are you talking about?"

"Remember, Albert, there were two men here the night the toxic waste was dumped. One, the Iraqi, was taping, the other...."

"Was dumping! Of course! The driver! We should go over every inch of ground the driver walked on."

"Precisely," the elf agreed.

Nelkie pushed off on his walking stick and headed off toward the larger set of tire tracks. Albert pointed ahead to a large patch of brown grass surrounded by several dead trees. "That must be the spot," he said. "Yup. The tracks end right there."

The elf was sadly shaking his head, while looking at the eighty-foot-tall hemlock trees that were vibrantly alive only a week ago. He silently renewed his vow to find out who committed this crime against nature and to see to it that he was caught and incarcerated.

Albert felt a wave of compassion rush over him. The ex-fighter could see from Nelkie's reaction that he was deeply troubled. Albert was beginning to understand that the elf's connection to the natural forces was more than an appreciation. It was a part of *his* life force as well. It was as if Nelkie were grieving for a relative who had met with a violent death. "Don't dwell on the dead trees, little guy. I know you're upset, but you gotta get past this so we can catch the bad guys, okay? C'mon, let's start searching the area. We might just come across something that everyone else missed."

Nelkie turned back to his new friend and forced himself to refocus.

"Yes, of course; thank you, Albert. It took a moment for me to get over the shock. I never could have imagined how someone could cause such a slaughter on purpose...but you're right; we must move on."

The elf paced back to where he thought the cab of the truck was parked, and began to scrutinize the ground. Albert said nothing and just walked over to where the tire tracks from the trailer stopped. Slowly and deliberately, he worked his way back to the area of the cab, looking for anything unusual in the dead brown grass.

Nelkie, meanwhile, was working the other way from the cab back toward the trailer. They passed each other at the halfway point and kept going, silently continuing their search. When they had reached opposite ends of where the truck had been parked, they both turned around to face each other. Albert called to Nelkie from the cab end. "Any luck back there?"

"Not yet, but let's make one more pass."

Again, they started at opposite ends, slowly moving toward the middle. Again, they met halfway, with no success.

"Well, it looks like we came up empty," Albert said.

"I'm afraid you are right, Albert. All I've seen is badly burnt grass, dirt, and a few rocks. I guess we'll have to check out the senator's office after all."

"I hope we have better luck there, but for now, we had better head back. Pat and Barbara should be almost home by now."

Nelkie was still looking down, about midway on the trailer side of the area, as Albert turned to go. When Albert's shadow moved over some small stones, Nelkie caught a glimpse of something shiny. The sunlight bounced off something between the rocks and Nelkie saw a split-second flash of light. "Wait! What's this?"

Albert turned back to see Nelkie pick up a small object. "Let me see what you've got there," he said, holding out his hand.

Nelkie was just two feet from his friend and about to hand over what he found, when the look on the elf's face turned from one of curiosity to an expression of sheer terror! Nelkie cried out in panic and threw the object as fast and as far as he could.

"Whut on God's green earth are you doing?" Albert ran to retrieve the tiny object over Nelkie's frenzied protests. "Albert! No! It's alive! I think it tried to bite me!"

As Albert bent over to pick up the cast-off cell phone, he was overcome by a fit of laughter.

"What's so funny? I'm telling you that thing attacked me when I picked it up! You had better be careful, Albert; I felt it growling."

Albert laughed even louder when he saw how insistent Nelkie was that his life was in danger. After a long moment, Albert finally calmed down enough to explain. "This thing is not alive, Nelkie; it's a machine," he said still struggling to hold back another fit of laughter. It's called a cell phone. It's a portable telephone, like the ones humans have in their homes, only you can take this one with you and send and receive calls almost anywhere. When someone calls you, the phone either rings...or, as you just found out, vibrates. You *have* heard about telephones, haven't you?"

"Of course I've heard of telephones. We elves aren't completely unenlightened. Hundreds, maybe thousands have gone before me on their quests. They have all brought back news and information about the world of humans. You might be surprised to know that we are aware of such things as the space shuttle, cable TV, and even the successful cloning of animals. It does appear, however, that we are having some difficulty keeping up with the rapid advances in your technology."

"That's to be expected," Albert said. "Believe me, there are millions of humans that have never even *seen* a cell phone, and probably never will. Your adopted country is the most technologically advanced nation in the world, but even here in the USA there are vast numbers of people who know what a cell phone is, but have no idea how to use one. This one, however, is just your very basic, cheap camera phone."

"Do you mean that phone takes pictures?"

"Yeah, but that's really no big deal nowadays. The newer phones now have so many applications it's truly staggering, especially when you think that a mere fifteen years ago, there were very few, if any, around and they were the size of a brick! Today's phones can help you do everything from watch movies, or read books, to get directions to anywhere by way of global positioning satellites that are orbiting the earth."

"Okay, Albert, all this is truly fascinating, but let me ask you something. Do you have enough knowledge in the use of this device to possibly find out who may have called the driver, and thereby help us to identify him?"

"You got it, pal," Albert said as he flipped open the phone.

Albert sat down on a flat rock so Nelkie could see what he was doing. "See this button up here?"

"The little one on your left?"

"Yeah. This is a list of all the text messages the driver received, and before you ask, I'll explain what that is. If either the caller or the receiver of the call can't talk for whatever reason, you can type a message and send it. It will show up instantly as a printed message."

"I see. This way you can read your conversation rather than speak it, thereby protecting your privacy."

"Exactly! You're a quick study, little guy; I like that. Now, look here. Our driver has three messages in his Inbox. One from someone named Kaye, a second one from Marvin, and the last little gem here simply says 'boss.' If we're really lucky, 'boss' is our Iraqi. Now, watch this." Albert hit the "contacts" button, and sure enough, Kaye, Marvin, and the boss's numbers came up.

"Does this mean you now have the ability to call the boss and find out if he's our man?"

"Absolutely, but I don't think I want to do that just yet."

"Why not?"

"Because, my curious little friend, our man, as you call him, is a professional bad guy. He's not about to tell us where he is…and I don't think I want to alert him that someone is looking for him--at least not yet."

"Okay. I do understand we must be careful. If our strategy is not sound, we could put Tommy Walsh in greater danger. So what *can* we do with the information from the driver's phone?"

"Well, I don't know who Marvin is, but it's probably a safe bet that Kaye is the driver's girlfriend. I think it would be safer all the way around if we try to find the driver through Kaye or Marvin. If we can catch up with the driver, then we let him lead us to the Iraqi. Whaddaya think?"

"I think you're right, Albert. That would be the safest way to proceed."

"Then we're in agreement--good. Now, I think we should get back to my cabin so we can pursue this in private."

They concurred that it would not be a good idea for them to ride the invisible trail bike back into the compound.

"If Pat and the Mrs. are back from their walk, things could get a little sticky," Albert pointed out.

"You can let me off when we're just out of sight of the main house," Nelkie said. "Then you can put the bike away and I'll meet you in the cabin."

Albert straddled the bike and fired it up. He held out an arm. "Time to fade out," he said as the elf grabbed hold and they became nothingness.

Chapter 36

Pat and Barbara returned from their walk with a strong feeling of renewed strength. Over a period of time, they had successfully overcome many of the problems and pitfalls that can occur during a marriage of twenty-six years. Although this was by far the worst crisis of their lives, there was never any doubt that they would see it through together. The relationship they had built over the years was substantially reinforced by a steadfast respect and admiration for one another. Whenever they faced a serious difficulty in the past, each of them was always able to draw strength from the other. They walked through the patio door still discussing their options.

"I was thinking," Barbara said. "I'm sure that by the time we get Tommy home safely, R.J. will have figured out who was behind all this. It will give me great pleasure to press charges and send this depraved person off to jail!"

"That would be great, but I'm afraid it's not that easy."

"Why not?" she asked. "If we can prove that this bum, whoever he is, committed a kidnapping, why wouldn't he go to jail?"

"Oh, I'm sure he would, but that would solve only half our problem."

"I don't understand," she said, as they seated themselves on the sofa.

"I guess what it comes down to is that unless we have irrefutable evidence that whoever is responsible for the kidnapping is also to blame for dumping the toxic chemicals on our property, I still have a major problem."

Barbara paused to consider what might happen if those who polluted the Walsh-owned property were never caught. "I think I know where you're going with this. If we can't prove that the hijackers were working with the kidnappers, it would make *you* look responsible for the illegal disposal of toxic waste."

"Absolutely. Look, it's obvious that our first priority is Tommy's safety. If the kidnappers are caught and Tommy is returned to us unhurt, the most important issue is resolved. We should also be able to keep our home and prevent the forest from being decimated. However, that is only the tip of the proverbial iceberg. If all those involved are not arrested, you can bet that video of our tanker truck will be on the evening news."

"I understand that, but don't you think that all your friends and colleagues will stand by your statement that this was an attempt at blackmail?"

"Honey, I've been in politics a long time. Whatever political savvy I've developed over the years is telling me that this would make me a political hot potato. People who we always thought we could rely on will be running from me as if I had the plague. My career, no matter how good it's been thus far, will be instantly in the crapper."

"I don't want to believe that," she said sadly, "but somehow, I know you're right. Let's hope R.J. can connect all the dots and end this nightmare."

Before Pat could agree, Albert entered the family room from the other end of the house. He had put the trail bike away and thought it best to check in. "Hey, I thought I heard voices in here. How was your walk?"

"Lovely, as always, Albert," Barbara answered. "It always does us good to walk among the tall trees. We saw about a half dozen deer about a mile up the trail."

"It is amazing" Pat added, "how these magnificent surroundings can help you to put things in perspective. We find that Mother Nature seems to have a knack for helping to clear one's head and allowing one to think a little more clearly. Barb and I are certain that if we can stay calm and think rationally, instead of letting fear and panic control our thoughts, we'll get through this. R.J. is more than capable, with a great organization behind him. I'm quite sure he will see to it that Tommy gets home safely and the Iraqi thug gets locked up for good."

"Now *that's* the kinda talk I wanna hear," Albert said, smiling. "In the meantime, if there's anything I can do for either of you, I'm here for ya."

"Thank you, Albert. We do appreciate your loyalty," Barbara said.

"I second that," Pat chimed in. "And there is something you can do for me that will help a great deal."

"I'm all ears, boss."

"After you drop me off at the airport tonight, I'd like you to come back to the compound and keep an eye on things until I get back on Friday night."

"You mean keep an eye on me." Barbara's tone was one of mock complaint. "Honestly, Pat, I'll be fine. I'm sure you will need Albert with you in Washington. I'm a big girl and you don't need anyone to babysit me. No offense, Albert."

"None taken, ma'am." Albert bowed slightly with respect.

When he spoke again, a look of genuine concern came over the senator's face. "You have always been fiercely independent, Babs, and I love you for it, but you know I'm going to be worried sick about you being up here alone. I would feel much better knowing Albert was here, just in case the unthinkable happens."

"Okay then. It's settled. I'll stay here with the Mrs. until I pick you up at the airport Friday night. If there's nothing further, I'll head down to the cottage."

"Great, Piston, thank you. We're just going to grill a couple of steaks around 6:00, so I guess you can bring the car around at about 7:30."

"See you after dinner." Albert waved and strolled out onto the patio. His pace quickened as he passed the garage. Anxious to get what information he could from the driver's cell phone, he took all three porch steps in one stride and rushed through his front door.

The four-room log cabin reflected Albert's masculine personality. A large stone fireplace made the living room look much like a hunting lodge. There was an antique flintlock rifle mounted over the mantle and a realistic-looking faux bearskin rug on the floor below.

Albert shut the door and walked around the room. Pointlessly, his eyes searched for his invisible ally.

"I'm over here," said a small voice from the couch. Turning his head toward the sound, Albert noticed his scrapbook open on the coffee table. "I retired twenty-one and three...not bad, huh?"

Nelkie became visible and Albert noticed an inquisitive look on the elf's face. "Are you confused about something?"

"Well, yes. Two things, actually. Firstly, twenty-one and three what? What does that mean?"

"Twenty-one wins against three losses. Any professional fighter would be proud of that record."

"I see, but not really...I mean I can understand your being proud of a winning record, but the rest doesn't make sense."

"Whattaya mean?"

"Well, your personality, as I read it, does not project such violence and brutality. Unless I'm way off, I read you as a caring and considerate person. It doesn't follow that such a man would beat men up for a living. You must have had quite a temper, as a young man."

"Not at all, Nelkie. Prizefighting was a job. It's an acquired skill, developed through years of specific training. The sport long ago was dubbed the 'sweet science,' because of all the technical aspects involved with defense, strategy, and the formulation of a fight plan expressly designed for each opponent. Emotion has nothing to do with it. The best fighters are the ones who can stay calm and execute what they were trained to do in a precise and workmanlike manner, while their opponent is trying his best to do the same. If you lose your temper, you've lost control and will probably lose the fight."

"Fascinating," Nelkie said, closing the book.

"Well, enough of that," Albert said while pulling out the driver's cell phone. "We have business to attend to. Now let's see what we've got here." Albert sat on the couch so Nelkie could see the cell phone screen. "The first text message is from someone named Kaye." Albert read the message aloud. "*Good news. Got Sat. nite off. Can watch u race. See u at track.*"

"Well I'm not sure what to make of that illiterate mess," the elf said.

Albert chuckled at Nelkie's innocence, but was patient enough to explain texting shorthand. "Everyone texts illiterately," he said, smiling. "This is the most informal means of communication. Proper English grammar and even punctuation are ignored by everyone. Shorter is better. If you haven't noticed yet, you will eventually realize that most of human society is always in a hurry. It even applies to communication. Text it fast, move on."

"So what can we garner from this cryptic message?"

"Well, as near as I can figure, our driver races cars, and I think he's racing tonight. The million-dollar question is...where? Let's check out the other texts. This one is from a guy named Marvin. *Sponsor wants pics of u and car call me 4 dtails.*"

Albert's broadening smile told the elf this was good news, but from Nelkie's perspective, humans communicated in gibberish. "This pretty much confirms what I thought, Nelkie. Are you familiar with the sport of stock car racing?"

"I know of its existence, but not much else."

"Okay. Brief explanation. Most professional racecar drivers have sponsors that invest money in the car in exchange for advertising their company name on the car. It appears that our guy's sponsor wants some photographs, perhaps to use in magazine ads. I think Marvin is the guy to call, but before I do, I want to read the other text message."

Albert scrolled down to "Boss," and brought up the text. "*Pay same place Sat nite.*"

"I'll tell ya what, little guy, I'd bet my next paycheck this message is from the Iraqi. This may or may not prove useful, but for now I'm sure if I call Marvin, he'll be more than happy to put me in touch with our driver."

"Can you call now?"

"Why wait?" Albert went to the driver's "contacts" and called Marvin. The phone was answered on the second ring.

"This is Marvin."

"Oh, ahh, Marvin, I'm calling you because I found this cell phone on the pump in a gas station and your number was in the contacts. I'm trying to find the owner. I know I'd be going nuts if I lost my cell. I called you because there was a text from you that said something like, sponsor wants pics of you, or something."

"Oh sure! I sent that message to Holeshot! So, the dummy lost his cell, huh? No wonder I haven't heard from him."

"Yeah, I guess so. Look, if he's a local guy, I'll be happy to deliver his phone. Who is Holeshot, anyway?"

"Oh, sorry. Terry 'Holeshot' Hannan. He's an up-and-coming stock car driver and my client, I'm his agent, Marvin Feinstein. Holeshot is in the feature at the race arena tonight. If you want to come down and watch the race, I'll call the track and have them hold a couple of passers for you at the gate."

"Sure, thanks, that would be great."

"I'll make sure they have a couple of pit passes for ya, so you can give him back his phone in person. You might want to get his autograph. It won't be long before Holeshot Hannan is a big name in NASCAR."

"Well thanks, Mr. Feinstein. We'll be there tonight. I can't wait to meet someone who's about to be famous!"

"Well, thank you for being a good Samaritan."

"No problem, I'm sure Holeshot will be thrilled to get his cell phone back. Bye."

As he hung up, Albert was grinning from one ear to the other. The elf smiled back at his friend and said, "I could hear both sides of your conversation easily. This is very good news, is it not?"

"It's great news. Mr. Feinstein has no idea how 'thrilled' Terry Holeshot Hannan is going to be, Nelkie. *We* are on a roll."

"Just one question, Albert, if I may."

"Shoot."

"Isn't 'Holeshot' a rather odd name for a human? What *is* a hole-shot, anyway?"

"Holeshot is what we call a nickname. Sometimes we humans give each other kind of fun or funny names that reflect our character or occupation. 'Holeshot' is an old street racing term. It means the first car away after the traffic light turns green has 'pulled a holeshot' on his opponent."

"I see. So Holeshot would be an apropos nickname for our Mr. Hannan, considering he drives racecars for a living."

"Yes, and also because his criminal activities revolve around driving."

"Ah yes, this is all beginning to make perfect sense. Now, am I to understand that using Mr. Feinstein's information, you have formu-lated a plan of action?"

"Oh yeah! I just have to figure out how to stash you in the front seat of the limo when I take Pat to the airport this evening. The race arena Mr. Feinstein spoke of is only a ten-minute ride from the air-port. If I can shake up our Mr. Hannan enough, he just might make a mistake we can capitalize on."

"So, do you plan to confront Mr. Hannan tonight?"

"Yes and no. I think we'll just go there and wing it. We have the element of surprise on our side and I want to use that to our advan-tage. I know I'll have a better feeling for how to handle this once

I'm at the track. I want to be careful and assess the situation before I make any moves."

"Very good. You are only the third human I have been in contact with, and I am very encouraged."

"Whaddaya mean?"

"I am encouraged because your last statement exhibits a degree of wisdom. Don't forget that I am still a novice when it comes to dealing with humans. I must judge each experience on its own merits. I already knew you not to be a fool. *Now* I know that I can trust your judgment, because it is tempered with wisdom."

Albert was humbled by the compliment and didn't know how to respond. Never before had anyone ever connected the word "wisdom" with Albert "Piston" Parker. Guts, cunning, toughness, sure. Wisdom? Not a chance.

"Well, thanks, Nelkie…and you're no dummy either, but that's enough of this mutual admiration nonsense, we have work to do. Are you hungry?"

"Famished."

"Alright. Lemme see if I can rummage up some dinner for us, then we hafta get up to the garage and get the limo ready."

"Sounds good to me. Do you have any meatballs?"

Chapter 37

Nelkie watched Albert ransack the garage as they prepared to leave. "What are you looking for?"

"Hang on a minute; I'll know it when I see it. Aha! There we are!" He picked up a cardboard box that once housed a room air conditioner. Albert turned around to explain what he was doing. His face showed a momentary shock, until he realized what happened. The limo was gone! "Nelkie!"

"What? There's really no reason for you to raise your voice, Albert. I'm only four feet away!"

"I'm sorry, but you should really pay more attention to what you lean against when you're invisible. You almost gave me heart failure!"

"Oops," Nelkie said, while quickly removing his arm from the fender, allowing the Lincoln to reappear. "Sorry, Albert. I'm still getting used to using these powers. I was watching you and didn't even notice the car had disappeared!"

"Well, you got away with it this time, but in a different situation, especially if there are witnesses, the result could spell disaster for us."

"Your point is well taken, my friend. It won't happen again."

"All right. Now, I'll just put this box in the front seat and then we'll put you in it. If you remain quiet, the senator will never know you're here."

Albert helped Nelkie into the box, trotted around the hood, got in, and started the car. Suddenly, the chauffeur started laughing uncontrollably.

"What? What's so funny?" said the voice from the invisible box.

Albert was pounding the steering wheel with both hands, trying to control the surprise attack of humor. "I just got the funniest picture in my head. Can you imagine if I didn't put you in that box and I just drove up to the main house with you sitting there? Pat would see me drive up, sitting on nothing, turning a steering wheel that wasn't there! He would surely think he had lost his mind, hah heh heh, oh boy."

Nelkie, seeing the pure ridiculousness of that scenario, joined his friend in an outburst of laughter. It took several moments before they were able to regain their emotional equilibrium, but finally, Nelkie became the voice of reason.

"Okay, okay. That was really funny, but we really must be serious here. Remember, the senator thinks you are alone. If you pull up to the house laughing like a hyena, he'll think you're the one who's lost his mind."

"Yes, of course. You're right," Albert said, still smiling. He put the big car in gear and promised to keep his mind on the job at hand.

The two friends took great pleasure in the lighter moments in the garage. For they knew things were about to become much more serious for both of them.

Chapter 38

Albert wheeled the big Lincoln up to the terminal, got out, and opened the door for Pat. "Thanks, Piston...oh, I need to ask you one more favor before I go." The senator handed his driver a stack of folders and asked him to drop them off at the office on his way home. "Just drop these on Anne's desk. She'll know what to do with them."

"Will do, boss." Albert put the folders on the front seat and then carried the senator's bag to the curb. "Have a safe trip, and try not to worry. I'll keep an eye on things at home."

"Thanks again, Albert. I'll see you back here Friday night, about 6:30."

The ex-fighter slid behind the wheel and nosed the car into traffic. "Okay, my little cohort, we are off to the races!"

It was only a matter of about fifteen minutes before Albert had pulled into the race arena parking lot and shut down the Lincoln. "Listen, Nelkie, maybe it would be best if you stayed here in the car. I really don't know how you'll be able to maneuver around a couple thousand people, even if you are invisible. I'll just go and poke around a bit. I won't be more than a half hour."

"As much as I want to go with you, I'm afraid you're right. I don't know how I could deal with crowds of humans running this way and that. I would probably get trampled."

"Good," Albert said. " I'm glad we agree on this point. On the brighter side, you get your wish to see the senator's office. When I get back, I have to shoot into town and drop off these files."

Albert made sure that his invisible friend was locked in. He left the front windows down an inch and reminded Nelkie not to touch anything.

After picking up his admission and pit passes at the box office, Albert found a vantage point in the lower grandstand, where he could see the track clearly. The feature race of the evening was being hotly contested. There were two cars far in front of the pack, battling for first place. The excited crowd was raising the already unbearable noise level even higher. Every time the pack went by the grandstand, Albert wondered if the tremendous noise and vibration would tear the place apart. The smells of high-octane exhaust and burning rubber made him nauseous. *I don't think my senses were assaulted this badly in the ring.*

Finally, he forced himself to pay attention to the race. It was then he realized that his man was one of the two drivers dueling for first place. As the leaders came streaking past the grandstand, the car on the outside put on an extra burst of speed and edged in front by maybe a foot. The crowd was going crazy and Albert soon figured out why. He had just enough time to see the name "Holeshot Hannan" on the door of the first-place car, as it zoomed under the checkered flag. The fans were screaming in appreciation for their hometown hero.

The winner was passing the grandstand on his victory lap when Albert made a mental note of the sponsor's name on the hood. Sierra Log Homes. The driver got out and waved to his fans. Albert thought, *Local boy makes good. If his fans knew this boy was up to his neck in blackmail, hijacking, and kidnapping, they would hang him by his thumbs.*

Albert walked down the grandstand steps until he reached the walkway in front of the first row of seats. Twisting and sidestepping around dozens of Hannan's fans, he finally secured a place at the wire mesh fence, just above the track. Terry Hannan was holding a checkered flag, his face beaming, as he was having his picture taken. *Well, at least now, I know what he looks like.*

Albert watched closely as Terry's eyes panned the grandstand.

The instant their eyes met, he seized the opportunity. He pulled the driver's cell phone from his pocket, flipped it open, and waved it over his head in an exaggerated motion. When he was sure Terry could see it, he yelled. "Hey, Holeshot! I know what you did! It's time to pay, Hannan." Albert read the panic on Terry's face. *He's probably turned his life upside-down looking for this thing, and now he knows he's got a boatload of trouble.*

Hannan turned and bolted for the pit area. Albert's eyes remained glued to his prey. He watched as Hannan leapt into a vintage Corvette and sped off toward the exit.

Thankful that he was still in good shape in his fifties, the ex-fighter flew up the grandstand steps three at a time. Like a charging bull, he bumped several unsuspecting fans out of his way as he made a mad dash for the parking lot. *I hope his only way out is through the parking lot.* Albert cleared the exit door and broke into a run for the Lincoln.

Nelkie was greatly relieved when the race was over. Even though he was in a car more than a hundred yards away, his sensitive ears could not take much more of the constant thunder of twenty-six racecars.

Albert was in the car and away in what seemed like one motion.

"Are we being pursued?" Nelkie asked

"No, we are pursuing," Albert answered, trying to catch his breath.

"Am I correct in the assumption that our Mr. Hannan is driving that car, speeding toward the exit?"

"Right you are, my astute little friend." Albert told Nelkie what transpired between the two of them when he confronted the driver.

"And you did this to see if he would run for help and maybe lead us to the Iraqi?" Nelkie inquired.

"Well, it seems to be working so far…and I can't just follow the guy around all night. I've got to get back to the compound at some point," he said while yanking the limo into gear. Albert cleared the race arena exit a mere fifteen seconds behind panicked Terry Hannan.

As they maneuvered into the downtown area, Albert slowly closed the gap between them. Hannan was forced to stop for a red light and by the time the light turned green, they were only two cars back.

"Look!" Nelkie said. "Did you see that?"

"No, what?"

"He must have a new phone. I saw him take it away from his ear when the light changed."

"I'll bet you dollars to doughnuts he's crying to his Arab boss. We'll just follow at a safe distance for a while and hope for the best."

After about ten minutes, the Corvette pulled over in front of a diner. Albert pulled in about three spaces back and cut the lights. As Hannan exited his vehicle, there was a tremendous flash of lightning. It was starting to rain. Holeshot put the top up on his car and walked into the diner.

Albert and Nelkie watched their prey drink three cups of coffee in a booth overlooking the Corvette. Hannan glanced at his watch and picked up his phone again.

"He sure looks nervous, little guy. I guess I really shook him up."

"Look," Nelkie interrupted. "He's making another call. Quickly, Albert, let me out! If I can get close enough to that window I'll be able to hear everything!"

Without saying a word, Albert flung the door open and tilted the box, so the elf could hop to the curb. Nelkie scampered under an over-hang just below Hannan's window. He had no problem hearing both sides of the conversation.

"Did ya get me the extra ten grand?"

"Relax, my friend. My boss is very satisfied with the job you did for us. He wants you to be safe. I have your money and I will meet you at the usual place as soon as I can get there."

"Oh, thank God! That guy, whoever he was, scared me half to death when he started waving my cell phone. I don't know where he found it, or how much he knows, but I can't take any chances. I'm on probation. If anything even looks suspicious, they'll send me back to jail in a heartbeat. I can't go back there, man! I gotta get outta here now, tonight!"

"Take it easy, Terry. I told you, my boss takes care of his own. We have a slush fund for these little emergencies. Stay calm, and I'll see you in a few minutes."

"Okay, okay. I'll leave now, and thanks for getting me out of this."

Nelkie ran back to the curb where Albert was waiting, and repeated what he had heard. "Get me back in the car--Hannan will be leaving momentarily."

As soon as they got back in the limo, they saw Hannan toss some bills on the table and rush out to his car.

"It's race time," Albert said, starting the car. They watched the Corvette dart away from the curb and accelerate into the rain. Albert had to let four cars go by before he could give chase. After about five minutes of sudden rights and lefts, they thought he had gotten away. Suddenly, Nelkie yelled, "There! Ahead on the right! He's turning again."

"There must be an alley up there," Albert said. "He's turning in the middle of the block."

They lost several valuable minutes desperately searching for a place to put the car. Finally, Albert pulled in front of a fire hydrant and they scrambled out of the car. They ran as fast as they could toward the alley, which was now a block away.

Chapter 39

A very shaky Terry Hannan sped down the alley. He was now only a minute or two from collecting his pay for the hijacking, and with the bonus ten thousand promised to him, he could now make good his escape. *Thirty-five grand should be enough to start my life over in Mexico. At least I won't have to worry about going back to jail.*

The Corvette's headlights illuminated the cinderblock wall at the alley's end. There was a small glint of light from a solitary bulb in an alcove off to his right. He stopped the car, shut off the lights, and headed for the alcove. The dim light was barely enough to see the two dumpsters at the kitchen door of Ming's Chinese Take-Out. The wheel man cautiously looked around. *I must have gotten here first, so I might as well check to see if my cash is in the usual place.* Down on his hands and knees, he felt along the underside of the dumpster nearest the door. Heaving a great sigh of relief, he freed the manila envelope from under the container. Hannan stood up and ripped open the envelope. In the faint light he could make out three strapped stacks of hundred dollar bills. Two were marked $10,000 and one $5000. *Now, if that little weasel would just show up with the rest of my...* "Aaawwak!"

Something had tightened around his neck. While looking at his money, he was unaware of the Iraqi moving silently out from behind the second dumpster. With the speed and accuracy of an experienced assassin, the Arab looped a steel guitar string over Hannan's head and around his neck. The murderer crossed his wrists and tightened the lethal wire. With his knee planted firmly in the small of his victim's back, he pulled the steel noose tighter still. The eyes of the executioner widened in his depraved exhilaration. He was consumed by the frenzied passion of the kill. A demonic smile spread across his face as he felt his prey twisting and squirming in vain.

Hannan was clawing at his own neck, desperately trying to force his fingertips under the deadly wire. In panicked desperation, he dropped to his knees, hoping to throw off his attacker's balance, but his tormentor anticipated the move and maintained his leverage. Terry "Holeshot" Hannan's life was slowly seeping away in a dingy garbage-strewn alley and he was powerless to stop it.

The murderer held his grip for a full minute after all movement from Hannan had stopped. Satisfied that his victim was dead, he dropped him face down in the rain-soaked alley, grabbed the money, and climbed atop the dumpster. He vaulted over the wall and was gone.

Albert and Nelkie cautiously approached the darkened alley in the pouring rain. Albert wished there were at least some moonlight to guide them. The rain had brought grease and oil from a thousand truck deliveries to the surface, making the ground slippery beneath their feet. Nelkie reached up without warning and tugged on Albert's sleeve, forcing the ex-fighter to lean over toward the elf.

"What? What is it?"

"Go slowly, my friend, and make not a sound," he whispered. "I fear something is very wrong. I can feel the presence of evil."

Albert said nothing, but nodded at his companion. Although he didn't understand it, he knew his odd little friend possessed a keen intuition that should not be ignored, but the ever- present steel nerve of a professional fighter allowed him to press on. With one hand feeling along the wall, he prudently led Nelkie down the corridor.

In the dim light of the recess, they could see the silhouette of Hannan's car. The driver's window was down and Albert could see the car was unoccupied. Silently and with extreme caution, the two amateur detectives made their way to the alley's end. As they passed along the front end the Corvette, Nelkie spoke. "There! By the garbage bin! I'm afraid we're too late. There is no life force here, other than our own."

The rain had done very little to hold down the stench of rotting garbage. When Albert rolled the body over, Nelkie thought for a moment that he was going to be sick. It was a sobering experience for the elf. He had never seen anything as gruesome as the deceased human at his feet. Hannan's sightless eyes stared up at Nelkie, revealing the horror of a violent death.

Albert was down on one knee, examining the body. He turned and directed his attention to his tiny friend. Peering through the rain, he could barely make out a see-through silhouette formed by the rain falling and bouncing off the invisible elf. "Hey, are you okay, little buddy?"

"I'll be all right, Albert," Nelkie replied. "I must tell you that whoever did this has the very essence of evil coursing through his veins. We must not become complacent or overconfident in our dealings with this individual. He is truly a demon in the flesh. Given the opportunity, he could kill us both and never suffer a moment of regret or remorse. This man could take a life and feel no more emotion than you would by taking a bath. Albert, I cannot stress enough how dangerous this person is. Although he is long gone, his evil presence remains. It hangs in the air like the oppressive August humidity. I have never felt such overpowering darkness and foreboding."

The rain was running off the bodyguard's short white beard in rivulets while he spoke. "You can bet this is the work of that rat-like Arab. Where there's garbage, there's bound to be rats, and our friend Hannan here is the kind of human garbage that attracts rats like Salaam. Look, we had better get outta here. If someone should happen to come by, we could be in a lot of trouble. We don't want to have to explain what happened here. C'mon, we gotta beat feet-- now!"

They were walking briskly past Hannan's now-abandoned car,

when a thought stuck Albert. "Hold on a minute," he said, opening the car door. He reached inside and grabbed Hannan's cell phone. I've got an idea that might help us."

They proceeded out of the alley onto the deserted sidewalk. The rain was keeping pedestrians at bay, at least for the moment. After several machinations to allow his friend to get back in the car without making it disappear, Albert slid in behind the wheel. He reached under the seat and produced a towel. "Here, little guy. I always have a couple of these on hand for emergencies. Once we stop dripping, I think I'm gonna make a phone call."

"To whom?"

"Our Iraqi adversary."

"What? I don't understand. He's certainly not going to volunteer any information. What do you expect to gain?"

"I want him to know that someone is on to him. He'll be racking his brain to figure out who's calling him on the dead man's phone. Maybe he'll think someone saw him commit the murder. At any rate, it's bound to make him nervous, and nervous people make mistakes."

Nelkie thought this through quickly. He realized there was no danger to himself or to Albert. The Arab was a smart, experienced career criminal, but there wasn't any way for him to figure out that it was the senator's bodyguard nipping at his heels.

"Make the call, Albert. I see your point. Hannan made a mistake by trusting the Iraqi to help him escape, probably because he was very afraid of going back to jail. He was foolish to trust a murderer, and it cost him his life."

"Right. I don't think Salaam is foolish enough to make a *fatal* mistake, but he might just trip himself up somewhere because we shook him up a bit." Albert pressed the "send" button after pulling up the number for "Boss." The call was answered on the first ring by a voice that Albert was more than familiar with.

"Who is this calling?"

"I know who you are, Salaam. I'm coming after you for kidnapping and murder. You are going to pay dearly for that mess you left in the alley, off Bradley Street."

The accented voice on the other end would not be intimidated. "I do not know who you are, nor do I care. I have done nothing and you cannot prove otherwise, or you wouldn't be making this call! I laugh at your accusations!" The line went dead. Nelkie, having heard both sides of the brief conversation, spoke first. "I guess Salaam is far too smart to make a mistake on the telephone."

"I didn't think he would, but now he knows he didn't get away clean…and you can bet he's worried."

"Good. What's next?"

"I can't just leave Holeshot in the alley like that. I have an old friend on the police force. I'll call him and give him what information I can. I don't want to bring more people into this mess, but I can't walk away and do nothing, knowing there's a corpse in that alley."

"You are a good man, Albert. Calling the police is the right thing to do."

Albert nodded his head in agreement while dialing police head-quarters. "Hello? Can you tell me if Lt. Frank Martini is on duty tonight? He is? Yes, thank you." The desk sergeant put Albert's call through to his friend.

"Lt. Martini."

"Hey Frank, it's Albert. How are ya?"

"Piston, you old pug! I'm up to my ears in paperwork, but other than that, great. So, to what do I owe this honor? Is everything okay with you?"

"I'm fine, but I'm afraid this is a business call, Frank. I think I'm about to create more paperwork for ya."

"Story of my life, Piston. What's up?"

"Are you familiar with a local thug and wanna be stock car driver named Terry 'Holeshot' Hannan?"

"Holeshot? You bet I'm familiar. I collared him a few years back. He was the wheel man on a botched warehouse heist over on fifth. The kid can drive anything that has wheels, but he can't stay out of jail. I think he's on probation now, unless he's screwed up again."

"He's screwed up, all right, but for the last time. He's been murdered. He has a mark around his neck. Looks to me like somebody strangled him. I thought you should know--his remains are in an alley between 24th and 25th off Bradley."

"Which begs the question, how on earth does a low-life like Hannan cross paths with the bodyguard of a US senator? Look, Piston, before we get any deeper into this, I gotta ask you something. Are you in any kind of trouble here?"

"It's a long, complicated story. I found Hannon's cell phone, but before I could return it, somebody iced him. All I know for sure is that Hannan was in pretty deep with some really seedy people, who are trying to squeeze the senator. I'm afraid the senator's son Tommy is in a life-or-death situation. Pat has his own PI on it, so I would appreciate it if you could keep a tight lid on this, at least until the kid is safe."

"Okay, Piston, I'll do what I can to keep it quiet. Oh, one more question--you didn't touch anything at the crime scene, did you? I mean, you could have created a forensics nightmare by stomping all around the area."

"Don't worry. I didn't do anything other than roll over the body to see who it was. and then I left. You know how much I value your friendship, Frank, and if I can help you get those captain's bars you've been itching for, I will. By the way, I need to ask you a small favor."

The lieutenant answered sarcastically. "Ya know, Piston, somehow I knew you didn't make this call out of the goodness of your heart. What do you need, champ?"

"There's a number in Hannan's contacts. I would really like to know who it belongs to."

"Look, Piston, I know you're a tough guy and you can handle

yourself--I've seen you fight--but I gotta tell you, If you go foolin' around with police work, you can get in way over your head. I'll get the information for you, but you've gotta promise me you won't do anything foolish."

"I appreciate your concern, Frank, but I can't just sit on my hands with this one. Pat's in trouble and I owe him big time. Don't worry, I'll watch my step."

Albert read off the number listed as "Boss" and Frank promised to get back to him soon.

"Thanks, pal. I can see those captain's bars on your collar already."

"Yeah, yeah." The detective lieutenant hung up.

With his call concluded, Albert turned to the elf. "I really hate to take advantage of my friendship with Frank, but I think he might get us a step closer to finding the Arab."

"Do you think your friend will find out where Salaam lives?"

"I doubt that, Nelkie, but I know Frank will find out who's paying the bill for that number, and maybe we can track him down that way."

"I understand. Do we go to the senator's office now?"

"Yeah. I still have to drop off these papers, and I suppose it won't hurt to have a look around."

"Absolutely. Don't worry, Albert. We'll find the Iraqi and we will find out who his boss is. I just know it."

"It won't be easy," the human answered, "but we will get to the bottom of this, or I'll die trying."

"That's all I need to hear, my friend. I'm with you all the way."

With a look of grim determination, Albert fired up the Lincoln and headed toward the federal building.

Chapter 40

Tommy Walsh stared into the rain outside the basement window of his dungeon. The nineteen-year-old college sophomore had lost track of how many days he had been held captive. *Was it a week?* he wondered. *Maybe a week and a half.* The only thing he knew for sure was that someone must want something from his father awfully bad. *It must be serious business if somebody is willing to kidnap the son of a US senator and risk the wrath of the FBI.*

He had gotten through the extreme depression and boredom of his captivity so far by spending several hours every day doing sit-ups and push-ups, along with improvising every other form of exercise he could think of. He also had the presence of mind to notice every detail concerning his captors. He had made mental notes about their physical appearance, as well as any oddity or distinction that would nail a positive identification. If and when he got the opportunity to describe his kidnappers to the authorities, he would do so with precision and clarity.

Tommy heard the key turn in the basement door and he backed away to the wall farthest from the entrance. His jailers had promised to pistol whip him mercilessly if they ever opened the door and found him anywhere but against the far wall.

The door opened and a huge bald man entered, carrying a small bag. The 280-pound monster tossed the bag of burgers and fries on the only table in the room, at which point, Tommy took note of the leaping black panther tattooed on his kidnapper's forearm.

His jailer mocked him. "Sorry punk, but they were out of caviar… yuh, haw haw."

Tommy clenched his fist behind his back and thought, *Just one spinning kick to that gigantic gut of yours, and you're done, flea brain.* He thought it better to change his mind when he caught a glimpse of the other goon in the doorway. He was a slight man, very thin, with narrow shoulders. A nose ring hung above a greasy-looking black goatee, and he was pointing a .357 magnum at Tommy's chest. *Discretion,* the prisoner told himself, *is the better part of valor.* He picked up the bag of fast food and asked, "Can you at least tell me when I'm getting out of here?"

"You better just shut up and eat, punk. You ain't gettin' no more food till noon tomorrow."

Having said his piece, the burly jailer backed out of the door until only his shaved head was still in the room. "And remember, don't try anything stupid, or all your father's money won't be able to save your rich-kid neck!"

You'll get yours, fat boy, and I'm gonna enjoy giving it to you! Tommy caught himself before his anger boiled into rage. His better judgment told him to try to be patient. It was obvious the miscreants that held him here were no match for the FBI. If he could just keep it together for a few more days, he was sure to be rescued.

Thomas Jefferson Walsh sighed deeply, braced his feet under a radiator, and set about breaking his record of 714 continuous sit-ups.

Chapter 41

Albert wheeled the limo into his parking space under the Federal Building. The two investigators got out and headed for the elevator. As Albert hit the "up" button, he thought it best to issue some instructions to his invisible companion. "There shouldn't be a lot of people in the lobby at this hour, but stay close to me, just in case."

The chauffeur flinched at the sound of a female voice behind him. "Well, that's very gallant of you, Albert, but I just ran four miles unmolested and I really don't think I need Senator Walsh's bodyguard to protect me from being mugged in the lobby." Her tone was one of a teasing, taunting nature, rather than one of anger or contempt.

Albert silently cursed himself for not looking around before he opened his mouth. He didn't hear the sneaker-clad woman walking behind them and now he was faced with an awkward situation. He turned around to see Susan Barnes, who worked in the DEA's office, one floor above Pat's. Susan was a fitness fanatic and often jogged after work to relieve the stress from her high-pressure job. They had known each other for years, which only made Albert's embarrassing moment even worse. "Ah, dah, sorry about that Susan, I guess my job has a tendency to make me overprotective at times."

She smiled at him and said, "Ya know, my job has a tendency to make me think I'm a big girl who can take care of herself. I should be flattered by your concern for my safety." The elevator door opened and Albert bowed slightly and waved the woman in ahead of him, hoping for all he was worth that she didn't trip over Nelkie.

When they arrived at the lobby, the jogger thanked him for what she thought was a clumsy attempt at chivalry, and strode off. The lobby was deserted, but there was the muffled conversation and clink of dinnerware from some of Rutha's patrons enjoying a late dinner. Albert removed his cap and wiped a few beads of sweat from his brow. "Well, that was embarrassing," he mumbled under his breath. He could barely make out the small voice behind him say, "Sorry, I couldn't warn you, she fell in right behind us before I could say anything."

"It's okay. No harm done, *this* time. I just hafta remember to stay on my toes when you're around."

"How will *that* help you?

"Oh, God, Nelkie…it's just an expression. It means I hafta stay sharp."

"Sharp?"

"Oh, never mind. C'mon, there's the main elevator bank."

It wasn't until the elevator doors closed that Nelkie became overwhelmed by the smell of garlic and herbs.

"Albert!"

"What? Jeez don't do that. I'm still jumpy from our last elevator ride."

"I just wanted to know something, sorry."

"Well, what is it?"

"Don't I smell meatballs?"

"Oh, for heaven's sake! How can you think of meatballs now?"

"Well I haven't eaten anything for several hours and the aroma is so strong, I feel like I'm smelling them with my stomach!"

"All right, all right. Just let me drop these papers off and I'll get you an order of meatballs to go. Okay?"

"Thank you, my friend. That would be spectacular."

Albert reached for his keys when they got off the elevator. They walked into the outer office and he snapped on the light.

"Marvelous thing, electricity," Nelkie commented.

"Yes, simply marvelous," Albert agreed, sarcastically. He dropped the folders on Anne's desk and headed for the door.

"Where are you going?"

"I thought you wanted those meatballs."

"I do, but first things first, my friend. I want to look around here for a minute. You never know what might turn up."

"Really, Nelkie. I'm sure R.J. went over this place as thoroughly as anyone can. I'm sure there's nothing here."

"Can you just indulge my curiosity for five minutes? If I don't find anything by then, we'll go."

"Okay," Albert acquiesced. "I wouldn't want to think we missed an opportunity, even if it's a small one."

"Good." Nelkie became visible so he could touch things without complicating matters. The elf wandered into the senator's private office and asked his friend to turn on the light.

"Now, let's see," he said, folding his arms across his chest. "If memory serves me, the senator said the first time he saw Salaam, he was sitting behind the desk." He strolled around the desk and climbed up on the chair. Standing, he surveyed a desk with memos, files, mail, and an assortment of pens and stationery, all of which were arranged in a neat and orderly fashion.

Nelkie moved a file folder toward himself and a small pad fell out from under it and onto the floor. Albert picked it up and casually tossed it back on the desk.

"Just one of his note pads," he said.

"Let me see that," Nelkie demanded. Albert slid the pad over to the curious elf. Across the top of the page were two printed lines. "From the desk of" was on top and underneath "Senator Patrick Henry Walsh"

"Nothing special about that," Albert said.

"I'm not so sure," Nelkie answered. "There's an imprint left on this page. Someone wrote something on the page above this one and then tore it off."

"Yeah. So what? That's what pads are for. You write something down, tear off the page and take it with you."

"I'd just like to know what was written on the page above this one," Nelkie insisted. "If my eyes were as keen as my ears, I could read it, but I just can't make it out."

"Well, I can fix that," Albert said, matter-of-factly. "I saw this trick once in an old detective movie." He produced a pencil and began to lightly rub the point across the pad from left to right. In about ten seconds, the message was as easy to read as a neon sign. There was a phone number, followed by the words "Downtown Sportsman's Athletic club."

"Nice work, Albert! Now we've got something."

"Well, thanks, but I don't see what we've got other than a number for some heath club that Pat wrote down."

"Ah, I think not," Nelkie replied. "I'll wager that if you take a closer look, you'll find this is *not* the senator's handwriting."

Albert turned the pad around to get a better look. "Amazing," he said. "It's not Pat's handwriting! How did you know that?"

"A lucky guess," the elf said modestly. "I just thought the senator, who has a complete exercise center in his home, with the very best professional equipment, would have no need to make note of a health club phone number. My guess is that Salaam was trying to reach someone--perhaps his boss--at that club."

"I think you hit the nail right on the head, little guy. You're right. We've got something here. Only I don't have a clue how we're going to find out who he was trying to reach at the club."

"Don't worry," Nelkie assured his friend. "The answer will present itself. Now, what about those meatballs?"

In a short while, Albert was heading the limo for the highway, while Nelkie was blissfully engaged in dining ecstasy.

Albert looked over at his passenger. Seeing the dreamy look on the elf's face made him laugh. "You really love those things, don't you?"

"Oh yes. A delicacy. Truly one of the most exquisite tastes on earth. How one can start with something as unappealing as a cow and end up with a food as deliciously singular as this...it must be magic."

Albert laughed again as the big car accelerated down the entrance ramp to the highway.

Chapter 42

The long limousine swooped down the exit ramp with all the grace of a gigantic soaring bird of prey.

"We're almost home," Albert said, with a note of relief in his voice. "Boy, this has been one heck of a day. I don't know about you, little guy, but I've had enough murder and mayhem to last me a good long time."

"Yes, undeniably. If I live to be as old as Daido himself, I hope never to behold a sight like the one in that alley. Poor Mr. Hannan. What a terrifying way to die. Even if he was not a very good human, that was a horrific way to meet one's end."

"He was playin' with fire, Nelkie. Hannan was just a small-time crook with a talent for driving fast. He was outa of his league. Salaam killed him at the first sign of trouble. We just hafta find a way to prove it…and by the way, who is Daido?"

"He is the oldest and wisest among the Circle of Elders. He has lived more than four hundred years and is revered by my race. Right now, we have more important things to talk about, but perhaps when this is over, I will tell you more about our culture. Anyway, if your friend Detective Martini can find out what we need to know about Salaam's phone, I'm sure things will start to fall together."

"I'm sure that will be a piece o' cake for Frank. He'll have the information we need tomorrow, or my name's not Albert Parker."

"Piece of cake?"

"Oh, don't start that again, little guy. It's just an expression. It means this is a small task for Frank. It will be easy for him to find out who owns the phone Hannan called."

"I guess I have a lot to learn about your 'expressions.' Most of them do not appear to make much sense, at least initially. Do all humans speak in riddles like that?"

"Nelkie, you're turnin' my brain into oatmeal. I'm just too tired to get into an explanation of American colloquialisms--and besides that, we're about to turn into the gate; we're home."

"Good. Maybe sometime in the future, I'll tell you about life in the treetops, and you can explain collo, er, colloq...oh whatever they are to me. In the meantime, I would like to ask you a small favor. If you would, drop me off as close as you can to the caretaker's house. I would greatly appreciate it. I must keep a promise I made."

"Sure," Albert said. He piloted the limo down the access road to the estate and came to a stop about a hundred yards from the Baxter house.

"I won't interfere with your private business," the chauffeur said, "but please be careful. We have a lot more work to do before this over and I would hate to have you discovered. That would really complicate things, if you get my drift."

"No need to worry, my friend. I have no intention of drifting. I will be along in an hour or so."

Nelkie vaulted out the car door and headed toward the house. Albert drove off, rolling his eyes skyward, as if pleading for help from above.

Nelkie was grateful to be back, close to his beloved forest. He found the city to be much too harsh and noisy. Even if he had not gone through the horror of Hannan's death, he was sure he could never be at ease in those surroundings. All the nuances of urban life, including the stale, acrid odor that permeated the air in the city, made him uneasy. He was a child of nature and needed desperately to be back among the trees. His ancestry could not be denied. Nelkie was, and always would be, a woodland elf. He smiled to himself as the cool evening breeze brought with it the welcoming scent of pine. He looked up at the tall conifers near the house. They swayed gently from side to side, as if they were beckoning him, leading him home. He forced himself to look away and continue his approach to the house.

From his vantage point, he could see Billy's parents on the couch in the living room. Realizing Billy must be in bed, he walked around to the back of the house in search of the little boy's bedroom. In the reflected moonlight, through an open window, Nelkie could see something on the wall. The elf managed to climb up a small dogwood tree for a better look. There was a wooden plaque on the wall, from which hung a small baseball glove and a child-sized bat. He shimmied out on a limb that was only inches from the window. Looking inside, he could see his little human friend was sound asleep. Carefully, Nelkie edged off the limb and onto the window sill. With a short, soundless jump, he was inside.

Ever so softly, he walked over to the bed. In a low gentle voice, he called the boy's name. "Billy, wake up, my young friend. It is I, Nelkie."

The little boy opened his eyes wide, then quickly shut them and rubbed both hands against his sleep-filled eyelids. He opened them again and looked around the room. The youngster wasn't sure if the voice he heard was in a dream, or not. Again, the low, gentle voice whispered. "I am here, Billy. Speak softly, or your parents may hear us."

"Nelkie? Is that you?"

"Yes, my friend; I told you I would be back." The elf made himself visible.

"Oh, there you are," Billy said. "Thank you for coming back. Did you find out how to save my dad's job? Can we stay in the house now?"

Nelkie looked into the seven-year-old's pleading eyes. A shaft of moonlight shone on the boy's face, giving him an angelic appearance. He felt an ache in his heart for this boy, who would become an innocent victim of someone else's greed, unless Nelkie was successful in his quest.

"Do not fear, Billy. I have powers that are reinforced by the Circle of Elders, and their combined great wisdom will not allow me to fail, but you must be patient. The loss of your father's job is only one small piece of a very large puzzle. It may take some time for me to bring the evil ones to justice, but you have my word that they have met their match. I will not rest until all those who share guilt in this matter are defeated."

"I knew you would come back, Nelkie, and I know you will help my dad keep his job. You are a good elf and I am very glad you are my friend."

"I am very proud to have you as my first human friend," Nelkie said. "It is rare to find one so young as you who is deeply concerned about his family. You will grow to be a fine and honorable man, Billy Baxter."

Nelkie told the boy that he had much to do and must be on his way. "I will get back to see you when I can, Billy," he whispered. "Next time I see you, I will bring you something special."

Before the boy could answer, the elf had disappeared. Billy listened, but Nelkie's soft shoes made no sound as he stepped upon the sill and alighted from the dogwood tree to the ground.

Billy rolled over in his bed, happy that Nelkie would make his father's problem go away.

Chapter 43

Nelkie made it back to the compound in record time. He entered Albert's cabin to find his friend with his feet up on the coffee table. The bodyguard was startled when he heard the door open, and looked up to see no one walk through the door. It took a moment, but then he realized the "nobody" was his see-through friend. Nelkie popped into view and shut the door.

"Thank you. I was hopin' you weren't a ghost. Barbara left me a note. She's up at her sister's for a day or two. We have the place to ourselves."

"That's great, Albert, but do me a favor and keep that giant canine locked up. He almost had me for dinner once and I don't want to give him a second chance."

"Oh yeah. We don't want you to have to go through another totem pole episode, do we?'

"It's a good thing he didn't knock it over," Nelkie said. "I would have been in real trouble. Can you even imagine how the senator or his wife would have reacted if I'd had to defend myself from that animal?"

"What would you have done?" Albert asked, now very curious.

"Oh, I'm not sure. I know I wouldn't hurt the beast, but I'm certainly not going to allow him to get close enough to make me an appetizer. I would probably just conjure up a strong wind to keep pushing him away from me."

Albert chuckled, thinking about Pat and Barbara standing on the patio, watching their 150-pound dog blow out into the pool. "Definitely one of your better photo ops," he said, still laughing. Suddenly, the phone rang and Albert dove on it.

"Hey, Piston. That phone number you gave me is billed to a company named Two Guys Plumbing Supplies. The address I got was their downtown offices, 348 Berkley. They have a huge warehouse out in the sticks. I think it's off Stevens Street."

"Frank, you're a prince. I owe ya big time."

"Listen, Albert, you watch your back out there. If things look like they might get sticky, you call me right away."

"Will do, Frank. Thanks again." Albert hung up and shrugged his shoulders at Nelkie. "Two Guys Plumbing Supplies? Does that make any sense to you?"

Nelkie looked thoughtful. He scratched his chin and then gave Albert his considered opinion. "One thing I'm sure of. There's no way on earth that Terry Hannan was inquiring about his plumbing at 10:30 on a Saturday night. I have a question."

"Shoot."

"You say this R.J. Abbott is very good at investigations?"

"His company is one of the best in the world. Why?"

"If you call them and say the senator needs to know a few things, will they do some investigating and possibly some research for you?"

"In a heartbeat."

"Splendid! Call him in the morning and ask if they can find out who at the plumbing company actually has possession of the phone in question. Next, see if they can find out if Sierra Log Homes and the plumbing company are connected in any way."

"I think I see where you're going with this. You think the Iraqi's boss is a big shot at one of these companies. Maybe the owner. It's worth checking out. I'll call R.J. in the morning. For now, my clever little friend, I'm going to bed. The couch is yours. G'night."

Nelkie curled up on the huge couch and thought this was the

first time since he left home that he got to sleep on something soft and fluffy. The elf fell asleep quickly, thinking that tomorrow would be the day they began to unravel the mystery that was Mohammad Abdul Salaam.

Chapter 44

A grey dawn fell over the cinderblock prison that held Tommy Walsh. After his morning exercises, he stared, for what seemed like the two thousandth time, out the only window of his basement jail. He had to stand on his toes to see anything outside. He figured out that the window must be at the rear of the building. All he could see were trees. No road, no cars, no people, only a heavily wooded area about fifty feet from where he stood.

Wherever I am, I must be miles away from any city. If only I could find a way to break that window quietly, I might be able to make a run for it.

The only items in his one room cell were a small army cot, a kitchen-type table, and in one corner of the room there were several crates filled with hundreds of elbow-shaped short pieces of pipe.

"Well, let's go look at the lovely pieces of pipe," he said aloud. He bent over the first crate and began to remove some of the elbows. *If I don't find something to do soon*, he thought, *I'm sure to go stir crazy.* Tommy began to arrange pieces of pipe on the floor. For lack of anything better to do, he found himself making designs and pictures on the floor.

After emptying one crate, he lifted it up to see what was underneath. "Oh, what great joy," he said, mocking himself. "A whole box of small straight pipes." He took several handfuls out of the crate. Some of the pieces were two or three inches long and some reached a length of about a foot. Mindlessly, he started to fashion a mural on the concrete floor. Like a small boy playing on the floor in kindergarten, he shaped houses, a road, and then a skyscraper. Tommy went back to his toy box to get some smaller pieces to make windows. He carelessly thrust his hand into the box and something jabbed him under a fingernail. He yanked his hand back as if it had been burnt. After shaking off the pain, he examined his index finger. A tiny bubble of blood oozed out from under the nail. "Damn! What the hell is in there?"

There, on the bottom of the crate, Tommy saw his salvation. More carefully now, he reached down and pulled out a foot-long rat-tailed file. The end that had jabbed him came to a point. The prisoner looked at the file and then at the window. Slowly, a smile grew across his face when he realized that escape was now a possibility.

He took the empty crate over to the window and turned it upside-down. Standing on the box, he jammed the pointed end of the file down where the glass met the wooden frame. Over and over, again and again, he pulled the file along the edge between the glass and the wood that held it in place. Pulling, scraping, digging. Slowly, the wood and putty began to come away from the glass. Little by little, tiny dust particles floated to the floor.

After about forty minutes of tedious work, a very small space, the same thickness as the pointed end of the file, began to develop between the glass and the wood. Encouraged by his progress, Tommy dug deeper. Pulling, scraping, digging. He repeated this movement so many times that his arm ached. He switched to his left arm and continued from the opposite corner.

An hour of maddening monotony had rewarded him with a space a little more than a quarter inch deep.

If I can get this down to where I can jam the point of the file under the glass, I might be able to pry one of these panes out from the bottom.

He was sure that if he could remove three or four panes of glass, he could knock out the divider with his palm and climb out the window!

Another forty minutes of hard labor and he had worn the wood frame down to where he could see the bottom edge of the glass. With great care, he inserted the point of his file under the glass and pried gently. The glass moved only a fraction of an inch. The disappointed prisoner realized that he would have to go through the same process along at least one of the side edges, in order to loosen the glass enough to remove it.

Undaunted, he dug his file in again and began pulling from top to bottom. Scraping, digging. His quest for freedom was far greater than the dull ache building up in his arms.

Chapter 45

Nelkie bounded off the couch at the crack of dawn. He was anxious to get on with his quest. His sharp ears picked up the sound of Albert's snoring in the adjacent bedroom. The elf decided against waking up his host, and strolled into the kitchen.

With his stomach demanding immediate attention, he looked around the room for some breakfast. With tremendous brute force, he managed to pry open the refrigerator with his bare hands. He propped the door open with a kitchen chair, climbed up on it and liberated a container of orange juice. Placing the container on his chair, he gingerly pushed it over to the sink. Nelkie retrieved a cup from the drain board and poured himself some juice. Next, he fetched a steak knife from the drain board and like a man hacking his way through a jungle, he separated a banana from the bunch on the counter. He put all his weight on the knife and sliced off a full third of the fruit. After surgically removing the skin, he sliced off four large pieces.

Nelkie was happily gorging himself when Albert shuffled into the kitchen in shorts and flip-flops.

"Good morning, Albert," he said, in a cheerful tone.

"I won't know if it's a good morning until I've had some coffee," came the sleepy reply.

"It's warm and sunny. How could it not be a good day?"

"I'm just not a good morning person," Albert replied. "After a coupla cups a coffee, I'm sure I'll appear more human."

"Where I come from, that may not be considered such a great thing."

Albert shot Nelkie a curious look. When it finally dawned on him that he was speaking with a non-human, he had to laugh. Nelkie joined in and the sound of the elf's infectious laughter forced Albert to put the coffee pot down and enjoy a good belly laugh.

"You're quite a character, Nelkie. I hafta tell you, I really do enjoy your company. It's nice to be around someone who has a positive attitude. It's invigorating. Although, every once in a while I look at you and think any moment now, I'm going to wake up in a sanitarium in a straitjacket."

"Fear not, my human friend, for I assure you, I am real, I am not human, and you are not crazy."

"Well, I thank you for that," Albert said, sitting down with his coffee. "But if I could be serious for a moment, I wanna tell you something. I truly admire you for what you're trying to do. This whole quest thing is a very noble idea. I also believe, judging by my experience with you, that elves are a highly intelligent race, but I think your philosophy is flawed."

"Oh?" Nelkie looked across the table with raised eyebrows.

"Well, it seems a little naïve to me, to have an entire race of intelligent beings truly believing that if you do something good for someone, they in turn will do something good for someone else. Personally, I don't think that most humans are like that. Do you really think that you can actually change the world by sending one elf at a time to face hatred, bigotry, and greed?"

"If you are asking me if we believe that one being can change the world, the answer is absolutely YES. I will use your own race as an example. Will you sit there and tell me that Jesus of Nazareth did not change the world? Will you claim that Christopher Columbus had no impact on the human race? Would you say that Gandhi's life was of no consequence, or likewise that of Dr. Martin Luther King Jr.? I think not, my doubting friend. Now, I do not mean to compare myself to any of these great ones of your past, but the fact remains that one singular life can indeed change the world."

"Your point is well taken, Nelkie. I guess I've seen so much of the ugly side of life that my faith has been a little shaken. Thanks for setting me straight. Now, let's see what we can do about changing our little corner of the world."

Albert picked up the phone and dialed R.J. Abbott's private number. As always, it was answered on the first ring.

"Abbott."

"R.J., it's Albert. How's it going?"

"Slow, but sure. A couple of my field operatives ran down a lead on a motorcycle. Traced the bike to a dealer in LA. The salesman remembered our Arab. Positive ID on his picture. Of course, the address on the sales receipt turned out to be an empty lot. My FBI connection tells me his people have spotted Salaam in Sacramento. We're running that one down as we speak. That's about it for now."

"Sounds like you're working hard, as usual. Look, I know you're really busy, but I need some information for the senator."

"What can I get for you, Albert?"

"We need to know if a company out here called Sierra Log Homes is connected in any way to another company called Two Guys Plumbing Supplies. Anything you can find out about these two companies would be a big help. Oh, one more thing. We also need to know who at Two Guys was issued a cell phone with the following number." Albert read off Salaam's cell number to R.J.

"Got it. I'll get back to you by early afternoon."

"I appreciate it, R.J. Thanks."

Albert hung up and shrugged his shoulders at Nelkie. "Well, that's all we can do until we have some additional information. I think I'll make another cuppa coffee and relax on the porch. Want one?"

"No thanks, but I'll join you on the porch."

Albert held the door open for his diminutive friend and settled into a rocking chair. He hung his feet over the porch railing and yawned. "Ah, I just love this place," he said. "Only about a hundred and fifty feet from some of the thickest unspoiled forest land in the whole country, right off my porch. I never tire of just looking at it."

"We are of one mind on that subject," the elf concurred. "Don't forget that about a week's walk into that unspoiled forest is my home, and the home of hundreds of my fellow elves."

"I hafta tell ya, Nelkie, that I find it a little hard to understand why you live the way you do."

"What is it that you find so mysterious?"

"Well, for one thing, you are well aware of all the modern conveniences that humans use, yet your entire race chooses to live inside of trees with no heat or hot water. Life must be very hard in the winter for your people."

"Let me explain a few things, Albert. First of all, as you know, we are not people. That reason alone is enough for us to live separately from humans. Can you even imagine if someone who looks like me applied for a job at The Home Depot, or Toys 'R' Us? I could probably start a small riot just by walking in the front door. One look at these ears, my friend, and that would be it. Pandemonium. Or, how about this; I walk into a bank and try to get a mortgage on a nice little house, so I don't have to live in a tree anymore. That would be an interesting conversation. As the loan officer looks over my application, he says something like, 'Let's see, Mr. Nelkie, it says here that you are a self-employed toymaker. How much money did you make last year?'

" 'Er, well, none. I gave all the toys away.' Somehow, I don't think that would go over too well. Anyway, as far as our lives being difficult in the winter, let me show you something."

Nelkie skipped down the porch steps and looked around. He pulled a small piece of wood planking from under the porch. It was almost a foot long and about six inches wide. He put the board on the walkway in front of the cabin. Next, he found a stone roughly the same size as a softball. With considerable effort, he placed the stone on the plank. Now he stepped back and picked up his walking stick and pushed back his sleeves. Albert couldn't help but notice the elf's face. It was contorted with deep concentration, as the little being directed the power of his mind through his walking stick. After a long moment, he touched his stick to the stone and said, "Behold, heat!"

Albert removed his feet from the railing to pay more attention to the event taking place in his front yard. With his eyes glued to the stone, Albert could swear it was starting to change color. It was sort of gray, but now it appeared to be brown…no, red. Then bright red. By the time Albert made it down the stairs, the stone was white-hot. When he got within six feet of it, he could feel the heat radiating from the stone. All of a sudden, with a great flash, the plank burst into flames!

"Whoa baby," Albert shouted as he stepped back, shielding his face with his arms.

"You humans have fireplaces," Nelkie said. "We would have a problem with the smoke. Even if we could somehow install a chimney, the escaping smoke could only cause problems. So, instead, every living area has several heat dispersal units. Small rocks and soil keep the heat from setting the floor on fire, while larger stones are piled high and heated white-hot. Crude maybe, but very effective. So you see, Albert, we really don't need electricity or water heaters. We simply apply the knowledge of the ancients, which was handed down to us millennia ago, and we are warm and comfortable."

Albert's eyebrows were arched so high in amazement, they nearly reached his hairline. "You sure can do some astonishing things, little guy. I think if I could perform this kind of magic, I'd be a very rich man!"

"Albert, my friend, this is not magic. At least it is not the hocus-pocus that humans believe to be magic. It is advanced knowl-edge, taught to our elders by the ancients, countless centuries ago. It is a tool, a means to achieve an end, nothing more. This is another reason why we cannot yet live among you. Even a good man like yourself will not think first to use this knowledge to help others. Your first thoughts are of money!"

"Nelkie, you make me feel like I did something wrong," the human said, looking at the ground.

"I apologize, Albert. You are a good man. I know this to be true. It's the way you humans think. Sometimes your thought process is misdirected. If you were raised in a society like I was, where each member is completely committed to helping everyone else in any way they can, you would not think of money or grand pos-sessions. You would know that working hard to help other people would make you feel an absolute joy in your heart that would far outweigh any jingle in your pocket. Consider this," Nelkie added. "Think back to all the best times of your life. I can assure you that when you remember the most exciting, the most humorous, and the most meaningful times in your memory, they will include other people. Good times cannot be enjoyed to the fullest if you are alone. At least half the pleasure of life is sharing it with some-one else."

"I hafta agree with you. I'm afraid most of us humans lose sight of the basic truths that can make life itself a beautiful thing."

"Don't be discouraged, Albert. I think we both know now that you will no longer be one of them. In time, others will absorb some of this wisdom from you. This, my enlightened friend, is what makes the challenge of an elf's quest worth the effort."

Nelkie was pleased that someone who used to knock men down for a living had come to understand and appreciate the humanitarian philosophy of the elf nation.

Albert had returned to his rocking chair and was lost in thought.

Nelkie sat on the top step of the porch, taking in the unspoiled beauty of the woodland. His memory was jogged when he noticed a large dead ash tree at the forest's edge.

"I'll be right back," he said, and scampered off toward the dead tree.

Albert watched his friend snap off a limb. The elf broke off several pieces until he wound up with one he was satisfied with. He returned with a stick about a half inch in diameter and a foot long. Reclaiming his perch on the top step of the porch, the elf produced a small knife from a sheath on his belt. The human leaned over the railing to watch.

"I just remembered another promise I must keep." Without saying another word, the elf set his knife into the nondescript piece of wood. Albert watched closely as Nelkie's hands moved faster and faster, up and down and around the small stick. Tiny pieces of bark and wood chips were flying around the little craftsman as if they were being ejected from a chainsaw. Nelkie's hands were moving at blurring speed. Albert was amazed that anyone could handle a knife at such a pace without causing injury to himself. In approximately three minutes, the apprentice toymaker stopped. He held out the finished flute at arm's length and studied his work. The once-dirty-looking little stick was now a clean, finely detailed instrument. The light-colored ash flute had six finger holes with which one could play several different notes.

"Hmm, it seems I'm a little out of practice," Nelkie said. After very closely scrutinizing the flute, he raised his knife and removed the tiniest imperfection on the wooden tube. Satisfied that his work was up to exacting standards, he turned the flute over and, at a much slower speed, carefully carved six stars in a circle.

"The American elf signature," Albert said, remembering his toy ferry boat.

"That's right," Nelkie said, smiling. "Now it's finished."

He wiped off any remaining wood dust and placed the flute in his pouch.

Albert was about to ask who the flute was for, when the phone rang and disrupted his thoughts. The voice on the other end introduced himself as Ellis Davenport, head of research investigations for R. J. Abbott.

"I have a good amount of information for you, Mr. Parker. You may want to write this down for your report to the senator."

"Okay, great. Just give me a second to find a pen."

Albert motioned to the elf to join him in the cabin. They sat on the couch as Albert picked up a large legal pad and a pen.

"Thank you for the fast service, Mr. Davenport. I'm sure the senator will be pleased."

"No problem. When Mr. Abbott called this morning and told me this information was for the senator, we got on it right away. Now, here's what we found. Sierra Log Homes is involved, either directly or indirectly, with several other companies. What I mean is, a few of these are related to Sierra's home-building business and are listed as wholly owned subsidiaries of Sierra. Others are connected either by limited partnerships, majority stock holders, or a series of holding companies and other legal mumbo-jumbo that would take a year to sort out. It seems to me, Mr. Parker, that for whatever reason, someone does not want it to be easy to connect these nine companies. What we have here is basically the tip of a very large legal iceberg."

"So what you're telling me, Mr. Davenport, is that you can prove on paper that these nine companies are all connected to one another, but some clever lawyer is probably trying to hide those connections in legal clap-trap."

"Precisely. I will give you the names of the nine companies in the order in which they opened for business."

Nelkie leaned over the table as Albert jotted down the list as follows:

1. Sierra Log Homes
2. Two Guys Plumbing Supplies
3. American Drywall Contractors
4. National Estate Services (maids, gardeners, etc.)
5. Foremost Nurseries (trees, shrubs, lawns.)
6. International Publishing (books)
7. Elite Importing (household items)
8. L'il Luke's Bar-B- Que (restaurant chain)
9. Design Technologies (custom alarm systems)

"That's the basic package," Davenport said. If you need more information, I can dig deeper, but it will take time."

"Thanks a million, Mr. Davenport. You've been a great help. Let me see what I can do with all of this and I'll get back to ya."

"You're very welcome, and call me Ellis."

"Okay. Thanks again, Ellis."

They ended their conversation and Albert stared at his notes, shaking his head.

"Is something wrong?" Nelkie could read the frustration on his friend's face.

"I was hoping for something a little more telling than just a list of companies. I don't see how this can help us at all. It seems like the farther along we get in this investigation, the more chaotic the facts become. I don't have the slightest idea what to make of this list."

Nelkie put a reassuring hand on his friend's shoulder and said, "One just needs to know where to look."

Albert looked at his notes, but found nothing helpful. He turned to Nelkie to see the elf grinning from one large ear to the other. He knew that Nelkie had spotted something on that list that he did not. Exasperated, he demanded to be enlightened. "All right, you pixillated little imp, I know you're onto something. Are you going to clue me in or not?"

"Of course, my friend," was Nelkie's reply. "You say the facts are becoming chaotic. Allow me to demonstrate how the seeds of harmony can grow roots in the soil of chaos."

"What in the world are you talking about, Nelkie?"

"Look out the window, Albert. Do you see that big spruce tree swaying back and forth in harmony with the wind? A thing of beauty, is it not?"

"Well, sure, but...."

"If you stood right next to that tree, you would see that all the separate needles would be blowing this way and that in a chaotic manner, yet from a distance, the whole tree is swaying in gentle harmony with the wind."

"Thanks for the nature lesson, but what does that have to do with this stupid list?"

Nelkie picked up the copy of *Ring* magazine from the coffee table. "The list as you see it is just a pile of useless information, but when one looks at the list a little differently, there is a glaring harmony that we may find useful."

With that statement, the elf placed the magazine over Albert's list, covering all but the first letter of each company's name. Albert's eyes widened with recognition as Nelkie ran his forefinger down the list from top to bottom. The first letter of each company, when read vertically, spelled out the name Stanfield!

"Holy smoke," Albert cried. "Stanfield! If that's Emil Stanfield, you really are on to something."

"Why? Who is Emil Stanfield?"

"The one man who would have a good motive to scam the senator's land away from him. He's a developer and one of the most successful businessmen on the West Coast. His picture is always in the paper. He attends every highly publicized charitable event and donates millions, but he can afford it. I think it's all done just to make him look good. It's rumored that he is really a vicious, vindictive creep. If he's connected with all the companies on that list, he would have the means to develop this land quickly and efficiently."

"This is very good," the elf said, scratching his chin. "I think we have two more calls to make in order to give our investigation a directional jolt."

"I don't follow," Albert said. "What are you thinking?"

"Well," Nelkie began, "I assume we are agreed that this Stanfield fellow is probably our man. I feel that is just too much of a coincidence for his name to turn up in such a prominent way, without him actually being involved."

"Oh, he's involved all right," Albert said emphatically. "I've followed this guy's career in the newspaper. Emil Stanfield has an ego as big as the great outdoors. He's in this right up to his egotistical neck. You can bet your pointed ears on that one."

"Good. Since we are in agreement," the elf went on, "I think you should call Mr. Davenport back. Ask him if the name Stanfield can be tied to any of the companies on that list. It would help immensely if there is some legal connection on paper. Next, I believe you should call the health club. Ask them if Stanfield is a member."

"Wow! That's it," Albert declared. "Nelkie, you're a genius! That's who the Iraqi was trying to reach from Pat's office! He must have called information, written the number down on Pat's memo pad, and called from his own cell phone."

"That's the way I see it," Nelkie agreed. "By the way, see if you can get an address for Stanfield's private office. We should have a look around the place tonight, when no one is there."

"Gotcha." Albert grabbed the phone and got Davenport on the line. After outlining what he needed, he thanked the researcher and dialed the Downtown Sportsman's Health Club.

"Hi. I'm trying to locate Emil Stanfield. Could you tell me if he's in the building?"

"Just one moment, sir, I'll check. Yes, he has reserved some court time. His card is here, so he must be on the squash court. Shall I page him for you, sir?"

"No, no. That won't be necessary. I'll just come down and meet him. Thank you."

"Outstanding, Albert! Now we know that Salaam and Stanfield are defiantly associated. We must get to Stanfield's office."

"I agree, Nelkie. Maybe something will turn up there that can help us locate T. J. Let's discuss strategy over lunch, shall we?"

"Capital idea, my friend. What culinary delights await?"

"Uh, I think I can grill a coupla burgers for us. How's that?"

"Great! What's a burger?"

Albert was extolling the virtues of cow meat, as Nelkie referred to it, while the elf helped him with plates, rolls, and condiments.

Nelkie thoroughly enjoyed his first cheeseburger, but was quick to point out that there was no comparison to the exquisite flavor of a well-prepared meatball.

"I think you've become a garlic freak," Albert said, only half joking.

Chapter 46

The ugly, hairless head appeared from behind the dungeon door. Supported by a massive, unwashed body, it entered the room. The head was smiling sardonically as it surveyed Tommy's crypt-like cell.

"Oh, ain't this cute. The poor little rich kid has been sooo busy making pretty pictures on the floor."

"Just trying to keep from going crazy," Tommy said. "You guys won't even bring me a newspaper. It gets a little boring, just sitting here all day, you know."

"Shut up, you spoiled little snot! You're lucky we don't pass the time beating on your rich little head. Hey Mung, come and take a look at what our artist has done here on the floor."

The man with the small nose ring and the large handgun walked into the room, gun first. "Whut's this supposed to be, Crusher? Are we runnin' a kindergarten here?"

"Yeah, I think this kid's been havin' too much fun. Get that push broom from the hallway, Mung."

The skinny man retreated and returned, gun in right hand, long-handled push broom in his left.

"Give that to snot-nose here," Crusher ordered. "Sweep all this crap out into the hall, Jr. Play time is over for you. Keep your gun on him, Mung. I'm gonna look around and make sure there aren't any more little surprises in here. The bald-headed monster turned around and started to walk toward the only window in the room.

Tommy saw the chance he had been waiting for. Trusting in his martial arts training, he acted swiftly and efficiently. He calmly accepted the broom from his captor and pretended to be trying to tighten the handle. As he clumsily fumbled, the broom separated from its handle. Before the bristles could reach the floor, Tommy had struck Mung twice with the handle. As the broomstick sliced through the air, the whirring sound made Crusher turn toward the noise. The big man had turned in time to see Mung take two shots to the face in rapid succession. Whack! Thwack! The first blow collapsed the bridge of his nose, then a hard shot to the temple put his lights out and he dropped to the floor.

Crusher was now running at Tommy with both arms fully extended, as if to try to strangle his prey. The walls of the basement room were ringing with the bald man's enraged growling. Unmoved, Tommy stood his ground and waited until the last possible split second, then dropped to one knee. With blurring speed, T.J. struck twice.

The pain radiating down the giant's right shin was too intense for him to remain standing. He was going down. Before his hands could break his fall, he felt the broomstick explode across his clenched teeth. The big man was on all fours. He spit out a mouthful of blood and the parts of seven broken teeth. "Now I'm gonna kill you," Crusher gurgled through his imploded incisors.

"I think not, fat man," came the reply.

Crusher looked up to see Tommy holding the gun. "Stay put, or I'll blow what's left of your brain all over this room."

The beaten jailer sat with his back against the wall looking very much like a 280-pound Jack o' Lantern.

Tommy backed out the door of his prison and locked it. He threw the key under the stairs and then, smelling freedom, he bounded up the stairs two at a time.

He arrived at the first floor and was surprised not to find any other guards or accomplices. He put the gun under his shirt and strode out into the sunshine.

Chapter 47

Nelkie was curiously examining Albert's movie library, when Ellis Davenport called back. The elf had learned about television and movies when he was in school, but he was fascinated by how far the technology had advanced in only a few years.

While Albert took the call, Nelkie investigated how the DVD player was wired into the television. Having the mechanical mind of a toy maker, he was naturally curious about what made these electronic marvels work. His studies were interrupted by his very excited partner.

"Bingo! Pay dirt! We hit the jackpot, Nelkie!"

Albert came into the living room waving a piece of paper.

"What have you got there?"

Albert showed Nelkie his notes and they both poured over the fruits of Ellis Davenport's labor.

"According to this," Albert pointed out, "Emil Stanfield is on the board of directors of every single company on our list! It would probably take a dozen lawyers a year to prove it, but I'll bet you dollars to doughnuts that sly weasel owns all nine of those corporations."

"What better way to find out what's going on in a company you own secretly, than to attend every board meeting," Nelkie observed.

"Yeah, and I'll betcha every other board member thinks he's just an outside observer, paid a fee for his managerial input. If they only knew the owner was sitting right there, watching their every move.

You gotta give this guy credit. He sure is a cunning fox."

"Any luck tracking down the Arab's phone, Albert?"

"Oh yeah, I almost forgot. All they could get out of the office help was that the phone was issued to some efficiency expert. He checks on everything from how well the warehouse is run, to how friendly the company operators and order takers are. Nobody likes him. They all have him pegged as a spy for upper management. It's rumored that he reports only to the board of directors. Here's the best part, though--aside from the fact that this guy is all business and friends with no one, he's of Middle Eastern decent! Ellis says his name is Ahmed Fazal."

"I think we both know who Ahmed Fazal really is," Nelkie said, scratching his chin.

"Yes, we do," Albert concurred. He was looking at his friend and smiling broadly.

"What's so amusing?" the elf asked, still scratching his chin.

Albert started to laugh. "Oh, I was just reminded of my young adult years. Has it occurred to you that you've been scratching your chin an awful lot lately?"

"Well, now that you mention it, yes. I hope I'm not getting some sort of malady. It would be terrible if I got sick now, just when we're making such wonderful progress."

Albert laughed out loud. His little friend had an absolutely brilliant mind, but the telltale signs of the advent of adulthood had eluded him completely. "Come with me, little man."

Nelkie followed Albert into the bathroom. "What are we doing in here?" he asked.

"Allow me," Albert answered as he picked the elf up and stood him on the sink, in front of the mirror. "Look closely at your chin, my friend, and you will see why it itches."

Nelkie peered into the mirror and discovered the slightest hint of red. "By Bindar's basket! My beard is coming in! Today I really am a mature elf. I have a beard!"

The elf was so excited that he did a series of cartwheels into the living room, the last of which sent him tumbling into the entertainment center. The two friends shared a hearty laugh as Albert's entire video library tumbled off the shelves until Nelkie was buried up to his knees in DVDs.

While they were cleaning up the mess, Albert gave the elf the last piece of good news. "Ellis gave me Stanfield's office address. He said it was the easiest job we gave him. A matter of public record."

"Things are really starting to work out well," the elf said. "How soon can we go to Stanfield's office?"

"Almost any time now. The office should be unoccupied in an hour or so, but I have no idea how we are going to get inside."

"You just leave that little detail to me. I still have a few more surprises for you. I have a positive feeling about this. I just know we will find out where Tommy is very soon."

"I hope you're right, Nelkie, but I have to tell ya that something's botherin' me."

Nelkie picked up the last movie from the floor and put it back on the shelf and picked up a palm corder that was on the shelf below. "Is this what I think it is?" he asked his host. "Oh, and what is it that's bothering you?"

"Well, that's a palm corder, or a small video camera, but I never use it anymore because I can record video from my phone. Anyway, I've been wondering if maybe we should share some of this information we've gathered with Martini of R.J."

"I believe we should handle this alone, Albert. I think we can do better than they would, even though we are not professional investigators."

"I appreciate your faith, Nelkie, but what if we get in over our heads? If anything bad ever happened to Tommy because we didn't get help, I could never forgive myself."

"Not to worry, my friend. You have a weapon the police do not...
ME! I can gain access to any building, and I can do so unseen. Even
your friend R.J. cannot make such a claim. Don't forget, it's not just
the senator's son that's facing grave danger here. Hundreds of my fellow elves are in jeopardy of being discovered, displaced, or worse.
Forgive me, but my instincts are telling me to trust the future of the
American elves to my own resources, not those of humans I do not
know. Don't worry, my stout-hearted friend; we will emerge victori-
ous and you will be a hero!"

"I don't care a fig about that hero stuff...I just want to be sure
Tommy gets home safely."

"I know you do. I promise, Albert, if a situation develops that I
think we cannot handle, or if Tommy would be in more danger if we
don't get help, I will be the first to ask for reinforcements."

"Then that's good enough for me, little guy."

"Good. Now, about recording video with your phone. How is
that possible?"

Albert took out his iPhone and said, "It's really very simple." He
bent down and showed his friend the proper procedure, and then
pointed the phone at Nelkie. "Do something," he commanded. The elf
obeyed and sprung into a tumbling routine across the three-cushioned
couch. He somersaulted off the arm and landed on his feet, like a dart
thrown into the floor.

"How's that for elfin agility?"

"Well, let's see how it turned out. Albert sat on the floor so they
could both see the video. They were both taken aback by what they
saw. The couch cushions were being depressed by some unseen force,
followed by a tiny voice saying, "How's that for elfin agility?"

"Well there's something I didn't know," Nelkie confessed. "Elves
don't have cameras of any kind, you know."

"Going by this, what would be the point? Anyway, this may be something we can use to our advantage somewhere down the line."

They watched the brief video once more, just to be sure they didn't miss anything. Not another word was spoken, as they both just shook their heads in disbelief and headed toward the door.

Chapter 48

The curious duo marched out to the barn, with Nelkie taking two hurried steps to every one of Albert's leisurely strides. "Barbara left the Jeep here, so let's take that. I think it will be a little less conspicuous than the limo, and I think you could remain visible. If anyone should notice you, I would guess they'd think you were a little kid on his way to a costume party."

"How many little kids do you know with a beard?" Nelkie asked indignantly.

Albert smiled and decided not to tell his friend that what he was calling a beard, most humans referred to as "peach fuzz."

The Jeep roared out of the compound and toward the highway. Both its occupants were filled with nervous anticipation. Most of their ride was passed in silence. Albert wondered what developments lay ahead, while Nelkie simply enjoyed the ride. Traveling by car was a stimulating experience for the elf. For this woodland creature to be rocketing down the interstate at a blazing sixty-five miles per hour could only be defined as living life to the fullest.

With both of them lost in thought, time passed quickly. Before they knew it, they were downtown looking for 368 Colorado Blvd. Nelkie spotted the building and pointed to the underground parking garage. Albert wheeled the Jeep into a vacant spot and killed the motor. A quick scan from the safety of the Jeep revealed a dozen parked cars, but no one was about. They got out, and Nelkie disappeared.

"Stay close, little guy; I'm not familiar with this building."

"Right behind you, Albert. Hey, what's that over to your right?"

Albert looked ahead and to his right to see a large steel door, right next to which was a vacant parking space. Stenciled on the wall above the empty space was a sign proclaiming a reserved spot for E. Stanfield. They approached the door and Albert peered through the steel mesh and glass window. He could see a smaller door with the gold-plated script letters E.S. above the threshold.

"It looks like you found Stanfield's private elevator." The chauffeur tried the outer door. It was locked. "Well, I guess we'll hafta go through the lobby. I'm sure his office will be listed in the directory." Albert started to walk away when Nelkie stopped him.

"Wait! This is perfect. I'll get us in."

Albert turned to make sure they were still alone, as the elf flipped open the knob on his walking stick and removed the tiny key. As he inserted his key into the lock, an almost imperceptible amber glow emanated from the keyhole. At the same time, the tiny key grew larger in his hand. When it had expanded to fill the entire keyhole, the amber glow dissipated and Nelkie turned the key. The human turned around when he heard a "click" and tried the door. It opened easily. The elf removed his key and they advanced to the elevator door. It was also locked. Nelkie repeated the procedure with his key and suddenly, the elevator door slid to the right, granting them entry.

They stepped into the private elevator and the door sealed them in. There were only three buttons on the panel: PH, L, and G. Albert pushed the button for the penthouse.

The door slid back to reveal the opulently decorated inner sanctum of Emil Stanfield. The trespassers entered a large private office and at once felt the reflected masculine power of its owner.

Highly polished mahogany walls rose to meet a twelve-foot ceiling. Elaborately framed original oil paintings hung at strategic points around the room, most of which depicted brutally violent scenes culled from contact sports. Directly opposite the mammoth desk stood a brass and glass trophy cabinet containing dozens of ribbons, plaques, and trophies. Albert had to get a closer look. "Hey, check this out! This guy has trophies for half a dozen sports! The dates go from this year all the way back to his high school football team...state champions. This guy is some athlete. Football, hockey, karate, squash, tennis, and even racquetball. Every award in here is for first place. That's Stanfield ,all right. Second place was never good enough for him. First or nothing. Win at any cost."

"That's all well and good, Albert, but we are not here to admire this man's athletic achievements. He is our adversary."

"I know, Nelkie, I know. It's just that I was a professional athlete for many years and I understand what kind of determination and skill it takes to own a collection like this one. I hafta respect that, even if the owner is a lowlife snake in the grass."

"I think I can understand your point of view, as long as you don't lose sight of who this evil man really is."

"Not a chance, buddy."

"I didn't think so. Anyway, I'm going to go through his desk. See if you can find a safe, or anywhere he might store private papers."

"Good idea." Albert began looking behind all the paintings for a hidden safe.

Nelkie was surprised to find the desk unlocked. He searched drawer after drawer with no success. The center drawer contained only pens, stationery, paper clips, and the like. Top right drawer, only an appointment calendar with business related meetings and Stanfield's workout schedule. The large bottom right drawer contained only toiletries. Nelkie tried the two drawers on the left side of the desk. Top left held file folders and various memoranda. Nothing useful or incriminating. The elf had his hand on the last drawer when Albert interrupted his progress.

"Would you mind becoming visible, please? I really don't like trying to talk to you when you're not here."

Nelkie voiced the words "I must return," and obliged his friend.

"Thank you. I can't find any safe, but there's a credenza over next to the trophy case. Do you think you can unlock it for me?"

Nelkie nodded. "Just let me look in this last drawer." He pulled the handle, but it wouldn't open. "Hmm, this one seems to be locked."

Albert walked over to Nelkie's side, so he could finally see how the elf was opening all these locks. Nelkie flipped open the handle of his walking stick again and removed the key. It was smaller than even the tiny keyhole in the desk. Albert watched with raised eyebrows as his friend placed the key in the locked drawer. Again, the amber glow emerged from the keyhole. Again, the key expanded until it filled the keyhole. Albert was going to ask how Nelkie did that, but thought better of it.

Nelkie opened the drawer and reached inside. The first item he removed was an eight-by-ten picture frame that was upside-down. He placed it right side up on the desktop. They both realized right away that they were looking at an eighteen-year-old Emil Stanfield in his high school football uniform. He was standing behind a large state championship trophy, with his arm around a very pretty Homecoming Queen.

Albert was already trying to dig something else out of the bottom of the drawer, when Nelkie stopped him.

"Hey! Wait a minute! Look at this picture!"

"Yeah, so? Stanfield with the first of his many trophies. So what?"

"You're missing the most important trophy of his life! Look at the girl, Albert. Look closely at the girl!"

Suddenly Albert looked like he had been hit by one of his own left hooks. "Holy Moses," he exclaimed. "Is that who I think it is?"

"Absolutely, my friend. This is a high school picture of the future Barbara Walsh!"

"Whoa. This is gettin' a little scary," Albert said, scratching his head. "Let's see what else is in here."

He pulled out a large photo album. When opened, the first things they came across were love letters from the then Barbara Brown to her high school sweetheart, Emil. One of the letters revealed how she did not want to leave her hero to travel east to college, but that a scholarship to Yale was not something she could turn down. She promised that they would be together all of next summer.

They were both going over several letters, when Albert grabbed Nelkie's arm. "Oh man, you gotta hear this. It's a bombshell." He read Nelkie a letter in which Barbara expressed extreme regret that she must confess to meeting a charming upperclassman. She admitted that he had swept her off her feet. He was studying political science and had the most patriotic name she had ever heard: Patrick Henry Walsh III!

As they went through the rest of the photo album, they came across a newspaper clipping of Barbara's wedding announcement, political campaign pictures, birth announcements of her children, and pictures of her receiving various awards for charity work.

"No wonder this guy is after Pat with a vengeance," Albert exclaimed. "He's still carrying a torch for Barbara!"

"Do you mean he's still in love with his high school sweetheart?"

"You can bet your walking stick on that one," Albert replied immediately. "Not only is he still stuck on her, but he hates Pat and wants to ruin the senator for stealin' her away from him."

"I guess you're right," the elf said, walking over to the credenza. "I'm sure Stanfield is not used to being bested at anything and this must have been a tremendous blow to that oversized ego you spoke of, but I can't help but think there's more to it than just a broken heart."

Nelkie unlocked the credenza and started spreading its contents out on the floor. There were several rolls of blueprints, along with estimates for everything from furniture to golf clubs.

"I knew there was more," Nelkie said confidently. "And here it is!"

Albert grabbed some books off a shelf and put them on the four corners of the blueprints so they could unroll them completely. "Well, I'll be dipped," the older man said. They were looking at plans for dozens of log cabin-type guest cottages, each with a rustic-style swimming pool and whirlpool bath. There were also plans for a high-end nightclub, which was to be a simulated forest, with artificial trees and an indoor waterfall. The entire resort was to have a "forest" theme and was to be called "Fantasy Forest."

I don't know if I can see any logic in this," Nelkie said, shaking his head. "Except for pure greed, that is. I mean, where is the sense in bulldozing a pristine natural forest, only to build an artificial one?"

"Of course you're right. It makes no sense to us, nor should it to any normal-thinking person. But Stanfield is not normal by any means. He is a very wealthy man, who is consumed by hate and the need for vengeance. That, at the very least, makes him extremely dangerous. He knows the rich and famous will flock to his trendy new resort and he'll make a ton of money, but the profits are only the cherry on top of the sundae. His real pleasure will be from forcing Pat to sell his beloved forest land for pennies on the dollar. Then he has the exquisite pleasure of breaking his rival's heart into bits by making millions by selling the timber and building a resort for the very rich. I'll bet, in his twisted mind, he thinks he'll be showing Barbara who the better man is after all, because if his plan works, he will have brought Pat to his knees."

"Well it won't work," the angered elf replied. "Let's put this stuff away and get out of here. I would like to see this Downtown Sportsman's Club."

"Yeah, I've seen enough to know he's our guy," Albert agreed. They put everything back the way they found it, and boarded Stanfield's private elevator.

In less than ten minutes, they were parked in the lot of Stanfield's health club. "Wait here for me," Albert said. "I'm gonna go inside and poke around a little."

"Okay, but be careful."

"Don't worry; I'll be right back."

Albert walked in the front door of the very upscale Sportsman's Club. He strode up to the reception desk as if he owned the place. There were trainers, attendants, and other staff all scurrying about, all dressed in whites.

"Ah, excuse me," Albert said, and drew the receptionist's attention.

"How may I help you, sir?"

"By any chance, could you tell me if Emil Stanfield is in the club?"

"Let me check the card file, sir. No, I'm sorry. His membership card is not here, sir, so he would not be in the club at this time. However, I know he has reserved court time for 9:00 a.m. tomorrow."

"Thank you very much," Albert said. "I'll see if I can catch him at home."

"Very good, sir."

The chauffeur walked back to the Jeep and informed Nelkie about Stanfield's 6:00 a.m. commitment.

"I would like to be here when he arrives," Nelkie told his friend. "The only thing we can do now is follow him around and hope he slips up somehow."

"We'll be waiting for him when he gets here. I just hope he gets careless sometime soon," said Albert. "I'm worried about Tommy. Time is getting short."

Chapter 49

As soon as he was sure there was no one else around, Tommy unloaded the pistol. He threw the bullets into the woods and the gun in a trash can.

He trotted down the driveway and through the chain-link gate. Looking around, he tried to get his bearings. Nothing looked familiar, but judging by his surroundings, it was easy to figure out that he was in an industrial park. T.J. Walsh made his way up the street, looking for the exit to the main road. Although he knew he had locked up his former captors, he couldn't help looking over his shoulder every few minutes.

Tommy's first thoughts were that he had to get into town, wherever that was, and find a cop, or at least a phone. *Maybe I could flag down a passing car and tell them what happened. If I could just get a ride out of here, I'd feel a lot safer.*

As if his prayers were answered, a Chevy Suburban turned the corner and was slowly heading in his direction. The young escapee ran into the street, waving his arms wildly, hoping that if he ran directly into the path of the oncoming car, the driver would stop. His luck seemed to be holding. The driver stopped and stuck his head out the window. "What's wrong? Are you all right?"

"Please help. I've been kidnapped and I just escaped! Can you take me to the police?"

"Kidnapped! Oh, my God! Get in!" The driver's voice had a tone of sincere concern. Tommy slid into the front seat and looked over, about to thank his rescuer. To his flabbergasted disbelief, he was staring at the business end of a .357 Magnum revolver.

"This is just not your day, kid." The voice had lost all its concern and was now mocking him. Tommy heard the electric door locks engage as the smiling Iraqi spoke. "Let's go back to the warehouse and see what kind of mischief you've been up to."

Salaam put the big car in gear and placed the barrel of the .357 against Tommy's knee. "I want you to consider this, before you entertain any thoughts of escape. If you should survive the attempt, which is doubtful, you will never again walk without a cane. If you even flinch, your knee joint will become part of the upholstery."

Just two minutes before meeting this unpleasant little man, Tommy was basking in the sunshine of his newly won freedom. Now he was being returned to relive the worst nightmare of his life. The reversal of fortune had left him in the clutches of despair and hopelessness. His spirits sunk even farther when they turned into the yard and he saw his former jailers running toward the suburban. They had simply smashed the window Tommy had spent hours working on.

The big man ran to the driver's side window and began spitting lame excuses through his shattered teeth. Salaam would have no part of it. He held up his hand and interrupted the blubbering buffoon. "You're just lucky I found him before he got to a phone, you brainless fool! Now get him back inside before I finish the job on you two myself!"

They pushed and shoved Tommy back down the stairs and into his former cell. The Arab pointed to a spot on the floor, near a radiator and looked at Tommy. All he said was, "Sit."

Salaam reached into his pocket and produced a pair of handcuffs. He put one cuff on Tommy's left wrist, and the other around the radiator pipe. He gave the smaller man the .357, along with some specific orders. "Don't screw this up again, or I swear I'll kill you both myself! If he has to go to the bathroom, you keep that gun touching his head until he's locked up again, got it?" Mung just nodded his ugly head. The Arab threw the key to Crusher and left.

Chapter 50

Long before dawn had edged in the new day, Nelkie was on his second cup of tea. Albert came scuffing out of the hallway into the living room in his flip-flops and shorts. "Don't you ever sleep?" he asked, rubbing his eyes.

"Yes, but not very well last night. I feel that if we don't find Tommy soon, something could go wrong and he may get hurt. It's just a feeling, but a nagging one that won't go away."

"Yeah, I know what you mean. I didn't sleep well either. I don't think that watching Stanfield is going to help us much. I mean, I believe we should--you never know what might happen--but I can't help thinking that he's just too smart to screw up now."

"You may be right," Nelkie offered, "but what else can we do? I can't think of any other course of action that could lead us to the boy."

Albert thought for a moment before he spoke. "Maybe we should consider this. If nothing changes in a day or two, I'll call R.J. and Frank and let them in on what we know. After all, as much as we want to find Tommy and put Stanfield in jail, we are not professional investigators. Those two guys are very good at this type of work and may be able to see something we missed."

Nelkie nodded his head in agreement. "Tommy's safety is our first concern. Let's give it two days. If we don't progress any farther, call for help."

"Agreed," Albert said. "Just give me a few minutes to clean up and we'll head outta here."

The telephone stopped Albert in mid-step. "Hello? Hi Barbara, have you heard from Pat?"

"Yes, I just got off the phone with him. Unfortunately, he had no good news. R.J.'s investigation has apparently hit a wall. It seems our Iraqi nemesis has left for the moon."

"What does R.J. recommend we do now?"

"He said to let our lawyers go ahead with the sale. Unless he gets a break, R.J. said it would be better to concentrate on getting Tommy home safely. The investigation will be ongoing and he feels that he will be able to follow a paper trail that will eventually expose these people. Anyway, I'll be home tomorrow night and Pat said he'll call around 8:00. He's been working on getting the freedom medal for that fireman that rescued nine children from a burning school."

"I heard about that guy on the radio. He should get a medal."

"I'm sure my husband will see that he does. Well, I guess that's about it, Albert. I'll see you tomorrow."

"Okay. Try not to worry. I'm sure Tommy will be home soon." They said their goodbyes and Albert flip-flopped off to the bathroom. When he returned, ready to leave, Nelkie stopped him at the door.

"Wait just a second. I have a question."

"Whut's up?"

"I was wondering about your camera phone-video recorder thing. Let's just speculate that we are present when Stanfield says or does something that could be considered incriminating. If we recorded him in the act, would that be enough evidence to convict him in your courts?"

"You can bet on it. I don't expect we'll have that kind of luck, but I hafta have my phone with me anyway, so if we see somethin' goin' down, we can record it for evidence."

The bodyguard tucked his phone into his shirt pocket as they climbed into the Jeep and headed for the Downtown Sportsman's Athletic Club.

Chapter 51

There were a few dozen cars in the parking lot of the club when they arrived, but no one was milling around outside.

"I hope he's not inside already," Nelkie said.

"I don't think so. I'm pretty sure Stanfield drives a white Bentley, and it's not here." Albert found a space a good distance away from the other cars. "I don't think anyone will notice us parked over here." He killed the motor and the two friends sat in silence for only a moment when quite unexpectedly, Nelkie grabbed Albert by the arm. "He's coming! Oh no, I didn't expect this," the elf said with a note of fear in his voice.

"What? Who's here? Whaddaya mean? Of course we expected him. He's scheduled to be on the court in fifteen minutes."

"Not Stanfield, Albert. The evil one! I can feel his presence. There is no mistaking the evil blackness that now approaches. Look," Nelkie said, pointing to the driveway. "The killer is here!"

Albert watched the black Suburban roll into the lot. A chill came over him. The big car circled the lot like some kind of steel predator stalking its kill.

"Get down," Nelkie urged. "If he should see us, we may never find out why he's here."

They ducked down as the Suburban snaked around the Jeep and rolled toward the opposite end of the lot. Satisfied that he was alone, the Arab parked, but remained in the car.

"Well, I guess we both know who he's waiting for," said Albert.

"Yes, but the question is why," Nelkie added.

Suddenly, Albert remembered his phone. "I have good news and bad news. Which do you want first?"

"What's the good news?"

"It's a bright sunny morning. If Stanfield talks to Salaam, there's no doubt the video will be clear and sharp."

"And the bad?"

"We're too far away to record any audio, and that's what we must have to incriminate these two and prove conspiracy."

Nelkie was sure Albert was right. A video without sound would prove only that Stanfield and the Arab knew each other. They must record the conversation in order to have any hope of bringing these two evil men to justice. At the same time, the elf found himself struggling to overcome an ever-intensifying feeling of foreboding. With each ticking second, Nelkie felt the rising tide of internal instinct, warning him of approaching danger. His sixth sense had escalated from the familiar tingling sensation to a state in which he resonated from head to toe with its gong-like effect. The strength of his will was being tested like never before. Strong feelings of self-preservation were telling him to flee, but he knew the success of his quest hinged on what he did in the next few minutes.

Nelkie's train of thought was abruptly intruded upon when Albert observed another car entering the lot. "Stanfield is here," the older man said. "There can't be more than one white Bentley around here."

Nelkie knew what must be done and that he was the only one who could do it. Without hesitation, he ignored nature's warning signal, seized the camera from the dashboard, and bounded over his chauffeur and out the window.

While the Jeep was shielding him from view, the elf held out the phone and asked, "How do I work this thing to record their conversation?"

Albert explained that it was basically a simple point and shoot procedure. "Just try to hold it steady so your subjects aren't jumpin' all over the screen."

"Okay, I've got it."

The elf tucked the phone under his arm and touched his medallion. He voiced the key words and instantly he and Albert's phone were gone.

Stanfield was now out of the Bentley. He was reaching into the trunk for his gym bag when Salaam got out of his car and called to him. "Emil! Wait! I must speak with you."

As Nelkie advanced, he could feel the intensity of the combined evil auras growing. He had been bothered by the Arab's presence all along. Now that he was in close proximity to both men, the very air around him stagnated with the malignancy of unrepentant, allied evil. The elf swallowed hard and penetrated the heinous aura. He drew slowly closer, careful to keep his approach noiseless.

The Arab was now standing next to his boss. Stanfield's expression was one of extreme anger. "Have you lost your mind, Salaam? What are you doing here? I told you we were never to meet in public!"

"Relax. No one followed me here and there's nobody out here in the lot. Anyway, I didn't want to tell you what I have to say on the phone. You never know who might be listening."

"This better be good. You're putting us both at risk by coming here."

"We had a little trouble, and I wanted you to know I took care of it before it became a problem."

"What are you talking about? What trouble?"

"Those two morons I hired to guard the warehouse bungled the job, and the Walsh kid escaped."

"WHAT?"

"Don't worry. I said I took care of it. I caught him only a block from the warehouse. I brought him back and cuffed him to the radiator; he's not going anywhere. I thought you should know that we may have underestimated this kid. He's no sissy. He beat the hell out of Mung and Crusher."

"I told you those two were a bad idea," Stanfield said heatedly. "What were you thinking, hiring a couple of dope fiends?"

"Look, Emil, they didn't have to perform brain surgery. All they had to do was watch the kid and feed him."

"Yeah, and they couldn't even do that! Look, before someone wanders out here and sees us together, get back over there and move the boy up to the Sierra model home. Get rid of those two clowns before they cause us any more trouble. I'll contact you tonight. Now, get moving!"

"All right. Just stay calm. This was only a minor setback. I'm on my way."

Stanfield stormed off into the club. Salaam trotted back to the Suburban and Nelkie ran jubilantly back to the Jeep.

"Did ya get anything we can use?" Albert asked

Nelkie handed the phone back to its owner and said, "With what's in there, those two are as good as behind bars already, but don't let that big car out of your sight. He's going to move the boy right now. All I know for sure is that Tommy is handcuffed to a radiator somewhere in a warehouse."

"Okay, okay, but lemme see whatcha got," the chauffeur said, holding out his hand. With one eye on the Suburban and the other on his phone, Albert reviewed Nelkie's footage. As he listened to the clandestine conversation, his face lit up as if he had just scratched off a million- dollar instant lottery ticket. "Holy crap! You did it! You *really* did it! They even mention Tommy by name! There ain't a lawyer on the planet that can keep these two out of jail now. They've just convicted themselves with their own words. I gotta call Frank."

Albert got the detective lieutenant on the phone and filled him in. "Great news, Frank, you're about to make captain!"

"Oh yeah? What do you know that I don't?"

"I'm holding solid video and audio evidence that a freelance Arab henchman, under orders from Emil Stanfield, has kidnapped the senator's son."

"What? Are you talking about *the* Emil Stanfield?"

"Pictures don't lie, Lieutenant...or should I say Captain?"

"Yeah, yeah. Let's worry about the promotion later. Are you sure you've absolutely got Stanfield dead to rights, because if I pull a guy with his connections in for questioning and I screw up...."

"I'm tellin' ya, Frank, he's a kidnapper and maybe an accessory to murder. Look, one video is worth a thousand words. I'll send it to ya as soon as we hang up. I just wanted to call you first and give ya the good news. Trust me, as soon as you hear this conversation, you'll be on your way to Stanfield's office as fast as you can get there!"

"Okay, Piston, send me the video. If there is conclusive evidence on it, I will go after Stanfield."

"Don't worry, I gotcha covered--but look, there's more. I ain't got a lotta time, 'cause I'm about to follow that Arab to where they're holding Tommy. Remember you told me if things get sticky to let you know? Well, now's the time. I'm not positive yet, but it's a good bet that the kid is in a warehouse owned by a company called Two Guys Plumbing Supplies. Can you have someone meet me out there before this gets ugly?"

"All right, Albert, I'll send a couple of uniforms out there right away. Try to stay out of trouble until they get there."

"I can't make any promises, Frank. I don't have any idea what I'm gonna find out there. I'll try to wait, but I think they're gonna move Tommy to another location. If that's the case, I'll have to do *something*."

"Okay, I understand. Just be careful and don't try to be a hero, Piston. I'll get my guys there as fast as possible."

"Gotcha. Thanks, Frank."

"I just hope you're dead-on with all of this, or I'll be pounding a beat again." Frank hung up before his friend had a chance to reassure him.

Chapter 52

Detective Lt. Frank Martini and his partner, Sgt. Bill Savas, watched Albert's video condemn Emil Stanfield beyond any reasonable doubt. "I don't know how Parker managed to get this, but he's right, this guy is toast." They pulled into the underground garage and parked their unmarked Ford right next to Stanfield's Bentley. They got out and Savas remarked that the Bentley was soon to be the most expensive car at the police impound garage.

"Yeah, if all goes according to plan," Frank cautioned. "Look, Bill, I don't want to rush in there like this is a drug bust. This guy has no idea that he's been found out. We can do this the easy way."

"Works for me, Lieutenant. If we play it casual, there's no hot pursuit, no sirens, and no shooting. Nobody gets hurt and the bad guy's locked up. Way to go."

After taking the public elevator up to the lobby, Martini checked the directory and was not at all surprised to find Stanfield's office listed as the Penthouse Suite. The detectives strode across the lobby to a bank of elevators, and Savas pushed PH.

The door slid back and they walked into a reception area that was both luxurious and elegant. An eighteenth-century desk stood unoccupied at the foot of a highly polished mahogany staircase that led to the executive suite. The rest of the waiting area was appointed with the finest hand-tooled Italian leather sofas, as well as several overstuffed armchairs. Savas nudged his partner and whispered, "Check out the oil paintings. I don't know much about art, but I'm willing to bet they are all originals."

"You can bet your badge on that one, Savas. There's more money invested in this room than you and I will make in both our lifetimes."

Presently, a bespectacled secretary descended the staircase. She could have been mistaken for a movie star with her full head of fiery red hair that seemed to roll over her shoulders. She was dressed in a tasteful business suit, but the hem of her skirt was clearly shorter than business length. When she noticed the two men, she quickly apologized for her absence. "I'm sorry, gentlemen. Were you waiting long?"

"No, not at all," Frank answered, flipping out his badge. "I'm Detective Martini and this is my partner, Sgt. Savas. We'd like to ask Mr. Stanfield a few questions. He may have some information that will help us with a case we're working on."

"I see. Do you have an appointment?"

Frank answered in a tone that was polite and sincere, but not urgent. "No, but this *is* a police matter and we need to speak with him as soon as possible."

"I understand. Let me inform his secretary that you're here." She picked up the phone and spoke briefly with Stanfield's personal secretary. "Yes, of course. I'll tell them. No, I don't think this is an emergency," she said, with one eye on Martini. "Right. Thank you, Beverly." She hung up and spoke directly to Frank. "Mr. Stanfield is on a conference call to Paris at the moment. He said that if you would be kind enough to give him about ten minutes, he would be more than happy to answer all your questions. Would either of you care for some coffee?"

Frank looked at his watch. "No, thank you. We'll just wait."

Everyone sat down and Frank's eyes drifted up to the large oil paintings that lined the walls. He was sure one of them was a Monet. Both Savas and Martini sat patiently, thinking Stanfield was the proverbial lamb about to be led to slaughter. They should have known Emil Stanfield was much more a lion than a lamb.

No one but Stanfield knew that months ago he had picked this day to launch the final stage of his plan to destroy Pat Walsh. The meeting with his Arab henchman outside the club had rattled him, but a rigorous morning workout had all but dissipated his anger. Now that his prisoner was being moved to a safe house, every piece on his chessboard was poised for the final checkmate. Tommy Walsh's whereabouts were untraceable, and the sale of the senator's beloved property would be finalized in a matter of a few days…at which point Thomas Jefferson Walsh would have mysteriously disappeared, and the video of toxic chemicals being drained out of a Walsh Trucking tanker would be anonymously delivered to C.N.N. Stanfield would revel in directing the rest of his plan from his private paradise on Grand Cayman Island. Once the deforestation was completed, profits from the sale of millions of board feet of prime lumber would finance construction of the Fantasy Forest Resort. With feelings of immense self- satisfaction, Stanfield opened the middle drawer of his desk and pulled out an envelope containing a first-class ticket on the Queen of the Seven Seas.

The only fly in the ointment was the presence of two detectives on the day of his planned departure. At first, it jangled his nerves a bit, but he was prepared. This just meant that his embarkation would have to be a bit more rushed than he would have liked.

When Beverly told him two detectives were downstairs, he hastily made up the conference call story to give himself some time. This was a red flag, an alarm. *I didn't get this far in life by leaving anything to chance. The odds that the police are here about some unrelated matter is unlikely at best. What's more likely is that those knuckleheads at the warehouse screwed up again and got caught. There's also the possibility the cops figured out that Salaam killed that buffoon Hannan. I can't risk a phone call. If all this has gone sour, phone records could put me away.*

He quickly decided the only option he had to ensure his freedom was to leave now. He had more than enough available funds to live in luxury, anywhere on earth. If the police were here to arrest him, he had time to make good his escape, and be safe from extradition in the

Cayman Islands.

Stanfield was confident that he would easily elude the police. After all, who had ever heard of anyone making their getaway on a cruise ship? The very idea bordered on the ridiculous. The Queen of the Seven Seas was his safe haven that even the most experienced detective would dismiss out of hand. He rushed to the closet and changed into a navy blue jogging suit and a baseball cap. The next step was to take his briefcase into the bathroom and empty its contents onto the floor. After placing the empty briefcase on the sink, he opened the medicine cabinet and began tossing everything off the top shelf. He then removed the glass shelf, which triggered a mechanism making the entire cabinet swing to one side, revealing a wall safe. Stanfield placed all five fingers of his right hand on a raised pad on the safe door. The machine recognized his fingerprints and the door opened. He removed several thousand dollars in cash, and his passport (along with another under an assumed name) and a small-caliber pistol. After packing everything in his briefcase, he grabbed his cell phone and ran to his private elevator. Four minutes later, the wolf in sheep's clothing had hailed a cab and was away.

When the cab pulled up to the ship terminal, Stanfield carefully scanned the area before getting out. No one sitting in a car reading a newspaper. Nobody milling around the entrance who might be a cop. With an arrogant smile, he paid the driver and got out, confident that the police were far too stupid to figure out where he was. One more look around and he pulled his cap down over the sunglasses and walked through the terminal entrance.

Almost fifteen minutes had passed, and Martini was getting antsy. He looked at his watch for the fourth time, and then at Savas. As if he could read his boss's mind, Savas said, "I got a bad feeling. Is there any chance there's another way out of here?"

Martini shot to his feet. "Damn it all! Let's go, Savas," he demanded while bolting for the stairs. "If this guy's got a private elevator, I'm gonna feel like an idiot." With Sgt. Savas on his heels, Martini steamed into Stanfield's outer office, only to be confronted by Beverly Bridges. "Excuse me, but you can't just barge in here...."

Martini flashed his badge. "Yes, I can. Police business." Savas got to the door first, but of course, it was locked. Without hesitation Frank pulled a credit card out of his wallet and shoved it between the door and the frame. The card caught the latch and he pulled the door open. Within seconds they knew they'd been had. Beverly ran into the room an instant behind the detectives, already apologizing to her absentee boss. "I'm sorry, Mr. Stanf...where is he?"

"That would be our question to you," Savas said, sarcasm overwhelming his tone.

"Well, I'm sure I don't know. He was supposed to be on a conference call."

Martini butted in. "Look, Ms....?"

"Bridges, Beverly Bridges."

"Ms. Bridges, we don't have a lot of time. I can't get into details, but your boss is a wanted man. Do you have any idea where he might have gone?"

"No clue, Lieutenant, but I'm not surprised to find out he's broken the law."

"Oh?"

"I don't know if you're aware of this, but the squeaky-clean philanthropist image you see in the news is *not* Emil Stanfield. I've been present at several meetings with his inner circle. The truth is that Mr. Stanfield is a ruthless, vindictive man, without a hint of conscience. He is an abusive, insulting boss and I can't stand him. I tolerate working for him only because he pays me twice what I would earn anywhere else, but I'm not so sure it's worth it. I would be more than happy to pay that SOB back for all the mistreatment that goes on here daily. Let me think a minute."

Savas was checking out the suite while Beverly was talking, and called to Frank from the bathroom. "He left here in a big hurry. There's toiletries all over the floor…the place is a mess!"

As Frank turned to investigate, Beverly picked up the phone. "I have an idea," she said. "Let me call Corporate World Travel. I book all of Mr. Stanfield's business trips through them. Maybe they can help."

"Take the shot, Ms. Bridges," Martini said. "Right now, it's all we've got."

The secretary got the travel agency on the phone and was stunned to find out her boss had booked first-class passage on a cruise ship three weeks ago. "This is a little weird," she said, as she hung up the phone. "It seems my boss called the travel agency himself, and told them he wanted to book first-class passage on the Queen of the Seven Seas. The ship is leaving today for the Caribbean."

"He's leaving by ship, Savas! We gotta get to the terminal right now!" He thanked Beverly on the run as the two detectives bolted for the elevator.

Chapter 53

Martini cut the lights and siren as they approached the ship terminal. The Queen of the Seven Seas, looking very much like a floating city, was in her berth waiting to take on her next multitude of vacationers.

They trotted into the terminal and were taken aback by the vast number of passengers going through the boarding process. Savas looked at Frank as if to say, "Where do we start?" Martini didn't wait for the question to be vocalized. "Bill, if you'll get up there and find out if Stanfield has boarded yet, I'll scan the crowd."

"I'm on it."

As soon as Bill Savas disappeared into the crowd, Martini got to work. Twenty-three years of surveillance participation had taught him how to look for his man in a crowd of this size. Expertly, he scanned the sea of humanity, automatically eliminating those males who were short, fat, young, or elderly. However, given the enormity of the crowd, it would have been hard to spot Ronald McDonald. Suddenly, his trained eye focused on something that seemed out of place, but Frank couldn't put his finger on it right away. Standing next to an elderly couple was a man in a navy-blue jogging suit. Frank looked closer, instinct telling him something was wrong with this guy, *but what was it?* The suspect had a baseball cap pulled down over a pair of dark-tinted sunglasses. *Nothing odd there.* A bright light went on in Frank's head when he realized the man was holding a briefcase. *Nobody takes a briefcase on vacation…especially a guy in a jogging suit!* Martini pulled out the card case bearing his gold shield and calmly walked in the direction of the suspect. He had hoped to catch Stanfield off guard and arrest him with little or no resistance. His hopes were dashed when he got within ten feet of his man.

Stanfield was also scanning the crowd. He spotted the approaching detective and panicked. Pandemonium exploded as his fight or flight instincts overwhelmed him. He shoved the old gentleman in front of him as hard as he could. Off balance, the old man collided with his wife at such a rate of speed that she went whirling into the oncoming detective, sending them both to the floor in a tangled ball. Stanfield headed for the exit, running for his life. Martini got to one knee and shouted, "Police!

Adrenalized and out of control, Stanfield pulled his pistol and turned toward his pursuer. The fugitive's face was contorted like that of a madman, as he squeezed off a shot.

As soon as Frank saw the gun, he dove on the old lady to shield her, screaming for all he was worth, "Gun! Everybody down!" A fraction of a second later, he felt a searing hot pain as the bullet entered and exited his right forearm. He cried out in pain, but hesitated only a split second before rising to his feet. The southpaw detective reached under his right arm and drew his service revolver, but he knew he couldn't risk returning fire in the crowded terminal full of screaming, panicked people. He shouted again, hoping Stanfield would come to his senses. "Stanfield! Give it up! It's over!"

The villain ignored him and made it to the door. Martini was bleeding profusely now. His right arm felt like someone was holding it to a blowtorch. Still, he pressed on. He stumbled through the door, his heart pounding wildly, forcing more blood out of the gaping hole in his forearm.

The cop hit the street in time to see Stanfield drag an unsuspecting cab driver out of his car, while hammering his face unmercifully with the butt of his pistol. The rampaging fugitive jumped behind the wheel, leaving the driver on his knees with both hands holding his pummeled face together. He slammed the car into gear and pounced on the accelerator.

Martini, still fifty feet away, dropped to one knee, every fiber of his being focused on steadying his aim. For Stanfield to make good his escape, the cab would have to cross Frank's path for at least two or three seconds. He went for it.

Sweat was pouring into the detective's eyes. The adrenaline rush pumped him up to an awareness level bordering on the extrasensory. Frank Martini's entire universe seemed to be moving in slow motion. As the stolen cab converged on the point where Frank would have two seconds to make a decision, everything became clear. He no longer felt the screaming pain in his arm. There were no civilians or traffic in his line of fire. It was time to act. The taxi was crossing Frank's path, accelerating with Stanfield hunched over the wheel. The fugitive's eyes were fixed on the exit.

In less than a heartbeat, Frank made the decision not to take the head shot. He wanted this guy alive. He went for the bigger target: the driver's side front tire. Calmly and with great concentration, he squeezed off one round. The projectile found its mark. The exploding tire rumbled off its rim, causing the cab into a spin like a gigantic yellow top. It careened off a parked car and then another before the taxi slammed into a light pole, nose first. The air bag in the old beat-up cab did not deploy, and with no seat belt to restrain him, Stanfield's face was catapulted into the steering wheel. His jawbone broke clean, then his nose and the bones around his right eye socket. He was left unconscious, the horn blaring his surrender.

Martini stepped up to the car, still pointing his service revolver at the unconscious fugitive. He removed Stanfield's pistol from the seat and checked his pulse. Satisfied that his man was still alive, he cuffed the suspect's left hand to the steering wheel and promptly passed out.

Bill Savas had started running off the ship as soon as he heard a shot fired. He made it outside in time to see his partner on one knee. Running as fast as he could, he drew his gun just as the taxi spun out of control. With his lungs blazing in fiery agony and his heart thumping like a kettle drum, he reached his passed out partner just in time to break his fall. Gingerly he let Frank down and removed his own jacket and tie. Savas rolled up his jacket and placed it under his partner's head, and then applied the tie/tourniquet above the wound on Frank's blood-soaked sleeve. The sergeant then pulled out his radio and announced to dispatch, "Officer down! Ambulance needed at pier forty-two!" His job was still not finished. As soon as he caught his breath, he had to deal with the crowd that had formed around the wrecked cab and his prostrate partner.

Chapter 54

Albert had waited to start the Jeep until Salaam was approaching the gate. When the Suburban hit the street, Albert followed at a safe distance. "That tank is big enough that I can stay four or five cars back and still see him."

"Just don't let him get away from you, Albert. This is the break we've been hoping for."

"You're right; this is a tremendous break, but what if the cops don't show up in time? Whatta we do then?"

"What's a dope fiend?"

"What?"

What's a dope fiend?" Nelkie repeated.

"A drug addict. Why?"

"Well, according to Stanfield, there are two drug addicts guarding Tommy."

"Oh, this is an interesting development," Albert said, sarcastically.

"Not to worry, my friend. The way Stanfield and Salaam were talking about those two, it didn't sound like they had one brain between them. We will have a distinct advantage. There are three of them and three of us, counting Tommy."

"Howd'ya figure we have an advantage, when it's three against three, and the other three will probably have guns?"

"Because we have a secret weapon: invisible me! Don't worry, Albert; if the police do not arrive in time and we must act, you'll know when I make my move. Just follow my lead and do what comes naturally. We will overpower them easily."

"Forgive me for feeling a little uncomfortable, but it's not all that reassuring when someone who is less than three feet tall talks about overpowering anybody!"

"Albert, my good friend, you of all people should not doubt the power of my elders. You have seen it firsthand. Believe me, I would not advise this course of action unless I was certain of the outcome. Of course, there are calculated risks, but they are superseded by the consequences of inaction. Tommy could be killed, the senator's career ended in disgrace, as well as our beloved forest being laid to waste, making refugees of my entire race!"

"Okay, little fella, we've come this far. In for a penny, in for a pound. Let's go get 'em!"

"That's what I wanted to hear, Albert. These evil ones are about to meet their match. In the end, good will always triumph over evil."

For the rest of their slow-motion pursuit, the elf was lost in thought. His reflections centered on how wrong he had been about his perception of humans and his quest in general. When he left his treetop home, Nelkie thought he would venture into the human world and spend a brief period of time enlightening the ignorant race with the ancient wisdom of woodland elves. The humans, of course, would be totally impressed and would immediately change their ways. Nelkie would then effectuate some deed or other for the betterment of hu-mankind and return home, mission accomplished--simple as that!

Ignorance, inexperience, and naïveté had fueled what the elf now knew to be the childish misconceptions of a cocky, overconfident ado-lescent. Once he was exposed to the greed, ambition, and ruthless revenge that was Emil Stanfield, and the bloodthirsty, remorseless evil of his Arab henchman, Nelkie was forced to accept his new reality or perish. When he stood over "Holeshot" Hannan's lifeless body, Nelkie was shaken to the very core of his being. Elves did not lie, cheat, or steal. Until now, Nelkie had at best only an abstract understanding of murder. When he stood over the dead human, who was brutally murdered only to ensure someone's petty revenge and financial gain, Nelkie's perception of the universe was turned inside out. He was catapulted from the benign, nonviolent fellowship of the elf community into a dark and terrifying nightmare world that he could easily have perceived as a decent into madness. Nelkie's inner courage, advanced intellect, and moral comprehension of right and wrong would not allow his fear to defeat him. Instead, this was the point where he came to understand the depth of human depravity. This was no longer just scary talk from the elders; this was real. Hannan was dead, and the man that killed him felt no regret or shame...on the contrary; he felt proud of a job well done!

From the moment he and Albert walked out of that garbage-strewn alley in the rain, Nelkie commanded himself to strengthen his resolve. *So this is really what my quest is all about! This is the spreading evil that has caused such great concern among the wise ones for centuries. I was sent here to stop this evil and cultivate tolerance and understanding amongst those who are virtuous and want to live in harmony...and I will! I will trust in the gifts given to me by the elders, and with the power of the ancients vested in me, I will do what is expected, and make my brothers proud.*

Nelkie had felt his powers growing in strength and intensity with every use. His ability to access these gifts had become easier, almost instantaneous. Trusting in these powers gave him the courage and confidence to face any enemy. These were no longer the thoughts of a foolish adolescent; it was the confidence of a mature adult with the conviction to accept his responsibilities. He trusted that the tough and loyal Albert Parker would do whatever was necessary to get Tommy home safely and clear the senator's name. Nelkie could already smell victory.

The Suburban was signaling to turn into an industrial park. The elf and his human driver were four cars back. By the time Albert had turned into the park, Salaam was signaling to turn again. They followed at a discreet distance. When they made the corner, they could see the Suburban pulling into the yard of Two Guys Plumbing Supplies. The Arab drove past the main entrance and around to the rear of the building. Albert pulled into the yard to survey the situation. The warehouse was a dull, industrial grey one-story building, about fifty yards long. There were steps in the exact center leading up to double glass entry/exit doors. The entrance was flanked on either side by three roll-up doors, surrounded on three sides by black rubber cushions with a bright-yellow stripe to allow trailer trucks to line up with the loading dock. There was only one truck backed in to the left of the entrance. The other five were unoccupied. The elf picked up the distant whine of materials-handling equipment, but before he could mention this fact, they both saw the trailer shake twice as a fork lift entered and exited the back the truck with a loaded pallet.

"Well, this must be the place, little guy. I don't think the Arab is goin' in there to get a price on faucets. I would guess Tommy is probably being held somewhere in the back of that building, or maybe in the basement, where he can't be seen or heard."

"I agree, Albert. Given what we know, there can't be any other reason for Salaam to be here other than to move the boy."

"All right, now what? I knew all along we'd beat the cops here. We can't let these thugs take the kid outta here. We gotta stall 'em until the troops arrive."

"You're right. Drive around back. I'm sure Salaam is inside by now. If we can't block their exit, or delay them in any other way, then by Bindar's belly, we'll fight!"

"Bindar's belly?"

"Never mind; it's just an expression."

Albert rolled the Jeep carefully around the corner and parked it at a perpendicular angle to the Suburban. With the warehouse wall in front and the Jeep behind, the big car was blocked in.

"Well, this is it…showtime! You had better make yourself scarce."

The elf got out of the car, touched his medallion and was gone. The human heard a small voice from nowhere say, "If they bring the boy out before the police get here, watch for my move and then just do what you do best."

"Check. I'm about to add another KO to my record. I can feel it in my bones."

While his eyes were trained on the rear door of the warehouse, Albert couldn't help but wonder what kind of little surprise his invisible friend had in store for the unsuspecting criminals. The one thing he knew for sure was that whatever Nelkie was planning, it was bound to be mind-boggling.

The two would-be rescuers didn't have time to investigate. Within two minutes of their arrival, the back door opened and the criminal parade marched out into the sunshine. The Arab was first out, followed by Tommy, whose hands were cuffed behind his back. Mung was next, brazenly brandishing a pistol. Crusher's big, bald-headed frame brought up the rear.

The ex-fighter was searching his brain to find some excuse to delay them without causing any harm to come to Tommy. He stepped out from behind the Jeep. "Hey, fellas, sorry to bother ya, but I'm lost. Can ya tell me how ta get outa here and back to the highway?"

Tommy looked up when he heard a familiar voice, but had the good sense not to give any sign of recognition.

The Arab, immediately suspicious when he saw the Jeep had hemmed him in, looked at Mung and nodded his head toward Albert. He stepped aside, grabbing Tommy's arm, to keep him close. The skinny thug stepped out from behind the prisoner, pointing his gun at Albert's chest. "On your knees, Grampy, *now!* Who are you, and what are you doin' here?"

If you're gonna do something Nelkie, now would be a good time.

While Albert was emotionally gearing up for the battle to start at any second, Nelkie had reconsidered. *I can't do anything as long as*

Tommy's mobility is limited. Our chances of success would be far greater if he had the use of his hands. The better strategy might be to divide and conquer, but how? Not being able to communicate with his partner, Nelkie had no choice but to let this scene play out and seize his opportunity when it presented itself. There was also the thought that the police were on their way. The elf decided to wait, because any delay would increase the chance that the cops would arrive in time.

Albert had no idea what to do now, but since there was no sign from Nelkie, he figured he had better do what he was told. He kneeled down and began to plead with his captors, but all the while he was watching for the elf to make a move, or for a chance to take out one or two of these guys on his own. He had no such luck.

The former New Yorker summoned up his best Flushing accent, hoping to make himself sound even more like an out-of-towner. "Look, guys, I don't want any trouble. It's none a my business what-ever's goin' on here, and I don't care! I just wanna find my way outta here, that's all."

Mung snapped the barrel of his gun across Albert's face hard enough to knock him over. "Shuddup, old man, and don't move, or I'll shoot ya right now!"

The skinny thug glanced up at his boss and asked, "Whadda we do with this jerk?"

Salaam had already removed Tommy's handcuffs. He tossed them over to Mung with instructions to take Albert into the warehouse. "We can't take him with us. We don't know who he is, or what he knows…and we don't have time to find out. Take him downstairs and cuff him to the radiator. I will deal with this one later."

Mung snatched Albert by his shirt collar while shoving the gun into the bodyguard's ribs. "Let's go, Grampy—inside, and don't get cute, or your life ends here."

Albert's blood was boiling. He knew he could take this creep out with one punch, but now was not the time. He had to wait for Nelkie's move before he made one of his own. He allowed the physically inferior Mung to push and shove him down the stairs and into Tommy's vacated former cell.

"Sit," his jailer demanded, while pointing to the radiator. Albert sat with his back to the radiator and Mung tossed the cuffs at him. "One on your wrist and one around the pipe, Gramps. Do it now."

Albert's situation was going from bad to worse. He saw his opportunity for a successful rescue evaporate like the morning fog. *What is Nelkie waiting for? I can't help him now, and where the hell are the cops?*

Mung was pushing the business end of his gun into Albert's chest, while checking to make sure his prisoner was secured. He wrenched Albert's arm, and the cuff clanged against the pipe, assuring him his man was helpless.

While his friend was being incarcerated, the elf had silently crept down the stairs. He walked into the basement room both pleased and confident. Once the Arab had given the order to take Albert inside, he had unwittingly executed Nelkie's plan to divide and conquer. The elf would set everything in motion by sending the hapless Mung's inferior mind reeling in terror. He smiled, knowing that what was about to happen was far beyond this skinny thug's ability to comprehend.

Nelkie focused his concentration and raised his walking stick directly over Mung's gun hand. With an almost imperceptible touch, he lightly tapped the first knuckle while whispering the word "thumbs."

The skinny man looked down at his hands, distracted when he thought something had touched him. Suddenly, he felt an odd tingling sensation surging through his fingers. The pistol was becoming difficult to hold on to.

"What's...what's happening to me?"

He looked down at his hands, terrified to find that all his fingers now had only one joint! He was literally all thumbs. Trembling with fear, and no longer able to point the gun with his ten thumbs, he dropped the pistol and ran out of the room and up the stairs, screaming in horror at his ungodly digits. He shouldered through the exit door and ran past the bewildered trio standing next to the Suburban. Mung ran for the gate and never stopped screaming.

The Arab reacted instantaneously. Handing his gun to Crusher, he said, "Shoot him if he moves," and ran into the building.

By the time Albert had risen to his knees, calling for his friend, Nelkie had already snapped open the lid on his stick and removed the key. "We must act quickly, Albert," he said, as he unlocked the handcuffs. "Salaam will be running down those stairs at any moment. Take the gun and position yourself by the door. I'll run upstairs and help Tommy dispose of the fat one."

As predicted, the Arab raced down the stairs, unaware of the tiny creature waiting for him on the landing. Nelkie thrust his stick between Salaam's legs and held on. As soon as the Arab went into free fall, the elf shot up the stairs, confident that the gun-toting Albert would take control.

Salaam rolled down the final flight, pinballing off the wall and the opposite railing. Albert stepped out from behind the door, pointing the gun at his adversary, and waited for him to roll to a stop.

The Arab had been in too many life-threatening situations in his many years as a paid assassin to ever be totally unprepared. Although he didn't know what he would find at the bottom of the staircase, he came up fighting. While tumbling out of control, he had somehow managed to reach behind his back and free up a razor-sharp stiletto from his belt. Before the unsuspecting Albert could react, Salaam had rolled to his feet, slashing the eight-inch blade across his opponent's knuckles, forcing the gun to skid across the floor. Having made his first move from right to left, the Arab prepared to bring the blade backhand into Albert's chest. This old man was easy prey and would be disposed of within the next split second. Of course, Salaam had no idea who he was dealing with.

With his right hand sliced open and bleeding, the Albert "Piston"

Parker of old emerged at the speed of thought. Once a fighter, always a fighter. Before Salaam could bring his arm back across his body to finish off his opponent, Albert's lightning left hook had found its mark. A bolt of pain exploded on his right side as Salaam's two lowest ribs shattered into glass-like shards. Automatically, the Arab's arms came down to protect his fragmented rib cage. He never saw the second hook that hit his temple with the force of a falling tree, rendering him unconscious. Albert used the knife to cut off one of the Arab's sleeves and used the makeshift bandage to wrap up his hand. He picked up the pistol, shoved it in his belt, left the unconscious Salaam on the basement floor, and dashed up the stairs.

Nelkie, meanwhile, had to use every ounce of strength he could summon to open the rear door of the warehouse, unconcerned that it would disappear as soon as he touched it. The metal door made a high-pitched squeal as Nelkie forced it open. Distracted by the noise, Crusher made the last mistake of his criminal life. He turned, expecting to see his boss, but saw nothing…not even the door itself! He was looking straight through where the door was, directly into the warehouse. "What the…?"

Tommy wasted no time. He seized the moment to deliver a spinning kick to the big man's solar plexus. Bent over, with the wind knocked out of him, he could do nothing to stop Tommy's knee from crushing his nose and what was left of his front teeth. The blow was delivered with such force that the 280-pound thug was sent sprawling into a backward somersault, as the gun skidded across the asphalt. The back of the big man's skull hit the concrete with an audible thud. His eyes had rolled back in his head and he was motionless.

"Not bad, kid. Not bad at all," Albert said, as he emerged from now-visible warehouse door.

Tommy and Albert embraced and performed a clumsy hooting, jumping dance as they spun in circles, celebrating their victory.

"Man, am I glad to see you," the younger man said. "How did you find me?"

"Kid, that's one heck of a long story. We'll have plenty of time for all that later. Right now, we have some business to attend to before these clowns wake up. I'll go back and drag the Arab out here. See if you can find somethin' to tie them up with and cuff 'em to the Suburban."

"With pleasure, Albert."

The excitement and commotion had ended in a whirlwind of energy—except, of course, for that of one tiny creature standing behind the Jeep, unseen to all. As he watched Albert and Tommy embrace, the enormity of the situation almost overwhelmed him. Feelings of relief, as well as that of accomplishment, filled his tiny heart. He desperately wanted to become visible and join Albert and Tommy in celebration, but he knew that would only complicate matters. The realization that his quest was rapidly coming to a successful conclusion filled him with mixed emotions as well. Nelkie's thoughts were not to be sorted out at this time, as he was physically jolted by the violent shrill of approaching sirens.

The senator's son helped Albert drag Crusher's drooping mass over to the Suburban. They pulled him up into a seated position with his back to the door. Next, they placed the semiconscious Arab between Crusher's legs and cuffed their wrists together. Tommy busied himself with a hundred feet of heavy-duty orange extension cord he found in a storeroom, while Albert stood guard. After looping the extension cord around the two thugs about fifty times, Tommy tied the two ends securely around the steering wheel. When they were satisfied that their prisoners were totally immobile, Albert dialed a number that had now been committed to memory. The phone was answered mid-ring.

"Abbott."

"R.J., it's Albert. It's all over. Tommy is tying up the Arab, and the police are on their way as we speak."

"Wow! That's great news, Al. How on earth did you catch the slippery devil? Where are you, anyway?"

Albert stated his location and R.J. replied that he was local and would be there in twenty minutes. Albert hung up and dialed Frank's cell. The tough lieutenant had insisted on walking out of the emergency room under his own power, after his wound was cleaned and dressed. Savas pulled the car up to the curb and Frank answered his phone as he slid in next to his partner. "Martini."

"Hey Frank, I think it's safe to say you're about to make captain."

"Well, I'll tell you what, Piston, if you're right, I think I've earned it. It's been a pretty tough day so far. I caught your boy Stanfield trying to board a cruise ship."

"Great! Is he in custody now?"

"Yeah, but he didn't go down without a fight. When he saw me, he pulled a gun and things got a little testy."

"What?"

"It's okay. I got away with just a flesh wound, nobody else got hurt--thank God--and Stanfield is locked up."

"Well, this ought to make your day a little brighter. You may have some work to do before you can prove Salaam killed Holeshot, but he's tied up in a neat little package, just waiting to transported to HQ."

"Thanks, Piston. I guess I'm gonna owe you one, big time."

"Nah, you don't owe me nothin', Frank. You worked this from your end, and I worked it from mine. It's all good. Look, I gotta make another phone call; I'll be in touch." Albert hung up to make the call that would be the most rewarding of all.

Pat Walsh was on the phone with a fellow senator, trying to drum up support for his anti-crime bill, when his secretary politely interrupted him. "I'm sorry, Senator, but Albert is on line one. He says it's urgent."

"Thanks, Anne." Fearing the worst, Pat cut the other senator off with no explanation. "Oh, my God! Gotta go. Call you later." He pushed the button for line one, his pulse pounding. "Albert! Is everything all right? Hello?"

Albert handed the phone to Tommy to spare himself the trouble of telling the story for a third time, and because he thought it would be better if the first voice Pat heard belonged to his son.

"Albert, are you there?"

"Hi, Dad! I'm okay. Albert just walked in here and we kicked the crap out of the bad guys. The cops are on their way."

Pat sat back in his chair and let out a long breath. The unexpected shock of hearing his son's voice was so great, he was momentarily speechless.

"Dad? Did you hear me? It's all over."

"Yes! Yes, thank God you're all right," he said, choking back tears of joy. "I was afraid I might never see you again. Are you sure you're all right? Did anyone hurt you?"

"I'm fine, Dad, but I can tell you I never want to look at another cheeseburger as long as I live! That's all these lowlifes would bring me to eat!"

Father and son both laughed. "Look, Tommy, before you do anything else, call Mom. I'm going to catch the first plane out."

"Okay, great! I'll see you in a few hours. Here's Albert."

"How's that for brightening up your day, boss?"

"Albert, my old friend, you are truly a prince among men. You must tell me how you accomplished such a feat. I'm forever in your debt."

"Nonsense," came the reply. " I'm the one who's *repaying* a debt. Anyway, an opportunity to help presented itself, and I just went with it. To be honest, Pat, I had help from someone who, shall we say, had a vested interest in our problem. He figured out that it was Emil Stanfield who was behind all of this. He was out to ruin your life."

"Stanfield? Are you sure? We've been friendly for years! Why would he want to ruin me?"

"There's no doubt that Stanfield is guilty. The police have already picked him up."

"Well, I would have never guessed in a hundred years. So who is the mystery man you helped to end this nightmare? Is he there with you?"

"Err, ah, no, Pat. He had to umm, disappear. Look, he told me that for reasons of his own, he must remain anonymous in this matter."

"I will respect that, Piston, but you tell him for me that my thanks and gratitude are endless. If he should ever be in any kind of need, *ever*, you tell this man to call me first."

"You bet."

"Thank you. I'll see you at the airport and you can fill me in on the rest of the details on the way home."

"I'll be there before your plane even lands, boss. Bye, Pat."

Pat got up from his desk, shoved a few papers in his briefcase and then, without a second thought, he picked up the small box that contained the Freedom Medal and tossed that in his briefcase also. He told Anne that the crisis was over, but that he had to go home right away. Four minutes later, he had already hailed a cab and was on his way.

Chapter 55

Tommy and his rescuer were sitting calmly on the Jeep's hood, as the patrol car screamed around the corner of the warehouse. A uniformed Sergeant got out from behind the wheel. "Albert Parker?"

"That would be me," Albert answered while sliding off the hood. "This is T. J. Walsh, Senator Pat Walsh's son. Those two," he said, pointing at Crusher and the Arab, "were holding him here against his will. The smaller one is also a suspect in the murder of Terry Hannan."

The sergeant took down all the pertinent information, while his partner undid the electrical cord and patted down the suspects. While searching the Arab's pockets, the patrolman exclaimed, "Hey Sarge, I found something! You might want to see this." As his partner walked over, the patrolman removed a rather large piece of wire from the suspect's pants pocket.

Looking straight into the Arab's eyes, the sergeant asked, "What's this?"

A momentary flash of fear passed over Salaam's face, but he quickly recovered. In a perfectly calm and matter-of-fact tone, he simply said, "I'm a musician; that's a guitar string."

After hearing this exchange, Albert walked over to the sergeant. He was grinning as if he had just answered the final jeopardy category with the game winning reply. "Sergeant, I know you are not aware of this, but you are holding the home run ball!"

"What?"

"Guard that guitar string like it was King Tut's treasure, until you can get it to the police lab. I know for a fact that after they run DNA tests, it will prove to be the murder weapon that ended Holeshot Hannan's life!"

The sergeant looked back at the Arab and said, "Oh yeah?"

Albert answered with, "There can be no other possible conclusion."

The cop stored the damning evidence in a large envelope. Salaam said nothing and just stared at his shoes.

As the patrolman was loading his charges into the squad car, a Land Rover wheeled around the corner and came to a stop. R.J. Abbott got out dragging a handcuffed man behind him. While holding the slightly built, muttering man up by his collar, the investigator asked, "Does anyone know who this miserable wretch is? I found him running out of the park, screaming some nonsense about his thumbs. Something told me I should grab him before he hurt someone, or himself, but I'll be damned if I can figure out why he was so upset about his thumbs!" R.J. held up his prisoner's hands by the small loop of chain between the cuffs. The hands, including thumbs, were perfectly normal.

"His name is Mung," Tommy said. "He was the other one who kept me under guard. I don't have the vaguest idea what happened to him. All I know is that he ran out the door babbling gibberish. He did stop for a second, as if he wanted Crusher over there to help him. I could see that his hands seemed to be all knotted up, as if he had arthritis or something, but before Crusher could even say anything, Mung just freaked out and ran off screaming like a lunatic."

"Well," R.J. said, "I almost ran him over. He jumped out from between two parked cars, looking like an escapee from a mental institution. I figured whatever the problem is here, this guy needs to be restrained."

While the Sergeant added the hapless Mung to the back seat of the patrol car, Albert filled R.J. in on the evidence found in Salaam's pocket. "I'm no scientist, R.J., but I'm willing to bet when that guitar string comes back from the lab, it's going to be playing 'Jailhouse

Rock' for Salaam here."

"I would say that pretty well seals it," R.J. agreed.

"One thing is still bothering me about this, R.J. This guy is supposed to be a professional assassin. The CIA and Interpol have been chasing his shadow for years, without success. Now it seems to me, Salaam should have been smart enough to throw that guitar string in the dumpster after he iced Holeshot. Now, all we would have on him would be the kidnapping charge, not murder. How could he have been so stupid, to keep the bloody thing in his pocket?"

"I think the answer to your question is as simple as the force of habit. He more than likely just put it in his pocket with the intention of using it again on his next victim. You know, we call this a string, but it really is not. The E string is actually made of wire wrapped around wire, which makes it unbreakable and lethal. The lab report indicated to us that this guitar string was probably one of the Arab's favorite tools."

"Well, it looks like we've got this pretty well wrapped up," Tommy said. "What's next?"

"I think I can answer that," the sergeant said. "If Mr. Walsh and Mr. Abbott would be kind enough to follow us back to HQ so we could get signed statements and secure the evidence, we can put this thing to bed."

"Of course, we would be happy to," R.J. said. The senator's son opened the passenger door to the Land Rover and turned to his rescuer. "Okay, what about you. Albert?"

"You go ahead with R.J. Tommy, I hafta get back to the compound and change, so I can pick your dad up at the airport. I'll catch up with you guys at home later."

Albert watched as the Land Rover fell in line behind the squad car. As soon as the two cars were around the corner of the warehouse, he called to his tiny partner. "All right, Nelkie, they're gone. Where are you?" He heard the small voice from the area directly in front of him, just above his knees.

"I must return."

"Ya know, no matter how many times I see you do that, it's always such a rush to see you pop out of thin air like that. What fun it must be, to be able to do that!"

"It does have its advantages. Anyway, Albert, I must tell you that you were spectacular! I think we make quite a team, you and I."

"Like no other team on earth, I'm sure. Well, I guess we had better get going. We have just enough time to get back to my cabin and grab something to eat before I have to clean up and get to the airport."

They got into the Jeep and headed for home. The human spoke first. "Wow. This has been one wild ride, Nelkie. I'm so proud that we actually figured this out. I mean, Stanfield and the Arab are in custody, Tommy is safe, the senator's reputation remains intact, and even little Billy's father gets to keep his job! That's pretty much the whole ball of wax!"

"Not to mention that the entire nation of American elves is no longer in danger of being evicted…or worse, discovered by the most criminal element of human society!"

As Albert pointed the Jeep north, toward the Great Redwood Forest, he was saddened by feelings that the wildest adventure of his life was drawing to a rapid conclusion. His voice took on a tone of genuine concern when he spoke to his tiny ally. "Nelkie, do you really have to head home right away? I've kinda gotten used to havin' you around. Maybe you could hang out awhile and we could celebrate our victory together."

"I would love to, Albert, but my quest will not be completed until I report to the elders. I have truly enjoyed and learned from our time together. I am sure that if I could stay longer, the bond that has grown between us would flourish and mature even more, but I am duty-bound to inform the elders in full detail of all that has taken place on my quest. Now that I know the evil ones are incarcerated and our beloved woodland has been wrested from their grasp, I must inform the wise ones that all is well. Then I can assume my rightful place as an adult among the elf society."

"I do understand, my little friend; you have a job to finish. I guess what I'm tryin' to say is that I'm gonna hate to see you go."

"Thank you, Albert. I too will miss your company."

The rest of their ride was filled with upbeat conversation and Nelkie's introduction to Beatles music. The elf listened intently and informed his friend that not only were these humans superb musicians, with a true gift for harmony, but surely they must be revered as some of the wisest of their race.

"Why would you think that?" Albert asked.

"Because they are unerring in their belief that all you need is love."

Albert had spent enough time with Nelkie to know that he could not argue this wisdom; in fact, he was starting to believe it himself.

Chapter 56

When they arrived at the compound, Albert dropped Nelkie off at the cabin and garaged the Jeep. The two friends enjoyed a quick meal of tuna sandwiches and tomato soup. Within an hour of their arrival, Albert was dressed in his suit and walking up the driveway to fire up the Lincoln.

He was opening up the garage door when he saw something moving out of the corner of his eye. He turned to see a very excited Barbara Walsh running down the driveway. She was wearing an elegant cream-colored suit and waving wildly at the chauffeur.

"Albert! Wait! I'm going with you. I had just gotten back from my trip when Pat called with the wonderful news," she said, as she approached. When she was close enough to touch him, she grabbed his suit jacket, pulled him closer, and planted a kiss on his cheek.

"Pat told me all that you have done for us. I know that praise makes you uncomfortable, but thank you with all my heart for rescuing our son."

"Glad I could help." He opened the door for her; they got in and headed for the airport.

Pat came striding into the terminal with his face glowing. All the stress and worry of the past few weeks were gone and he now had the look of a man who was glad to be alive. Barbara ran to him and they embraced. Their eyes welled up with happy tears and they stayed locked in each other's arms for an extended moment, sharing their joy and relief.

Albert stood back, savoring every second. He was filled with pride to be a part of this heartwarming reunion.

Pat opened his tear-filled eyes to see his chauffeur smiling at them. Albert reached out to take Pat's briefcase. Instead of relinquishing the case, the senator seized Albert's hand and shook it vigorously. Much to the ex-fighter's surprise, Pat's left arm scooped around Albert's shoulders and squeezed him with such force that they both almost lost their balance.

"Albert, my friend and protector. I will never find the words to express my grateful thanks. How can I ever repay you for saving my life from devastation?"

The chauffeur's face had turned bright red with embarrassment. Other travelers, passing by the emotional scene and staring, were making him very uncomfortable. Albert politely extricated himself from the senator's grateful death grip and with a nervous smile, and took the briefcase.

"No sweat, Pat. I'm the one doing the repaying. I think we might finally be even. Anyway, let's go home, I hate crowds."

Chapter 57

Albert wheeled the limo around to the main house to find R.J.'s Land Rover parked just beyond the front porch. As he pulled behind it, Tommy and R.J. came charging down the stairs, yelling welcome home greetings.

It was a joyous reunion. Barbara was tearfully telling her son that he must gain some weight back before he got sick, and Pat was professing his pride in his son's courage. With an awkward display of clumsiness, the three of them managed to get through the front door. Albert and R.J. followed with the luggage.

Once they were all settled in the family room and caught up on all the recent events, Pat addressed the group.

"I have an announcement to make. In the light of what has happened, I have made a decision concerning the future of this very precious and fragile forest we all love. I have decided to donate all but the thirty acres surrounding the compound to the National Parks System. I think I have enough contacts in the Department of the Interior to secure the superintendent's job for Pete Baxter. I believe that with the power of the federal government behind us and a bit more security around here, we can prevent any more threats to our home and to the preservation of this wilderness."

The announcement was applauded by all as a wise move. R.J. suggested that a few more judiciously placed security cameras would be a good place to start. Pat agreed.

Seemingly preoccupied, the senator rose from his chair and left the room. He returned a few moments later holding a small box, about six inches square.

"Albert, if you would be kind enough to present this to your anonymous friend with our heartfelt thanks, I would be most appreciative." He handed him the box and Albert opened it, revealing the gleaming Freedom Medal.

"Thank you," the chauffeur said earnestly. "I know this person well. Believe me, he is like no one I have ever met. I know he will be very proud and deeply honored to accept this."

Albert then politely excused himself. He left the main house, thinking, *If they only knew, if they only knew*.... He shook his head slowly and proceeded down the driveway to his cabin.

Chapter 58

Albert walked through his cabin door feeling physically drained. The emotional overload of the past twelve hours had finally caught up with the ex-fighter. In the course of one day, he had experienced a range of emotions that were of an overwhelming intensity. Fear, Joy, pride, relief and now one more sentiment he did not expect to feel this deeply. The tough guy smiled softly as he heard the slow, rhythmic breathing coming from the small depression on the couch. The events of the day had taken their toll on his little buddy, who was sound asleep. Aware that his trusted ally would probably be leaving in the morning, he felt a deep sadness. He would miss this magical little creature. He wished there was someone he could tell about Nelkie's wonderful wisdom, his strong spirit, and the incredible power he wielded with such poise. Who would believe me? If I told anyone this story, they would have me taken away in a net!

He pulled a spare blanket out of the cedar chest and gently placed it over the small depression. His smile widened as he watched it disappear.

Nelkie's nose and stomach worked together to arouse the elf from a deep and much-needed rest. A delicious breakfast aroma filled the cabin. Albert peered out of the kitchen to see a pair of tiny hands appear on the back of the couch. Slowly, the familiar mop of curly red hair emerged over the couch back. When Albert could see a pair of sleepy deep-blue eyes between those hands, he spoke.

"I thought you were going to sleep the whole day away, so I decided to cook breakfast."

"It smells great! What are you cooking?"

"French toast, a la Parker. Potato bread done golden brown, with a touch of powdered cinnamon and maple syrup. Come and get it." Albert poured his friend a cup of tea. "I put a couple of phone books on your chair, so you could sit a little higher," he said.

Nelkie thanked his host and dug into his morning feast with great enthusiasm. "This is wonderful, Albert! I had no idea you were such an accomplished chef."

"Glad you like it. Listen, I've got some news for you. Frank Martini called while you were asleep. He said that when the Arab was confronted with the blood evidence on the guitar string, he sang like a bird. He thought if he corroborated all the evidence against Stanfield, he might be able to cut a deal with the prosecutor for a lesser sentence for himself. Of course, the whole session was recorded by the police. I think they are both gonna go away for a long, long time."

"Well, that about finishes it, my friend," Nelkie said, patting his stomach. "My quest has reached its human conclusion. I can start my trip home."

"I have more good news from the senator," Albert went on. He explained Pat's plan to annex most of his property to the National Redwood Preserve and how he was sure he could keep Pete Baxter on as superintendent.

"That's more than good news, Albert. That means that the homeland of my race is secure. The elders will be very pleased to know this."

"Yes, of course. As long as the United States remains a sovereign nation, your home will be protected by the power of the federal government. Oh, I almost forgot. I have something for you." He went into the living room and retrieved a small box. "The senator wants you to have this," he said, and opened the box.

The elf's eyes widened when he saw the red, white, and blue ribbon. Moving closer, he read the inscription: "With the thanks of a grateful nation."

Albert removed the medal from its case and placed it ceremoniously around his friend's neck. "It is my great honor to award you this Medal of Freedom from the United States of America."

"Thank you. Thank you very much, my friend. Please tell the senator for me that the honor is mine and that I am proud to have played a small part in the elimination of any threat to his home and family." The elf slid off the kitchen chair and marched into the living room. He donned his hat and slung his provisions pouch over his shoulder. Stroking his chin, he smiled and said, "Even my beard is almost completely grown in. I have successfully completed my mission and now I even *look* like a mature elf! I have become what you humans call a 'man.'"

"Congratulations," Albert said, "but don't be in too much of a hurry to grow up. Time passes much too quickly. I know that I would give almost anything to get back twenty years or so."

They laughed, but it was more of a nervous laugh because both of them were uncomfortable, knowing that the moment of Nelkie's departure had arrived.

Albert bent over slightly and stuck out his large-knuckled right hand. Nelkie grasped it firmly in both of his. The ex-fighter thought for a second that he had seen a twinkle in Nelkie's eyes that had never been there before. At that very moment, he felt a barely noticeable jolt. It was about half the intensity of a static electricity shock that one would get upon touching a metal doorknob, after walking across a rug. It almost felt like some sort of transference of energy from Nelkie's body into his. The feeling vanished in less time than it takes to blink, so Albert mentally shrugged it off. Nelkie's voice brought his focus back to their farewell.

"Albert, my friend and ally. I am proud to have known you. I know," the elf said, his eyes again showing that momentary twinkle, "that you will have a long and healthy life. You and your friend, Senator Walsh, are prime examples of what all humans should aspire to."

"Thanks, Nelkie. Our time together has taught me that a human can receive no greater honor than the respect and friendship of someone of your race. I only hope that someday, the high moral standard of American elves will become the rule, rather than the exception among humans. C'mon, I'll walk you out."

Albert opened the screen door and they walked onto the porch, greeted by the warm early-morning sun.

"Have a safe journey home, my friend."

"Thank you," the elf said, bowing with respect.

Albert watched the elf stride off toward his beloved forest. Before he was out of earshot, Nelkie turned, waved his stick in a gesture of farewell and said, "Be well, Albert."

The tiny figure turned back toward the trees. Albert watched him blend into the underbrush, leaving the older man alone with his thoughts. "I'm sure gonna miss that little fella," he said aloud.

He went into the cabin, still bugged by the fact that there would never be anyone he could tell about the greatest adventure of his life. Albert thought that maybe he would feel better after a long, hot shower. After tossing a towel onto the bathroom sink, he glanced into the mirror. He did an instant double take. Albert leaned over the sink and looked closely at his reflection. He couldn't believe his eyes! His hands moved slowly across his face, as if feeling it would confirm what his eyes told him had happened. His prematurely white hair and beard had darkened. The dark-brown hair of his youth had returned! Albert looked closer to see the crow feet-like wrinkles around his eyes had softened. Even his skin appeared less leathery. Eyes that could not be brought to tears by dozens of tough professional fighters were now overflowing as a result of the touch of one tiny elf. When Albert realized that Nelkie had somehow given him back his twenty years, he could not hold back the tears.

Chapter 59

Nelkie was excited about being back in the forest. He marched along, wearing his new medal proudly. *I have only one more service to render before I can go home*, he thought, and at that moment, he turned onto the path that would take him to the Baxter's caretaker cottage.

It was still early and Nelkie was hoping he would find Billy playing in his tree house. In a short while Nelkie found himself standing at the foot of Billy's ladder. His keen ears told him he was in luck. He could hear the little boy above his head. Not knowing for sure if anyone else were up there, Nelkie touched his medallion and vanished before ascending the steps.

The elf looked through the narrow doorway to see Billy holding a toy biplane aloft. The boy was making rat-ta-tat machine gun noises as he whooshed the plane through the air.

Nelkie took a seat on the floor and waited for Billy to land his plane. When the boy finally put the plane down, Nelkie whispered softly, "Bill-ly."

The child jumped, taken by surprise, but when he heard a giggle coming from the floor, he knew right away who had called him.

"Nelkie! Where are you?" His voice was high-pitched with excitement, as his eyes scanned the floor.

A warm smile was the first thing Billy saw as the elf suddenly appeared before his first human friend. "I have good news for you, Billy, as I promised."

"Were you able to help my daddy? Can he keep his job?'

"Yes to both questions, my young friend. The senator's problems have been solved. Your father will keep his job and your family will not have to move away."

"Yippee," Billy cried. "I knew you could do it! I just knew it!"

"Shh! Please don't talk so loud. Someone may want to know who you're talking to."

"Oops, sorry. I'm just so happy! Thank you Nelkie, I am so lucky to have met an elf. Thank you for helping my dad and me."

"You're welcome. Look," Nelkie said, reaching into his pouch. "I brought you a present." He produced the wooden flute he'd carved, and played a short melody.

"Can I try?" the boy asked impatiently.

"In just a minute," came the reply. "I must do something first." The elf placed the flute on Billy's table and held his walking stick above it. The little boy watched closely as the look on his friend's face changed from his normal warm and friendly countenance to one of intense concentration. Nelkie placed his walking stick on top of the flute and slowly began to roll the instrument back and forth across the table. Billy's eyebrows were raised in delightful surprise as a series of six musical tones arose from the table and gently floated around the tree house. Nelkie repeated the rolling motion once more and again, the room was filled with music. Satisfied with the completion of his task, Nelkie put down his stick and handed the flute to his friend. "I have empowered this instrument for you in two ways. First, the flute knows how to make music. All you have to do is move your fingers over these holes as you blow into this end."

The boy did as he was told and the flute responded with the most delightful tune, as the boy played on with ever-widening eyes. Nelkie danced gleefully around the tree house, while Billy astounded himself with his newfound musical talent. They carried on, entertaining each other until they were both forced to stop to catch their breath.

Nelkie patted Billy on his shoulder and the elf's expression became a little less animated. "I must be on my way, Billy, but I would like to show you something before I go." Nelkie reached for the flute, and Billy complied.

"Keep this flute in a safe place, my young friend, for someday you may use it to call for help."

"What do you mean?"

"If you cover all the holes except the first one, and then blow softly, the flute will play the same series of notes that you heard when I was rolling it across the table. I hope you will never have to use them, but if you do, these notes are a distress call. If ever in your life you find yourself in bad trouble and there is no one to help you, play those notes. I promise you, Billy Baxter, that I will hear them and I will come as soon as I can. Just remember, you are to use the flute to call me only if you are in grave danger, or you are in trouble beyond your ability to save yourself."

"Yes, I understand. I am not to call you because I miss you," Billy said. "Only in a 'mergency, right?"

"Right," Nelkie answered. "Now, my young friend, I really must be leaving." Nelkie gathered up his few belongings and before he could say anything, Billy rushed over in tears and hugged him so hard, he could hardly breathe.

"Whoa! Easy there, Billy; you're a lot stronger than you think!"

"Oh! I'm sorry! I just wanted to thank you again and give you a goodbye hug."

"It's okay. I understand." Nelkie reached up and returned a gentle hug to the much taller, much younger little boy. "Goodbye and be well, my friend," Nelkie said as he touched his medallion. In half a heartbeat, he was gone.

"Wait! Nelkie, wait a minute!"

A small voice answered from the bottom of the ladder. "What is it, Billy?"

"I just remembered, I have something for you too, but it's back in the house. Just give me a minute; I'll be right back."

The seven-year-old hurried down the ladder and ran for the kitchen door. He returned in less than five minutes, clutching a large brown grocery bag. "Here, put this stuff in your pouch, so you don't get hungry."

"Well, thank you very much, Billy. This is very kind of you." Nelkie packed his treats in the pouch until it was so full, he could barely button it. They said their final goodbyes as Billy's mom called him from the kitchen. Nelkie started homeward and Billy ran to answer his mother's call.

"Billy, come in here right now! I have to talk to you!" Her tone was something less than happy. When he walked into the kitchen, she questioned him. "Can you tell me what happened to that bowl of tomato sauce and meatballs I put in the refrigerator? It seems to have disappeared!"

The little boy knew he had some explaining to do. His young brain was desperately trying to fabricate a believable story.

"Well, I'm waiting."

Knowing he was in trouble, he decided to come clean. "I, umm, gave them to my friend Nelkie, so he wouldn't be hungry on his long trip home."

"Nelkie? She looked at her son unbelievingly and shook her finger at him in pseudo reprimand. "William Wyatt Baxter, if you don't stop making up these stories and blaming everything on your imaginary playmates, you're going to make me crazy! Now go outside and play and stay out of my kitchen until lunchtime!"

Billy scampered out the door as his mom threw her hands in the air in exasperation. "Good grief! Nelkie! Where does he get this stuff from?"

Billy sat in his tree house, his heart filled with magic and wonder. He played his precious flute, and its melodious happy music took his mind and spirit to an enchanting place, known only to children.

A half mile into the forest, Nelkie's finely tuned ears could still make out the delightful music coming from the tree house. He savored another bite of meatball and thought, *What a joyous life I lead!*

Chapter 60

Nelkie skipped and danced along the forest path, delighted to be headed home. He had formed a strong bond with Albert and would miss his trusted ally, but for now, he longed for the treetops that were his home. He looked forward with great pride to addressing the Circle of Elders on the successful completion of his quest. He had faced the evil that lurks among humans and defeated its disciples. He was fulfilled.

Summer was in full bloom. He enjoyed snacking from the endless supply of ripe berries as he took in the carnival of sights, sounds, and smells that surrounded him.

By midday, he had covered several miles. Not wanting to lose any time, he decided not to stop for lunch. When hunger struck him, he would open his provisions pouch and eat on the move. Billy had provided well for his friend. There was enough fruit, nuts, corn muffins, and meatballs to last him for days.

Nelkie's excitement never abated as the day wore on. Before he realized it, dusk was rapidly approaching and he was forced off the well-traveled path to search for a place to bed down.

He found a stand of ten or twelve mature hemlocks. A thick bed of soft, dry needles lay under the long downward-sloping boughs. Like a camper entering his tent, Nelkie brushed aside a flap of limbs and entered his shelter. He curled up under the protective branches and touched his medallion. Within minutes, he was dreaming of a girl with wildflowers in her hair.

Just after dawn, he was jolted awake by a very determined wood-pecker. He was jack-hammering away at the trunk above the elf, persistently pecking a hole to get at his breakfast.

Nelkie sat up and yawned. After scanning the area and concluding that he was alone with the alarm-bird, he stretched and took a deep breath of cool morning air. He enjoyed a large, juicy orange and felt energized and ready for another day's march. The elf packed up his things and found his way back to the path. He turned toward home, his spirits light and his pace steady.

Although he pressed on all morning without stopping, he did not tire. In fact, he seemed to gain energy with each step. On his way, he watched dozens of squirrels chasing each other up and down tree trunks, and marveled at the variety and multitude of birds soaring through the forest's high canopy.

He felt his first hunger pangs since breakfast when the sun was a little more that straight overhead. *I guess I should stop for a while*, he told himself. His strategy was based on the thought that if he ate now and rested for a short while, he would have no trouble hiking into the late afternoon.

Sitting under a tall pine tree, the elf feasted on a corn muffin and some shelled walnuts, and washed it all down with a few deliciously juicy grapes. After resting his legs for a good half hour, he could sit no longer. The elf resumed his journey, proceeding ever deeper into the forest.

Several miles from his lunch break, Nelkie came upon something odd. Just off the path, he saw a small grouping of yew bushes. He strolled over for a closer look. Something here just didn't make sense. Upon closer examination, he realized that they were freshly planted! Nelkie racked his brain, trying to figure out why anyone would plant shrubs this deep in the forest. Surely he had come twenty-five miles from the forest's edge. Finding no logical answer to this enigma, he shrugged his tiny shoulders and resumed his trek.

As the afternoon wore on, Nelkie noticed an odd pattern developing. Every three miles or so, he would come upon another small grouping of freshly planted young yew bushes. After he happened onto the fourth grouping of these shrubs, he was severely perplexed. First of all, he thought, the only vehicle one could navigate along the forest pathways would be a small motorcycle. There were no tire tracks anywhere.

After much consideration, Nelkie concluded that some person or persons had carried all these shrubs into the forest and planted them. What he had seen already would take one man five or six trips. Try as he would, he could not come up with a reason why anyone would go through such hard physical labor to plant shrubs where no one would ever see them. If there was any wisdom in this arboreal endeavor, it was lost on Nelkie. He resolved to consult the elders about this mystery and pressed on, deeper into the forest.

Late afternoon wore on into early evening. Nelkie began to feel a little weary. It had been a long day's walk and his need for food was gnawing away at his stomach. He was looking for a suitable place to sit and enjoy his evening meal when the familiar tingling began.

"Uh-oh," he said aloud. "Someone is coming."

The tingling rapidly escalated into a thumping, pounding alarm! Whoever was approaching was doing so at a tremendous rate of speed!

The elf touched his medallion and took a few backward steps off the path. He could hear the rhythmic sounds of hooves advancing toward him. Suddenly, he could make out the shape of the oncoming animal. The strength and grace of the beast's movements were unmistakable. The great creature slowed and then came to a stop within ten feet of the elf. He raised his head in the air, searching for a familiar scent.

Nelkie saw the great crown of antlers and his heart leaped. He grabbed his medallion and ran toward the great stag.

"Rajah, my friend! I have returned. It's so good to see you!"

"Nelkie! I knew it was your scent I picked up back there. I didn't think you would be back so soon, but I had to make sure. Did you complete your quest?"

"Oh yes. It was wonderful. I met some humans that were truly the best of their race and, unfortunately, some that were the worst."

The regal beast lowered his head while tilting his massive antlers toward Nelkie. "Well, climb on up, my friend, and you can tell me all about it. If you ride on my back, I can cut your travel time home in half."

Nelkie held on while the stag lifted him effortlessly. Rajah told his friend that while Nelkie was away, there had been trouble.

"What kind of trouble?" Nelkie asked.

"Death has come to many of our brothers of the forest. It rains down on us from above. They hide and wait silently in the trees. They wear garments that make them blend in with their surroundings. They are above even the keenest sense of smell. All creatures except myself, thanks to you, are defenseless."

"This is very bad news, Rajah. I don't know what I can do, if anything, to help. However, I can do something to keep you and me from harm." Nelkie immediately touched his medallion and voiced the words that rendered both of them invisible.

Rajah stopped in his tracks. "Nelkie! I can't see myself! Did you do that?"

"Yes," the elf answered. "Don't worry, my noble friend. I can bring you back at will."

"This is a wondrous thing," Rajah said, starting forward again on legs that were a little unsteady. "It feels very strange to walk and not see my legs under me."

"I know. It takes a little getting used to."

"Tell me, can you do this for all you wish to protect?"

"If you mean can I turn all the animals in these woods invisible, I'm afraid not. I must be touching them to enable them to disappear. If I jumped off your back right now, you would be visible before I touched the ground."

"That's too bad, Nelkie, but I should have known the answer would not be as easy as that."

"Give me a little time, big fella. I may come up with something."

They traveled on into the early evening. Rajah asked many questions about humans and Nelkie did his best to answer all of them. He told his friend how the forest had come within a breath of being mowed down at the hands of Emmett Stanfield. The great stag was spellbound as he listened to stories about the murderous Arab and the eminent respect and friendship that grew between Albert and Nelkie.

"So, if this human, Stanfield, had not been stopped," Rajah said, "you and I would both be out of a home."

"You and I and every creature that lives in this woodland," Nelkie replied.

"I'm sure I will never understand the humans," concluded the big stag.

They walked on until twilight. Rajah found a cozy thicket where they could bed down for the night. The two tired wayfarers found a comfortable place to lie down and in a few short minutes, the soft summer breeze had lulled them both into a very sound sleep.

Chapter 61

"What do you say to a brisk morning run, Nelkie?"

"You've been awake for only ten minutes, and you want to run?"

"I run every morning for a few miles. It gets my heart pumping and keeps me strong. C'mon, it's invigorating."

Nelkie wiped the sleep from his eyes and reluctantly straddled the beast's broad back.

Rajah started off at a canter. Nelkie was holding on tightly at first, but soon relaxed his grip as he fell into the steady rocking rhythm of Rajah's stride. A smile grew across the elf's face. This was fun! "Can we go faster?" he asked, his smile now forming a continuous line from one pointed ear to the other.

The stag obliged silently with a blinding burst of speed. Nelkie's grip tightened on his friend's antlers as the streaked through the forest. With his eyes tearing from the wind and his heart racing, the elf threw back his head and let out a gleeful yell. "Hoo-yah!"

Rajah raced on. Nelkie felt as if at any second, the great beast would leap above the treetops and fly him over the canopy, all the way home.

Finally, Rajah slowed to a trot. The constant jostling bounced and bumped the elf into a fit of uncontrollable laughter. The stag jogged on until Nelkie, his little voice reverberating as if he were pounding on his chest with his fists, pleaded with his friend to stop. When the stag slowed to a walk, it was Nelkie who was out of breath. It took him a few moments to get enough wind to speak. "You sure know the meaning of the word invigorating. I don't think I've ever been more awake!"

"Nothing like an early-morning run to make you feel alive," the stag said. "It will also make you feel hungry," he added.

"I have a pouch full of fruit, nuts, and even meatballs. Would you like some of this?"

"Thank you, but no--I see what I want right ahead." The buck stepped off the path about twenty feet and stopped in front of yet another newly planted group of yews. "These are my favorite," he said. "The young shoots are so sweet and tender."

"That's great, Rajah, but I would really like to know how they got here."

"Why?"

"Well," Nelkie said, "obviously they didn't grow here naturally. Doesn't it strike you odd, that someone is planting your favorite food this deep in the forest?"

The stag answered with a mouthful of greens. "I never gave it much thought. I'm just glad there's more of it."

"Well, I don't get it," Nelkie continued. "If someone is providing you with food, I would just like to know who, and why."

A light breeze drifted over the two friends and suddenly, Rajah's massive head turned. He informed Nelkie that they had company. "There's a human among us, not too far ahead. We should investigate. I fear the hunters may have returned."

Nelkie agreed and advised his friend to follow the scent as quietly as possible. They had advanced only a hundred yards or so when Nelkie's built-in alarm system began to go off. "We're getting close, Rajah," he whispered. "Be careful."

As they inched closer, Nelkie saw something moving. "There," the elf whispered. "Climbing that tree!'

Rajah followed Nelkie's pointed finger to see a man ascending a large oak and whispered back to his friend. "Is he a hunter?"

"I don't know. I don't see a gun. We must get closer."

They got within earshot and Nelkie's heart sank. He saw the man standing on a limb, next to a hunter's tree stand that had been nailed to the trunk. There was no doubt as to the man's identity. A fierce anger was building up from deep inside the elf. He clenched his fists. His first thoughts were to strike an avenging blow for all who had suffered at the hands of Andrew Slater!

Rajah felt his friend stiffen his posture and instinctively knew Nelkie was very upset. "What's wrong, Nelkie?"

"I know this human. His name is Andrew Slater and he has hunted and trapped illegally, for years, in this woodland." Nelkie went on to explain about his confrontation with the poacher and his promise to reform.

"How could he not heed my warning? Is he fool enough to think that I wouldn't keep my word?" Nelkie's voice had taken on a tone of disbelief. His anger had risen to a point where it could affect his reason. Sensing this, he forced himself to back off emotionally. "Rajah, my friend, I want you to know that I must summon every ounce of self-control I possess to keep from rushing to judgment. If I submit to my gut reaction to this situation, I could unleash my full wrath upon this human and strike him blind, but I will not. Although it certainly looks like Slater has returned to his old ways, I will wait and observe and be sure of his intentions before I act."

The stag assured Nekie that this was the only sensible course of action. Rajah's deep, soothing voice did much to bring the elf's rapidly boiling anger down to a more rational simmer. "If this Slater human is killing our innocent brothers, no punishment would be too severe. However, we should be absolutely certain of his intentions before we seek retribution."

At that moment, they saw Slater steady himself against a large branch opposite the tree stand. He was withdrawing something from the deepest pocket of his overalls. The two spies were cringing in suspense as they waited to see what kind of weapon this unrepentant human would produce.

To their utter amazement, Slater began to whistle a delightful tune as he retrieved a small crowbar from his pocket. He placed one end between the trunk and the tree stand and pounded with his palm on the other. Shortly afterward, he had pried the entire contraption from its home. It hit the ground with a loud clang. The human then climbed down the back side of the oak and stepped out from behind the tree, carrying a shovel. Still whistling, he carried the tree stand about thirty feet from the oak and buried it.

"Well, I'll be," Nelkie said. "I thought for sure he was back to his old habits."

"I guess we both learned something about rushing to judgment, huh?"

"Something told me to wait, Rajah. Now I'm glad I did. I could have made a terrible mistake."

Nelkie's feelings of relief were quickly replaced by the familiar tingling of his sixth sense. "Let's get back off the path, Rajah. Someone's coming."

The stag complied, while raising his head into the wind. "More than one, Nelkie. At least two, definitely humans."

Both of them could now hear muffled laughter off in the distance. Knowing he could trust his built-in alarm system, Nelkie informed his friend that there were three humans approaching.

At the same time, unaware of any imminent intrusion, Slater had carried three small yews out from behind the great oak. He removed the burlap bags from around their root balls and started digging.

"He has done well," Nelkie observed. "Not only has he removed all the hunter's aids, he has taken it upon himself to provide extra food. He should be rewarded, for all is good."

"I'm afraid not all," came the stern reply. Rajah nudged his friend toward the path. Three men were drawing closer. Nelkie could make them out clearly now. The three were dressed in hunting garb and carrying rifles. They were also passing around a bottle.

"Whiskey," Nelkie said, anger again rising in his voice. "It makes humans irrational. The combination of guns and whiskey will make them even more dangerous than they already are."

The trio arrived at the base of the great oak. The man in the middle waved the bottle at the tree as he spoke to the others. "Hey, someone ripped this one down too!"

"Maybe it was him," another chimed in, pointing at Slater.

The third man began shouting at the former poacher. "Hey pal, didn't your mother ever tell you not to touch other people's stuff?"

Though he knew he was in trouble, Slater would not back down. "Didn't anyone ever tell you guys that killing animals in these woods is illegal?" he answered.

Rajah could no longer watch in silence. From inside his head, Nelkie heard the big stag's voice. "Nelkie, I think you had better do something. This is escalating into a confrontation. Slater is bound to get hurt!'

"Don't worry, big fella, I'm already working on it. We are about to give these hapless humans an experience they will never forget." The elf raised his walking stick skyward and concentrated his powers of telepathy. He stretched his sensory muscles to their limit and sent an urgent message throughout the forest. He asked for assistance and unity to combat and defeat a threat to all.

As he was doing this, the inebriated hunters were becoming more belligerent. The man with the whiskey bottle was growing more impatient with Slater, and he wanted answers. "What did you do with our tree stands? There are more than a half dozen missing. You had better have a good answer--and I mean right now!"

Nelkie moved his focus to Andrew Slater. He transferred the energy of his thoughts into the mind of the former poacher. "Andrew, you have proven yourself to your brothers of the forest and they have accepted you as one of their own. You may call on them for help and they will answer. Your brothers will not abandon you to fight a common enemy alone. Concentrate, Andrew. Call upon your brothers and they will come to your aid."

An awareness he had never felt before filled his consciousness. He did not understand it, but he could not deny it. Suddenly, he felt stronger, more confident, and certain that he was not alone. In an unearthly moment, he was compelled to follow the spiritual voice in his head and call for help. The three antagonists before him disappeared from view as Andrew Slater spoke to the forest with his mind. "Help me, my brothers. Our enemies confront me, and I am alone. Unite, my brothers, and we will rid ourselves of this threat together."

"All right, pal. You got about five seconds to tell us where our property is before we beat it outta you!"

Slater calmly put down his shovel, looked his adversary in the eye and simply said, "I think not."

The three hunters moved as one. They were going to beat this man senseless, until they got their property back. Before they could get within ten feet of their victim, they heard a great whooshing noise from above. The three looked up, astonished to see three peregrine falcons bearing down on them. The birds seemed to come out of nowhere, and their blinding speed combined with wingspans of almost four feet terrified their would-be prey. The falcons banked within inches of the hunters' faces. With no time to raise their weapons, they dropped them in a panic and turned to run. As soon as they had turned their backs to Slater, they were confronted by a sight that would haunt them for years to come. Blocking their escape were a dozen black bears on their hind legs, stretched out to a height of almost six feet. Confronted by more than 6000 pounds of snarling omnivores, their blood froze. Instinctively the trio reversed direction in hopes of escape. One step in that direction, and they were facing certain death. Circling between the hunters and their weapons were four eight-foot-long, 200-pound mountain lions. Two of the big cats let loose with an ear-piercing screech that assured the hunters that they would hunt no more.

Slater now stepped forward and stoked one of the cougars on the neck and back. "Patience, my prince. Let me speak with these men, before you decide to eat them." He stared with distaste at the hunters as he spoke. "You three have gone too far. I am the protector of this woodland and my friends and I have found you guilty of the worst of all crimes against nature. Killing for sport! There is nothing more cruel or uncaring. My friends here, as well as those furry fellows behind you, believe this is a crime punishable by death. I can give you a choice. If being eaten alive does not suit you, maybe the answer lies in the trees above your head." The doomed trio looked up into the great oak to see scores of California mountain king snakes suspended from its limbs. "These fellows will be happy to crush you to death, so you don't have to be eaten alive."

Convinced he was about to die, the middle hunter pleaded for mercy. "Look, mister... I don't understand how you made this happen, but we don't want to die. Please, I beg you, we have wives and children. I swear, we'll never hunt again anywhere, ever!"

"I told you, I am the protector of this woodland. You have committed heinous crimes against my brothers. Did it ever occur to you that those you killed had wives and children as well? Probably not. Give me one reason why I should deny my brothers their dinner."

The three were babbling incoherently, alternately pleading and promising anything to save themselves from a horrible death.

Slater held his hand up in angry frustration. "All right, shut up! Shut up, all of you! I'll tell you what I'm gonna do. I will tell my brothers to let you go this time and I'll tell you why." The hunters let out a simultaneous sigh of relief as Slater explained. "My friends will spare your miserable lives because even these dumb animals, as so many of you call them, know that all life, even yours, is precious, and should not be taken in revenge. If your well-deserved death sentence was carried out now, my brothers would be no better than you. This would be wrong. We have more respect for life than that. However, if any of you set foot in this forest again, we will have no choice but to see to it that the sentence you received today is carried out at once. Now go, before we change our minds."

As they turned back to the path, the men were astounded to see the black bears, now on all fours, lining the path on both sides. Inexplicable as it was, these men knew that somehow, Slater had the ability to communicate with these beasts. The bears had opened the path to allow them to pass. They briefly looked at one another in shock and disbelief. What they had just seen was impossible, yet undeniable. Without a word, all three hunters seized their opportunity and broke into a run. They never looked back. As soon as they were out of sight, Andrew picked up their abandoned weapons and his shovel. Before he could set about the task of burying the rifles, he heard a clear and unmistakable male voice resonate throughout his mind. "Thank you, my brother. We welcome you and we stand ready to defend our home together." Slater observed one of the larger bears rearing up on his hind legs. When the beast had reached his full height, Andrew peered into his eyes. The human saw and felt great power and grace in those eyes, but there was something more. Acceptance. The bear threw his head back and let out an ear- splitting roar, as if it were a statement to seal their new alliance. Slater watched as the bear gently returned to all fours and slowly lumbered away with his brethren. Movement caught Andrew's attention. It was coming from a hilly area off to his right. The mountain lions had since slinked away, but there was one large female on an outcropping of rocks. Slater felt her eyes on him and soon, her voice. "Call and we shall come. We are all family now." Her statement made, the cougar leapt from one rock to another and in two graceful moves, was gone.

Slater was deeply moved by the spiritual nature of his experience with his new found family. He searched his mind for an explanation for how this could have happened to him. While digging a fresh grave for the rifles, he considered the possibility of his own insanity. He had heard stories about people who had heard voices in their head and acted upon them. These people were almost always proved to be insane and their actions were usually of a violent nature. *This was different,* he thought. *These creatures didn't just communicate with my mind; they responded to my call for help and reacted to the situation!*

Nelkie and Rajah were still watching from a short distance away, when the elf said, "We must go to him. I am quite sure that all that has happened has left this poor man in a confused state, and he deserves an explanation." Nelkie touched his medallion, and he and the stag materialized.

As the pair intersected Slater's burial site, he stared at them, convinced that he had most certainly lost his mind. "Oh man, I must have lost it…this can't be happening! First, I think I can speak with man-eaters, and now I think I see a tiny elf riding on the back of a giant stag! What's next, elephants riding tricycles?"

"Don't worry, Mr. Slater. You are not losing your mind," Nelkie said, while lowering himself from his mount. "You are, however, one of the chosen few."

Positive that he was addressing a hallucination, he looked curiously at the elf and said, "Chosen for what?"

"To be one of the very few humans who have the capability to communicate with the animal world telepathically." Nelkie strode over and offered his hand. Still confused and uncertain, Slater bent over and shook hands with what he knew was his imagination.

"I am Nelkie, son of Balthazar, and I wish to congratulate you on your reformation from poacher to protector."

"Forgive me, little man, but you're really scaring me. How did you know my name and how did you know I was a poacher?"

"I was the one, although in a very different form at the time, who warned you of the dire consequences that awaited you if you did not change your ways."

Slater's eyes opened wide with fear upon remembering the monster floating above him as he lay dying. "That was you?"

"Yes Andrew. If you don't believe me, I would be happy to…."

"No no, I believe you, I believe you. I think I like you much more at this size, if it's all the same to you!"

"I understand. Anyway, as to what has just happened to you, I am responsible. As a reward for your commitment to turning from a life of crime and showing genuine concern for the inhabitants of this woodland, I have made you a brother of the forest. This means you may communicate with all the forest creatures, and they with you. In your own words, you are their protector. You can warn our brothers of any impending danger. If any hunters should intrude on our domain, or if a wildfire threatens, you can make your brothers aware. They will likewise be watching out for your safety from the sky and the trees, as well as the hills and valleys of the woodland. Oh, by the way, this is my friend Rajah."

The stag politely bowed his antlers and Slater suddenly heard, "I am pleased to meet you."

"Believe me, big guy, the pleasure is all mine." Turning back to the elf, Slater thanked him for his wonderful gift. "Nelkie, I can't tell you how awesome and fascinating this is. Not only does this help me to protect the innocent creatures that live in this wood, but it gives me the opportunity to get to know all of them as no human ever has. This is the most exciting day of my life! Thank you!"

"No thanks are necessary, my brother. You have more than proved your worth today, and I am proud and comforted to have you among us. I must leave you now, for my family await my return. Good luck to you and be well."

Taking the cue, Rajah stepped over to Nelkie and lowered his wide rack of antlers. The elf held on and Rajah gently raised his friend off the ground and onto his back. As they returned to the forest path, the great stag turned his head back in Slater's direction, at which point Andrew heard, "I wish to thank you for planting all of those yews; they are delicious."

Slater watched, misty-eyed, as they cantered off along the forest path. With his hands on his hips and his chest swelling with pride, he said aloud, "I am one of the chosen few!"

Chapter 62

Nelkie and his trusted friend traveled on until nightfall. After finding a safe place to settle in for the night, they had a short discussion about their highly successful day before turning in. Not yet asleep, yet not really awake, Nelkie became aware of a glowing golden light above him. As sleep had almost claimed him, it took the elf a long moment to shake the cobwebs from his brain and open his eyes. He concentrated his focus on the golden swirling light above him until his vision cleared and he could make out the hundreds of tiny shapes floating gracefully through the canopy.

"Rajah! Wake up! Look who's here!" The stag raised his massive head to join Nelkie's observance of the golden light ballet.

"Fairies," he said. They rose to stand, as one minute form flitted down from the formation.

"Welcome home, Nelkie. We have heard from our brothers that your quest has been successful. Congratulations to you. We have come out this evening to tell you that you are now only one day's walk from home."

The elf bowed with deep respect before he spoke. "Thank you, my queen. As always, a delight to see your highness. Of course you have met my friend and protector, Rajah. He has volunteered to carry me home on his back and has saved me many long days of solitary travel."

"Yes," she said. "We have long been acquainted with this noble stag. Thank you for bringing our brother back to us so soon, Rajah."

"My privilege, your majesty."

"Your arrival at this time, on this night of nights, is most fortu-itous," she said.

"How so, my queen?" the elf asked.

"Tonight, my subjects and I, along with a few honored guests, will celebrate the bounty of the first summer harvest. It is the first rite of summer, and there will be much song and dance. The merriment and feasting will go on until dawn. We would be honored to have both of you attend this, our most sacred of observances."

"Thank you, your majesty," Nelkie said, while bowing deeply. "The honor is most assuredly ours."

"An honor and a privilege, ma'am," Rajah agreed.

"Then come, follow us off the path and deeper into the wood. The festivities are just beginning." She flew off with the speed of a lightning bolt, while leaving behind a trail of golden light for them to follow.

"This is so exciting, Rajah. Not many outsiders have been allowed to witness the sacred rites of the nocturnal forest fairies. They fiercely guard their privacy."

The stag lowered his antlers for his friend, and said, "I'm quite sure this promises to be a night to be remembered for all time."

They followed the light trail for several thousand yards, through the thickest part of the woodland, until they came upon a clearing that was alive with movement and light. They stopped at the edge of the clearing to stare in amazement at the sights before them.

At the center of the clearing was a great bonfire blazing a good twenty feet high. There were thousands of the tiny creatures flutter-ing, hovering, and whisking about in preparation. They worked in groups of fifty to a hundred, flying about to transport nature's bounty to the area set aside for the feast. Several dozen fairies were hanging the last of a multitude of flower garlands from the trees surrounding the bonfire. While Nelkie and Rajah were watching all the activity, six females floated over to them at eye level to the stag. They all had the same high- pitched voice and spoke in unison. "Our queen wishes us to seat you at the banquet. The celebration is about to begin."

The honored guests followed their winged ushers and were seated far enough back from the bonfire so they could enjoy its beauty, but not feel its intense heat. In front of them, the ground was covered with a variety of giant greenery upon which were displayed a cornucopia of all the abundant provisions the forest provided. Fruits and nuts of every variety imaginable, along with lush greens, and freshly picked vegetables were the bill of fare. Rajah dug into the greens with gusto, as his friend delighted in a fruit and nut appetizer. They sat back enjoying the glow of the fire and the wonderful taste of freshly picked produce, when the celebration began in earnest. First, the smaller brothers and sisters of the forest paraded out of the underbrush to seat themselves at Mother Nature's table. Rabbits, squirrels, raccoons, and foxes padded, hopped, and trotted into the clearing. Birds of several species fluttered in to join the feast. Throughout the meal, hundreds of pairs of fairies oscillated to and fro, bearing large blossoms filled with a blend of liquid nectars, the recipe for which was known only to a select few of their realm. Nelkie stood and held a nectar-filled flower up for his friend to drink. "Try some of this; I think you'll like it," he said.

His friend, reluctant at first, only stuck the tip of his tongue into the nectar for a small taste. He swallowed the first few drops, and said, "Umm, have you tasted this? It's delicious. Sweet, but with a lingering aftertaste, very good. Without waiting for a reply from the elf, he plunged his tongue back into the blossom and lapped up the remaining nectar. Nelkie was about to take a sip and looked into the flower to find it empty.

"Wow. This stuff must be good. you finished it!" Momentarily, several of their winged servers set down more of the "flower cups," filled to their brim. Nelkie took a few sips and thought there was something vaguely familiar about the aftertaste. He couldn't put his finger on it because he had only one time in his life tasted elf-brewed beer. What neither he nor Rajah realized was that the familiar aftertaste was produced as a result of the nectar's high content of alcohol! Unconcerned, the two went on eating and drinking to their hearts' content.

Suddenly, they heard a low, soft blending of voices rising up from behind them. It was a female harmony of many parts. They were not spoken words, but notes. The voices rose gradually in volume and were joined by others coming from the entire perimeter of the clearing. The soothing harmonies changed in pitch as the female voices were joined by the males at the far end of the clearing. As this was happening, several hundred fairies had formed a circle around the bonfire. They performed their ceremonial dance as one entity by forming a chain of connected arms. All eyes were on the dancers as they raised their arms together above their heads. Their wings beat in exactly the same cadence, which was increasing in speed as the glorious harmonies from the perimeter increased in volume. These harmonies, now incalculable in number and more heavenly in mood and timbre than any choir of human origin, escalated and intensified until they exploded into a crescendo of a thousand blended voices.

As the vocal crescendo detonated high into the trees, the hundreds of bonfire fairies erupted as one into the highest reaches of the upper canopy and exploded into a fountain of golden light, streaming continuously back to earth.

With each change of pitch, tone, or melody created by the fairy choir, the flyers displayed another kaleidoscope of light and design throughout their treetop theater. They formed geometric shapes of every description, and blended them from one into the other continuously. Their spectacular display culminated with the aerial artists forming the shape of a gigantic eagle, its wings beating in concert with the voices below. Each feather of this golden bird of prey was a single fairy, moving with precise choreography that allowed the eagle to dive and swoop above the clearing. Soaring in song, the voices of the vocal orchestra accompanied the bird lower and lower into the meadow. The harmonies grew higher in pitch and volume, as the eagle approached the ground with its wings flapping furiously. The pageant reached its dramatic finale as the eagle's talons touched the forest floor. In perfect synchronicity with the climactic halting of a thousand voices, the eagle exploded into as many parts and dissipated into the tree-lined backdrop in a fading golden mist.

"Wow! Never have I seen and heard such magnificence!" Nelkie said, while applauding vigorously.

"Nor I," the stag agreed. "The beauty of this woodland has just been enhanced a thousandfold."

Queen Katherine fluttered down to them as the two attempted to stand. Her regal countenance faded as she succumbed to a fit of the giggles. She watched the inebriated elf trying to maintain his balance, which immediately resulted in his taking several quick backward steps, only to wind up on his butt, laughing uncontrollably.

Rajah, not understanding what was happening, tried to go to his friend's aid. The not-so- majestic stag was flabbergasted to find that he could walk only sideways, on very wobbly legs. Nelkie joined the queen in shrieks of laughter when it appeared that Rajah's massive antlers were too heavy to hold up. His head was severely tilted to his left as he stumbled wildly on teetering legs, reducing his once-dignified image to sheer goofiness. Nelkie was holding his stomach with both hands, trying to stop laughing before it started to hurt; still, he couldn't resist teasing his friend. "Hey Rajah, I think I know where the name 'stag' comes from! I think it's short for 'stagger'!"

"Not funny," his friend replied, while still trying to find his legs.

With tears of laughter streaming down her royal face, Queen Katherine found it next to impossible to regain any sense of decorum, but she did manage to calm herself enough to speak to her two confused guests.

"I apologize, my dear friends. I should have warned you about consuming too much nectar. I had planned to guide you back to the forest path tonight, but I believe, given your current condition, that would prove to be far too hazardous. Come, if you can make it to the edge of the clearing, I will have soft beds prepared for both of you."

It took several attempts, but after a time Katherine's guests found themselves curled up and comfortable on a bed of soft fir. "Thank you, my queen," Nelkie said. "I feel I have embarrassed myself tonight and I would…(hic)… like to apologize for my lack of control."

Katherine looked down and smiled at the already snoring stag. Turning back to the elf, she said, "Nonsense. No apology is necessary. Now please get comfortable and get some much- deserved rest. We will keep watch from above until dawn. Sleep well, and know that you are safe." Queen Katherine, sovereign ruler of all nocturnal forest fairies, executed an aerial curtsy and swiftly flitted into the upper canopy, to join her subjects.

Shortly after dawn, Rajah woke, stretched, and glanced up into the canopy. His movement had awakened the elf. Nelkie patted his friend's broad back and greeted him warmly. "G' mornin', big fella. Sleep well?"

"Like a fawn at his mother's side."

"Ah, good. I feel well-rested myself. I'm sure we both slept more soundly, knowing that someone was keeping watch."

"I'm sure you're right…but speaking of our guardians, where are they?"

"You will never see nocturnal forest fairies out in the wood after dawn, for a variety of reasons. They have outstanding vision in low light, but are almost blind in bright sunlight. As you can imagine, this handicap would make them easy prey."

"I've often wondered why no one has ever seen them during the day. As it is, very few have claimed to see them at all. Their very existence has been disputed to the point that they have become a legend. I have heard many stories of these creatures holding ritual ceremonies and great feasts that celebrate the seasons. Rumor has it that these

NELKIE'S QUEST

events are a feast for the eyes and ears and last well into the night, but this is the stuff of legend and only a few of my brothers have claimed to be eyewitnesses."

"We elves have a long-standing alliance, but I have seen them only a few times," Nelkie said. "Once when I was very young, we were privileged to be invited to attend their midnight harvest celebration. I will never forget the spectacle of seeing them fill the late-night canopy with their song and dance of light. It was like fireworks set to music. The only other time was at my presentation to the elders, when I was introduced to Queen Katherine."

"You were indeed privileged. Maybe if I should choose to reside in this part of the forest, I too will be able to attend these wondrous events."

"I sincerely hope you stay, Rajah. I'm getting used to your being around, and I do enjoy your company."

"And I yours. Now, my friend, are you awake enough for our morning run?"

"I'm really not sure, but I know that after less than a minute on your back, I will be, and the faster we travel, the sooner I will be home...so let me get up there, big guy."

Without further hesitation, the two were off. Nelkie held on as his beloved forest streaked by in a blur of greens and browns. When the stag had finally slowed to a walk, Nelkie spotted a stream a few feet off the path. "Hey, look! There's a perfect place for us to stop and get a drink and a bite to eat."

"I'm with you. That run made me thirsty." Rajah lowered his friend to the ground and they both enjoyed a long, cool drink. Nelkie found sustenance in his pouch, while the stag feasted on the local flora.

The sun had risen to the point where it was penetrating the canopy here and there, dotting the forest path with its mosaic beauty. A warm summer breeze drifted slowly through the trees as the two wayfarers resumed their trek.

Nelkie was growing more and more excited with every passing mile. Memories of family and friends pervaded his thoughts. Not to mention the image of one particular girl, who had hair the color of sunshine.

As the day progressed, the elf began to recognize landmarks that told him he was very close to the end of his long and exhilarating quest. It was early afternoon when Nelkie spotted the most important milestone of his journey.

Chapter 63

"Look! Rajah! The heart-shaped rocks! By Bindar's berries, I'm home!" The two companions had been traveling together for more than a week and now their journey was at its end.

Nelkie's excitement was cut short by the warning tingle of his "I wonder who or what could be milling about this close to home."

At that moment, he heard a familiar voice. It was soft, friendly and feminine. "Nelkie, is that you?"

The doe's graceful movement caught his eye as she stepped out from behind the boulders. "It is you! And look at that bright red beard! You look so handsome and worldly!"

"Why, thank you, Lilly. It's great to see you! How have you been?"

"Just fine, Nelkie. All is well here." Nelkie noticed her soft eyes had drifted over to Rajah and he immediately apologized.

"Forgive me, Lilly. This handsome stag is my good friend, Rajah. He has carried me for the past week so I could arrive home sooner. Rajah, Lilly is the first friend I made in the forest. She saved the life of my best friend, Bartholemew."

"Hello, Rajah, and thank you for bringing our Nelkie home safely."

"The pleasure is mine," the stag answered, with a noble bow. "And I am pleased to meet anyone who calls Nelkie 'friend.'"

While the elf climbed down, he whispered in Rajah's ear. "Her mate was killed long ago by hunters. It strikes me that you two would make an ideal couple!"

Before he could reply, Lilly was speaking to the elf. "Nelkie, I have something wonderful to tell you. Sometime after you left, a human showed up here. He was alone. I watched from behind the heart-shaped rocks as he picked up every single one of those horrible steel traps and buried them. When he was done, he just walked off into the forest whistling the happiest tune. Can you imagine that?"

"I can more than imagine it. I could swear to it." He explained to the doe that the man who buried the traps was the very man who set them. "He has reformed and now dedicates his life to protecting our brothers."

"That is wonderful. Well, I don't want to keep you from your family, my friend; you should go to them now, and we will talk another time."

"Yes, of course; thank you, Lilly…and it really is great to see you again."

The elf turned to Rajah and reached up to stroke the stag's shoulder. "Well, this is it, my good friend. Family and friends await me, not to mention the elders. You know, now that I have completed my quest, I will be out in the forest from time to time, helping to retrieve resources. In other words, if you should find a reason to stay in this part of the woods," he said, his eyes rolling up toward the doe behind him, "we could run into each other fairly often."

"I would like that very much, Nelkie."

"All right, then. I will not bid you farewell, for I know we shall see each other again soon. I thank you again for the ride home, my brother, but now I must be off."

He nodded to the doe and then quickly ran off in the direction of the giant redwood that was his home.

Lilly walked over to Rajah and they both watched the jubilant elf dash off. "His parents will be very proud," the stag declared. "He is one very special individual."

"He belongs to a race of special individuals," she added. "I'm so glad he was successful."

"I too am very happy, but not at all surprised by his success. Nelkie is a very clever and resourceful elf. Failure was never a consideration for him. I am sure that someday he will prove to be a leader, with great wisdom."

"I would love to see that," she said, "but unfortunately, you and I will not live another three hundred years to see Nelkie the Elder! Come, let's take a cool drink from Nelkie's pool. You must be awfully dry after your journey."

They walked over to the elf's first accomplishment and drank their fill. "I have never been this deep in the forest," he told her. "The woods seem much thicker and the vegetation more lush."

"Our part of the forest is still unspoiled," Lilly said. "Very few humans will venture this far into the wood, so our environment has stayed clean and comparatively safe."

"I think I may want to stay here awhile. Would you care to show me around your lovely neighborhood?"

"I would be delighted," she answered.

Chapter 64

Nelkie was almost at the entrance of his treetop home when he noticed some of the bark on the enormous redwood moving. Suddenly, the little doorway took shape out of the numerous furrows in the massive trunk. As the door opened, he quickly stepped inside to be greeted by the towering Coobik. The watcher shut the door behind Nelkie and bellowed a warm greeting. "Welcome home, Nelkie! Word arrived this morning that you were close to home. I have been expecting you."

"Greetings to you, brave one. How did you know I was here?"

"Shortly after you left, I established a sentry system with the help of some of our winged friends. I have made quite a few changes around here, to make things run more efficiently. Come with me and I'll show you my latest innovation."

They walked over to the podium where Coobik kept his log. The watcher waved his arm in the direction of a chair positioned directly below a rather odd-looking item to the right of the podium. Nelkie climbed up on the chair and examined the long, leather-covered tube about three inches in diameter. It extended from the lectern up a good thirty feet and then disappeared into the trunk at a forty-five degree angle. The end nearest Nelkie was covered by a small leather bag that was cinched shut. Coobik removed the bag, exposing a small mirror. "Look into that mirror while I log in your return. Tell me what you see."

Nelkie peered into the mirror, which was pitched at an angle.

Momentarily stunned by what he saw, Nelkie looked back at Coobik. The older elf was busily writing in his log. Nelkie looked back into the mirror. Coobik had definitely made some improvements. "Wow! This is great! I can actually see the approach to the passage tree from the outside! It looks like the area ten feet or so in front of the door."

Coobik put down his quill and smiled proudly. "It's called a periscope. There is another mirror at the end of the tube that is positioned so that I no longer have to open the door to see outside."

"I must say, I really am impressed, wise one. Now you really are Coobik the Watcher."

"Yes, thank you. Well, enough of this. There will be plenty of time for you and me to catch up after you've settled back in. You must be anxious to see your parents. Go on up, my young friend, and welcome home."

"Thank you, Coobik. I'll see you later."

Nelkie hopped into the elevator and gleefully worked the ropes. He ascended rapidly into the towering redwood. When he reached the top, he exited and bounded outside into the never- ending canopy. He moved through nature's great umbrella, traversing leader and limb until he arrived at the entryway to his home.

The smell of fresh cornbread caressed his nose as he stepped through the threshold. He peeked around the corner to the kitchen area and spotted a freshly tossed salad on the table. His mother, with her back to him, was dutifully mixing herbs for tea.

"Am I in time for lunch?" he asked, in a soft and gentle voice.

"Nelkie! You're home," she shrieked, as she waddled over and smothered her son with a warm and loving hug. She squeezed half the breath out of him before she stepped back, holding him at arm's length. "Let me look at you," she said. "Oh, you're much too thin! Come, sit and eat. Your father will be home any minute." A happy tear rolled down her cheek as she ushered her boy into a chair. She stared at him for a moment before she spoke. "I must say, now that your beard has grown in, you look so much older. It gives you a look of maturity that was not there the last time I looked upon that innocent face."

"I am more mature, Mother. The knowledge and experience I have gained in the past few months is easily three times what I learned in my first sixteen years."

"Who is that stranger at my table?" called a familiar voice from the doorway.

"Father!" Nelkie leaped to his feet and ran to embrace the older elf.

"My son, it is so good to have you home. Did your quest go well?"

"Yes, Father. I have been successful. You and Mother will be very proud when the elders enter my name into the Book of Deeds. Look, I even have a medal, presented to me by a human!"

Balthazar examined his son's award. "I know these two images on the front. They are two of America's finest presidents, Washington and Lincoln."

"Turn it over, Father."

"With the thanks of a grateful nation," Balthazar read aloud. "Nelkie, my son, I don't yet know what you have accomplished, but I am very proud of you already."

"Thank you, Father. Now please sit. I have a surprise for you and Mother." Nelkie unbuttoned his provisions pouch and handed his mother the plastic bag containing the last three meatballs. "If you will heat these up, we can have them with our meal. I think you will find them uniquely delicious."

She obliged her son and soon they were all in agreement that this was indeed a special treat.

"It's a shame you could not get me the recipe for these meatballs," she said. "I would love to make more."

"Unfortunately the recipe would not help us much, Mother, since I believe the first ingredient would be a cow."

The smiling Balthazar couldn't help adding a little good-natured sarcasm. "It has come to my attention," he said, "that there is a very distinct shortage of wild cows, this deep in the forest...pity."

The family all laughed out loud together and when they finally stopped Nelkie told his parents how good it felt to be home again.

"It's wonderful to have you back," his mother answered.

"Yes," his father added. "I'm looking forward to having you work beside me in the woodshop once again. On a more serious note, Son, I have to ask...what was your impression of the human world ?"

"It's a marvelously modern world, Father, but it is fraught with danger. Deception, deceit, even murder can and do occur with too much frequency. I did find, however, that even in this unstable environment, there are great numbers of honest, self-sacrificing humans who have dedicated their lives to helping or protecting the less fortunate."

"So you believe there is still hope that the humans will one day evolve from their barbaric nature?"

"Yes, Father, I do. I believe that their evolution from barbarism is well on its way. There is much evidence that large numbers of humans can work together for the common good. Humans will evolve; it will just take a bit more time."

"Well spoken, my son. Your opinions show that you have gained wisdom on your quest, as well as maturity."

"Thank you, Father. Now, speaking of my quest, I must seek an audience with the elders. If they grant me permission, I will make my report."

"Yes, you should go right away. I'm sure the wise ones are already aware of your arrival."

Nelkie got up, kissed his mother's cheek, and promised to be back soon. He left their living quarters and made his way through the canopy to the elders' chamber.

Chapter 65

Upon his arrival, Nelkie was met at the entrance by Daido himself. The ancient one put an arm around Nelkie's shoulder and pointing with his staff, he led the Nelkie into the elders' private chamber.

"Come, young one. My fellow elders are waiting to receive you. We have had unconfirmed reports that you have enjoyed great success. When word reached us of your imminent homecoming this morning, we convened to await your report."

"I thought I would have to request an audience with the wise ones. I should have known that the elders would be well aware of my arrival."

They walked into the inner chamber to find the five remaining elders at their places around the time-worn oak table. Daido took his seat in the high-backed chair that was reserved for the senior elder. He motioned Nelkie to take the only vacant seat at the circular table.

Respectful greetings were exchanged before Daido called the meeting to order. "Before you start your narrative, there are some questions that must be asked," Daido pronounced. "I will start with perhaps the most important of them all. As a direct result of any word or deed for which you are responsible, does any human know the exact location of this dominion?"

"No, sir. Well, not exactly."

The elder in charge of security spoke next. Hannibal demanded that Nelkie elaborate.

"Well, sir," he said with a slight bow, "I was compelled to enlist the aid of a human to insure the completion of my quest. Without his help

I would not have succeeded. He knows of our existence in this forest, but he does not know exactly where in this vast woodland we actually reside. I assure you, most honored one, that this was not a decision I made in haste. Our secret is still safe."

"I will accept your word," Hannibal said. "Now, we must also be informed as to how many humans with whom you have had personal contact."

"Three, sir. One by mistake, one by happenstance, and one by design. Perhaps it would be easier to explain if I just start my report."

The elders conferred briefly and agreed to let Nelkie begin his narrative.

The young elf explained that the mistake was when he forgot to use his medallion and was discovered by Billy Baxter. "I will not make excuses for this breach of my personal security, but I would like to explain the circumstances in the hopes that the wise ones will see my mistake as understandable."

As the others nodded, Daido asked Nelkie to "please continue."

"I had been walking in the dark for more than an hour, looking in vain for any kind of suitable shelter from the heavy rain. I came upon a ladder that led up to a small tree house. I was cold and hungry and soaked to my skin. After determining that I was alone in the tree house, I fell victim to my depleted physical condition and was overcome by sleep. In hindsight, I see this mistake as being fortuitous. When I was discovered the following morning, it was by the seven-year-old human that owned the tree house. He told me of his father's misfortune and that was where my quest began in earnest. You could say that our entire nation is secure today because of concern of one little boy!"

"A most interesting perception," Hannibal stated. "Please go on."

"The accident happened shortly after I began my investigation into the father's problem. I was inside the home of a United States senator, looking for information, when an accidental fall rendered me unconscious. Although I had used my medallion this time, I was discovered by the senator's bodyguard/chauffeur. This became the man I recruited to help me, after much confusion and distrust was sorted out."

"I see," Daido said. "The picture of your trials is becoming clearer. I recall your appeal to us for help early on your journey. Am I to understand that your request to the Circle of Elders to intensify your power had something to do with the human you revealed yourself to by design?"

"Yes, wise one. Absolutely." Nelkie went on to explain the particulars involved in his dealing with Andrew Slater. When he finished, the elders knew that by revealing himself to Slater in the manner he chose, Nelkie had assured a safer life for all the inhabitants of their beloved forest.

With those points clarified, Nelkie went on to explain in detail how he became aware of Stanfield's evil plan and how he and Albert had worked together to stop him. When he finished, the elders understood how close they had all come to a total upheaval in their way of life.

Daido once again, spoke for the group. "Nelkie, son of Balthazar, you have completed a task with great skill and intelligence. We, the Circle of Elders, are proud to welcome you back to your community as a mature adult. Every creature in this forest owes you a solemn debt of thanks for saving our home. I will send word that at 6:00 this evening, all are called to attend your formal introduction into the Ancient Book of Deeds. Well done, Nelkie!"

The Circle of Elders all rose from their chairs and applauded the young elf, who bowed in gratitude for their acceptance. "Thank you, most wise ones. With your permission, I will withdraw."

Daido, apparently more than pleased with Nelkie's report, smiled and with a gentle wave of his arm, simply said, "Granted."

As Nelkie rose, Voltor the historian called to him. "We will meet you in the foyer of the great hall after everyone is seated. Your parents will then be escorted to the front row, after which we will begin our procession to the dais."

"I understand, honored one. Thank you."

Nelkie left the inner chamber filled with excited anticipation. After tonight's formal ceremony, he would be given a hero's welcome. There was always a wonderful banquet after an elf was inducted. The merriment would usually last until sunrise. This would be the biggest night of his life. He would be officially welcomed and accepted into his community as an adult. Tonight every American elf in the great redwood forest would pay homage to the elf that saved their home from demolition.

Chapter 66

"My report went very well, Mother. Daido has decreed that my induction will be tonight at 6:00."

"How wonderful! I must find an appropriate dress and pull out your father's best formal robes. I made some new clothes for you while you were away. I've laid them on your bed. They are very special, befitting an elf of your accomplishments."

"Thank you, Mother. I can't wait to see them. I think I'd like to go up and lie on my own bed for a little while. It's been a long time."

"Go on up, my son; you have more than earned a good rest in your own bed. I'll call you when it's time to get dressed."

Nelkie ascended the ladder and slowly took in the comforting sight of his own bedroom. On his bed were clothes the likes of which he had never seen. The new tunic had been carefully crafted with his mother's love, and was as bright red as the suit of Santa himself, only much more elegant and formal. The long sleeves flowed into a bell at the wrist and were trimmed in sparkling gold, as were the neckline and the jagged up-and-down cut of the hip-length hem. A new pair of green leggings was laid out next to the tunic. Nelkie picked them up to find them flecked with the tiniest specs of gold, which shimmered with reflected light. There was a finely tooled black leather belt with a large gold buckle, along with a pair of brand new ankle-length earth-toned boots. He knew his parents must have bartered a good amount of their time and talent with Poco, the master leather crafter, in order to receive such finely made goods. To complete his outfit was a three-toned hat. The band that went over his forehead was the same earth tone as his boots. Green flecked with gold covered the body and long tail of the hat, which was embellished with a bright red pom-pom at the end of the tail. He thought, *Tonight I will look like the prince of elves!* Nelkie carefully folded his new clothes and placed them on top of his clothes chest.

He fell backward on his bed, stretching out his 27-inch frame to its maximum. "Ahh," he said aloud. "If there were a king of the world, he could possess no finer bed than this one." His belly full and his heart content, he was asleep within seconds.

Chapter 67

Nelkie, accompanied by his proud parents, entered the foyer just outside the Great Elf Hall. He peeked into the room from the rear doors. A sea of elves was seated in the banquet hall. The multitude was dressed in an endless rainbow of bright, happy colors.

In the front of the seated assembly was a raised platform, which held a long table and six high-backed chairs. High above the table, suspended in front of a shimmering light-blue curtain, was a five-foot-wide representation of the American elf signature emblem. Six stars in a circle were carved into a highly polished disc of white oak.

The entire hall was bathed in multi-colored light reflected through the strategically placed huge glass prisms. Candles were everywhere.

"What beautiful colors," Anitra said, while looking over her son's shoulder. "What could work better to set a mood than to decorate with colored light?"

"Yes, it is breathtaking," Nelkie agreed.

A booming baritone startled the family, when Coobik came up behind them. "Ah, there's the proud family," he proclaimed. The watcher was dressed in full ceremonial battle gear, complete with a jewel-encrusted helmet and scabbard. He was followed closely by Ivar the Crier, whose official duty it was to inform the family of the proper protocol. "The elders will be along at any moment," he said. "When they are ready, I will announce the parents; Coobik will draw his sword and escort them to the front of the hall, where they will take their seats. Then I will announce the Circle of Elders and Daido will lead the procession to the dais. The last elder in line will be Voltor, who will be carrying the Book of Deeds. Once they are seated, I will announce our inductee, who will proceed to front and center, facing our elders."

Nelkie bowed politely to the crier, and said, "Understood, Ivar; thank you."

The rustling of robes became audible behind them as the wise ones entered the foyer. Even in the dim light of the anteroom, the leaders projected an aura of nobility and boundless wisdom. They were met with respectful bows from their brethren.

The senior elder embraced Anitra and shook Balthazar's hand, while telling them both how honored he was to induct their son into the Book of Deeds. "Nelkie has done us all proud, and I am certain that this is only the first of many accomplishments your son will achieve."

"I thank you, wise one," she said. "Your words are both a comfort and a source of pride." A polite curtsy brought their conversation to a respectful conclusion.

Daido now addressed the crier. "Ivar, are we ready to proceed?"

"Upon your order, wise one."

With a wave of his robed arm, the senior elder directed Ivar to perform his official function.

All in attendance turned to the rear of the hall when the crier rapped his staff three times on the oaken floor. "Hear ye, hear ye! These ancient proceedings now commence. Honor ye now the bearers of this evening's inductee."

The warrior elf drew his sword in salute and led the proud parents down the center aisle. When the advance party took their seats, the crowd turned their attention to the rear doors in anticipation of the imminent ceremony.

The crier slowly but loudly pounded his staff three more times and announced: "It is my honor and privilege to now call your most honored Circle of Elders to the dais."

Daido led his brother elders into the hall. The senior elder raised his crystal-topped staff high above his head while taking slow, deliberate steps. The assemblage watched in awestruck wonder as he seemed to will the crystal atop his staff to emit a soft blue light that spiraled across the great hall with ever-increasing speed. The light was magnified as it passed through prism after prism, bathing the hall from floor to ceiling in an avalanche of color from pale yellow through deep purple. Daido was leading the procession in single file. When the leader had reached the halfway point, followed by Voltor cradling the Book of Deeds, Nelkie was just setting foot into the hall. The Great One, still holding his staff aloft, spoke to his nation in a thunderous voice. "Behold him who reclaimed your forest from evil, who prevailed against an enemy of great wealth and power! His courage and conviction have set a standard that will be aspired-to throughout the ages. My brethren, I give you: Brother Nelkie!

The young elf was profoundly moved by the sanctity of the ceremony. The time had come for his name to be entered beside the heroes of his race that spanned thousands of years. He walked proudly through the center of the auditorium with his Freedom Medal announcing to all that he had the respect and admiration of humans, as well as his brother elves.

A hush fell over the congregation as they all stood to witness what they knew to be greatness in the making. After the elders took their seats, the assemblage followed suit.

Daido, the last to remain standing, rapped his staff on the floor. Like an obedient puppy returning to its master, the spiraling blue light reversed direction and returned to the crystal atop the elder's staff. The great room remained colorful, due to the abundance of prisms, but now the light was more subtle, befitting a formal ceremony.

Now that the processional had reached the stage, the ancient one's eyes came to rest on Nelkie and he smiled. "We, the Circle of Elders and all of your brothers and sisters welcome you home, Nelkie.

Witness now your inauguration into our Ancient Book of Deeds."

Voltor the Historian, held the great book aloft for all to see. It took all the strength he had to hold the heavy volume above his head for just a few seconds. He reverently placed the book down and opened it, gingerly turning the pages until he found his place. The historian dipped his quill in the provided inkwell and entered the date. Now ready to record the events of Nelkie's Quest, he nodded to the senior elder.

Daido addressed the congregation. "The elf heretofore known as Nelkie, son of Balthazar and Anitra, became aware of a human in need of help, by way of a seven-year-old boy. Nelkie's intention was to try to save the job of this boy's father, but he soon found out the problem was *not* the father's pending unemployment. This was only a symptom of a much greater problem, the consequences of which could reach this very assemblage."

While Voltor recorded every word into the age-old book, Daido continued. "If Nelkie's evil adversary had his way, this forest would have been obliterated in order to increase his personal fortune. This most wicked of men was responsible for a kidnapping, as well as a murder. Answering the call of his responsibility, Nelkie faced this man with courage and cunning, defeating him. The evil one is now in custody and will answer for his crimes. The most important development for the nation of American elves is that this forest will never be under assault again. We are protected by the United States Government and shall remain so as long as this sovereign nation exists. Along with these accomplishments, Nelkie also orchestrated the rescue of the kidnapped human. These actions resulted in the continued employment of the little boy's father. In recognition of the swift and efficient execution of your quest, we, the Circle of Elders have decreed that from this day forward you shall be known as Nelkie the Achiever. You may now turn and face your brethren. Let it be known on this day, the name of Nelkie the Achiever was entered into the Ancient Book of Deeds as a true champion of the forest."

The Senior Elder then asked Voltor for Nelkie's official documentation.

The historian handed Daido a sheepskin, framed in oak, which the elder read to the audience. "We, the undersigned Circle of Elders, do proclaim that Nelkie the Achiever, having met all requirements upon the completion of his quest, has been awarded the adult title of 'brother of the forest,' and is hereby welcomed into the community of mature elves."

In most instances, after the young inductee was given his proclamation, he was met with polite applause, befitting a formal occasion. In this case, the entire community understood the consequences if Nelkie had failed, and they responded with an uncharacteristic cheer, which carried throughout the Great Hall. They raised their voices in gleeful appreciation, knowing that because of this one princely-looking elf, their way of life was no longer in jeopardy.

The crowd demanded to be addressed by their hero. Cries of "Speech! Speech!" rose from every corner.

Nelkie the Achiever raised his hands and quieted the congregation. "My fellow elves, most honored elders; I thank you with all my heart. You are most kind. I want you to know that I was very fortunate to be allied during my quest with one of the finest of humans. His name was Albert Parker. If there were more men of his caliber in this world, we would all benefit greatly. I am very proud of my award," he said, fingering his medal, "and my new title, but I am most proud to be a member of a race whose compassion for all living things makes a success like mine possible. Thank you."

Daido rose from his chair and declared an end to the formal part of the evening. "Now let's bring on the musicians, and let the feast begin."

Cheers and laughter abounded as Balthazar appeared before his honored son. In each hand he held a frothy mug of elf-brewed ale. As was the ancient custom, Nelkie hooked arms with his father and robustly gulped down his ceremonial first ale as an adult. Balthazar also emptied his mug and embraced his son. "Your success has exceeded my most hopeful expectations, and I am proud."

"Thank you, Father. I would rather hear those words from you than from Daido himself."

The newly proclaimed adult stepped down from the stage into a swarm of admiring friends and neighbors. Everyone wanted a closer look at his medal. He was asked countless questions about the details of his astonishing adventure. The honoree graciously accommodated all.

The festive atmosphere accelerated when the elf orchestra filled the hall with the spirited sound of the drendaga. Suddenly preoccupied, all conversation around Nelkie was reduced to a distant mumble as his eyes scanned the crowd. He searched the sea of faces hoping to find the one that would elevate this evening to its peak. Nelkie was about to submit to the hopelessness of the situation when he felt a soft hand slide into his from behind. He turned to see a beautiful crown of wildflowers above the prettiest face in his entire world. Arnora gently took his other hand in hers before she spoke.

"Would the returning hero consider one dance before he is swept away by his admirers?"

"I can have only one?"

She laughed and led him out to the middle of the floor. The crowd circled around them and clapped in time to the music, as the young couple performed in joyous celebration.

When the music stopped and the applause diminished, the couple bowed to each other, and then to the audience.

"Would you care for a drink and maybe some fresh air?" he asked.

"Yes to both questions," she said.

Nelkie flagged down one of the servers and handed her a mug of cider. He secured another ale for himself and offered her his arm.

She tucked her arm in his and they strolled outside together. Finding a comfortable nook, they sat down to take in the view. Looking through the higher limbs, they could see that the sky was several shades of pink and purple as the setting sun put on its nightly display.

"It's so peaceful and beautiful here," she said. "I can't even imagine what terrible fate would have befallen us if your mission had failed."

"I was lucky to have stumbled into the problem in the first place," he answered. "I don't want to think about what could have gone wrong. I'm just very glad to be home. While I was away, many times I would be alone with my thoughts, especially at night. I would often think about home, my parents, or my friend Bart, but when thoughts of you would come to me, I would enjoy those the most. Thinking of you just made me feel good."

"That's very sweet of you, Nelkie; thank you. Oh, by the way, I saw Bart only minutes before he embarked on his quest last month. He was so excited. He asked me to tell you that the elders had given him several gifts. After the empowerment ceremony, he was granted the gift of speed. He said that at will, he could now summon the energy and speed to outrun a deer!"

"Wow! What a thrill that must be. I'm sure Bartholomew will do well. He is very smart--and by nature, more cautious than I. Hopefully, he will meet with success early on. He is my best friend and I miss him already."

Twilight was upon them as the sun melted into the mountains to the west. She stood and took his hand. When they looked into each other's eyes, they both knew that something extraordinary was growing between them. It was undeniable. She was bright and beautiful, and he was the handsome hero. Arnora reluctantly broke the silence of their moment of magic when she spoke. "I would really love to stay out here with you for hours, Nelkie, but that would not be proper. This is a special night for you as well as all the members of our community, and I must share your company. Let's go back and join the others."

"I guess you're right," he said. "It would be ill-mannered of me to leave my own party for any length of time…even if it was with the prettiest girl in the realm."

She blushed slightly as they started back, and asked him what his plans for the future were.

"Well, I'm really anxious to resume my apprenticeship with my father. Before I left, I was working on a problem with a see-saw. I need to work out the degree of angle at which to cut the rocker supports."

He held the door open for her and said, "I also hope to spend a lot more time with you."

"I look forward to that," she said, smiling at him.

They walked into the hall arm in arm. Their entrance did not go unnoticed by his parents. Anitra tugged on her husband's sleeve and nodded her head in the direction of the young couple. "They appear to be quite taken with each other, don't you think?"

"Yes, quite. Do you think our grandchildren will have bright red hair, or golden blond?" he asked with a broad smile.

She laughed a short giggly kind of laugh and simply said, "Strawberry blond."

Epilogue

Albert had just hung up the phone when there was a knock on his cabin door. The chauffeur pulled his door open to see Pat and Barbara Walsh standing on the porch. The senator was holding a large file folder which he dropped, suddenly stunned at Albert's appearance. Barbara stood next to her husband with her mouth agape for several seconds until she forced herself to recover.

"Forgive us for staring," she said, "but you've obviously dyed your hair and beard. I have to tell you, Albert, the result is absolutely stunning!"

"I agree," Pat added. "My God, Albert, you look twenty years younger! I've never seen anything like it. You should have done this several years ago."

"Thanks, guys. I was kinda nervous about what kind of reaction this sudden move would generate. It was one of those things that just sort of, uh, happened. I thought it was an improvement, but you never know what people will think."

"Well, I swear," Barbara gasped, "it makes you look like you have found the fountain of youth!"

"You always were one of my favorite people," Albert said, with a smile. "Anyway," he went on, "if I may change the subject, you'll never guess who I just got off the phone with. Our newly promoted Captain Frank Martini!"

Genuine excitement shone in Barbara's eyes when she said, "Oh, that's wonderful--be sure to offer our congratulations!

"He has certainly earned that promotion," Pat added. "How's he feeling?"

"Just great! His wound has almost completely healed, and he feels like celebrating. I'll be joining Frank and his wife Lynn for dinner tonight. Say, what was that you dropped, Pat?"

"Oh, I was so taken with your new look, my friend, I almost forgot to give these to you. There are copies in this folder of all the official documents finalizing the annexation of this property to the National Parks System. Barb and I are going for a walk. Would you take the Jeep and run these down to Pete?"

"Be glad to."

"Tell him that I've highlighted all the parts pertaining to him on page five. He'll still be superintendent, but now he will have easier access to park rangers and the Forestry Service. If he has any questions, tell him not to hesitate to call. We'll be back in about an hour."

"Will do. Enjoy your walk."

Fifteen minutes later, Albert pulled up in front of the Baxter home. When he received no response to the bell, he decided to check around behind the house. He soon found Mary Baxter tending her garden. As Albert's shadow moved across the pepper plants, she looked up. Not recognizing the chauffeur, she said, "Can I help you, sir?"

"Mary, it's me, Albert."

"My lord, Albert, you look so, so…well, so young!"

"Thank you. I dyed my hair. I guess the change turned out to be a little more than I expected. You look great yourself," he said, trying to change the subject.

"Oh yes, I'm sure the mud makeup is quite striking," she joked.

"It does project a rather earthy, natural look," he said, unable to suppress a laugh.

She smiled at him and said, "Albert, your charm is almost unbearable. What have you got there?"

"Oh, uh, the senator wanted me to drop these off for Pete to look over. Especially page five."

She removed her gardening gloves and reached for the folder. "He's up testing the pond water at the north end. I'll put these on his desk and make sure he sees them as soon as he gets back."

"Okay. Oh, Pat said if there were any questions, just call. They will be home in about an hour."

"Thanks, Albert. I'll be sure to tell him. You have a good day now."

"Thanks, Mary; you too."

Mary took her husband's package into the house and Albert started to walk around back to the Jeep. Suddenly he heard something that made him stop and listen more closely. It was music. Flute music. Not just a happy little ditty, but a beautiful, flowing melody that captivated him. *Where is that coming from? Whoever is playing that flute should be with a symphony orchestra! I've never heard more beautiful music!*

It seemed, oddly enough, that the music was flowing from the tree house at the edge of the woods. Albert walked briskly toward the tree house, his head full of unanswered questions. He climbed the ladder, not knowing what to expect, but surely not expecting what he saw.

Little Billy Baxter was sitting on the floor, with his back to the wall. Between his lips was a flute that Albert had seen before. He stood, dumbstruck on the top step, and could not have been more surprised if he had found a giraffe playing that flute. The boy sat with his eyes closed and continued to fill the air with the most soothing melody, while Albert tried to figure out how this could be possible. Momentarily, Billy brought the concert to a conclusion, opened his eyes, and grinned when he saw Albert.

"Wow! Mr. Parker! What did you do to your hair? You look so different!"

"I just put some color in it, Billy. Uh, listen. Would you mind if I asked you where you got that flute?"

"Umm, no. I guess I can tell you, if you can keep a secret."

"I sure can, Billy, I promise."

"It was a present from my friend, Nelkie. My mom thinks he a 'maginary friend, but he's really not. He's really real!"

Albert's face lit up at the mention of his friend's name. He looked at Billy with the same expression one sees on the face of a child on Christmas morning. Albert climbed the rest of the way into the tree house and sat next to Billy.

"Now I'll tell you a secret. I am the only other person in the world who knows Nelkie is real! I know he is a red-headed elf!"

The boy was astonished. "You do know him! You know he's real too!"

"Yes. I know him very well. I think you and I should have a long talk, okay?"

The End

CPSIA information can be obtained at www.ICGtesting.com
Printed in the USA
BVOW07s1148220614

356693BV00005B/440/P